FALLEN STONES

For: MARNI
From: Tom

"EMBRACE THE FEAR"

Thomas M. Malafarina
9/25/13

THOMAS M. MALAFARINA

FALLEN STONES

FIRST SUNBURY PRESS EDITION
Printed in the United States of America
October 2012

Trade Paperback ISBN: 978-1-62006-116-9
Mobipocket format (Kindle) ISBN: 978-1- 62006-117-6
ePub format (Nook) ISBN: 978-1-62006-118-3

Published by:
Sunbury Press
Mechanicsburg, PA
www.sunburypress.com

Mechanicsburg, Pennsylvania   USA

This book is dedicated to my incredible wife Joanne. Thank you for being you.

Introduction

One thing, which never ceases to amaze me no matter how many times I experience it, is the creative process. This may sound a bit strange coming from someone whose entire life has been spent engaged in one form of creativity or another whether art, music or writing. Nevertheless, the creative process still manages to fascinate me to no end.

Producing something from where there was once nothing provides such an amazing and exhilarating feeling that it is practically addictive (or perhaps "practically" is not correct - it is very addictive). To take for example, a blank sheet of paper, representing the absence of everything and turn it into a song, or a poem, or a sketch or a story is an amazing feeling akin to nothing else as far as I am concerned.

The same could be true of taking an empty pan or pot, adding ingredients without the aid of a recipe and coming up with new meal or desert concoction. I have absolutely no skill whatsoever when it comes to cooking or baking but I truly appreciate the creativity it takes to do either properly. For example, every time my wife JoAnne comes up with one of her delicious "inventions" as she calls them, I encourage her to write down the recipe so she can either make it again or perhaps someday turn it into a cookbook. But she has no interest in doing so. For her the thrill comes from making something new from nothing and that satisfaction is enough for her. Although she might disagree with my assessment, I consider that creativity. The same is true with any imaginative endeavor you can envision.

A while back I was interviewed for an Internet author's radio program and I explained to the host, "Creative people don't create because they want to... they create because they have to." Although that might seem a bit exaggerated, it is actually quite true. Even though the creative process brings pleasure and is something one might desire to do, it is something the innovative person must do. The inability to express oneself artistically can be devastating to a creative person, as the ideas back up like the waters behind a dam, unable to be allowed to flow freely at their desired rate. Eventually the ideas have to be permitted to escape or the dam will break. Expressing one's originality is a pressure release valve like no other.

This book, *Fallen Stones,* is a good example of the creative process in action. In early 2011, my publisher, Lawrence Knorr of Sunbury Press contacted me and asked if I would have an interest

1

in co-writing a book with him sometime. He had a very rough concept for a ghost story. I was finishing up my short story collection *Gallery Of Horror* with artist Nunzio Barbera and was planning to start another novel.

I told Larry I would be willing to put off starting my new novel and work with him for a time if I was motivated enough to come up with some good imaginative ideas. I asked him for a summary of what he thought the novel should be about. Little did I realize at that time I would be working on the book for more than a year and a half and would end up hijacking the novel and writing the entire thing myself.

At this point in the discussion, I should point out the reason why I ended up writing it myself. It was not because of any lack of desire to participate on Larry's part but because when it comes to my creative endeavors, I can be a bit of a control freak. I should apologize to Larry for that sometime. Also once my creative juices start flowing, I just write and write and write like a maniac and can't stop. This leaves little time for as they say "playing well with others", so fortunately for me Larry was extremely magnanimous in allowing me to take his crux of an idea and carry on by myself. In the back of the book is a list of what suggestions Larry gave me on the day I agreed to work on the story. You might not want to read them until you have finished the book however, because they could spoil things for you.

This is where the creative process comes into play. From those eleven lines of story suggestions, which constitute Larry's overview of the book, an entire novel of close to 150 thousand words evolved. That is the beauty of the creative process, and what still amazes me.

When you do read Larry's overview, you will notice that I took a few liberties with the original concept and went off in a variety of directions. But if I am correct, you will likely shake your head and wonder "How the heck did he get all of that from those eleven lines?"

That, my friends, is the creative process in action and why I love to do what I do.

Enjoy the book and thank you for your continued support.

Thomas M. Malafarina
September, 2012

Prologue

Scarcely a sound could be heard in the dimly lit chamber, save for the gentle rustling of papers, the almost silent breathing of the room's sole occupant and the occasional dripping of water from the faucet; a noise which seemed to echo loudly in the otherwise soundless space. The quiet was both serene yet at the same time somehow ominous, as if to suggest a sinister, evil presence might be lurking somewhere just beneath the all-encompassing cloak of silence.

The outermost areas of the room were cast in darkness. The time was just after midnight on a moonless, cloudy late April night. However, even had the moon been full and bright, the thick hand-blown leaded antique Italian glass windows along the ceiling would not have allowed for much additional illumination to enter from the world outside. What meager light was present came from the center-most section of the room, where numerous tapered candles, perhaps twenty or more, of the variety one might normally find in a candlestick or candelabra, surrounded most of the rim of a refurbished pearl-white claw-foot bathtub. The design of the fixture's four claws was representative of the talons of an eagle grasping firmly onto a round ball; a typical design used in many tubs of that style and early twentieth century period.

The large cast-iron tub was elevated atop a three foot high polished imported gray marble rectangular platform, with a set of three stairs surrounding it on all four sides, giving the feature the appearance an ancient sacrificial altar, which ironically and unknown to the current occupant, it would soon even more closely resemble.

A man soaked inside the porcelain-recoated tub with steaming water filled high, close to his chest level. He reclined as if relaxing against the back of the tub, although relaxing was the furthest thing from his mind. With his thin right leg bent at a forty-five degree angle, he was provided with a resting place for his reading material, although he was not actually reading the document any longer. He stared at the paper through red-rimmed dark-circled sunken eyes for a few minutes at a time, occasionally absentmindedly turning the pages, yet he was much too preoccupied and unable to concentrate sufficiently enough to actually read and comprehend its contents. He appeared to not be acting completely of his own volition, as if to suggest he was being coerced into a situation not of his own choosing. The skeleton-thin man looked exhausted, beaten, fatigued like he had finally lost a long and futile battle and had simply surrendered to what he saw to be an inevitable conclusion. His eyes left the document yet again and locked onto one of the flickering candle flames, which danced peculiarly on its wick.

He had fastened each of the individual blood-red candles to the rim of the tub with melted wax, and as they burned, more of the substance dripped slowly down their dwindling lengths, which were now shortened to half of their original size; an indication of just how long he had been soaking there, waiting. Although the man who was named Emerson had no recollection of doing so, he had refreshed the continuously cooling bath water on several occasions during that time. He would drain off several inches of the tepid water then once again turn on the faucet to replenish the tub with new, steaming hot water.

The wax of many of the candles had dripped down past the surface of the tub and some of the wax had oozed further down along the inside faces of the tub, slowly and perhaps symbolically making their way toward the water's surface resembling rivulets of coagulating blood.

A cell phone and a straight razor lie on the floor next to the tub. The gleaming silver blade of the razor shone in the candlelight. It was most definitely an antique, perhaps eighty or more years old, encased in an ivory handle, engraved with three initials DCL. Emerson Washburn had found the razor in an old wooden cigar box in the cellar of the main farmhouse shortly after moving in along with several other trinkets, equally as old. These included a set of gold cufflinks, bearing the same three-letter monogram as the razor.

Washburn had carefully sharpened and used the blade often since then. In fact, only a few moments earlier he had given himself an excellent shave with the old-fashioned implement. Had Emerson been able to think more rationally, he might have realized most of his current problems had coincided with the discovery and subsequent use of that particular straight razor. But his days of thinking clearly had passed many months preceding.

Emerson Charles Washburn broke his transfixed stare away from the dancing flame and looked absently about the room, appearing somewhat anxious, as if in anticipation of someone's arrival; someone of great importance. He still held the document in his now slightly-trembling hand but seemed to pay little attention to it. He no longer had any need to read it since he had practically known its contents verbatim, which was not at all surprising since he had written most of the text himself. After that he had handed it over to his local attorney for re-writing, in order that the lawyer could add of all of the mandatory legalese or "mumbo jumbo", as he was often fond of referring to it.

He had used a different attorney back when he lived in New Jersey, but that now seemed a lifetime ago, as if to suggest the person he once was no longer existed and the person he had become during the past year was someone entirely different. Washburn had once been tough, a fighter, a real brawler to be more precise, someone who took no lip from anyone. He had been a man in charge.

Now, however, he was a frail, thin, pale, weak shell of a man; a ghost of his former self, barely capable of functioning on his own. It was frightening how his health had declined over the past year. In his heyday, Emerson Washburn had beaten and actually killed many men with his own bare hands. He understood if enemies from his former life were able to see what a pathetic, wretched physical wreck he had become they would no doubt take great pleasure in his decline. Some might even seize the opportunity to pay him back for his past misdeeds. He had thought about this on several occasions, but in his weakened condition and obsessed mental state he could do little but hope no one had taken the time to track him down.

He looked slowly around the unusual room, absorbing the essence of the space and marveling at the fine craftsmanship the numerous contractors he had employed to turn what was once a rundown, dilapidated hexagonal shaped out-building into a luxurious spa retreat for the ultimate in relaxation. Washburn had spared no expense in funding the project as was typical of the man. After all, he had so much money at his disposal, acquired from his various past illegal enterprises, that spending it lacked any real significance to him. He had given up tracking the cost of the spa's luxurious restoration at around the sixty thousand dollar mark, and that was much earlier and a substantial amount of additional money as well.

A large stone fireplace, which Washburn assumed had once been used many years ago for heat, had been rebuilt into the wall behind him. When he had purchased the property, the fireplace was practically in ruins and no longer functioned. It now looked strong, with a thick highly polished handcrafted mahogany mantel. The entire edifice had been dismantled, stone-by-stone, then restored to a state far more luxurious than its original condition and was retrofitted with a natural gas burner for instant, convenient ambient lighting as well as heat. It could also burn wood if Washburn desired to do so.

Surrounding the tub area on four of the remaining five walls were large single piece mirrors, perhaps six feet tall and ten feet wide, which Washburn had ordered custom-made to the exact specifications of the six-sided room. Above the mirrored walls, weathered varnished boards of varying lengths, cut from oaks, which had been harvested from the many large trees on the property, were placed at forty-five degree angles to form a series of repeating triangular patterns around the room.

This pattern served to draw the viewer's eyes toward the incredible vaulted cathedral-like ceiling with its many arches of heavy timbers, which were originally part of three hundred year old church in Spain, and had been salvaged after the building had succumbed to a fire. Most of these amazing aesthetic features were scarcely visible in the gloominess of the shadowy room, but Washburn knew they were there, and somehow that simple knowledge helped to relax him enough to prepare him for the unwanted visitor he knew would soon arrive.

Washburn thought about the pitiful shape the building had been in when he discovered it shortly after purchasing the farmette. Structurally, the original building was similar to its present state, but it was in a deplorable condition; with sections of wood missing from the roof and walls, as well as broken windows and severe water damage throughout. Bats, rats, birds and other such wildlife had all found sanctuary in the ruins of the building.

There had been no plumbing or electricity in the original building, and the floor had been constructed of flat flagstone laid over compacted dirt. Washburn had never been able to determine the actual purpose for the original structure, but he had assumed from its contents and design it might have been used for bathing. That was why he thought of the room as a spa and why he had chosen to remodel it for that particular purpose.

A large, severely rusted and weather damaged cast iron bathtub had been sitting in the middle of the floor, at the center of the building. In fact, the ancient tub, now beautifully restored was the very same bathtub in which he now soaked. However, when he had discovered it, the old claw-foot tub had not been designed with plumbing or faucets. He had gone to great expense to have the tub properly drilled to allow for hardware and appropriate plumbing fixtures. Then he had it refurbished to its current immaculate condition. Washburn assumed when it was originally used, water must have had to be brought to the room from a nearby well or stream, heated in the old fireplace and then poured into the tub as required.

He also was of the impression the original fireplace must have been the only heat source for the entire building. He had never heard of any early twentieth century Pennsylvania coal region homes or farms with such frivolous and luxuriant bathhouses. To the best of his knowledge, bathing had always been done inside the main house. But based on what he discovered about the former owners and their level of affluence, construction of such a structure to be used for such a purpose might actually have been plausible.

After an extensive and costly amount of research, Washburn had learned the original builders and owners of the property were actually his maternal grandparents, Dwight and Marie Livingston. He had not known or heard much about his grandparents while he was growing up, but after hiring a private investigator to research the property as well as to find out as much as possible about his own family heritage, Washburn learned the Livingstons had been quite wealthy, having owned much land in the area as well as several coal companies. They had apparently purchased the land and built the house in the early 1900's.

Washburn had also learned his grandparents were not the first settlers to build on the property. Houses of one sort or another had existed on the land for several hundred years. However, at the time his grandparents bought the land, most of the outbuildings as well as the main farmhouse had ceased to exist; perhaps burned in fires or destroyed by other forces of nature. As a result, his grandparents hand started with a clean slate, so to speak, and built everything from the ground up.

Emerson Washburn's mother had never told either he or his younger brother Nathan about their grandparents, and neither of them had much interest in such things as either children or as young men. Washburn knew his grandparents had both died fairly young, in their early thirties, and he always felt that prior to their deaths they may have done something unspeakable because none of their living decedents ever spoke their names or even acknowledged they ever once existed.

On several occasions as a young boy, Washburn would catch his mother or father discussing something in hushed voices, wearing looks of disapproval. He might hear the occasional snippet of a phrase or the occasional word such as, "mother", "father" or even words like "tragic" and "horrendous" and he knew they were speaking about his mother's parents. His mother always got a look of anger, or perhaps hatred whenever they spoke this way, as if to suggest she despised her mother.

This often served to confuse young Washburn as he had also heard that his grandparents had died when his mother was only about two years old. He couldn't comprehend how she could have such hatred for someone she never really knew and certainly could not recall.

Washburn's young imagination often went wild with ideas trying to determine what his grandparents may have done to warrant such a family shunning. As soon as his parents would see him trying to eavesdrop, they would immediately cease their conversation and order him to go outside and play with his brother. They had no intention of allowing him to learn the mysterious family secret.

Then years later, after Washburn had grown to be a man and had found his way into a life of crime, he often wondered if he had chosen the lifestyle because of some genetic predisposition. He often wondered what sort of evil his grandparents had perpetrated, which was so vile as to have their very names banished from all family discussions? As a child he often thought he would give anything to learn the horrible family secret, but now that he did know everything, he wished to God he did not.

Growing up he often thought about what he heard adults refer to as "bad blood". Later when he had broken all ties with his immediate family, having been branded a "black sheep", he became more certain than ever that he had chosen a life of crime because he had been born for it. Whatever "bad blood" had coursed through his grandparents veins must obviously run through his own.

Since then he had spent many years building his criminal empire, dealing in virtually every known vice modern man could desire, from stolen goods to drugs to prostitution. Although his activities were considered evil in the eyes of society, they felt perfectly right and normal to him. For Washburn, it was as if the idea of right and wrong had no meaning. His parents had tried to instill in both himself and Nathan what society considered proper values. The concepts seemed to stick when it came to Nathan, but Washburn couldn't quite come to grips with them.

As he lie soaking in the tub, Washburn recalled the life-changing event which made him cast aside his life of crime and which brought him home. As if ordained by fate, many years earlier during one of his "business trips" to Pennsylvania, Berks County to be specific, something happened that spurred him not only to suddenly become interested in his heritage but also to eventually have it become an obsession for him. While staying in the area around the city of Reading, he read a story in the local newspaper about the tragic death of a couple in a car accident. A drunk driver had plowed into the couple's vehicle head-on as they were driving home from a movie.

To Washburn's surprise, the names of the couple, which seemed to scream out at him from the first paragraph of the story, were those of his estranged brother Nathan and his wife, Mary. Washburn had not spoken with either of them in many years and despite their lack of closeness, he felt a deep sadness, knowing he could very well be alone in the world, since he had never married and had no children of his own.

Perhaps he was simply overcome with a bit of melancholy that might have accompanied growing older without either a wife or children, he didn't know, but the feeling was quite disheartening. That particular event had sparked what would grow through the years to become an obsession with learning about his ancestors. The death of his brother and wife was likely also the catalyst for him to leave his life of crime, eventually retire and then hire a private investigator to search for any possible living relatives many years later.

As a recent unforeseen result of that investigation, he had learned a little over a year earlier about the existence of the farmette and its availability for purchase. It was when he discovered the property had originally been his ancestors' family homestead, he immediately decided to buy it; on the spot, sight unseen. This was not how Emerson Washburn normally conducted his business, but the idea seemed so right that he did so without forethought. It had been over ten years since he had first read about the death of his brother.

Washburn had purchased the property from a holding company, which had bought it many years earlier. The farmhouse and out buildings had been abandoned and unused for over thirty years and had been allowed to fall into disrepair. The buildings were uninhabitable shells, which appeared to have been vandalized over the years. The original Livingston farm had been much larger, hundreds of acres but through the years, parcels of land had been sold off, reducing it to a forty-acre farmette. Prior to the holding company taking possession the property had hands many times with residents never staying more than a few months and Washburn now understood the reason why. No wonder the former residents had fled leaving the structures to fall to ruin.

Washburn suddenly felt a slight prickling sensation at the back of his neck and knew from previous experience what was about to happen. He reached down over the side of the huge tub and allowed the document he was holding to fall to the floor with a slap, echoing loudly in the silent empty chamber. The cover of the document read "Last Will and Testament of Emerson Charles Washburn".

As he slowly returned to a sitting position in the tub he noticed a familiar change occurring to the wall-sized mirror located directly in front of him; a change he had seen many times before, but one which nonetheless always brought a disturbing sensation, which radiated to the very core of his soul. The mirrored glass seemed to slowly shimmer at first, and then begin to ripple like it was liquid in composition and as if someone had dropped a pebble into it. Then the ripples began to work outward in ever growing concentric circles. Washburn smelled a recognizable foul and dank odor like that of rotting vegetation and decomposing long-dead animals. During his lifetime, Washburn's illegal business dealings had required he dispose of more than his share of dead bodies and as such, he knew well the stench of decomposition.

The candles surrounding the tub started to flicker as if a breeze had suddenly blown across them. Within a few seconds, the image of a man gradually took shape in the undulating glass surface and Washburn knew the time he had anticipated with dread had finally arrived.

From inside the liquefied glass, the visage of a man slowly emerged. He was dressed in the type of clothing an early twentieth century gentleman of wealth would have worn. His form was translucent and his movements appeared jerky and irregular as if he was but the projection of a man. The creature moved with the same spastic motion one would see if watching an old silent movie, filmed with an obsolete and possibly damaged camera, using substandard film. However, Washburn knew the likeness, which had visited him many times before was not an illusion but was actually the spirit of his long-dead grandfather Dwight Charles Livingston, somehow made manifest. The ghost was tall and thin, perhaps gaunt would be a better description and appeared to be in his early thirties with dark brown hair and stylish mustache. He wore wire-rimmed glasses and carried a cane or walking stick with what appeared to be an ivory handle fashioned in the shape of an animal's head, a wolf. Washburn had seen a similar cane in a large portrait of Dwight and Marie

Livingston, which he had professionally restored and which currently hung in the living room of the main farmhouse.

One site he could never fail to notice, but always wished he did not have to endure, was the long gash sliced across the specter's throat. It was like a giant gaping toothless mouth of tattered flesh hanging in a flap across the wretched creature's neck. Several times Washburn thought he had seen some sort of insects, perhaps worms or maggots crawling about inside the cavernous slash.

Over the past year, Washburn had been haunted and tormented relentlessly by the specter, ever since the start of the restoration. In fact, he had first seen the image shortly after discovering the straight razor, which now lay on the floor next to the tub. Since then he had been forced against his ever-weakening will to do whatever the spirit commanded. In fact, the reason Washburn had been in that very room, soaking in the tub that very night was because he was carrying out a set of specific instructions the tormenting specter had ordered him to complete.

Many months earlier, he had manage to resist the spirit's commandments, but after countless hours of relentless torment, sleep deprivation, weight loss and declining health, he found he had to either bend to the will of his long-dead grandfather or be driven mad by the ghost's taunting. Now, since what he hoped would be the creature's final demand had been met, Washburn prayed the spirit would be satisfied, would return to whatever corner of Hell it had arisen from and would leave him at peace.

Washburn often wondered why he simply hadn't just cut his losses and run away early on in the conflict, rather than staying and continuing to fight a losing battle against the specter at the sacrifice of his fortune and his health. But such was not his way. Anyone who knew Emerson Washburn understood the man would never give up a fight until he or his adversary were either unconscious or dead. Like the legendary John Henry battling against modern mechanization, Washburn never gave in to an enemy.

But there was more to his remaining on the property than simple stubbornness and willpower. Unknown to Washburn, there was force controlling his destiny, which was keeping him in the game, and making him believe it was all his own idea. He was being controlled and manipulated at a point far below the flesh, far below even the cellular level. His very soul was lost and was being controlled not just by the ghost of his grandfather but by another spirit in the house; that of his grandmother, Marie. They had set into motion a plan, which had to be carried out at the exact time and place of their designation and which would not only affect him, but also another unsuspecting group of Livingston decedents.

The apparition looming before him had a face a white as chalk, and its blood red eyes were sunken deep into dark-rimmed sockets. If Washburn had looked at his own sickly reflection in the surrounding mirrors, he would have been shocked at how his countenance was almost as deplorable as the long dead being before him. The creature's once fine garments were soiled and smelled as musty as a tomb. What must have once been the man's white linen shirt now hung askew was yellowed and covered with blood and filth. Washburn knew the reason the specter appeared to be much younger than Washburn's own sixty-three years, was because of the couple's early death.

Washburn sat stock still in the rapidly chilling bath water, feeling especially vulnerable in his nakedness. He was having second thoughts about reading the agreement from the confines of the tub, even though the spirit had demanded it. Then again it was not as if he had either a choice or the willpower any longer to oppose the specter's orders. After months of anguish, he knew it was futile to resist the commands of his tormenter. He started to wonder if perhaps he actually was losing his mind or if he might have already gone mad several months earlier. He no longer understood his own actions, nor could he seem to be able to control them.

The image began to emerge from the mirror, slowly floating through the air, finally hovering near the document, which rested on the marble floor. With a wave of its ghostly hand, the pages of the document quickly flipped open, and turned rapidly until the thing found what it was looking for. It stared down at the document on the floor for a moment and a look of satisfaction spread over its withered dead face. It had seen what it needed to see; the circle finally was about to be closed. What had happened before was destined to happen once again, and he would see to it.

Washburn had not taken his eyes off of the specter and with caution said "Dwight... Grandfather... I... I have done... what you requested... I have named her as my heir... the one you said... will you now please go and leave me be?" The creature did not speak but simply floated and stared blankly at the man.

Washburn asked once again, "What more can you possibly want from me? I have done as you ordered... I always do what you wish ...I have left all of my property, all of my money and all of my earthly possessions to a niece I have never even met... isn't that what you requested? Isn't that enough? Please, I beg of you... I am a sick and tormented soul... Go now and leave me in peace."

But the image did not fade, did not leave nor did it melt back into the glass as Washburn had hoped against all hope. Instead, it stared silently at Washburn. It did not speak, nor did it convey any message through its typical mysterious telepathic means, which it had used on previous occasion. Instead it simply stood and stared expressionlessly at Washburn, as if uncertain of, or deciding what its next move would be.

No, Washburn did not quite believe that to be true. He knew the creature had a plan; it always had a plan, and Washburn was certain the ghost was moving events in the direction necessary to carry out that specific plan. This time surely the situation would be no different although he feared it might not end well for him.

Then the translucent image began to dissolve before Washburn's eyes, breaking down into a mass of millions of tiny glowing, sparkling particles. It had never done any such transformation in his presence before. The sight transfixed Washburn. A moment later, the cloud of luminous white iridescent specks floated over toward Washburn and surrounded his head like a throng of flying insects. Next the collection began to grip tightly against his skull and slowly absorbed themselves through his pores, into his body. Washburn sat motionless in the tub, his eyes glazing over as if in a trance. He was clearly no longer in control of his actions. Then like a mindless robot, he slowly reached his right arm down over the side of the tub, grasping the handle of the straight razor firmly.

Sitting upright in the bathtub, Washburn, or the creature that now inhabited his body, looked down at the blade of the razor, glimmering in the candlelight. Then he took special notice to the blood red candle wax dripping down the sides of the bathtub and a sly smile appeared on his lips. Calmly looking down at his chest, the man methodically began cutting a series of diagonal wounds into his flesh, making a number of "V" shapes. The point of each "V" was located where the two diagonal lines met at the center of his chest. Washburn neither flinched nor cried out in pain even though he felt the burning, sizzling agony as if every nerve ending in his body was explode. Instead, he sat calmly as the blood streamed down from one "V" to the next like thick, muddy water running over a terraced hillside, before it began to turn the bathwater a hideous shade of crimson. He looked upward, seeming somewhat strangely amused at how the newly sliced furrows in his chest matched the patterns of the wood surrounding the walls of his spa.

Next, he made a series of incisions across his face, his forehead and cheeks before reaching up and slicing off his left ear, which fell into the water with a moist sickening plopping sound. He then made a number of deep incisions across his left arm and wrist allowing the arm to hang limply in the bloody water. As the spirit felt Washburn's body becoming weak with blood loss, the phantom reached down into the water where it systematically began to hack at Washburn's testicals and penis, castrating them from his body, allowing them to float almost comically in the ruby water like some sick, perverse bath toys.

The glowing mass of glittering elements slowly left Washburn's body and within a few seconds, the specter was once again standing next to the tub looking down at the bloody carnage it had left behind. The ghost, which had once been Dwight Livingston, floated calmly toward the mirror wall and once again was quickly absorbed into whatever horrible world existed beyond the glass.

Washburn's eyes suddenly opened, filled with shock, pain and terror upon the realization of the irreparable damage, which had been inflicted on his now dying body. Too weak to help himself, unable to move, the ravaged man moaned and cried with agony as the last of his lifeblood flowed into the tub.

Seconds before his body finally shut down, he noticed something or someone watching him from one of the other mirror walls. It appeared to be the image of two young boys, their faces hovering in the glass. Washburn could see no bodies, just floating faces. Although he had never seen the pair before, they looked familiar to Washburn. Perhaps it was because they reminded him of he and his younger brother Nathan as little boys. The one boy looked to be about six years old while the other was perhaps a year or two younger. Then, because of the extensive research he had conducted he suddenly realized who they were.

The two did not seem to have the same sort of evil countenance as the spirit of Dwight Livingston, but instead appeared to be filled with sorrow. There was an almost angelic aura about the pair as they watched with a look of grief as the last few moments of Emerson Washburn's life fade from his mutilated body. Soon the image faded from his sight as did all vision.

Washburn lie dead in the bloody cauldron his head tilted to the right against the back of the tub, his right arm dangling limply over the over side of the tub, resembling the familiar pose in the famous painting "The Death Of Marat" by Jacques-Louis David. The bloody straight razor had fallen to the floor and the tips of his fingers rested against the face of his cell phone, which lay near his last will and testament. Suddenly the phone sprang to life and began automatically dialing a number. After a series of rings, a man's deep voice answered. After several minutes in which the faint echoes of a conversation could be barely heard, the phone went dead.

As Washburn's spirit left his body, it was quickly pulled as if by some unseen magnetic force into the still undulating glass. Then the surface of the mirror returned to its normal appearance, and the room was once again silent. Inside the mirror, the emaciated, naked genital-less image of Emerson Washburn appeared looking distraught, beaten, tormented; yet sadly accepting of his fate.

The floating faces of the two young boys looked on from the adjacent mirror wall as they slowly shook their heads as if in sad resignation. A sudden cold wind swept through the room as all of the candles were extinguished and the room was plummeted into total darkness. A slight glow appeared at the center of the wall of mirrors and wild maniacal laughter echoed through the pitch-black space.

Chapter 1

The young woman sat at her kitchen table bewildered, staring down at the sealed envelope she held tightly in her trembling hands. She assumed the mysterious packet contained an important letter of some sort, and she was quite certain it would not be any typical letter. It had arrived as a certified, registered letter, requiring her signature before acceptance. Never in her life had Stephanie needed to sign for a letter, nor had she ever been required to confirm her identity by showing the postman her driver's license. It was all very new and quite disconcerting for her. She felt a strange hollow sensation deep in the pit of her stomach, as if to suggest any such letter could not possibly be good news.

She tried to think of any bills, which she might have forgotten to pay recently. Perhaps she had inadvertently forgotten to send a check for some important invoice for several months in a row, and now that particular account may have gone delinquent and had been turned over to a collection agency. She wondered if that could be possible. She didn't believe so, as she was quite fastidious about her record keeping and bill paying. No, she was quite certain this had nothing to do with any late bill payment.

She looked apprehensively at the return address, twisting her longish brown hair in circles, as was her habit. The name printed in an ornate, pretentious calligraphic gold script read, "H. Mason Armstrong, Attorney At Law". Stephanie's lips moved silently as she read the name over and over to herself, one of those childhood practices which she had never been able to overcome. "H. Mason Armstrong, Attorney At Law", she finally said aloud. Yes, this definitely seemed like quite a pretentious name indeed.

Stephanie always had a negative prejudice toward anyone who used the initial of their first name and then used their middle name as their actual name. For Stephanie, it was to suggest the name Mason Armstrong was a powerful moniker for a lawyer, whereas the owner might feel his first name, which could be Harold, or Henry or something along those lines, was not strong enough for a man so grand and in such a prestigious position. Most people would not have even given any consideration to such an thought, but Stephanie always seemed to notice things like that; she always believed she could tell when people were "putting on the dog" as her mother used to call it.

The address for the law firm was in the town of Ashton, Pennsylvania in Schuylkill County. She could not imagine what an attorney from Schuylkill County could possibly want with her. Stephanie was not overly familiar with that part of the state, having been born and raised in western Berks County some fifty-plus miles south of Ashton. The only times she had been in the county was as she passed through it when heading north for one reason or another, and those occasions had been few and far between. Once again she looked down at the ornate lettering of the return address and was convinced this lawyer was most definitely "putting on the dog", trying to appear as if he were some big-time, big city law firm, when in fact he was more likely simply a small time storefront solicitor from a small coal region town.

Stephanie was familiar with the names of many of the small towns and cities in Schuylkill County from reading various articles in the local Berks County newspaper. She knew of the city of Yuengsville, because that was one of the larger cities in the county and where the county courthouse was located. It was also the home of America's oldest brewery. She knew of the town of Ashton, which was located some fifteen or twenty miles north of Yuengsville. She recalled Ashton had a tourist attraction, a coal mine called the Miner's Tunnel where visitors could ride in coal cars over a mile down under the ground inside what was once a working coal mine. She had been meaning to take her family up there soon before Jeremy was too old and too "cool" to appreciate it, but just hadn't been able to find the time. Perhaps they could get there this year over the summer.

She also was familiar with Ashton because the manufacturing company where her husband, Jason worked as an engineer, had a sister facility just outside of the town at its lower end. Since Ashton was built along the slope of a hill, locals often referred to its east end as "downtown" or the "lower end of town" and its western end as "up town". On occasion Jason would have to make trips to the facility to coordinate some sort of manufacturing related activities. She didn't understand exactly what Jason did, but knew it was important enough for him to be paid a decent salary. And as long as he was able to earn a living and the bills got paid, that was good enough for her.

Jason would always come home from his visits to the small community with stories of how that particular manufacturing plant was one of the few places in the area where anyone could hope to earn an adequate wage and he would tell her of how hard the local people had to struggle to make ends meet. He would often joke that if they could live in Ashton while still earning his higher Berks County salary, they could live like royalty. However, since both of them had spent their lives among the rolling farmlands of western Berks County, they believed they could never be happy living anywhere else.

As a young girl, Stephanie had also heard stories of how some of her ancestors had once lived in Schuylkill County. She knew her grandmother had moved to Berks County as a young woman seeking employment opportunities and had met her grandfather, fallen in love, married and the rest, as they say, was history. Once in passing, Jason had also mentioned that one of his grandmothers was originally from Schuylkill County as well.

Her parents as well as Jason's parents were also natives of Berks County and had attended local schools. Unlike some of their high school friends who couldn't wait to graduate and get as far away from the area as possible, both she a Jason loved the calm and quite of Berks County and had no desire to ever move.

Stephanie turned the letter over and over in her moist hands, unsure if she should open it or wait until Jason returned home from work. It might be easier to face whatever potential bad news awaited her inside the letter with Jason by her side. Jason had a stalwart, logical mind men in his profession often seemed to possess, and having him with her would make it all less stressful; no matter what the news might be.

Then she realized by the time he got home from work, her stepson Jeremy, and her daughter Cindy would be home from school as well, and the house would be thrust into the type of chaos that only a twelve and ten year old could create. Not to mention the fact that the baby, eighteen-month-old Samuel would soon wake up from his afternoon nap, adding to the pandemonium. No, she supposed she would have to open the letter now, while the house was quiet and she had to time to give it her full attention.

She thought about how much she treasured these quiet times when the two older kids were at school and the baby was asleep. These were times when she could get some housework done, or perhaps work on her book, or just sit around and contemplate life. She knew such precious moments would be available less and less when little Sammy eventually grew out of his need for afternoon naps. Plus it was the end of May, and school would soon be letting out for summer vacation. She had no idea how she would ever find time to work on her book when that happened.

She knew Jason would be willing to do what he could to help her and give her some of the time she so desperately required, but there was always so much to do and she seemed to be pulled constantly in so many different directions. Stephanie feared her writing might once again fall by the wayside as it had before. She had only been able to resume writing for the first time in over ten years when school started last fall, and she had only agreed to do so after Jason had talked her into it.

He had found one of her earlier children's books while he was unpacking a box when they moved into their townhouse. The book had been written years before they met. Jason was amazed to discover his new wife was a published author, and he encouraged her to return to her obvious passion. He learned how she had all but given up writing and illustrating children's books when her daughter Cindy was born.

At that time she had still been married to her first husband, Bill Sanders. Bill had not been in any way supportive of her writing, and there had always been so much tension and stress in their lives in the form of money problems, arguing and just general bickering. Each day the couple became more distant, drifting further apart and it became impossible for her to find the right mood to stimulate her creativity. Then later, when she caught old Billy boy in the act, so to speak, with the divorcee who lived in the house across the street, it was all over but the shouting.

After her divorce, Stephanie was a single mom with primary custody of an infant daughter and practically no time for much of anything else, let alone time to consider working on books, so she simply stopped, promising herself she would get back to her work if things ever settled down. During that time, she worked a full-time job and had to put Cindy into daycare. It was a vicious cycle for her. She needed the job and the medical benefits it provided to survive, and the cost of daycare was high and took a great deal of her money, so she had to keep working to be able to afford daycare. She also hated the idea of not being home with Cindy, but she had no choice.

As a result, her evenings and weekends were dedicated to spending what little free time she had with Cindy. This designation of her free time was often like having a second a full-time job. Stephanie seemed to be constantly exhausted and stressed almost to the breaking point during those difficult years.

Even when Cindy started elementary school, things had not yet settled down. Stephanie was still a single parent, still a working mom and still had to deal with all of the pressure and expense of the heavy responsibility. When she came home at night she had to make dinner, clean the house, do the laundry and try to find quality time for Cindy, who often helped her mother with the chores not only to free up some of her mother's time but also to be able to spend more time with her.

The child support checks, which came regularly from Bill helped a bit, and on those two weekends a month when Cindy went to stay with Bill and his new wife, who Cindy liked to call "Jane the evil stepmother", Stephanie spent her time trying to catch up on whatever housework she was not normally able to do. Still there was no time for writing, only dreaming about someday resuming that part of her life once again. Whenever the rare idea for a story would pop into her already busy mind, Stephanie would quickly jot it onto a piece of note paper or a napkin the put it into a shoebox filled with hundreds of similar scraps of ideas. Someday she hoped these notes would become the seeds of a new story or a new book, but for now they were just a mess of disjointed thoughts written on snippets of paper.

Stephanie had a friend from work named Cheryl who liked to go out to the local hot spots on the prowl for single men. Cheryl was always asking Stephanie to join her on one of her weekend expeditions. Stephanie and Cheryl's relationship was a case of opposites attracting. Stephanie was basically a quiet, reserved homebody, a conservative, and a mom with a young daughter and little if any time for going out on the town. She was not looking for either another husband or a boyfriend; she was simply too busy surviving.

Cheryl on the other hand, was a wild child. She would go out almost every weekend and was well known at all of the local dance clubs and restaurants. Like Stephanie, she was divorced, but Cheryl had no kids, no responsibilities, was very liberal, friendly, outgoing, dressed in provocative clothing and occasionally would end up spending the night with one of the men she happened to meet. The two women had almost nothing in common other than their place of employment, but somehow they had become the best of friends. Although Stephanie had no desire to live Cheryl's lifestyle or vice versa, they both seemed to fill a need for each other. Stephanie provided normalcy for Cheryl, and Cheryl provided a bit of insanity for Stephanie.

One night, while Cindy was spending the weekend with Bill, Stephanie had agreed to meet Cheryl at a local restaurant and dance club for happy hour. Stephanie got there about a half hour earlier than Cheryl and went to the bar to get a drink while she waited. As she stood at the bar, a slightly nerdy looking man about her age with brown hair and wire rimmed glasses walked up to the bar with a small plate of snacks from a nearby table and ordered a drink. He seemed out of place and a bit nervous standing with his polyester pants and rumpled dress shirt.

He glanced over at Stephanie and after a substantial gulp of liquid courage he said "Hi. I'm Jason Wright", and extended his right hand in a very business-like handshake gesture. Somehow, despite his unfashionable appearance, and clumsy social skills, Stephanie saw something very innocent and at the same time appealing in the awkward man. So smiling she replied, "Hi. I'm Stephanie," and she shook his hand. She could not help but feel an instant sense of comfort just being near them man, as if she might have known him all of her life.

Neither of them was skilled at small talk, but fortunately Cheryl arrived a few minutes later and with her flamboyant personality, she quickly took charge and kept the conversation going. She could see the immediate attraction between the couple and did all she could to help them learn more about each other.

Stephanie learned Jason was also divorced and had a young son named Jeremy, two years older than Cindy was. Unlike Stephanie, Jason had only been single for about two years and had full custody of his son. His ex-wife Sarah and her new husband, Brad now lived in Ohio. Stephanie and Jason were amazed at how they both immediately seemed to get along and how much they had in common. The learned they had both graduated from the same high school. Stephanie was two years behind Jason, but they had never met or even known of each other. This was likely because they were both so quiet and socially reserved.

Six months later, Stephanie and Jason were married and a little over a year later, they discovered she was pregnant with little Sammy. Stephanie often joked affectionately with Jason how when she met him she had finally found "Mr. Right", playing on her new family surname, Wright.

Financially, things were a bit tough for the young couple as they were rebuilding their new lives together. Fortunately, Jason earned enough money for them to afford to buy a small townhouse with room for both of the kids and a small nursery for the baby. This smaller house also meant Stephanie could quit her job and stay home. Then when Jason discovered one of Stephanie's earlier published books packed away in a storage box, he encouraged her to start up her writing once more. After some resistance brought on by her own apprehension and self-doubt, Stephanie resumed writing whenever she could find the time.

She had completed the story portion of her book before Samuel was born and was struggling to complete the illustrations.

Her old publisher was so happy to learn she was back in the game he signed her to a contract without her even having to pitch the book. Stephanie had never made any significant money with her books but still got the occasional fifty or sixty-dollar royalty check from her earlier books. Her publisher believed she had what it took to create a best seller and hoped this latest book would be the one to make her a household name. Stephanie did not particularly care about wealth or fame but did hope her books might be successful. She didn't want to let her publisher or Jason down, so she worked whenever she could find time to complete what she hoped would be her best book yet...

...but not today. Today there would be no work done on this or any other book. Today she held the strange and baffling envelope in her hands. Her natural curiosity was getting the better of her. Stephanie always had a very inquisitive mind. Her mother would tell her about curiosity killing the cat when she was a young girl and although the expression often frightened her, she could not shut off her questioning mind. And now, with her mother more than fifteen years in her grave, Stephanie heard the woman's voice echoing in her head once again, speaking the words, "Remember, Stephanie, curiosity killed the cat."

But that was not exactly correct. She initially heard her mother's voice, that sweet, pleasant voice she had loved as a child. But then something frightening began to happen. The voice started out sounding like her mother's but then terrifyingly began to transform into something horrid, something evil sounding. The voice became that of a hideous old crone, cackling madly; as if to suggest in death, her mother had become some sort of hell-born demonic creature. "Curiosity killed the cat, Stephanie, and it will kill you too." The horrid voice seemed to scream inside her skull.

For a moment Stephanie's breath caught in her throat and her chest hitched as if her heart skipped a beat. She sat silently, breathing deeply, allowing her mind to clear and her heart to resume its normal rhythm. Then she realized how foolish such a thought had been. In life, her mother had been a wonderful woman and if there was a heaven, and she believed there was, surely both of Stephanie's parents were enjoying the fruits of paradise. She had no idea where such a horrible nightmarish thought of her mother would have possibly come from, but it terrified her to the very center of her soul.

A strange tingle ran down her spine. She was unsure if it were brought on as a result of the horrible previous imagining or if it was because of the letter she held tightly in her hands. She looked down at the envelope and saw it was moist with the sweat from her fingers, which had held the envelope so tightly as to leave deep damp impressions on its face.

She knew now she had no choice, she had to find out what the letter meant and if it held good or bad news. She slowly slid her finger under the flap of the envelope and carefully tore it open, revealing a single, off-white sheet of paper adorned across the top with the letterhead of the lawyer, H. Mason Armstrong, in the same pretentious gold-leaf calligraphy as the envelope.

Stephanie held the letter in her now less-than-steady hands and gradually began reading it. After completing the three short paragraphs, she read it in its entirety once again; and then a third, then forth time. The first time she read it, she understood what she had read yet did not fully comprehend the personal ramifications of its meaning as if she had been reading a letter meant for someone else. The second time she read the letter was to make sure she truly read what she thought she had read the first time. The third time she read it to get all the facts straight and the last time was simply to read it calmly and to completely understand what its contents might mean to her and her family.

According to the letter, a previously unknown uncle of hers by the name of Emerson Washburn had recently passed away. His last will and testament had been probated a few days earlier, and he had named her as the sole heir to his estate. She had no idea she had even had an Uncle Emerson. This man was apparently her late father's brother. Neither he nor her mother had ever mentioned him having a brother when she was a child. And since they had both died in a tragic car accident shortly after her eighteenth birthday, any opportunity to learn of his existence died with them.

Washburn apparently owned some sort of farm or large plot of land in a rural region outside of the town of Ashton. "Ashton?" She wondered. She found it quite strange how she had just been thinking of the town a few moments earlier, and suddenly that same town appeared as a focal point of her inheritance. The letter said she was to contact the lawyer at her earliest convenience to make arrangements to collect her inheritance and take possession of the property.

Stephanie sat with her mouth hanging slack-jawed in disbelief. Try as she might, she could not grasp what everything the letter meant. She had no idea if the mysterious Uncle Emerson had been a wealthy man or if he had just been a man of average means. Did he have a substantial insurance policy? She recalled how when her parents were killed, between the lawsuit and the money from their own life insurance her older brother

Chuck had been able to finish his last year of college and there was enough money for Stephanie to get her degree as well. She at first felt a bit guilty, thinking about the money when someone she had never known had been kind enough to name her as his heir, but she had to admit, living on a single income with three kids made money very tight and every penny would help, no matter how small the inheritance might be.

She was already thinking far into the future; about selling the inherited Schuylkill County farm as soon as she was able, for whatever she could get and then using the proceeds to buy a nice single home on a large lot in western Berks County with a big back yard for the kids to enjoy. She didn't know the condition of the buildings on the farm, but understood that land was something that always held its value, even in poor economic times. Surely she would be able to find someone to purchase the land.

Again, she felt somewhat guilty spending money she did not yet have and especially when she considered how it had come to being. Suddenly she experienced a second cold chill race down her spine and the fine hairs on the back of her neck seemed to stand on end. She felt as if someone was watching her. Stephanie quickly glanced around the room but could see no one. For the briefest of moments she thought she saw a man out of the corner of her eye, but when she turned to look, all she could see was the large oval mirror out in the hall leading to the front door. She gave a nervous laugh, thinking about how she had managed to somehow spook herself. Stephanie shook her head in disbelief and read the letter several more times.

She decided not to call Jason at work to tell him, but instead to surprise him with the news after dinner. It was Friday afternoon, the start of a weekend. His work had been so very stressful lately and with their struggling, living from paycheck to paycheck, this windfall of whatever amount of money would be just what he would need to hear about, at the end of his long workweek.

Chapter 2

Jason sat at his desk running his fingers through his tousled brown hair in frustration. He was certain this project would be the death of him, even at his young age. Jason Wright was a manufacturing engineer for a high tech multinational manufacturing company called Technofacture International. This latest project was beginning to work on the very last of his already frayed nerves.

He was writing a financial justification for the purchase of a state-of-the-art half-million-dollar computer controlled machining center. According to his estimates and calculations, the automated machining cell would most certainly pay for itself in less than two years, which was an incredible return on investment. But the justification process was completely out of his comfort zone, and he was certain no matter how many times he checked and rechecked his figures something would be wrong which might endanger the project's approval.

And that was just the tip of the stress-inducing iceberg for him. Even if the project was approved, he still had to arrange for the purchase of the machine as well as all of the related components and subcomponents of the manufacturing cell including a cutting tool package consisting of more than two hundred tools. Plus he had to see to the design and purchase of work-holding devices, an overhead crane, cabinets, utility carts and so forth. Then he had to coordinate the machine installation as well as learn to write programs to control the machine, train the machine operators, prepare operator manuals and about a thousand other incidental items. During more prosperous economic times, this would have been handled by a team of at least two or possibly three different engineers, but in the lean, mean world of twenty-first century manufacturing the sole responsibility fell on his young shoulders. In addition, he had to keep up with his normal shop floor support duties while simultaneously juggling the project.

The success of this project was paramount. It had been eight years since his facility had been given capital funds for the purchase of new equipment and if this project was not just a success, but also a resounding, knock-one-out-of-the-ballpark type of success it might be the beginning of the end for his facility.

Most of the other machines in the plant were so old and so antiquated, just keeping them running was a daunting task for their maintenance department despite the high skill level of the technicians. Not to mention the difficulty maintenance personnel had trying to locate and acquire replacement parts for machines that were considered obsolete. His company was falling far behind in their manufacturing productivity and efficiencies, so much so, he feared if things did not soon turn around, he and many others might be losing their well-paid jobs.

The facility where he worked was in Lancaster County, Pennsylvania and was just one of dozens of plants the company owned around the world. Jason's site was also one of the few sites to still have a labor union. The company's once cooperative relationship with their bargaining unit had been damaged over the previous few years and seemed to continue to degenerate almost weekly. Most of the grievances filed by union members were unable to be handled at the local level and ended up being resolved by the corporate lawyers. This brought a great deal of unwanted attention by corporate management to the plant's labor-relations problems.

As the company's productivity figures fell, more and more of the manufacturing work was being shipped to other Technofacture facilities around the world. With the dirt-cheap labor rates in China and India, this had the potential of becoming a major problem for his plant. Fortunately, at least for the time being, the quality of the work returning from those foreign facilities was sub-standard, especially when compared to the superior craftsmanship his site could produce. But with each shipment received, it was clear the foreign division's manufacturing skills were improving, and Jason suspected within a year or two they would either equal or surpass the quality of his facility, and they would produce the product at a fraction of the cost stateside.

As if to make matters worse, foreign manufacturing plants were not the only threat to his future. His company also had a manufacturing plant some sixty miles northeast of Lancaster outside of the small town of Ashton. It was a non-union facility with a highly skilled highly-motivated workforce, more modern machinery and a much lower labor rate then at the Lancaster site. In addition, the workforce was known throughout the corporation for their strong work ethic, high productivity, low absenteeism and general dedication to getting the job done.

These facts alone were enough to make Jason concerned about his job security, but with his facility falling farther behind every day he was beginning to believe corporate would never approve the money for a new piece of equipment, no matter how good the numbers looked or how appealing the payback might be. Approval for the justification for the machine had already passed the company's local financial controller as well as all of the essential managers at the Lancaster facility and was currently in the hands of the division president. That corporate executive would be the one to deliver the final verdict. Jason felt like the weight of the world was resting on his shoulders, as if the fate of his small manufacturing plant might very well be spelled out by the direction this single project would take. He had no idea at that moment just how accurate his concerns were.

As Jason sat staring at the computer screen reviewing his massive spreadsheet full of efficiency calculations, machine rates, productivity estimates and capital equipment costs, his phone rang startling him back to reality and breaking his concentration. It was a double ring which meant it was an inside call; Jason assumed it might be the shop floor with a problem; it seemed lately his day was nothing but interruptions in the form of one crisis or another. Jason took a deep breath, composing himself then answered the phone.

"Jason Wright, Manufacturing Engineering," he said in his typical cheerful greeting, preparing himself for the noisy background sounds of manufacturing machinery to resonate through the phone; but there were no such sounds. Jason instantly realized it was someone calling from inside the office building.

"Jason," the voice said. "This is Walt. Can you come into my office?" Walter Williams was Jason's department manager. He was a kindly, even-tempered man just a year or so from retirement. He had been grooming Jason to take his place whenever he chose to finally leave the workforce. And although Jason was flattered by the vote of confidence, he had a lot of concerns about moving into the role of department manager.

Jason was an outstanding engineer and loved his work, attacking problems with all of his energy, but he had heard stories of other competent engineers who had tried their hand at management positions and just could not seem to make the transition very well. He had actually known several such men himself. He feared he too might be one of those people. Jason considered himself a doer and not someone who had the ability to get the job done by directing the efforts of others. He possessed a good deal of natural leadership capabilities, but he knew having such abilities to use at his choosing and being required to use them constantly to get the job done were two entirely different animals.

As Jason approached his boss's office, he was suddenly filled with an overwhelming sense of dread as if some sort of impending doom awaited him inside. He walked toward the door feeling as if he were moving in slow motion, reluctant to place his hand on the gleaming metal knob. It was a strange, unexplainable surrealistic sensation of anxiety as if he were experiencing some sort of premonition. But Jason did not believe in omens, precognitions or any such things. He was an engineer, educated in the ways of logic and problem solving. He assumed the stress he was feeling from the project was affecting him in other ways; such as the bizarre emotions, he was currently experiencing. Taking another deep cleansing breath, forcing the odd sensation from his body, Jason gripped the knob and began to turn it as the door slowly opened inward.

Walter was seated behind his huge desk, which was in its typical state of disarray with papers stacked high on uneven piles, some of which had fallen and scattered across the top of his desk, intermingling with other collapsed piles in a mass of papers accumulated in the middle of his desk. It never ceased to amaze Jason how no matter how cluttered and disorganized Walt's desk looked, as soon as he needed some particular document he would simply reach into one of the impossibly cluttered piles and with the flick of a wrist, pull out the exact document in question without ever having to search.

Walter leaned back in his huge chair, attempting to appear relaxed with his two beefy forearms resting on its own thick leather arms. Jason thought he noticed some poorly disguised tension in the way the man's fingers held tightly onto the fronts of the chair arms as if his boss was bracing himself to deliver some bad news. Walter was a big man, not big in the tall sense but big in the weight sense. Only about five-foot eight inches tall and well over three hundred pounds of unexercised fat, the man was a prime candidate for a stroke or heart attack and the way his brow seemed to be glistening with sweat, Jason feared such an attack might be imminent.

"What's wrong, Walt?" Jason asked, seeing the uncertainty and displeasure on the man's face. Walter was not just Jason's boss but over the years he had become his close friend and mentor as well. Jason didn't like to see his friend appearing so overwrought.

"Well," the man said reluctantly, "it's about the justification you wrote and sent to me for the new machine."

Jason asked, "Did they approve it? Are they going to give us the money?"

"Not exactly," Walter said rather cryptically, his large bulk appearing to almost squirm with discomfort. "The suits up at corporate believe the project is a good one and one which they'd have to be crazy not to approve." Then after a moment of silent hesitation, he said wiping the sweat from his brow with a handkerchief he kept handy for just such occasions, "But they don't want to approve it for our facility."

"Let me cut to the chase here, Jason," Walter said and Jason knew he was definitely in for bad news. Whenever Walter used clichés like "cut to the chase" or "the bottom line is..." Jason understood he was about to deliver some bad news and wanted to get to it as quickly as possible. Walter said, "They like the project and are going to approve the machine's purchase, but the machine won't be installed at this facility."

Jason asked, "Won't be installed here? But it's our project, hell it's my project, where else would it be installed?"

"The machine is going to be installed in the facility up in Ashton..." Walter explained, "The boys at corporate are in love with that operation and at this point in time feel the folks in Ashton can do no wrong; whereas they believe we can do nothing right. So they decided to go ahead and purchase the machine, but the entire project is being handed over to the Ashton facility."

"They can't do that!" Jason said with frustration, "How can they do that?"

"Look, Jason." Walter consoled, "I know you are upset and justifiably so. This pisses me off as well. But you must understand; unfortunately the suits can do whatever they damn well choose to do. It's their company, their money and this just happens to be what they have decided to do."

"But what about us? What about all of us here?" Jason asked, leaning forward in his seat.

For a moment, Walter did not reply. He looked down at his hands now tee-peed on his lap, his elbows leaning on the huge arms of his chair. Then after taking a deep breath he looked directly at Jason and said with frustrated resignation, "We can't be expected to keep competitively manufacturing parts without outdated equipment...and the fact is we won't be doing so for very much longer."

Jason felt as if he had been hit in the face with a baseball bat. He sat stunned looking at Walter with great trepidation. "By the end of July, this year, Lancaster will cease all machining of products. From that point on all machining operations will be transferred to the Ashton facility."

Walter explained further, "Now, Jason, what I just told you and what I'm about to tell you is extremely confidential. It cannot leave this office. Is that clear?" Jason numbly nodded his head. "Alright then. Next Monday and Tuesday, a delegation from the Ashton organization will be visiting our plant to evaluate our machinery to determine which, if any machines they might want to take to their facility. When the group is touring the shop, if anyone from the shop asks you anything, you are to simply reply that you are not sure who the people are or why they are here. You have got to play dumb about all of this."

"Wa... wa..." Jason mumbled, suddenly unable to put two words together to form a cohesive thought.

"But what is going to happen to everyone here in the office?" Jason said, gesturing to the door, indicating his salaried coworkers.

"Well." Walter said, "Let's start with me. They offered me an early retirement package, you know, a golden handshake as they call it. The way it looks, I will be retiring sometime before the end of July."

Jason stared dumfounded at Walter for a moment, thinking about the implications of what he had just said, then realized with a bit of building anger that Walter was being given a great offer. After all, he was planning to retire soon anyway and now with the manufacturing operations ceasing, he would be receiving a good financial package, allowing him to retire earlier than he originally planned.

Then Jason said sarcastically and with a bit of attempted self-deprecating humor aimed both at his boss's good fortune and his own apparent misfortune, "Let me guess... you get the golden handshake and the rest of us get the golden shower... right?"

Walter smiled knowingly, despite the circumstances, understanding that Jason was simply letting off a bit of steam with his off-color yet sadly accurate assessment.

"I suppose you're almost right about that." Walter said reluctantly, "A lot of my direct employees will definitely get pissed on before all of this is over. Almost everyone in this department will be losing their jobs that is...except for you."

Jason suddenly sat up straight in his chair realizing what Walt had just said. "Wa... what do you mean, except for me? Are you saying I will still have a job? How can I still have a job?"

Walter smiled a fatherly smile and said with a certain degree of pride, "Jason, as you are aware, for some time I've been grooming you to fill my shoes when I retire. As such, I have always spoken highly about you not only to the management here in Lancaster, but to the managers at our other facilities, as well as to the boys in corporate. As a result, they have instructed me to offer you an alternative to being laid off, and I must say it is a very generous offer, considering the current world economic situation."

Suddenly Jason became hopeful. Maybe he wasn't going to lose his job after all. He hadn't realized it but all the while he was listening to Walter he was subconsciously dreading   having to break the news to Stephanie. But now, from what Walt was saying, perhaps there might be a small ray of hope.

"What sore of alternative?" he asked.

Walter hesitated for a beat then said, "Everyone was impressed with your work on this project and they are prepared to offer you the 'Manager Of Manufacturing Engineering' position at the facility in Ashton."

"Ashton?" Jason said in disbelief, "But what about Jim Dodson? Isn't he still the manager at the Ashton facility?"

"He is... or I should say he was." Walter replied, "But he too was offered a chance to take early retirement and he jumped at the opportunity even faster than I did."

That was when the realization hit Jason. He was going to have to uproot and relocate his family. Sure, it would only be about fifty miles north of where they currently lived, and probably would not be a major inconvenience for visitations with his stepdaughter Cindy's dad, but still it was a major adjustment to put his family through; a new place to live and a new school in the fall.

"Jason," Walter confided, "I don't know that you have a lot of choices here. However, I still would like you to take the weekend and talk it over with Stephanie. Maybe you two can take the kids and drive up through the area around Ashton and see what sort of house you might want to buy. You can get a lot more for your dollar up there and your salary will be substantially higher, so I see no reason why you would not be able to buy or even build a much bigger home...

"And I'll tell you what... I'm going to need you here the early part of next week for a few days until the Ashton group is finished, but if you decide to take the offer, you can take off next Wednesday through Friday to drive up to Schuylkill County and maybe meet with some realtors. I'll speak with the personal folks at Ashton to see who they recommend.

"Look," Walter said. "It's two fifteen. Why don't you head out for the weekend, drive around for a bit, maybe go and sit under a tree or something and think about how you want to present this to Stephanie. It's a great opportunity, Jason, and a lot better than the alternative for sure. But it's also a very big step, and you both need to be onboard with whatever decision you make."

Jason stood on wobbly legs, his mind reeling. He had so many things to consider, so much to think about. He thanked Walter once again and headed for the door. As he passed a large mirror, which hung on the wall behind the office door, he thought he saw a strange man staring out at him. Although he only got a split-second glimpse, the image made his breath catch in his throat. Jason swore the man appeared as if he had wild and insane eyes. His face was a mass of bloody cuts, and his left ear appeared to have been severed from his head as well. Jason blinked and the image was gone.

Walter noticed Jason's reaction and asked "Are you all right, Jason? You look like you just saw the devil, himself."

Jason realized he must have had one of those strange moments when you see something out of the corner of your eye; something you swear you actually saw only to discover it was all an illusion or a trick of light, shadow and imagination. "Man," he replied, "all of this is so much to absorb. I think maybe I need a drink to calm my nerves; this stuff must be really getting to me."

"Well, that's probably not a bad idea, Jason, my boy." God knows I've had my share of drinks while trying to cope with everything that's happening. The best advice I can give you is to do whatever it takes to help you relax and then figure out what you think is best for Steph and the kids. I'll be right here for you whenever you make up your mind. And if you think of any more questions you have for me just call me anytime. You have all my numbers."

On his drive home, Jason tried to figure out how he was going to break the news to Stephanie. Neither of them had ever even considered moving before, but now they would have to give it some serious thought, as his only other option would be to try and find another job locally or else to be unemployed. He had enough severance and vacation to carry him for a few months at best, but regardless, he would have to try to land another position right away. He was the sole source of income for his family, supporting not only Stephanie but their three kids as well. He didn't like the idea of relocating north but with the economy in the toilet, he might have to face the fact that he likely might not have any alternative.

He hated the idea of introducing more change into his kids' lives. It was only a few years earlier that Jason had gotten divorced from his unfaithful first wife and then young Jeremy had to get used to living with Jason alone, with essentially no mother.

His ex-wife and her new husband had moved to Ohio and although she always said she missed Jeremy badly, she never seemed to be short on excuses for why she was not able to either come to Pennsylvania to see Jeremy or to allow him to go out to Ohio as well.

Jeremy had only seen his mother once since the divorce. And then to complicate matters further, the young boy then had to adjust to Jason's marriage to Stephanie as well as moving into their new townhouse and getting to know his new younger stepsister Cindy. Jason was grateful Jeremy and Cindy did not have to change schools or that might have made a tough situation even worse. And then when Stephanie became pregnant, the two step-siblings, formerly only children, suddenly found themselves with a new baby brother. Jason realized it was quite an adjustment for them to make and was pleased with how, despite everything, they seemed to adapt quite well.

Cindy's father, Bill, who lived in northern Berks County, almost at the Schuylkill county border, was still an active part of her life, and she saw him regularly. Since he lived about half way between where they currently lived and Ashton, any move they might consider would not impact his relationship with Cindy or his visitation significantly.

However, no matter how much he might hope for the contrary, Jason knew that moving would definitely impact the children to a greater extent than he would prefer. The two kids had been in the same school system since pre-school, and at ten and twelve years old had a large network of close friends. There was no way he could imagine pulling off a move to Ashton without affecting them in a very negative way. Jason decided neither he nor Stephanie should mention anything to the kids until they both had at least an initial chance to discuss their limited alternatives.

Jason also didn't look forward to adding the stress of this new situation to his current work stress and wondered how badly it could affect what he considered his otherwise perfect home life. Yet knew he would have little choice but to face the problem head-on as he did all similar situations and try to find the best solution. He was seriously considering the possibility of commuting the fifty plus miles north every day. He already had a forty-five minute drive to work. So what would another fifteen or twenty-five minutes matter; especially as a temporary solution? But he knew it would eventually begin to take its toll, physically and mentally not to mention the wear and tear on his car as well as physical dangers associated with such a long and unpredictable commute when the cold winter months arrived.

Jason thought back to a time during the early part of his career when he had worked for a Berks County manufacturer and had known some shop employees who commuted daily from Schuylkill County to the Reading area in order to take advantage of the higher paying jobs. They enjoyed benefiting from the higher wages they earned but had no desire to relocate their families out of their native county. They were a tightly knit group of workers which some of Jason's co-workers jokingly referred to as the "Coal Region Mafia".

Some of these men carpooled while others paid drivers for the right to have a seat in their vans full of commuters. This allowed them to still commute to work but sleep during the more than one-hour trip while the van owners drove. Jason knew of three or four workers who owned large vans and charged people to ride with them daily; these entrepreneurs always seemed to have a list of people waiting and never had empty seats. It was a nice little under-the-table business, which allowed the owners to always drive brand new automobiles, which their passengers helped to pay for.

However, he never heard of anyone heading in the opposite direction as jobs in Schuylkill County were few and the wages were not up to par with their neighboring counties. So if he planned to commute, Jason knew he would likely be doing so alone and with the price of gas he wondered how much of his raise he would end up pouring directly into his gas tank. But nevertheless he decided riding alone might be for the best, as he often had to arrive early and occasionally leave late, which he suspected might occur more frequently with his new managerial responsibilities.

Jason really didn't mind the idea of a long commute to work. With his present daily drive to Lancaster, he had become an avid listener to audio books. He would regularly got to the local library and borrow numerous audio books. Jason found that it not only made great use of the commuting time and was relaxing, but it also provided him with an opportunity to listen to the writings of authors he might not normally take the time to read.

During his long drive home, Jason realized this was going to be one of the toughest weekends of his life and he and Stephanie would have to do a lot of soul searching before making their final decision.

Suddenly he felt a prickling sensation on the back of his neck and felt as if someone was watching him. He looked into the rearview mirror and within a split second took in all of the details of what he believed he saw. For a brief second, Jason was certain he there was a man sitting in the back seat of his car. The man appeared to be in his sixties, rail thin and shirtless. The man had long slashes down his chest forming a series of V-shapes from which blood flowed freely. The man's face was likewise slashed as if with a razor and one of his ears was missing. Jason was certain it was the same tortured man who he thought he had seen in Walt's mirror; but he know was impossible.

Startled he blinked his eyes and just as quickly as it had appeared, the horrific vision in the back seat was gone from sight. Jason felt a steady rough bumping and realized his car was heading off the highway. He quickly brought the car back under control and reluctantly looked again into the rearview mirror, and to his gratitude unspeakable creature was gone.

"Wow." Jason said aloud, "I really have to find some way to relieve some of this stress. It must really be getting to me."

The rest of the way home Jason's eyes darted between the highway and the rearview mirror as if he believed the horrible vision would return. Despite the mild May temperature and the fact his air conditioning was running full blast, Jason was drenched with a cold sweat beneath his clothing.

Chapter 3

Forty-eight hours earlier...

A darkly clad man hunched silently in the shadows, feeling the tumblers of the lock gradually give way beneath the pressure of his special burglar's lock pick held tightly in his right hand. He had practiced this task many times during the past several weeks, honing his technique for this special moment. Soon he heard the familiar click, indicating the locking mechanism had released and he was clear to go inside. Opening the door ever so slowly, he waited a moment to hear if there was an alarm system present and if so, if it was activated. He was pleased to have his patient anticipation greeted with nothing but wonderful silence. Apparently, there really was no security system to worry about. This wasn't what he would consider the smartest move on the homeowner's part, but perhaps in this area of the country locals didn't deem such countermeasures necessary. Or maybe the owner simply never got around to installing one. And now of course it was much too late for that. Knowing what he did about the owner, the man assumed the owner's arrogance would not have permitted him to install such a system.

He opened the back door of the house and slid quickly into the darkened rear kitchen, shutting the door behind him. He stood silently in the room; his back pressed tightly against the door, feeling the cool glass of the small window panes against the back of his head, the only sound in the kitchen being that of his own shallow breath escaping in barely audible puffs.

He waited, giving his eyes time to adjust to the near total darkness, which was scarcely supplemented by the meager light of the moon coming in through the windows with their curtains drawn tightly shut. Jack thought about how long he had searched to find his enemy; all the years he had planned to exact his revenge. He looked down at his left hand, which he stretched open, palm up, fingers extended, appearing as nothing more than a black-silhouetted form. But in that charcoal shadow, he could see the one missing element of the shape, the place where his ring finger had once been. It was the finger, which had once held his precious wedding ring, but now both the ring and the finger were long gone; taken years ago by his enemy; taken by the rotten black-hearted bastard known as Emerson Washburn.

Jack Moran thought again, of how angry and frustrated he had become a month ago, when after he had finally been released from prison, and had spent six months tracking Emerson Washburn, he finally learned of his location only to hear of the man's recent death. Jack had planned his revenge for so many years while he wasted away in that prison cell. He often thought of how someday he would track down Emerson Washburn and torture him mercilessly. Jack planned on making the man endure the same agony he, himself had suffered at Washburn's own hand so many years earlier, but he intended to make Washburn's suffering a thousand times worse.

But now, since Washburn was already dead, likely rotting away in some lost hole in Hell, Jack would unfortunately never have the opportunity to properly seek his retribution. He had originally heard through his street connections that Washburn was dead and then later heard from a few talkative residents at a local bar how Washburn had apparently committed suicide.

For some reason, the regional newspaper chose not to mention anything about Washburn's suicide, but simply stated he had been found dead in his bathtub. Anyone reading it might assume a heart attack or stroke, but not suicide. He wondered if Washburn had managed to gain control of several important local officials with the power to control such things. Jack didn't know for certain and didn't particularly care, but it sounded like something Washburn might do. As far as Jack was concerned, dead was dead and the once great Emerson Washburn was now as dead as anyone could be. However, he was frustrated he had missed his opportunity to be the bringer of that death.

"Suicide was too good for that rotten pig," Jack had thought to himself. "He saved himself from the Hell on earth I planned to bring down on him." Perhaps the ghosts of the people Washburn had killed in his sordid past had come back to haunt him, and had driven him mad. That thought brought a slight smile to Jack's silhouetted face. Ironically, Jack had no idea how close to the truth his statement had been.

Jack turned slightly to look out through the kitchen door window, out onto the huge rear deck making sure the five-gallon can of gasoline he bought with him was readily available. He could see in-ground swimming pool he had walked around to access the deck. Jack placed the lock pick into his jacket pocket and felt for the lighter, which he had put there to use later. Then he reached around to touch the thirty-eight-caliber revolver he had loaded and tucked into his jeans at the small of his back. He didn't actually believe he would need the weapon but it never hurt to be prepared, and if he suddenly did need it, the weapon would be easily accessible.

Jack had heard that Washburn had left his old life of crime in New Jersey behind him and had retired to a new quiet life in Pennsylvania. Jack was shocked to see the isolated and serene atmosphere the former gangster had chosen. Then he thought "No wonder he had killed himself. Such an environment would drive any self-respecting city boy crazy." He suppressed a laugh.

He also wondered how the man could survive alone without his entourage of goons to watch his back or how Washburn could live without hurting someone at least once a week. He had experienced Washburn's propensity for incredible violence first-hand, and understood just how much the man enjoyed inflicting pain. Jack was not at all surprised when, throughout the years, he also heard stories of other horrendous acts Washburn had committed, which were even more deplorable than what Washburn had done to him.

For over twelve long years, Jack Moran had dreamed of capturing and binding the man so he was helpless and then yanking out his fingernails one at a time. Next, he would use a tin shear to systematically remove each of the bastard's fingers, one knuckle joint at a time. Then he would have started on Washburn's toes. He had planned to keep the man alive for as long as possible, making the torture seem endless, until Washburn finally succumbed to his trauma and blood loss. But now, that dream was never to be realized. But that didn't mean Jack couldn't still exact some form of revenge. And that was exactly why Jack Moran had broken into Washburn's home this very evening; for a little bit of R and R: revenge and retribution. Also, he had to retrieve something of his own; something very precious to him.

Standing in the darkness he thought back to the night when it had all happened, that unforgettable night when he had been overpowered and knocked unconscious by several of Washburn's goons. Although he was not a large or powerful man, Jack always prided himself on being able to hold his own in any type of physical altercation. But on the night Washburn's men took him, Jack had been caught off guard and never had the opportunity to even attempt to defend himself.

Jack Moran was not a career criminal or even a petty thief at the time he unfortunately crossed paths with Emerson Washburn. He had however, been a compulsive gambler and a chronic liar, two undesirable vices which when combined always seemed to bring with them very negative consequences. But no matter how unsavory or distasteful, neither of these traits was considered illegal in the eyes of the law.

Unfortunately, for John "Jack" Michael Moran II, his inalienable right to gamble had become much more than the occasional legal vice, it had instead become a compulsion, an addiction. As a result, Jack found himself expanding his gambling activities beyond those legal games of chance and into the dark underworld of illegal gambling. Even more unfortunate for Jack, when it came to gambling, his propensity for good luck fell far short of his compulsive need to gamble. That was how he found himself owing over fifty large to a bookie representing the interests of one Camden, New Jersey businessman of sorts by the name of Emerson Washburn.

About a year earlier, Jack's wife Christina to whom he had been married for seventeen years and their only child, a lovely fifteen-year-old beauty named Samantha died in a tragic automobile accident. Prior to the accident, Jack had been attending Gamblers Anonymous meetings regularly, trying to get his head straight and was doing quite well at fighting his addiction. He always wore his wedding ring proudly, affirming a new commitment to staying away from gambling of any type and rededicating himself to his wife and daughter. His ring became more than just a symbol of his love and his marriage; it became a talisman, and a source of strength, which he used to battle the war raging daily inside of him.

However, once his loving wife and daughter were taken from him, he fell into an uncontrollable downward spiral of drinking, followed by reckless gambling. He still treasured the ring, what it symbolized for him, and always would. But it no longer seemed to hold any of its original power, real or imagined, to help him fight his inner demons. The accident left him a broken, empty husk of a man and killed any desire to refrain from acting on his impulses. Jack fell off the gambling wagon in a big way and headed full speed down the road to self-destruction. Before long, he was over fifty thousand dollars in debt to Emerson Washburn.

Washburn was a large and powerful man who had come to Camden as a young man without a penny to his name. Washburn had scraped and clawed his way up from the streets to a position of power in local New Jersey back-alley gambling activities. Rumor had it that Washburn was also into extortion, prostitution, pornography, drugs and other such vices. He made a very lucrative living with his small, close-knit group of thugs and yet still managed somehow to operate below the radar of the police as well as the major New Jersey crime syndicates.

Washburn understood his own limitations and always made sure not to step on the wrong toes or to allow his business to grow bigger than it absolutely needed to be. The bad thing about this philosophy was it kept him from making a lot more money. However, the good thing about it was his low-key operation permitted him to not be of interest to the police, which in turn kept him out of jail; or the mob, which kept him alive. Although many people in the business knew and feared Washburn, he understood and accepted his place in the pecking order of the New Jersey crime families and prided himself on knowing how to make a lot of money while still keeping a low profile.

He occasionally did a favor for and when necessary, paid fees to competing crime syndicates, just to kept them all happy and off his back. A shrewd businessman, Washburn understood he had to keep his ego and greed in check and never cross the syndicate bosses. This was because no matter how powerful he thought he might be, they could easily crush him like an insect in a heartbeat, and they would not hesitate to do so.

Another negative aspect of running such a limited size operation was he had to do some of the muscle work himself. This was not to suggest Washburn didn't enjoy doing that sort of thing, but it did take him away from the more important duties of running his enterprises. As a result, he always had a few of his crew who specialized in doing whatever was necessary to convince anyone who was late with a payment how important it was to not keep Mr. Washburn waiting for his money.

However, whenever someone was in debt to the tune of say fifty thousand or more as Jack Moran had been, Washburn often found it critical that he take care of such situations personally. It was a matter of his need to command respect; and not just the respect of the person who might be behind in his payment, but also the respect of his crew. Washburn wanted his boys to know he was not opposed to getting his own hands dirty. Washburn did not like asking someone to do something he would not be willing to do himself.

That was how one night, almost thirteen years earlier, Jack Moran had been brought before him, bleeding and beaten, pleading for his life, swearing on the departed souls of his wife and daughter he would find a way to pay Washburn back and would do so quickly. Washburn had no desire to kill the man, since it was impossible to get money from a corpse. Likewise, he knew crippling the man would hinder his ability to earn a living and pay back the debt as well. However, he did think the insolent actions of this Jack Moran could not be ignored and the man needed to be taught a lesson.

His boys has roughed the man up a bit, and Jack had been crying and pleading for another chance, but Washburn felt something more meaningful was needed to drive home the fact that he would not tolerate any more impudent actions on the man's part. When the word spread on the street, it would also serve to remind others of what would most definitely happen to them, should they likewise cross Emerson Washburn.

That was when Washburn decided what action he would take. So with two of his goons holding Jack down, with the man's hand positioned flat on a table top; Washburn pulled out a short tin shear and without showing the slightest bit of emotion he methodically cut off Jack's ring finger, ring and all.

Jack screamed in agony as his blood pooled onto the top of the table, pumping and spurting from the severed stump in perfect rhythm with his now racing heartbeat. Washburn nodded to one of his henchmen; one of the two remaining men who were not busy holding Jack down, and the man secured a gag tightly across Jack's mouth, muffling his screams. Tears streamed from Jack's eyes as he moaned uncontrollably beneath the gag.

Washburn backhanded Jack across the face and the shock of the blow brought Jack back from his world of pain to the reality of his current potentially fatal situation. He realized he could very well die within the next few minutes depending entirely upon Washburn's mood. Jack forced down his agony as he eyes blazed with a mixture of hatred and terror. Washburn sat quietly staring at Jack contemplating the direction his decision would take. After a few moments, Washburn held the bloody severed finger with the ring still in place, just a few inches from Jack's eyes and spoke.

"I know how much this ring means to you Jack, not to mention, I suppose, the finger it was attached to." The goons holding Jack began to chuckle until Washburn gave them a hard look and once again all sound ceased. "I know about the accident which took your wife and daughter, and I know what this ring symbolizes to you. I'm afraid it's obviously too late for the finger, but I may be willing to give you back your ring and spare your life."

"I'll tell you what I am going to do with you, Jack, my boy," Washburn said. "You seem like a reasonable, level headed young man. I think perhaps I will give you one more opportunity to make restitution."

Jack's look of defiance disappeared, quickly replaced by one of hope, of acquiescence to whatever demand Washburn might make.

Washburn said, "I hope you realize what I am about to suggest to you is going to make my associate, Gino, over there quite angry, since he would like nothing better than to make you suffer long and hard. Isn't that right, Gino?" Washburn looked over Jack's shoulder toward a mountain of a man standing in the shadows. He had not been one of the men holding Jack down but a much bigger, more menacing figure. From his vantage point and because of the poor lighting in the room, Jack could not determine if the figure said was that of a man or if it were some sort of horrible inhuman creature. The shadowed figure said nothing but instead made an unintelligible grunting sound.

"You see, Jack," Washburn explained, "It's not that Gino is angry or upset with you as I am, or that he even cares about you in the slightest. He's simply one of those special individuals that enjoy hurting other people. He is very serious about his work and tends to become disappointed when I decide to take away one of his playthings such as you. But sadly, I'm afraid he will have to live with his disappointment for now and wait for another opportunity. And we all know when it comes to gambling addicts such as you; there will always be another opportunity. Your type always ends up right back here in the same exact predicament."

Washburn hesitated for a beat then said; "So then, let's get down to business, Jack. I realize you are not really an experienced thief, but simply an out of control gambler and liar who has had a few bad breaks. But I think I've come up with a way for you to get me the money you own me by tomorrow night and still manage to keep yourself alive in the process." This made Jack look suspiciously at Washburn. He didn't trust the large man as far as he could throw him, yet he was eager to learn about what he might have to do in order to survive this ordeal. He had no desire to even look back again at the huge man named Gino who was still hiding in the shadows, nor could he begin to imagine the idea of the man-monster actually torturing him to death.

"I am going to offer you one of two alternatives," Washburn said. "Either you can go out between now and twenty-four hours from now and do what I tell you to do to get me my money by tomorrow night or else I will hand you over to Gino. I realize it doesn't sound like much of a choice, but unfortunately for you, Jack, it's all I am offering. Either you get me my money or Gino gets you."

Jack mumbled beneath his gag, and Washburn nodded his head to one of the henchman to remove the obstruction. Jack sobbed for a moment, took a deep hitching breath and asked.

"But... but... what can I do? How... how... can I possibly... get that much money?"

Washburn said as if speaking to a child, "Now don't worry about that, Jack. I have a plan; it's called armed robbery."

"But...I...never robbed anyone before... I wouldn't even know... where to start," Jack said terrified.

"Well, Jack," Washburn countered, "lucky for you, Johnny and Santos here do." Washburn indicated the two men who had been holding Jack. First, they are going to take you to get you hand stitched up Then they'll take you to places we know have cash. They'll give you a big unloaded   gun and then you will just walk into the stores and rob them. Then you bring the money out to Johnny and Santos and move onto the next target. By the end of the night if the cops don't catch you or you don't get killed, you will have brought me more than enough money to pay me back. Then maybe you will get your precious ring back."

'But... but..." Jack tried to interject.

"No buts, Jack," Washburn warned. Then he signaled to the dark figure in the back of the room and the massive man-beast walked slowly to toward Jack. The hulking creature was beyond huge and was rippling with muscles. His enormous Neanderthal head was colossal with a low hanging hairy brow and deep-set dark eyes. His eyes appeared to be void of any emotion, what Jack thought of as "dead eyes". The man's face was covered with scars and his nose was broken and twisted. He wore a tight black tee shirt and dark pants that did little to disguise his massive muscles.

"Now Jack, if you don't do what I say then Gino here is going to take you into the other room to get to know you better, and I would guess that after only a few minutes alone with Gino, you'll be cursing your own mother for ever giving you life."

The huge ape-man's eyes began to sparkle with obvious pleasure at the thought of having Jack to himself as a sinister smile curled up on his thick simian lips. Jack was unable to come to grips with the idea that the monstrous creature looming before him was actually human. The term "sub-human" came to mind, but that didn't feel quite right to him. Perhaps "non-human" or "other-than human" would be a more accurate way to describe the heinous man-beast. Whatever the man's true nature, Jack understood no matter how much he might try to imagine the horror which would await him in that back room, he would never be able to come up with any image equal to that of the actual pain and agony he knew he would endure at the hands of this animal.

Jack quickly turned back to Washburn, unable to keep looking at the monster of a man. "Alright... I'll do it... I'll get you your money...but after I do what you ask...will you keep your word and let me go?"

Washburn looked at jack with such a fury that Jack began to wonder if perhaps the man would kill him immediately, himself instead of giving him another chance. "I always keep my word, Jack!" Washburn shouted angrily. "You should know that."

Then Washburn seemed to visually push his anger aside as the dark cloud of fury left his face returning him to a calmer demeanor. He said with confidence, "And, Jack, we both know that even if you succeed and get me my money, it will only be a matter of time until you are in the same boat and will end up owing me again. When that day comes, Jack, maybe I will let Gino work on your remaining fingers or some other part of your body instead." Washburn looked deliberately down at the crotch of Jack's pants.

Jack felt a cold chill run down his spine, as he recalled how the stump of his finger screamed with agony and throbbed unmercifully bringing with it the realization of just how true Washburn's words were. Even if somehow he managed to get himself out of that scrape, as long as he continued to stay in New Jersey and gamble the way he had been doing, he would once again find himself in debt to Washburn or someone just like him and once again be facing the consequences.

As Jack Moran stood in the dark kitchen of the now dead Emerson Washburn, looking down at the missing shadow, which was once his finger, he recalled the rest of that night and how he had dutifully done his best to rob the various businesses, which Washburn's goons had designated.

The first several attempts had all gone surprisingly well with little or no resistance; the menacing gun Jack was brandishing helped quite a bit with that aspect of the process. Everything had been going so smoothly, Jack believed he was well on the way to getting all of Washburn's money in no time at all. In addition, whatever drugs the back-alley physician had given him for his pain, had not only numbed his aching hand, but it had also seemed to numb his emotions, removing all of his fear and anxiety. He actually felt very much at ease during each of the robberies, almost as if he were invincible.

That was until he got to the sixth target of the night, a convenience store, where everything suddenly went wrong. Jack recalled how while in the middle of the robbery he had been overpowered by an off-duty policeman as rotten luck would have it, who happened to be in the store at the time. Then Jack thought about the twelve long years of an original fifteen-year sentence he had spent in prison paying for his failed crime.

As one might suspect, Washburn's men had not come to his aid. They fled the scene at the first sign of trouble, which Jack assumed they had been instructed to do by their boss. For all Jack knew, the last store he was told to rob might have been one frequented by cops, and Washburn and his goons may have known it as well. Jack estimated by the time he was caught he had probably gotten most of Washburn's money anyway. Maybe this was the sadistic Washburn's idea of a sick joke. Sure Washburn may have lost some of his money, but Jack was certain the man didn't care. He assumed the man got more pleasure out of knowing Jack would be rotting away in a prison cell than he ever would have ever gotten from the money alone.

That was what Jack Moran thought about every day while he was stuck in prison, fighting off rapists, perverts and psychos and simply hoping to stay alive for one day longer. Each day he thought of nothing but revenge and reclaiming his precious wedding ring. For all he knew, Washburn may have flushed his most treasured memento down the nearest toilet, but he didn't believe so. He had a feeling Washburn would have kept it as some form of perverse leverage to hold over him, in the event they met again someday. Jack was certain Washburn knew their last encounter would not be able to go unanswered.

And now some twelve years later thanks to good behavior, crowded prison conditions and early release, Jack was standing in the kitchen of the Pennsylvania home of the man he despised with all of his heart and soul; the man he had sworn revenge against; the man who had apparently killed himself in a bathtub, several months earlier.

Jack put aside his thoughts of the past and tried to focus on the business at hand. He believed somewhere in the house the ring, his ring, was still hidden. Most would think such an idea preposterous. Why would a man of great wealth and power like Emerson Washburn keep a ring with virtually no monetary value? And if the ring was worth anything why would he have not sold it years ago? So then, the question became, would Washburn hold onto a worthless ring out of spite, just out of some twisted sentimental purpose or perhaps to remind him of the night he took it from Moran along with his finger, his dignity and his freedom? Jack believed so. He also thought Washburn might be just vile enough to hold onto his memento for the past twelve long years. If the ring was still in the house, Jack would find it and he planned to search all night if necessary to do just that.

Being careful to keep the flashlight pointed downward, Jack switched it on and was startled when the dark kitchen was suddenly awash with extremely bright light. He would have dropped the thing to the kitchen floor had he not first passed his hand through the security wrist strap. Jack realized flashlights certainly had changed over the previous decade or so. He never expected to see such a bright illumination from such a small light. He quickly switched the light off once again, but not before he was able to get a quick glimpse of the large kitchen layout. He instinctively looked behind him to make sure no one was outside, but the coast was clear, as he knew it would be. The momentary flash of brightness had simply set off his already tense nerves.

With the brief glimpse he saw of the kitchen, Jack was able to determine the room was an extremely oversized country-style kitchen. There was a large table and eating area off to his left with six chairs surrounding it. The table had appeared to be a high-end expensive piece of furniture. The floor on which the table rested had looked to be some type of imported Italian tile, equally expensive he was certain. He had seen a brief image of a stainless-steel refrigerator and industrial grade stove, also off to his left as well but could not recall any particulars. All he could say was the area appeared to be immense. To his right he believed he had seen a long granite counter with a double-bowl sink halfway up its length, and a curtained double window above it. In front of the sink was a large island also with a granite top. Directly across the kitchen from where he stood, Jack had seen a door, which was somehow braced open, apparently leading to a darkened hallway. He could not believe the size of the kitchen and wondered just how much money Washburn had sunk into its renovation.

Feeling his way cautiously along the island, Jack passed carefully through the kitchen and toward the hall. As soon as he got beyond the open doorway into the darkened hall, Jack bent down and removed a doorstop allowing the door to close behind him. Once the door was completely shut and Jack was in pitch-blackness he again switched on the flashlight, cupping his hand over the front to try to keep the brightness to a minimum.

Jack looked down along the hallway to determine which direction to head next. He could immediately tell that Washburn truly had spared no expense in remodeling the home. Since it had been so dark when he arrived outside, Jack did not have the opportunity to see what improvements Washburn may have made to the outside, but if this was any indication of the degree to which the man had gone, the outside likewise must no doubt be a sight to behold.

Jack removed his cupped hand from the front of the flashlight, allowing it to shine to its fullest potential, flooding the long hallway with bright illumination. Jack immediately noticed what appeared to be either new or refinished hardwood floors, covered with an oriental-styled carpet runner, which extended completely down to the end of the hall. Since it seemed to be one solid piece Jack assumed it must have been custom-made specifically for the house.

The walls were covered in tastefully designed striped pattern wallpaper with a solid pattern border on top and the wooden baseboard had been restored to its natural wood beauty. The chandeliers in the hall were made of what appeared to be expensive imported hand-cut crystal. Jack could practically smell the money that had been poured into the place.

Halfway down the hall to his left Jack saw an open doorway, which he assumed, led to a formal dining room. To his right he saw another door he suspected opened to either a closet under a stairway or perhaps led to the house's cellar steps. He tried to recall if he had seen a door in the kitchen, which may have opened to the cellar but couldn't recall if one had been present.

He could see the large handcrafted front door, with its beautiful stained glass sidelight looming in the distance at the end of the long hallway. He also saw a walnut banister traveling up along what had to be a flight of steps leading to the upstairs bedrooms. Those rooms were his destination; his main reason for coming to the house on this dark night. He sensed the ring he so desperately desired was in one of those bedrooms. He didn't know how he knew this, but still understood he had to be correct.

Jack placed his back tightly along the right wall and slowly worked his way down the hallway, keeping his eye on the large open dining room doorway. He kept his flashlight pointed downward and held it behind him to prevent anyone outside from seeing the light. Although Jack was quite certain there was no one on the isolated property except him, he still took any necessary precautions.

He passed the empty darkened doorway without incident and without going inside to investigate. If it were a dining room as he suspected, there would be little of interest to him in there. Likewise as he passed the closed door behind his back, he didn't bother to open it either, assuming he could always do so later, if things didn't work out for him upstairs; although he believed they surely would.

As he approached the area near the front door, Jack saw another wide doorway on the left side of the hall, just inside the foyer. When he stood directly in front of the opening, Jack was suddenly hit with an unexplainable and overwhelming curious desire and briefly shown his flashlight into the opening. So strong was the need to find out more about the room, that he completely forgot his original concern with the flashlight beam. Upon examining the interior of the space, he recognized it immediately as an oversized formal living room, much larger than he had expected to find. Even from out in the hall, Jack could see the room was as expensively renovated and professionally decorated, as the rest of the house seemed to be. He assumed this living room opened up to the adjacent dining room as was typical of most houses of that style, but he was still surprised by its size.

Jack lifted the flashlight for another quick look and saw the walls were adorned with a variety of paintings. Knowing Washburn's reputation as Jack believed he did, the artwork was likely one-of-a-kind original works and likely very valuable. He started to wonder if he should help himself to some of the wealth hanging on the walls. But then he realized he would have to find some way to fence the stolen paintings, and he had absolutely no knowledge of how to do such a thing. He decided instead to leave them hanging where they were so they could burn along with the rest of the house when he was finally ready to start his blaze.

Among the paintings directly visible from the entrance hanging above the mantel of a large fireplace, Jack saw a portrait of a couple. It appeared to be a formal wedding pose, perhaps an oil painting. Both the man and the woman in the portrait seemed to bare some family resemblance to the way Jack remembered Washburn looking. Jack wondered who they might be. The work seemed to be too old for the couple to be Washburn's parents, so Jack determined they must have been his grandparents.

The man in the picture held some sort of cane or walking stick with what appeared to be an ivory handle shaped like the head of a wolf. The man's hair was dark brown under a formal top hat as was his stylish mustache. He also wore wire-rimmed glasses and was dressed in an expensive looking suit typical of early twentieth century gentlemen. The woman in the picture had long dark brown hair pulled up in a stylish bun and wore white silk wedding gown. Jack realized the image must have been rendered on the obviously affluent couples' wedding day.

As Jack shone his light along the front wall of the room, it came to rest on something shiny and large positioned between two windows, both of which were covered with heavy drapes. He realized the object was an ornate gold leaf framed mirror. As he started to look away, not really having an interest in the mirror, his breath suddenly caught in his throat. A sinking feeling struck in the pit of his stomach and he broke out in a cold sweat.

Jack thought he had seen something in the mirror; a face, a hideous countenance. But surely, that could not have been possible. When he pointed the light back toward the mysterious mirror once again, whatever he may have thought he had seen was gone and the shining glass was back to normal. At first, Jack thought he might have mistaken his own reflection for the image in the mirror but now he could plainly see that his reflection was not even present in the mirror. It was obviously too far away and much too far off center to catch his reflection.

This did very little to quell the unsettling feeling he was experiencing. He wondered if he really could have seen what he thought he had seen. Jack didn't believe so; it seemed impossible, obviously a trick of the light. However, within that millisecond of time, Jack saw the vision in such complete detail, that it seemed unbelievably real.

He thought he had seen the face of the recently deceased Emerson Washburn, but not as Jack had remembered the man. The Washburn he believed he saw was not the large, strong, dangerous man he once encountered on that long ago fateful night, but instead appeared to be much older; and not just thirteen years older but almost ancient. The man was skeleton-thin and his flesh hung in layered wrinkles from his boney skull. What had once been a full head of thick black hair was now nothing more than thin wisps of grey and white, scarcely covering his blotched head. There were places where clumps of hair were missing, leaving patches of mottled grey flesh in their wake. The man's sagging skin was likewise grey and was prominently covered with darker age spots. His once thick broken nose was now a thin and twisted remnant, barely recognizable as it former shape.

The image's lips had been thin dark-grey slits and his practically toothless mouth seemed to go from hanging slack-jawed to slowly moving open and closed in an almost animatronic manner as if trying to speak. A steady stream of mucus filled drool leaked from the corner of the wretched creature's mouth. Jack was amazed at how much his mind had captured of the image in such a short span of time. In hindsight, the image might not have appeared as frightening to Jack as it did pathetic, but nonetheless the instantaneous image had sent chills of terror racing down his spine.

However, once Jack had directed his flashlight the second time and the image had disappeared, he logically began to rationalize what he had seen as nothing more than a brief figment of his imagination. He knew he was alone in the house and was well armed against anyone who tried to interfere with his plans.

He refocused on his goal and worked his way around to the base of the stairs, always being careful not to turn his back on the darkened living room. Just because his rational mind told him there was nothing to fear, a small part of him still had the creeps and he decided not to take any chances. He discovered another opening to a room behind him at the base of the stairs but he didn't believe it was where he needed to go. His destination was up the stairs and in a certain bedroom.

Jack slowly and carefully walked up the long and squeaky stairway to the upstairs hall. Once there, he shone his light into several of the open bedrooms hoping to find the one he wanted most, that being Emerson Washburn's private sleeping quarters. During his search, he was extra careful, watching for any mirrors, which might produce more of the strange optical illusions, but he didn't see the hideous image again. This helped to build his confidence and gave him the encouragement to move on.

At the far end of the hall, he came upon the final room, which he correctly assumed to be Washburn's bedroom. The door was closed, but upon trying the knob, Jack was pleased to see it was not locked. He slowly opened the door and raising the flashlight walked cautiously inside. Unlike what he had seen in the rest of the house, the master bedroom, although remodeled, was not nearly as tastefully decorated. In fact, it was quite dark and dismal in appearance, filled with heavy, thick antique furnishings and some of the most thread-bear carpeting Jack had ever seen. It was as if he had entered an entirely different world, a private sanctuary of antiquities. It was like the room existed in another period in time, separate from the rest of the house, furnished in a manner Washburn preferred. Jack had no idea how the man could have slept in a place, which smelled so dank, musty and old.

As if guided by some unseen, magnetic force, Jack immediately went straight toward a large well-worn dresser where he found an ornately decorated man's jewelry box sitting on top. He lifted the lid and was astounded by the number of fine pieces of jewelry inside the box. He decided he would help himself to pockets full of the treasures once he had found what he was looking for. He pulled handfuls of rings, gold chains, expensive watches and medallions from inside of the box as well as what appeared to be gold collector's coins, haphazardly dropping them on the top of the dresser.

When the box was almost empty, he lifted it up, turned it at an angle and dumped the remainder of the items on the dresser. Jack placed the flashlight on the dresser so it shone in his direction, and then began sifting through the mounds of jewelry searching for his precious wedding band. After several minutes, he realized his search was futile, and the ring was not present among the treasures. Angrily Jack picked up the jewelry box and threw it to the floor. It struck hard against the worn carpeting raising a small plume of dust.

The box was damaged upon impact, and Jack noticed the bottom jutting out at a strange angle where it had broken away. Upon closer examination, Jack discovered there was a false bottom, a secret hiding place, in the box and in his rage he had accidentally uncovered it. He bent down, picked up the box and pulled hard, prying the bottom from the box. It suddenly tore free and both parts flew from Jack's hand. As they did, a cylindrical wad of yellowed, brown-stained tissues fell from the compartment landing on the dirty torn cover of the bed next to the dresser.

Jack walked slowly toward the rolled up tissues already knowing what he would find inside. He cautiously reached down and began unraveling the tissues. As he did so, he saw the skeletal remains of his own severed finger, its flesh mummified and shriveled. And at the center of the decayed mass, he found his ring; his precious wedding ring still attached to the boney, remnant. Jack suddenly got a sickening feeling in his gut as if he might vomit, knowing the rotted, decayed stump lying on the bed before him had once been his own finger.

Jack suddenly felt a sharp pain in his left hand at the place where his ring finger had one been. He knew it as a ghost pain, a phantom ache which he had not felt for years. But now in the presence of his long missing digit, the pain felt almost a real as the night Washburn had taken his finger from him.

Struggling desperately to maintain his composure, Jack took a piece of the tissue, wrapped it around the back end of the finger so he would not actually have to come into contact with the dead appendage and slowly slid the ring off the rotted tip with the other hand. Still using the tissue, he tossed the hideous finger bone across the room where it clacked against the face of a large full-length antique dressing mirror. The sickening bone-on-glass clattering sound sent chill through Jack's body. He took some more tissues and turning so that he was once again positioned in the beam of the flashlight, wiped some of the tarnish and fleshy remnants from the ring, attempting to bring back enough of its original luster to be able to read its inscription. Then he saw what he had been waiting almost thirteen years to see. The inscription on the inside of the ring read, Jack and Christina 7/14/1979, the date he and his wife had been married.

Jack's eyes fill with tears for the loss of his wife and daughter so many years ago, for the misdeeds, which led to his encounter with Washburn, for the loss of his finger and finally his landing in prison. Perhaps some of the tears were for the happiness he now felt at regaining his special treasure. So many different emotions seemed to flood through Jack simultaneously; thoughts of happier times with his wife and daughter, sadness at their loss and thoughts of hatred and revenge for what Emerson Washburn had cost him.

He looked down at the expensive jewelry on the dusty dresser top and realized he no longer was interested in those stupid trinkets, nor was he interested in the paintings in the living room downstairs. He had gotten what he came for, and now it was time for him to exact his revenge. Even in death, Emerson Washburn would pay for what he did to Jack. If he had any living heirs then they could suffer the loss in his stead; Jack didn't particularly care. The anger was much too strong within him. He knew exactly what he had to do next.

Jack slid the ring onto the third finger of his right hand, picked up the flashlight and headed toward the doorway. He was going to go downstairs and retrieve the can of gasoline then starting at the top floor he would saturate Washburn's precious rugs and custom draperies with the flammable fluid and subsequently burn the place to the ground. Somehow, the idea of having all of Washburn's treasures turned to ashes gave Jack more pleasure than simply stealing and reselling them ever would have. He would finally get his revenge on the man responsible for ruining his life. He had waited over twelve long years for vengeance and vengeance would be his this night.

As Jack approached the doorway he heard a strange noise, a whisper like sound coming from somewhere behind him. It seemed to call his name in a quiet, drawn out breathy sigh, "Jaaaaaaaakkkk." The cold chill he had felt several times earlier returned to crawl its way down his tingling spine on invisible icy spider-legs. He also felt a cold sweat forming on the back of his neck and his upper lip. His stomach clenched as he natural internal warning system began screaming to him, telling him something was about to go very, very wrong.

Chapter 4

Dinnertime at the Wright household the evening Stephanie received the letter was out of sorts to say the least. There was little conversation between the couple, as both Stephanie and Jason were mulling over in their minds the best way to tell the other of their potentially life-changing news. If it weren't for the kids talking about their respective days at school and the baby yelling for either food or attention, the change in atmosphere would have been much more noticeable. Neither Jason nor Stephanie was aware of the difference, however, as they were both deep in thought about their own individual dilemmas.

As far as she could tell, Stephanie's news was what she considered to be of the good variety. After all, some relative she had never known had died and left her an inheritance, hopefully a substantial one. Although at first it seemed as unbelievable and as unlikely as something she might read on a Monopoly "CHANCE" card, Stephanie was finally starting to realize it actually was true.

For a while that afternoon as she waited for the kids to come home from school, she wondered about the mysterious unknown relative, this Emerson Washburn character. What sort of man had he been? Why had her father never mentioned his having a brother before? What was it about this man, which had caused his alienation from his family? Was his exile by his own choice or had the family shunned him and cast him out? And more importantly, why had he named her as his sole heir to his estate? Had he no children or family of his own? Was he like one of those eccentric lonely old recluses she often heard about whom always seem to die all alone wallowing in their own filth, confined to a type of self-imposed prison?

She decided when things settled down she might want to learn more not only about Emerson Washburn, but about her family history in general. She had never really had much interest in such things but for some reason the discovery of this missing relative seemed to spark a sudden curiosity in finding out more about her own genealogy. Yes, she decided she would definitely find some available time to do some research into her own family and maybe even look into Jason's family tree as well.

Across the table, Jason was likewise struggling with how best to present his news to Stephanie. What he had to tell her was for the most part bad news and yet this particular dark cloud seemed to have something of a silver lining. That was assuming they were both willing to uproot their family and relocate fifty miles north. The change of jobs would mean a promotion for Jason and more money, but that also meant more responsibility. It would provide Jason with the job security he no longer had in his present position. In fact, his current position essentially no longer existed. He knew it might be a challenge for his newly blended family but Jason could see no way around the fact that eventually they were going to have to relocate. He was the breadwinner, the sole source of income. Jason had to work in order to provide for his family and for the time being with the economy in such turmoil the only game in town was actually taking place in an entirely different town; the small Schuylkill County town of Ashton.

Both Stephanie and Jason sat in silence picking absently at their dinner, moving the food about as if interested although neither of them was really very hungry. As the mealtime wound down, the two older kids, Jeremy and Cindy wiped their faces with their napkins and got up from the table with a quick "Bye Mom, Bye Dad" before racing off to the living room to either watch TV or play video games. Seventeen-month-old Sammy was caught up in the excitement and began banging on the tray of his highchair chanting, "Down, down, down." He always wanted to do whatever his older siblings were doing.

Stephanie wiped the baby's face and hands clean, and then lifted little Sammy down. No sooner had his feet touched the kitchen floor then like two tiny rapid-firing pistons they carried him scurrying into the living room in search of his brother and sister. After a few seconds, the parents both heard the two older children complaining loudly, "No Sammy... Don't touch that.... no, no, no... Mom... Dad!"

This was followed promptly by a halfhearted admonishment from Jason shouting from the kitchen "Be nice and play with your little brother." The delivery sounded less like a scolding and more like an automatic reaction given with little thought or sincerity. A statement he and thousands of other parents before him likely said more often than they wanted to. He looked over at Stephanie and smiled lovingly, but she seemed to be preoccupied with other thoughts.

Stephanie and Jason loved all of their children and tried to never show any favoritism between them, but there was something so very special about little Sammy. They often referred to him as the glue, which helped to hold all of them together. Jeremy and Cindy were unrelated stepsiblings, yet they both were related to Sammy through one parent. Likewise, Jason was not related to Cindy and Stephanie was not related to Jeremy, yet little Sammy was a blood relative to every single member of the family. He was their common bond, the strongest link in the chain that bound them all together. Jason and Stephanie often referred to their family as a *Yours, Mine and Ours* type of family, making reference to the old 2005 movie which was actually a remake of a 1968 classic.

When things sounded like they were under control in the living room, Stephanie returned to the kitchen table and put her hands on the back of the chair with a sigh, seeming to allow all of the concerns of the day to flow out with that single stress-relieving breath. It was then she noticed for the first time, Jason was not quite himself. She had been so busy worrying about her own concerns; she hadn't noticed the cloud of worry, which seemed to envelop Jason like a dark shroud.

"Jason, honey", Stephanie asked, "Baby. What's the matter? I can see something's wrong."

Jason looked up and as he eyes met Stephanie's he felt the all-familiar pangs of love he experienced every time their eyes met. She was the one true love of his life. He realized it the day they met and sometimes just thinking about just how precious she was to him was overwhelming. This only made the news he was about to deliver all the more difficult.

"Well..." Jason hesitated taking a deep breath, "I have some unpleasant news." Stephanie visibly tensed, as her fingers felt as though they would dig into the back of the chair, which now seemed to support her and prepare her for the bad news she was sure would follow. "My boss, you know Walt, called me into his office and gave me some unfortunate news. It's not good news and it's something we cannot repeat to anyone. Stephanie nodded her head silently. You remember that project I've been talking about for months; that new machine tool?"

"Oh no!" Stephanie said with audible concern, "Don't tell me they didn't agree to give you the money. Not after all the work you put into it!"

Jason shook his head and explained, "No, that's not quite it. The project had too good of a payback for them not to approve it."

"Well...then what happened? What is the problem?"

Jason replied, "They didn't approve it for our facility."

"I...I don't understand," Stephanie said. Then she asked, "How can it be approved yet not approved for your plant?"

"The project itself was definitely accepted," Jason corrected, "but corporate does not want the machine to be located in our plant... they want to send it to the Ashton facility, up north in Schuylkill County."

"What?" Stephanie complained, "You know more about that project than anyone up there. How can they do that?"

"Unfortunately, they can and will do whatever they choose, Steph. They're paying the bills and paying my salary." Jason said, "The Ashton factory is a non-union facility with a great track record for quality, productivity and management-shop employee relations, while our place has a strong and radical union with a history of a confrontation with management. And our production numbers are in the toilet too. Remember three years ago when the union went on strike for several weeks?"

"Yes. How could I forget? You had to go out with your other office coworkers and run the machines in the shop. That was a bad one and the company almost closed the plant over that strike." Stephanie said, "But I thought they both came to an agreement and everything worked out."

Jason explained, "Well, not quite. You see, the company agreed to many of the union's demands just because they felt shutting down the plant in the middle of a strike was bad public relations, plus they needed to keep producing product. However, the boys at corporate have a very long memory and while the union was bragging to the media about how they brought the company to its knees, the suits must have been planning a way to eventually get what they wanted. They always get what they want in the end. And here is the really bad part of the story. Not only are they putting the new machine in Ashton, but they're also moving our entire machining operation up to that facility. All that will remain in Lancaster is some assembly, sales, purchasing and product design."

"But you're a manufacturing engineer," she said, suddenly realizing the implication of what Jason had just said then she asked. "What will happen to you? Are they going to let you go, you know, are they going to fire you?" She pulled out the chair and carefully walked around it, deciding to sit down for the news, which she was certain, would follow.

Jason took another deep breath and said, "Well, that's up to me, or I should say up to us." Stephanie said nothing, just stared at Jason with some confusion. "Bottom line is, I can either take the layoff and go try to find another job somewhere else..." He hesitated for a moment and then with as much enthusiasm as he could muster said, "... or I can take a promotion and be the manager of manufacturing engineering at the Ashton Plant."

"What?" Stephanie asked again, her face beaming with surprise and pleasure.

"Yep," Jason said with a bit of obvious pride. "More money... more responsibility...a definite promotion."

Suddenly, Stephanie began to shake and for a moment Jason was afraid she was going to cry, until he realized she was actually chuckling, laughing. To say the least, this was not the reaction he had expected. He could have understood anger, frustration, sadness and worry but laughter was not at all what he would have anticipated.

"Steph, are you OK?" he asked perplexed. Then, being an engineer and a man, he unsurprisingly tried to smooth things over somewhat by offering a more palatable solution. It was his nature to find solutions to problems. He quickly suggested "I mean...there are many ways we can approach this...I could commute back and forth for a while...and then in a year or so if the job works out we could find a place to live either up in Schuylkill County or even somewhere in northern Berks County... I mean...if that is what you...I mean we...want to do...and if it didn't work out, I could continue to commute until I find another job closer to home. Don't worry, Steph; there are a lot of solutions to this, I promise you."

Stephanie leaned back in her chair not looking at Jason but staring at the floor while shaking her head in amazement. She said, "Well, honey, it looks like you're not the only one with a surprise today."

Jason suddenly got an extremely concerned look and asked "What? You're not...not pregnant again are you?" He slapped his hand against his forehead in surprise. Jason had recalled from when Stephanie was pregnant with little Sammy her emotions seemed to be a bit topsy-turvy and her mood swings were many. He feared Stephanie's strange out of place laughter might be attributed to a pregnancy.

The question caused Stephanie to burst into fresh fits of deep belly laughter. When she calmed somewhat she said, "No, silly, I'm not pregnant. Here look at this." She handed him the manila envelope with its ornate gold-leaf return address. She had been laughing so hard that tears came to her eyes. She dabbed them with the sleeve of her shirt.

"What's this?" Jason asked as he read the return address. "H. Mason Armstrong? A lawyer? I hope we aren't being sued. I don't get it."

"You will... Just read it," Stephanie said still chuckling.

"Why are you laughing?" he asked. "This wasn't exactly the greatest news I just dumped on you."

She replied, "I'm not really sure why I am laughing. I think I'm either just amazed by the strange turn of events today or perhaps I am simply relieved. This has been a really bizarre day. Please, just read the letter, honey. You know how I always say things happen for a reason, even things that seem to be bad at first? Read the letter and you'll understand."

Jason gave her a quizzical look and then read the letter first by quickly skimming, which was his habit, then after looking up wide-eyed at his wife; he read it again using his finger to follow across the critical lines, just to make sure he had read it correctly.

"Inheritance?" he asked, "How much?" It was the first thought he had and he had blurted out the words without even thinking. Then he realized how crass it was to ask such a question and said, "I mean, I know it was probably in bad taste to ask something like that, but I assume you didn't even know this guy, this Emerson Washburn, right?"

She said, "No I never heard of him. I had no idea he even existed. Apparently he was my father's estranged brother, and I assume he was single with no kids. He must have thought I was his only living relative. So it looks like he must have either known about me or learned about me somehow and for some reason chose to leave his estate, whatever that might be to me."

"Speaking of which, what about your brother Chuck? I wonder why he wasn't named in the will," Jason asked.

Stephanie thought for a moment and then said, "That's a very good question. Maybe Washburn didn't know about him or for some reason chose to exclude him. I would have thought it was possible that Chuck might have gotten a similar letter, if this one didn't specify that I was the sole heir to his estate. Maybe we will find out more a little later on during the whole settlement process."

"This is so weird" Jason added, "I mean the whole strange series of coincidences. First, I all but get canned from my job... and the only spot available for me is with the division in Ashton. Then you get this inheritance letter from some unknown relative, also from Ashton...and you are left an estate with property in the area of Ashton... I mean this is so unbelievable it seems like the type of setup you would find in a movie or maybe a novel."

Stephanie replied, "I have to agree. There are so many strange coincidences all coming together at one time; it almost feels like someone else is controlling our destiny; like we have no say in the matter."

Jason said, "Luckily, I don't believe in such things, even though I was the one to point it out. I suppose it is just a weird set of coincidences that happen sometimes, and now it is happening to us...hopefully with very positive results. Do you realize, depending upon how much money is involved, this could change everything?"

"Yes." She replied, "And maybe that's one of the reasons why I'm laughing. I've spent all afternoon thinking about the letter, the inheritance and what to tell you. And I realize you've been struggling with how to tell me your news as well. So depending upon how this turns out, all of our worries might have been for nothing and our troubles may be over." She laughed again, but then suddenly her face took on a more serious expression.

"I hope you realize it might not be worth much, maybe not much at all." She cautioned, "I mean who knows what land or property is worth up north. I suspect a lot less than here. But if by some miracle it is a lot of money... Oh my, just imagine... then we will have the freedom to do whatever we want. You could simply take the layoff and try to find another company locally to work for, or take some time off to relax. I know manufacturing type jobs are few and far between nowadays but this inheritance might be enough to carry us for a while. Or you could even start that private consulting firm you have been dreaming about. Who knows?"

"No matter how insensitive this might sound, I have to wonder how much is actually involved in the estate." Jason said. "I mean is it land, is it property, money jewelry, cash, whatever?"

"I don't know." Stephanie confessed, "I only received the letter late today and the whole idea hasn't really sunken in yet."

"Have you spoken with the lawyer or were you waiting to tell me first?" he asked.

"No, I haven't called him yet," Stephanie replied. "I didn't want to call him until after we spoke."

Jason said, "Well then, we have to give this Armstrong guy a call and see what's what. You know, this could be really big."

"I was going to try to call tomorrow, but then I was thinking tomorrow's Saturday and he may not be in the office until Monday," Stephanie explained.

"Monday?" Jason exclaimed, "There's no way we can wait until Monday! I mean this is like when we play the lottery and fantasize about how we would spend the money if we won. This is too important to wait until Monday. We have to try him first thing tomorrow. Maybe we could leave him a voicemail at the very least. If he checks his messages he might get back to us sooner. Hey.

What about email?" Jason again skimmed the document looking for an email address and with a disappointed look said, "Crap! No email, but I just got another idea. What time is it?"

Stephanie looked at the wall clock behind Jason and replied, "It's about 5:45."

"You don't suppose he might be working late tonight do you? I know it's Friday night, but he could be still in the office," Jason suggested. "I mean its Ashton for Pete's sake. Nothing happens there on a Friday night other than almost everyone is going to bed early, hanging out at the fire company social hall or working late. Being a lawyer, I would go with working late. It certainly wouldn't hurt to try and see if he is in, would it?"

Looking surprised and at the same time exhilarated, Stephanie said "You mean call him... tonight... right now?"

"No time like the present." Jason suggested, "We might as well find out where we stand before we spend the whole weekend imagining what we might do with a would-be fortune only to discover it might be nothing more than a few dollars."

"Yes, I suppose you're right," Stephanie agreed. "It wouldn't hurt to give him a call and at least introduce ourselves and see what we have to do next."

Jason handed the letter with the lawyer's phone number to Stephanie who already had her cell phone in hand. She quickly dialed the number and told Jason excitedly, "It's ringing."

After only two rings, the phone was picked up, and Stephanie was stunned to hear a man's deep baritone voice say, "Good evening, Mrs. Wright, this is H. Mason Armstrong. I've been expecting your call."

Chapter 5

"Jaaaaaaaakkkk." Jack heard the mysterious voice calling once again. He wanted to run, to escape to somewhere safe, but his feet felt as though they were frozen in place as they often did in horrible nightmares. But this was no nightmare; as least not one of the sleeping variety as he was very much awake. He instinctively knew if he were to try to take a step, it would feel as if he were walking in a bog of mud several feet deep. This too was another sensation he recalled from some of the worst bad dreams he had experienced. This preternatural feeling enshrouding him was very much like that of a surrealistic nightmare. He started to turn as if in slow motion, feeling like he was trying to do so in an atmosphere thick with gelatinous fluid. Both of his feet seemed to plod heavily, as he suspected they would, but eventually he managed to turn completely around and faced the inside of the bedroom once more.

He was uncertain if he actually wanted to discover who had been calling his name in that strange ghostly, whispering voice, but he was unable to resist looking. He could not imagine what type of force other than perhaps his own subconscious and irrational fear, which might have had the capability of causing his feet to feel and behave as if they had turned to lead weights. On the surface, he didn't think he had fallen into a state of paralyzing fear over what he might discover, but it was possible he was mistaken. Maybe on the surface he believed he was not afraid, but perhaps at some subconscious level, he might actually be terrified; he just didn't know. Regardless, his curiosity was still very strong although it had taken on a more cautious, ominous edge as if he was straddling the line between circumspection and impending terror.

As he looked into the near darkness, his flashlight being the only source of illumination in the dismal room, his eyes immediately focused in the direction of a large dressing mirror across the room. It was about six feet tall, constructed of wood, perhaps once polished and fine looking but now worn, dull and scratched. It was oval and was suspended in a rectangular framework with two large supporting feet anchoring it to the tattered carpet. Halfway up the weathered frame two iron handles, their black paint chipped and tarnished held the mirror in place and allowed it to tilt as necessary, enabling the user to attain the best view possible.

When Jack had first observed the mirror upon entering the room he noticed it had been tilted back slightly, however now it was slowly moving into a vertical position, as if someone were standing in the darkness behind the piece pushing it into a specific position, although he could see no one. He suspected if a person was actually hiding behind the mirror somewhere in the shadows, then that person would likely be the one who had called his name, perhaps trying to spook him, to frighten him into leaving the property. Jack slowly reached around to the small of his back, each movement feeling as awkward and cumbersome as if made while neck-deep in quicksand, and carefully removed the revolver he had stashed there earlier. Then he laboriously brought it around to be ready to use on whoever might be found lurking in the darkness.

The now vertical surface of the mirror suddenly seemed to change before his eyes; looking less like a mirror and more like the surface of a reflecting pond. From a point in the center of the mirror a series of ever-growing concentric circles seemed to emanate, resembling the ripples one sees after dropping a stone into a still body of water. "Jaaaaaaakkk" he heard the voice call somewhat louder and more distinct than before as if to suggest whoever was summoning him was getting closer. Unbelievably, the voice with its liquid quality seemed to be coming from deep inside the mirror itself. Jack's common sense told him such a thing was not possible, yet regardless of what he believed, it truly was nonetheless occurring.

From within the undulating ripples in the mirror, Jack saw a form begin to take shape and to his dismay and horror, he realized it was the same image; the same skeletal face he thought he had briefly seen downstairs. He recognized the face as that of his recently deceased enemy, Emerson Washburn. He had convinced himself the countenance in the downstairs living room mirror had been a product of stress or an overactive imagination. However now it was obvious to Jack the thing was far too real. The creature looking out from the glass was not only as hideous as it had appeared to be earlier, but Jack could see immediately it was far worse than he had thought. It was not quite Emerson Washburn, but was some sort of Washburn-like incarnation born of some unimaginable accursed womb of Hell, now manifesting from the rippling mirrored surface. Its face blurred in and out of focus twitching spasmodically, which left Jack uncertain of what he was actually seeing.

The creature looked to Jack to be skeleton-thin and its flesh seemed to hang in folds, as flesh often does when an overweight person suddenly takes ill and sheds far too many pounds much too quickly. The skin covering the hideous being was mottled, rotting and even sloughing off in places revealing the glistening white bone beneath and resembling some sort of horror movie zombie. Jack could see what appeared to be small white insects; he suspected maggots of some sort, crawling in and out of holes they had bored sporadically about the specter's face. The vision continued to twitch and move in and out of focus, in a jerky motion reminiscent of an old fashioned black and white silent movie. In fact, the image itself appeared to be almost entirely black and white, save for a few slivers of crimson where its flesh was cracking, preparing to slip from its skull and in those places the red was far too pronounced; almost phosphorescent with its eerie ruby glow.

It seemed to Jack that perhaps the unimaginable world from which this atrocious version of the now dead Emerson Washburn was trying to emerge, might be one virtually void of all color except for the vibrant luminescent red which seemed to captivate if not hypnotize him. In his mind he seemed to be repeating the words "red, red, red" as if his brain was unable to comprehend the existence of any other colors save red.

Jack wondered if it could be possible the unholy being might be planting this unimaginable black, white and crimson fantasy in his mind and in reality did not look quite as revolting as the image portrayed. If Jack could bring himself to accept the fact that Washburn had been able to pull himself forth from the world of the damned, then it seemed logical the undead specter could also be capable of creating such an illusion. Before this thought had a chance to complete shape itself into a cohesive idea, something more unacceptable and even more revolting occurred, which Jack was certain was beyond his own imagination's ability to fabricate.

The mouth of the hideous being hung wide open and when it once again whispered his name Jack could smell a vile and nauseating odor coming from the mirror, like that of a dead animal carcass baking in the broiling summer sun along a country road; the smell of decay; the smell of death. Coming back to reality from his near hypnotic state, Jack didn't take the time to consider what he might or might not be seeing; instead, he did his best to muster all of his strength to lift his hand pointing the revolver directly at the mirror. He had made up his mind, if the origin of the ungodly specter before him was that mirror; then he would shoot the glass and hopefully send the Washburn-like thing back to whichever torturous pit in Hell it was trying to crawl from. Then when he regained his ability to move he would go from room to room destroying every mirror until there was no possible way for the creature to manifest itself again.

But he discovered he could not pull the trigger; his ability to will his finger to do so was suddenly gone. Mysteriously, the gun felt as though it weighed a ton as his right hand dropped back to his side, unable to continuing pointing, hanging uselessly at the end of an arm, which dangled helplessly like some useless vestigial appendage.

"I see...you found...your precious ring," the image in the watery mirror hissed. The being sounded as if speech might be something which was very difficult for it to accomplish from deep inside the glass. Jack wanted to reply, wanted to scream and curse at the heinous ghost of the man he had hated for so many years, but he was unable to speak or move.

The water-like film on the face of the mirror began to ripple more rapidly as Jack saw that the thing, which might have once been Emerson Washburn and was now some sort of Hell-spawned demon, was slowly beginning to emerge from within the mirror. Jack wanted to turn and run screaming from the unbelievable living nightmare unfolding before him but was now completely paralyzed; perhaps by some unknown power this ghastly thing possessed; perhaps by his own primal terror. The twitching specter floated out of the mirror and within a few seconds drifted across the room until it loomed just a few feet in front of Jack. It hideous face was still all that was visible in the glow of the flashlight, but Jack knew there were more horrors lurking in the blackness below that head.

Jack was thankful for the shadowy darkness of the room. He had absolutely no desire to see the revolting creature in its entirety. Seeing only its hideous maggot infested face in blurry twitching glimpses was horrifying enough. Jack could only imagine how the rest of the thing might appear, and he tried his best not to do so.

"Oh...Jack," the specter said with a condescending, almost mocking tone, its voice now clearer outside the confines of the mirror. "You didn't really think...you could get the better of me... did you? Even in death...you must understand...I am better than you... I see everything... I know everything... I even know what you were planning... I know about your scheme to burn my lovely house...to the ground... But sadly for you...you will never have that opportunity... You see, I have left this house...and all my possessions...to my long-lost niece. And I must keep it safe for her...the others have commanded it...as they have very special plans for her...and for her family.

Jack had no idea what the specter was talking about, nor did he care. He had come here to find his ring, then destroy the house and everything inside it. Now all he wanted was to escape with his life and his immortal soul intact.

Then suddenly, the ghostly phantom began to dissolve right before Jack's astonished eyes, breaking up into billions of tiny glowing particles. For the briefest of moments, Jack began to believe the repulsive thing was about to vanish, when abruptly, the mass of glowing specks flew rapidly toward him encircling his head like honeybees swarming to protect their queen.

Jack felt the accumulation of the luminous flecks tightening around his skull, felt tiny barely detectable elements slithering up into his nostrils and creeping between his tightly closed lips. His eyes burned, and he assumed the particles were even working their way inside him through his tear ducts. Then the entire swarm seemed to melt into the very pores of his flesh. Jack could feel a tingling sensation all around his skull as each microscopic glowing element passed into his body.

Within a few seconds, he felt an incredible cold spreading throughout his body. It started with his head, the crept down along his spine into his chest, down into the pit of his stomach and eventually all the way to the tips of his toes. Whatever the Washburn-thing had been, Jack understood it had now somehow become part of him. Jack realized he was no longer just Jack Moran. In fact, he could sense the very co-consciousness of Emerson Washburn inside his mind and his body.

The sensation was far beyond terrifying. Jack could still sense his own presence but could also feel Washburn's persona in there with him. Jack suddenly had an instantaneous recollection of Washburn's entire life. It was as if all of the man's memories had directly downloaded into his own brain, and they had become his own memories. One specific recollection, which seemed to keep repeating simultaneously from both Jack's own memory as well as Washburn's was from that life-changing night when Washburn severed Jack's finger. It was almost incomprehensible to Jack how he could see the same scene played out from two different perspectives at the same time; his own and that of Emerson Washburn. And what was even stranger was Jack actually reliving the emotions of that excruciating experience from two separate and opposite points of view simultaneously.

Jack's own personal impression of the event was filled with pain and terror, while the Washburn side of the memory was one of sheer pleasure; the sick thrill the twisted man had gotten from inflicting incredible agony on another human being. Although

Jack as Jack could have never experienced such a sensation, Jack combined with the presence of Washburn most certainly could. It was then Jack realized, although Washburn was someone deserving of his hatred and disgust, the man was also a mentally deranged creature incapable of distinguishing right from wrong or from controlling his sadistic homicidal impulses.

Then Jack realized it was not simply that Washburn was sharing space in his body, but Jack could instantly tell Washburn was in physical control of him. Although Jack's persona was still present it was now only a spectator, helpless to work any of his own bodily motor control. Washburn was operating Jacks body like a puppet master with a marionette. Jack felt his right hand reach around and tuck the revolver back into his pants. He still held the flashlight in his left hand and could feel Washburn position that hand downward to provide light for him to see ahead. In the mirror across the room Jack could see his own reflection moving without his actually being in control. For the briefest of moments, Jack looked at his own face in the mirror at his own eyes but no longer recognized the look they held. His eyes now reflected the violent and deranged soul of Emerson Washburn.

Jack felt his body begin to turn slowly as he clumsily staggered out of the dismal bedroom, then travel along the upstairs hall toward the stairs. He was terrified at not being able to control his own motion and feared the being, which now inhabited his body, might throw that same helpless body down the stairs, not necessarily to kill him outright, but to injure him and make him suffer. Washburn could simply cripple him and leave his broken body to die alone, helpless and in agony. He envisioned himself in a heap of shattered bone and flesh crumpled at the bottom of the stairs. No sooner had Jack experienced the mental image than he became concerned that the horrific thought might not actually have been his own, but might have been one that Washburn actually had planned for him. Had he known what fate actually awaited him, Jack would have been grateful to be thrown down the stairs instead.

Jack made it safely down the stairway without incident, and then his body continued shuffling awkwardly along the downstairs hall occasionally banging against the wall, stumbling past the living room and dining room, out into the kitchen then finally out the back door onto the deck. After the door was closed and locked, Jack's left hand clicked off the flashlight and tucked it into his pants pocket while his right hand reached down and picked up the gasoline can. Jack's fear began to increase as he sensed for the first time what the creature might have in store for him. He had no way of distinguishing between his own thoughts and those of Washburn.

Next, his remotely controlled body trudged through the back yard past the swimming pool, around the back of the house, through the side yard, around to the front of the house then down the long moonlit driveway. The stolen car Jack had used to travel to the property was parked a few hundred feet up the main road from where it intersected with Washburn's driveway.

Jack felt his body move toward his car, which he had hidden to the best of his ability along the side of the road, where it was concealed in the shadows of dense overhanging trees. When Moran reached the sedan, Washburn commanded his arm to open the driver's door, as well as the door to the back seat. Next Jack was forced to dump the gasoline inside the car, allowing it to soak into the cloth carpeting in both the front and back. He then took what was left in the can and lifted it high over his own head, allowing it to trickle down over his face completely saturating his clothing. His eyes, which Washburn had forced to stay open, burned unmercifully as the gasoline streamed over and into them. His sinuses were likewise singed by the caustic vapors emanating from the flowing fuel, and Jack's lungs burned from the vapors, which were apparently damaging him internally; not that such a problem would be a concern for very much longer.

Before Jack had sufficient time to realize the extent of his suffering, Washburn commanded Jack's helpless body to sit in the front driver's seat and start the engine while leaving the door open. Jack looked into the rearview mirror and at first saw only his own blurry, reddened and terrified eyes looking back at him. After a moment, Jack once again saw someone else looking at him through those same eyes as they changed to reflect a much more hateful and sinister appearance. At that moment, Jack heard Washburn's voice speaking to him from inside his own head.

Washburn said, "Too bad you just couldn't let things go, Jack; too bad for you indeed." Jack sat in the car smelling the pungent odor of raw gasoline as it permeated the air in the close confines of the sedan. He started to feel dizzy and nauseous from the gas fumes. His lungs burned as if on fire. Suddenly Jack's body revolted from the ordeal, and he vomited involuntarily down the front of his shirt and onto his lap. After a moment or two of silence, while Jack sat smelling the sickening sour stench of his own puke mixed with the gasoline fumes, Washburn said in Jack's mind, "Well I suppose we had better get on with this." Then Jack felt his right hand reach into his right pocket and grasp tightly on his cigarette lighter; the same lighter he had brought with him with the intention of burning down Washburn's home.

"Oh my Lord in Heaven, no!" Jack's thoughts screamed in his mind. "Please, please don't do this" But Jack realized Washburn's plan was irreversibly set in motion and no power could do anything to stop the unearthly fiend.

"I suppose I'll see you in Hell someday, Jack my boy," he heard Washburn say as his right hand flicked the thumbwheel on the lighter. It didn't light or even spark and for the briefest of moments, Jack thought he might be spared the fate he saw ahead of him. Then two clicks later, it finally sparked to life, and the car was engulfed in a flaming inferno.

The sparkling particles began to stream from Jack's body and rapidly reassemble themselves outside of the fiery conflagration by the side of the road. Then the specter of Emerson Washburn, having completed the task which he had been required to perform floated back through the darkness toward his home to prepare for the coming of the new homeowners: the Wright family.

Jack sat helpless in the car, paralyzed but still able to feel everything that was happening to him. Emerson Washburn had made certain of that. Washburn did not want the man to miss one single moment of his flaming agony and, as always, he had gotten his wish.

Jack Moran experienced unfathomable pain as his flesh, bubbled, broiled and eventually either melted from his body or was charred to his bones, while every single nerve ending in his body simultaneously fired electronic impulses to his brain synapses, which silently screamed with unbearable agony. In his mind, Jack discovered he was now alone and in his dying misery, he mentally howled a final death shriek. He could smell his own skin and hair burning from his body as the world around him eventually, mercifully faded to blackness.

Chapter 6

"Excuse...me?" Stephanie questioned, obviously discomforted by the way the lawyer had answered his phone. Suddenly she felt as if a squirming centipede was gently scooting across the back of her neck with its feather-light legs, as an icy chill shivered down her spine. She had been taken completely by surprise and she asked, "Wa...what? Mr. Armstrong? Yes...um...yes, this is Stephanie Wright, but...how...how did you know...it was me?"

"Good evening, Mrs. Wright," the lawyer repeated with a deep baritone voice; one which sounded accustom to public speaking. "Of course I knew it was you. Please allow me to explain. First of all, I assumed you would be calling me sometime today after receiving your registered letter. And since you had not yet called, I deduced you would do so after speaking with your husband when he got home from work. Secondly, I am not expecting calls from any of my other clients this evening. Third, and perhaps most important, is that I have caller ID on my phone and your name came up." He gave a bit of a chuckle, "You see, it was as simple as that. No mystery whatsoever."

"Oh..." she said with surprise, feeling a bit foolish, "I suppose... I guess I didn't think you... I mean I didn't realize...you know, Ashton is such a small town. I mean...you are...way up there... " Stephanie was fumbling to find the right words. However, the harder she tried to get out of the embarrassing hole she had dug herself into, the deeper it got.

Armstrong seemed to understand her dilemma and chose to have a bit of pleasure from her obvious discomfort suggesting, "Believe it or not, way up here in the coal region we actually have such modern conveniences as running water, electricity and even flushing indoor toilets. Not to mention other amenities such as cable TV, cell phones, the Internet and yes, even caller ID.

"I'm so terribly sorry, Mr. Armstrong" Stephanie said when she heard the obvious sarcasm in his reply. She didn't mean to suggest Schuylkill County was akin to some sort of third-world country by any means, although she and many of her friends often did think of that part of the state as being a bit "behind the times". The truth was she had not expected Armstrong to be in his office and was caught by surprise not only when he answered the phone, but also when he did so by using her name. She hoped the man had good sense of humor and had been simply offering the self-deprecating comment to break the ice. She couldn't be certain if she had genuinely offended the man by insulting his hometown but most definitely hoped she had not.

"You...you just caught me by surprise, is all," she said in a feeble attempt at explanation.

He replied, "No need to apologize, Mrs. Wright. I understand completely. You see, I have to admit I am actually a transplant to the area and not a native. I moved to Ashton some thirty years ago when I married my late wife, Margaret, and have been living here ever since. We met back when we were in college; she was born and raised in Ashton. After we moved here I realized there was something so inherently special about this area that I found very appealing and still do lo these many years later." He hesitated for a beat and said, "But then again, you didn't call to hear my life story. No doubt you called regarding the inheritance you were bequeathed by my client, the late Mr. Emerson Charles Washburn."

For a moment, this statement also caught Stephanie by off guard. The document she had received listed the deceased man as Emerson C. Washburn. For some reason, she had never considered his middle name might have been Charles. Her older brother Chuck had been given the name Charles David Washburn. She wondered for a moment if Chuck's name might have come from the same family source as Washburn's middle name; perhaps an ancestor several generations removed. Once again, she found herself thinking and wondering about her genealogy and about a growing desire she was experiencing to do something sometime soon about tracking down her family history.

After a moment, Stephanie replied distractedly, "Um... Yes. That's exactly why I called. Sorry. I am a bit confused by all of this...you see...well, I have never inherited anything before...and I didn't even know this Emerson Washburn existed... I guess it's just that I have so many questions...and absolutely no idea where to begin."

"Not a problem at all, Mrs. Wright." He said, "That's why I am here. If I do my job correctly, and I always do, I should be able to make all of this flow smoothly for you. I suppose the first thing we need to do is to get you and your husband up here to get started on the paperwork at your earliest convenience."

Stephanie held the phone against her chest and said to Jason, "He wants us to get started on the paperwork for the estate as soon as possible." Armstrong was able to understand everything she was saying though it sounded a bit muffled yet nonetheless still audible. He heard Jason say, "Tell him we can come up tomorrow morning if he would like us to." Then he heard

Stephanie reply, "I can't ask him that... He may not work on Saturday."

Then she spoke into the cell phone again, "Mr. Armstrong?"

"Please Mrs. Wright. Call me Mason," the attorney corrected.

"Very well." She said, "Then you can call me Stephanie, and my husband's name is Jason. Um...well...we were wondering if tomorrow would be too soon for us to stop up to see you...that is...if you work on Saturday."

The lawyer replied, "That's not a problem at all. In fact, I was hoping you might be available tomorrow sometime. I set my own hours, and to be honest I am generally in the office on a Saturday morning catching up on paperwork almost every weekend. So if you both would like to stop by tomorrow that would be perfectly fine with me. What time can I expect you?"

Again, he heard the phone being muffled against her shirt as said asked her husband, "What time can we be up there tomorrow morning?"

"Ask him if eleven is a good time. It takes about an hour or so to get up there so we should be able to have everyone awake, dressed and ready to go by nine forty-five," Jason quickly calculated.

Stephanie asked, "Mr. Armstr...I mean Mason. Would eleven o'clock be a good time or would some other time work better for you?"

"Eleven o'clock will be just fine. That will allow me to sleep in tomorrow then head down to the office after a brief stop at Maggie's for a hearty breakfast."

At first Stephanie wondered if perhaps Maggie might be a lady friend of Armstrong's, then she recalled something Jason had once told here. There was a small eatery at the top end of Ashton called Maggie's Restaurant, which he described as a quaint local gathering place; especially known for their breakfast menu.

"By the way," she mentioned, "we will have to bring our kids along with us. I hope that will not be a problem."

The lawyer replied, "Absolutely no problem whatsoever. On the contrary, I was hoping you would bring them along. After we take care of all the legal paperwork, I plan to take you all out to show you around the Washburn property, which will shortly become your property. I think it would be great if your kids could see it as well."

"Property?" Stephanie asked. "Oh, yes, the farm. What does it look like?"

"Well, I prefer not to get into too much detail over the phone, as there are a number of things we will need to discuss first tomorrow. However, I don't think it would hurt to give you a little tidbit to whet your appetite. What I was referring to was the Washburn family homestead. It is about a forty-acre or better farmette with buildings built by your great grandparents about a hundred years ago. When Emerson took ownership of the property, he put a lot of money into it and remodeled the living quarters as well as all of the out buildings. It is quite impressive and although I can't wait to show it to you, I really don't want to spoil the effect by telling you too much over the phone. But please allow me to simply say you will be quite surprised and pleased by your inheritance. I hope you will be kind enough to humor me on this. Let's just save any more discussion on this subject until tomorrow when you all arrive."

Stephanie said slightly stunned, "Alright then. We'll see you tomorrow morning at eleven at your office. Is there anything special we need to bring along with us?"

The lawyer replied, "No, not really; perhaps just your driver's license and birth certificate for official proof of your identity. But honestly, all you have to do is show up, and we should be able to get our paperwork completed by noon. I would offer to buy you lunch, but I have another appointment at three o'clock and have to get you out to the property and back before then. Besides, I assume with three young children you will likely be stopping for fast food on the way here. Lord knows I have used a similar tactic many years ago on long trips with my own kids."

Stephanie saw Jason leave the kitchen, she assumed to check on the children in the living room. Things had become quiet in the room and the only thing parents feared more than kids noisily misbehaving and getting into trouble was when they were quiet. When there was no noise, there was likely real trouble brewing.

"But I will make a deal with you," he insisted. "After we finish our business, you and your family can take an hour or so to become familiar with the area. I will have a set of complimentary tickets to Ashton's main tourist attraction here for you. We have a steam train ride, a coalmine tour and a state run coal museum. I think you and your family will enjoy all three; especially the mine tour. Then when you are finished, if you would consider staying around a bit longer, I will be more than happy to take you and your family out to dinner at one of our local dining establishments."

"Thank you very much, Mr. Arms.., I mean Mason. I greatly appreciate it. I think the mine tour is a great idea. And coincidentally, I was thinking about that very tourist attraction earlier this morning. It's almost like you were able to read my mind," Stephanie said quietly, not wanting the kids to hear. Then she experienced a strange unsettling feeling not unlike the one she had when Armstrong answered the phone earlier, calling her by name. She realized how ridiculous the thought was. There was no way this small town lawyer could be able to read her mind or even know of her interest in the Miner's Tunnel.

It had to have been simply coincidence. After all, she was quite certain the mine, the train and the coal museum, all located within a few hundred feet of each other were not only Ashton's main attractions but also likely the town's only attractions. The more she thought about it the more she realized it was all simply coincidence.

Then she became conscious of the fact that Armstrong's offer for dinner was one she had to decline. She apologized and told the lawyer, "Unfortunately, we will have to pass on the dinner invitation, as I'm certain the baby will be ready for a nap after the long day and will likely be getting cranky around dinner time. In fact, I suspect all three kids will likely sleep on the way home, as I suppose I will too."

"Not a problem at all," the lawyer replied. "Whatever works best for you and your family is fine with me."

Stephanie said, "Thanks again. But come to think of it, maybe we should be buying you dinner sometime since we are the ones getting the inheritance."

"That is certainly a generous offer," Armstrong said, "but keep in mind that I'm not only a lawyer but also a businessman and I have been well compensated for carrying out the wishes of your late uncle, my client. And I'm always looking for the next potential client. Since I hope you will consider hiring me to continue to handle your legal needs in the future, the least I can do is to attempt to make a positive impression on you and your family."

"Well, if it's any consolation," she replied, "you already have made a very fine impression. So we'll see you tomorrow morning then."

"Oh by the way," the lawyer suggested, "Please, remember to dress casually. You know, feel free to wear jeans and sneakers or comfortable shoes. We will likely be walking around out at the farmette and dress shoes won't cut it once we get off the walkways to look about the property."

"Farmette." Stephanie tossed the word around in her head. She thought about the rolling fields of Western Berks County and wondered if such land existed in Schuylkill County. Although she had not considered it before, she suddenly realized it must. After all, it was only fifty or so miles north and the area couldn't all be small towns and coal dirt. There had to be the possibility of at least some outlying rural farm area.

She always wanted to own a nice single home on a small piece of farmland, but realized she and Jason might never be able to afford such a dream. Yet, here was one literally being handed to her free of charge. When she first read the letter, she had envisioned the property as perhaps being run-down and in total disrepair, but now she thought about how Armstrong had mentioned the buildings had been refurbished. Then she recalled how he had also said it had been her family homestead built by her great-grandparents.

Suddenly the urge to learn more about her ancestry once again seemed to pop into the forefront of her mind. As she had just told Jason, she believed things in life happen for a reason and now she was beginning to wonder if all of the situations which had occurred that day and been some sort of serendipitous cosmic assemblage, the sum total of which was pointing her and her family in the direction of Schuylkill County; more specifically in the direction of Ashton and her family's past. First, she had received the notification of the inheritance, and then Jason learned of his job loss and potential promotion, which meant transferring to the Ashton facility. Then she learned from the attorney that the property in question was a farmette of over forty acres just outside of Ashton.

She had immediately thought of its potential resale value until she learned it had been her own family homestead. Suddenly resale was no longer the main thing on her mind. Learning more about the property was. Then finally Armstrong had explained how the property had been completely remodeled under the direction of Emerson Washburn. Stephanie realized the property apparently was not the rundown disaster she had feared it might be; instead, it was likely a nice and livable little piece of real estate. "Livable?" Stephanie questioned in her mind, "Where had that idea come from?" Up until a few moments earlier, she never would have considered entertaining the idea of actually moving north and living on the property. But now...

For the first time Stephanie was seriously thinking about the possibility, she might actually be willing to consider relocating her family to Schuylkill County. She of course understood such an idea was extremely premature, as she had not even seen the property. Yet it was as if a switch had suddenly been turned on inside her mind and an idea, which was once something inconceivable suddenly had some appeal to it.

"Mrs. Wright? Stephanie?" Armstrong called through the cell phone, "Are you still there?"

Startled back to reality, Stephanie said "Um...yes...sorry. I'm just a bit distracted...and as I said earlier, this is all so much for me to absorb."

He replied, "Not to worry, Stephanie. I promise I will do everything I can to help you and your family deal with this. I would suggest you forget about it for now and get a good night's sleep. Then we can take care of everything tomorrow."

Jason walked back into the kitchen giving her the OK sign with his right thumb and index finger. He wanted her to know the children weren't killing each other in the other room nor where they destroying the house. Stephanie nodded back at him in unspoken understanding.

"Ok...you're probably right," she said into the phone. "We'll see you tomorrow morning. Thank you again, and good bye."

When Stephanie pressed the call end button, Jason could see she seemed to have a distant, slightly confused expression. "What did he say?" Jason asked with some urgency "What did he tell you?"

After a moment, she replied. "Well...he wouldn't tell me much... he wants to save it 'till we meet with him tomorrow in person... but we already know there is a substantial amount of land and some buildings as well."

"Wow!" Jason said. "Ca-ching! That's great to hear. Land always maintains it value, so it has to be worth a good deal of money; especially with a farmhouse and other buildings. This is almost too good to be true."

She interrupted, "There's more. He told me the property was actually built by my great-grand parents back in the early part of the twentieth century. It's our original family homestead. How strange. It's only an hour or so away and yet, I never knew anything about it. That place represents my family's past, my history."

Jason was caught by surprise, realizing the significance of what Stephanie had just said. The property was now suddenly more than some unseen piece of real estate to be randomly discarded and sold for a profit. It had instantly been transformed into a significant part of Stephanie's family history. Neither of them had known much about their ancestry. Jason had never realized something until that very moment, but a void existed in both of their lives, a lineage about which they were for the most part, ignorant. Although neither he nor Stephanie had discussed her recent desire to learn more in that regard, he was suddenly wondering if he should find some time to start researching his own family history as well. It was an unusual thought for him to have, one he had never even considered before, yet here he was suddenly thinking seriously about it.

Jason wasn't sure what was causing him to have such a sudden interest. Maybe it was because he and Stephanie had created a new family, blending two families and then adding a new member to the mix. Since Sammy had heritage on both sides of their families, it suddenly seemed more important that Jason know more as well.

Then he heard Stephanie say distantly as if being perceived in a dream, "And that's pretty much all he would tell me over the phone. He said anything else would have to wait until tomorrow morning."

"Um... well..." Jason said coming back from his distant thoughts, having not actually heard everything his wife had said, "I guess... we had better say something to the kids, since we will be coming along with us tomorrow."

Stephanie replied, "Yes, it's much too late to try to find a sitter to stay with them so I suppose since we're taking them we should let them know." She was already preparing herself for the complaining she would surely hear. "But I was thinking. Maybe we should just explain that we have to travel north for some business tomorrow. We could tell them we are going to stop for some fast food and goodies along the way, but not mention anything else. The last thing we need is for them to get all wired and excited imagining we may have inherited untold riches. They would never get to sleep."

Stephanie finished cleaning up the kitchen while Jason went into to further monitor the kids' activities while getting some work done on his computer. Every few minutes she could hear him saying something like "No, Sammy," "Don't touch that, Sammy," or "Here's your favorite toy, Sammy." She was grateful he had gone in to take over watching the herd so she could start to relax her mind.

About 8:30 that night Stephanie entered the living room and told the two older kids they were all going away on a day trip the next day and they had to get showers so they would be clean and presentable in the morning. She told Cindy to go first since she was the younger of the two and because she took the longest. Trying to stall she asked, "Where are we going tomorrow and what are we doing?"

Stephanie answered, "We have to go up to the coal region, which is about an hour away to take care of some important business." As she said this, she noticed Jason was busy at his desk doing something on his laptop.

"What the heck is the coal region?" Jeremy inquired, "It sounds like a dirty place...coal is dirty right?"

"What kind of business?" Cindy chimed in. "Why do we have to go? We're big enough to stay home."

Stephanie had anticipated this sort of response. Lately, both of the kids were insisting they were too old for baby sitters and could take care of themselves. But despite the fact that they were both quite mature and responsible for their ages, Stephanie was not ready to cross that particular line just yet. Whenever she and Jason wanted to go out together for special occasions and they didn't want to take the kids along, they would hire one of two seventeen-year-old neighborhood girls to watch them. Either of the girls, Lynn or Janet were each very reliable. And thanks to their generation's love of technology, both of them had smart phones and whenever they were babysitting, Stephanie could reach them instantly when she wanted to check in on the kids.

Stephanie countered, "You two may think you're old enough, but believe me you aren't. Come on, kids; don't give me a hard time about this. We don't have a choice. We have to go see someone tomorrow morning, and I promise I will tell you all about it on the way up there."

"But it's Saturday!" Jeremy complained. "I was going to play some multi-player online games with my friends tomorrow."

"Well you'll just have to postpone that until we get home. So, Cindy, get your butt upstairs right now and get that shower!" Stephanie said more sternly.

Cindy turned reluctantly, obeying her mother as she trudged out of the room dragging her feet all along the way. Stephanie figured in a few years the eye rolling and door slamming would start, recalling her own frustrating teen years.

"Cindy? Wait a minute," Jason said from across the room. "I have a great idea for tomorrow. If we can finish up our business in time, how would you both like to do something you've never done before? It's something exciting and probably a bit scary, that is if you're both not too young to try it."

Stephanie looked at Jason perplexed. She had no idea what he had in mind, but it was clear that he had gotten both kids' attention. He continued, "How would both of you like to go down into a real coal mine?"

Both children's eyes got as wide as saucers, and then Stephanie realized what Jason had been doing on his computer.

He must have found the web site for the "Miners' Tunnel" tourist attraction in Ashton.

At first, Stephanie was startled by this latest coincidence. Not five minutes earlier, she had been discussing the exact same topic with Armstrong over the phone. Also, that afternoon before she had even read the lawyer's letter, she had been thinking about the attraction herself. And here was Jason not only telling the kids about the same thing, but he was also making plans to visit the mine the next day. Now in hindsight, it all seemed so strange and serendipitous to Stephanie, as if she were a passenger in a vehicle being driven by someone else and unable to determine its mysterious, unknown destination. Initially it was a bit unsettling to her, then she remembered her own philosophy of life, and the way things always seemed to happen to her for a reason. This idea comforted her and she relaxed, deciding to just go with the flow as people often said.

"I checked on the web, and there's an honest-to-goodness authentic coal mine in the town where we are going, and they take you down into the mine, like a mile under the earth in real mine cars," Jason told the kids enthusiastically. "The place is open until 5:00, and I'm sure we will have our business finished in time to go there. I don't know if you two are up for it, but I think it would be a really cool thing to do. That is, if you guys aren't too scared to try it. But if you are, I understand and we can skip it." Stephanie was enjoying watching Jason trying reverse psychology on the kids. "There is also an old steam train ride there and a coal mining museum. They both sound interesting too but not nearly as neat as the mine tour."

Jeremy said boldly, "I'm not afraid. I can do it. So can Cindy. Ain't that right, Cind?"

Jason corrected Jeremy's English, "Isn't that right. Not ain't. Ain't isn't a word, Jeremy."

"Ain't fell in a bucket of paint and now there ain't no ain't." Jeremy recited, "Ok...we AREN'T afraid. ISN'T that right Cindy?"

"Uh...yes...I guess..." Cindy said a bit more reluctantly and with a noticeable edge of uncertainty in her voice. She was not exactly sure what a coal mine was or what the uncertain and mystifying experience might be like, but she knew neither Jason or her Mom would take them anywhere which that be potentially dangerous. They were both very protective of their children and never let the kids participate in any activities in which they might be in danger of getting hurt.

"Alright then," Jason said. "It's a deal. We'll make sure we finish up our work in time to take the mine tour. Now, Cindy, get upstairs and get your shower; we have an early start tomorrow and won't have a lot of time to get ready."

Cindy left the room quickly, now thoroughly motivated to finish and get ready for bed. Stephanie picked up the baby and started up the stairs after Cindy. Jason said to Jeremy, "Mom and I are going up to give Sammy a bath in our bathroom a while. So as soon as Cindy is finished, I want you to shut off the TV and get your shower."

"Can't I stay up a little later? I'm twelve!" Jeremy complained.

"Nope. Shower then bed," Jason insisted. "And if it's any consolation, Mom and I are heading to bed right away as well. We have to get up early, drive far and we have a very busy day ahead of us. Everyone has to be well rested." Then after a moment's thought he said "And don't think of trying to pull a fast one on us either. As soon as Cindy is done, I'll be checking to make sure you have gotten into the shower. Understand?"

Jeremy said reluctantly, "Yes, I understand." Then he got a gleam in his eye and asked "Are we really going down inside of a coal mine tomorrow?"

Jason said, "You bet." Then he bent down and tousled Jeremy's hair. "I'll see you before bed, buddy. "Gotta go give the little stinker a bath."

"Ok, Dad," Jeremy replied. "I'll watch TV until Cindy is done. I can't wait to see what the inside of a mine looks like."

Jason wondered if telling the kids about the mine was such a good idea. He and Stephanie had chosen not to tell them about the inheritance so they wouldn't become wired and too excited to sleep, and then he opened his big mouth and mentioned the mine tour. In hindsight, he was starting to doubt the logic of his possibly poorly planned announcement. He suspected there was very little that didn't get young kids excited. Regardless, the damage had already been done, so all he could do is hope the kids were tired enough to go to sleep. Otherwise, he suspected Jeremy and Cindy would both be asleep during the hour trip north the next day.

He checked to make sure the front door and the kitchen door was locked, then he grabbed two nighttime pain tablets, one he immediately took and the other he was taking up to Stephanie. He turned out the lights in the kitchen and headed up the stairs.

Chapter 7

H. Mason Armstrong lowered the telephone receiver gently back down into its cradle, which was situated in the exact place it had previously been atop his large mahogany desk. He sat with his hands folded in front of him, hunched over with the elbows of his suit jacket resting on his clean and unblemished desk blotter. He was deep in the throes of contemplation. He was distressed, burdened by the troubles, which had plagued him during the past month starting shortly after the suicide of Emerson Washburn.

Armstrong was by nature an extremely neat and orderly man with a desk organized to a level most people might consider obsessive. The fact was if he were blind and sitting in his large leather armchair behind his desk, he would be able to effortlessly reach out and instantly grab a phone, a paperclip, a pen or any other office supply he required. Armstrong's motto regarding office decorum was "a place for everything and everything in its place".

The desk was exactly as it had been since he started practicing law many, many years ago. He didn't even allow the advent of new modern technology to infringe upon the way his desk was organized. When he eventually decided to become part of the computer revolution, he made sure he purchased a separate table for the device so it would not interfere with his system. It was still easily accessible from his large, comfortable office chair as well. He was not exactly opposed to new technology, but he simply would never allow it to infringe on his traditional organizational preferences.

His carefully arranged desk and for that matter his entire personal office space, would rival some of the most stringent of the modern attempts at office organization such as the "Lean Office" initiatives of the early twenty-first century. And ironically, Armstrong had never even heard of such methodologies. He simply had always been a man who liked things to be exactly where they belonged and right where he could find them with ease.

His soul, on the other hand was anything be ordered. In fact, it was in utter chaos, filled with overwhelming trepidation due to the unknown series of events he suspected he had just set into motion. As he had been instructed, Armstrong had sent the certified letter to Stephanie Wright notifying her of her inheritance, which was also his legal responsibility as executor of

Emerson Washburn's estate, but he had neglected to tell her everything.

He had not warned her about the dark and tragic history surrounding the property. In the spirit of full disclosure he should have told her about the numerous catastrophes which seemed to plague the homestead, starting with its original owners, her great grand-parents, and ending with her Uncle Emerson's suicide just a month earlier. But despite his legal responsibility and the heavy weight of despair his conscience was now forced to endure, he knew he would not be speaking a single word about the property's tragic history to her nor to anyone else. He would not because he could not. He understood that whether alive, dead or otherwise, Emerson Washburn would never allow such an infraction to occur.

Then dreadfully as if on cue, Armstrong heard an odd yet frighteningly familiar noise coming from the darkened rear of his office. It sounded like a thousand worm-like insects were squirming madly atop a crinkled sheet of aluminum foil, their writhing bodies sliding in their own slimy secretions, creating a sickening wet yet hauntingly metallic sound. Armstrong looked at his desk clock and saw it was about ten o'clock.

He felt as if he had just hung up the phone from speaking with the Wright woman, but that would mean it would have only been about six thirty or so. However, according to his desk clock and the fact that his office was in total darkness, save for the light from his desk lamp, he must have fallen asleep or perhaps fallen into some type of hypnotic trance while contemplating his numerous problems. That had to be the only viable explanation for the loss of several hours.

In the meager light from his brass banker's light with its translucent green glass shade, H. Mason Armstrong could see a slight reflection of the semi-dark room around him in a long mirror mounted on a door leading to his private bathroom in the back of the office. Just outside of the room was a closet where Armstrong kept several suits and changes of clothing so that he would always be ready for whatever sort of business or social event he might be required to attend.

More times, than he cared to mention, his busy schedule had required him to freshen up and change clothes at work. His children were all grown now and had families of their own. They also no longer lived in the area, having scattered themselves all around the country. And with his wife now dead and gone as well; he often slept in the office on the large leather sofa, not particularly wanting to go home to his empty house. The bathroom as well as the tall mirror had assisted him to quickly become presentable for important appointments. But now, that same mirror was serving a much more sinister and unwelcome purpose.

Staring intently at his barely visible reflection in the glass hanging on the open door, Armstrong noticed the surface begin to ripple in the shadows, as a voice seemed to call from deep below the surface. At first, the sound was a distant, barely audible whisper but all too soon, it became more clearly defined. He was not shocked by the voice as he had been on the very first occasion he had heard it but he was nonetheless terrified not only by the voice itself, but by what it represented.

As the hardly visible ripples increased their intensity back among the shadows, as did the unsettling noise, Armstrong saw an all too familiar thin, bony bare foot extending from the mirror and setting down hovering just above the luxurious oriental carpet adorning his office floor. It never came in direct contact with the carpet but seemed to float an inch or so in the air just above it.

As his eyes reluctantly followed up along the length of the limbs, Armstrong could catch occasional glimpses of the all too familiar skeletal legs as the hideous creature stepped naked from the mirror into the shadows of his back office. Thankfully, Mason had never seen the abysmal creature in its entirety before and hoped he would not do so tonight, since the thing was still floating largely silhouetted at the back of the room. From what Mason could determine, the wretched being was gaunt and hunched, and Mason barely recognized the nude and emaciated specter as his recently deceased client Emerson Washburn.

When Washburn had first purchased the property and contacted Armstrong to handle his legal needs, the man had been tall, well over six feet in height and as broad as a refrigerator. He had looked to Armstrong very much like a typical Hollywood interpretation of how an enforcer for the mob might appear. Although Washburn had been dressed in an expensive top of the line business suit at the time, there was an obvious underlying sense of brutality to the man, which Armstrong suspected would find its way through any sort of expensive attire Washburn might use in a feeble attempt to cloak his real persona.

As such, Armstrong had been able to see right through the gangster's attempted ruse. He realized the mysterious new client who seemed to have more money than the lawyer had ever imagined, was not a well-educated gentleman, although he seemed fairly well-spoken in a self-educated sort of way. But

Armstrong sensed he was actually some sort of hardened street-smart thug; likely a criminal who had acquired his money through illegal means.

Armstrong had requested a very brief and discreet background check on Washburn as he did with all potential clients of obvious means. Although he had discovered many unsavory tidbits in the man's past, he nonetheless accepted Washburn as a new client. H. Mason Armstrong understood his place in the world. He knew at best, he was a small-town lawyer who currently had scarcely enough paying clients to make ends meet. The simple fact was with the addition of Washburn to his client list he would receive a windfall of funds to help his ailing business. So Armstrong chose to overlook any apprehension he might have about Washburn and immediately began handling his legal needs.

As a result of the various often high pressure demands of his new client, Armstrong often found himself going beyond the call of duty on Washburn's behalf often performing tasks, which some might consider outside of the scope of a typical lawyer's responsibility to a client. Mason did his best to try to think several steps ahead of Washburn so he didn't inadvertently find himself in a less than legal situation on his employer's behalf. Washburn was shrewd and street-smart, but Armstrong was intelligent and quite cunning himself.

One service Washburn had requested was for Armstrong to coordinate the renovation of his property. During the remodeling, Armstrong handled the disbursement of funds and payment to the army of contractors Washburn had requested he hire. These sorts of activities were things he normally didn't do for his clients, but when called on to do so he often worked with local banks and sometimes would even subcontract an area accounting firm. However, Washburn had demanded that Armstrong handle everything personally with no outside help.

Armstrong also found himself coordinating all of their construction activities, and acting as a middleman between the workers and Washburn. This type of construction project management and liaison efforts were definitely outside of Armstrong's comfort zone. But he was able to quickly adapt to the role.

The lawyer found a great deal of satisfaction, of both a personal and financial nature, in carrying out his duties as project coordinator throughout the renovation. It had been, in fact, Armstrong himself who had recommended most of the contractors used on the project. And it was far more than coincidental that those same contractors also happened to be

Armstrong's clients. As such, in as much as they began to prosper so too did he further prosper. At first, he had balked at the idea of doing everything himself, but once he was able to realize the financial benefits of the arrangement, he wouldn't have changed a thing. He liked being the fox in charge of that particular financial hen house.

Emerson Washburn had requested Armstrong find and hire the best of the best to do the work on his property, but Armstrong was always careful to never hire anyone who was not one of his clients, or any contractor who would not agree to sign on with him in order to get the work, regardless of their superior skills.

Since Washburn was a stranger in the area while Armstrong was a well-known pillar of the community with a great deal of assumed influence and political power, none of the contractors dared to challenge him. They always agreed to his terms. One more than one occasion, it became apparent to Armstrong that he and Washburn were not so different after all. Washburn had used threats and physical coercion to make his fortune in his criminal enterprises, while Armstrong used his own brand of persuasion to get what he wanted.

But in Armstrong's case, he believed what he was doing was legal, or at least straddled the line between legal and illegal, if not completely ethical. He figured if he was the project manager in charge of everything, it was his right to hire whomever he chose to hire, and Emerson Washburn would be none the wiser.

Besides, in Armstrong's opinion, it was not as if he were hiring anyone who would provide shoddy workmanship by any means, as all of his clients were top-notch contractors. But if one were to press him or were for example, to threaten to sever his finger or hand in order to get to the truth; and if they were then to ask him who the best candidates for the various positions truly were, there were only a few of his clients who could have hoped to have met those qualifications.

As the project progressed during the previous year, Armstrong noticed a dramatic and continually declining physical and mental transformation in Emerson Washburn. As the months passed, the man began to lose a great deal of weight, eventually shrinking down to less than half his original size. In the weeks preceding his suicide, Washburn's clothing had hung limply on his bony frame. The man had seemed to have aged by decades; his once coal black head of thick hair had grayed, thinned and actually seemed to have fallen out in places. His formerly charming and charismatic smile had turned into what appeared to be a permanent scowl.

Armstrong was shocked to see Washburn had actually lost several of his teeth as well. He was beginning to resemble a victim of radiation poisoning during his last days on earth. That same shadow of a man, over a month in his grave, or some twisted and perverse incarnation of what was once that man, now stood across the room from Armstrong. However, the unimaginable being now appeared more like some nightmarish creature from the warped mind of a deranged horror fiction writer.

The thing, which was how Armstrong thought of him, appeared to be above average height, yet was noticeably stooped as if its skeleton could not support the weight of its empty withered skin. Flesh hung from its shadowed naked form like deflated balloons. Between glimpses in the darkness, Armstrong thought he saw a dark empty spot where the man's genitalia had once been.

The lawyer was perfectly aware of the horrible ending Washburn had apparently chosen for himself. Armstrong recalled the self-mutilation, which Washburn had so gruesomely carried out, the slashing of his wrist, the V-shaped furrows carved in his chest, the severing of his ear and finally the removal of his own genitals. Armstrong would never be able to forget that repugnant sight.

He had been the person called to the scene by Ashton police Chief Max Seiler Jr. to officially identify and claim the body. He recalled how as he stared down into the crimson, blood-soaked bath water, Armstrong had no idea how the man could have inflicted such incredible damage upon himself. Mason had almost passed out when he saw Washburn's severed penis bobbing along the top of the ruby tub water.

The lawyer recalled how Seiler, a veteran police officer nearing retirement, had blanched white at the unimaginable carnage. Seiler was a tall muscular man who was no stranger to horrifying scenes of human disaster. He was a second generation Ashton police chief, his father Max Seiler Sr. having been chief during the 1950's through the mid 1980's. Max Jr.'s son, Max III was a member of the Ashton force destined to succeed his father someday, carrying on the Seiler dynasty.

Seiler had seen many horrifying sights during his tenure on the force, but none as mentally challenging as the sight of Washburn's decimated remains. Although he had heard stories of worse atrocities from his father he had never been seen anything so horrible in his career. Seiler' father had told him of an incident, which happened back in 1965, outside of an abandoned coalmine, the Coogan Coal Mine on the northern outskirts of Ashton. A young boy had apparently been attacked and disemboweled by some sort of wild animal while he and his friends were playing near the mine.

Rumors began to spread about an old local legend of a soul-sucking demon living in the mine. The legend said the demon was a 19th century coal miner who had become trapped and sold his soul to Satan for a chance to escape. Apparently, the great deceiver had tricked the man and transformed him into a demon. The monster had to remain in the mine until he collected the souls of ninety-nine victims. Of course many people blamed the demon on the boy's death, but a conclusive answer was never determined as the mine collapsed the next day and was never reopened.

Seiler had asked his father once about the incident, but the man refused to speak of it. That particular scene haunted Seiler's father until the day he died. Armstrong suspected the incident with Washburn would be Max Seiler Jr.'s equivalent.

Armstrong looked at the horrifying creature, now standing far across the main office from him. The thing's chest appeared to have become shrunken and still bore the marred V-shaped gashes occasionally visible in partial, shadowy glimpses. Armstrong remembered from one of his previous encounters with the spirit how the thing's mottled flesh had folded downward from the savagely ripped incisions in flaps, loose and shredded, and how from deep inside each of the ghastly tears worms and larvae seemed to crawl freely. He hoped against hope that he would not be forced to see so much grizzly detail this time. He prayed the beast would stay back in the shadows.

He had no idea what the insects inhabiting the ghost actually were. He was quite certain they were not creatures of this world, as they only slightly resembled any insects he had ever seen; enough of a likeness that he was able to think of them as insectile in nature. Although Washburn was now some type of non-corpulent being, Armstrong assumed perhaps on the other side, in that unimaginable hellish world where Washburn now resided, his body must have taken on some strange new form.

It seemed logical that if such an alternate manifestation of the man existed in such a bizarre world then it would also stand to reason other strange creatures, similar but different than those in our world, would likewise exist over there as well. And just as such similar creatures find their way into open festering wounds on this side; those particular things must have been able to do something quite similar on the other side.

He recalled how in some past encounters with Washburn, some of the disgusting creeping maggot-like things occasionally would drop from the specter's open wounds, falling to the carpet where they would writhe as if in agony for a few moments before they simply flattened out then vanished in a puff of foul smelling smoke. Apparently, the creatures from that world beyond the grave could survive in this world only as long as they stayed attached to Washburn. However, once they contacted the physical aspects of this world, they simply could not survive. The lawyer noticed how Washburn's shriveled and blackened feet never actually touched the carpet but floated an inch or so above it. Armstrong began to wonder if perhaps this small tidbit of information would come in handy at some time in the future. He had always believed knowledge was power, so he tucked it away for reference, although he had no idea when or if he would ever find an opportunity to use it.

Now Armstrong could clearly see the creature's face, which was a mask of slashes and its left ear was missing, as he remembered it had been. From within the gaping hole where once Washburn's ear had hung, a long worm-like thing emerged as if sniffing the air. Then the disgusting creature retreated, squirming back inside of the specter's skull.

As far as Armstrong could recall, this was the sixth time he had been confronted by the specter of his deceased client, but its inexplicable sight still nonetheless revolted him; not to mention the foul and disgusting odor, which accompanied its countenance. Trailing in its wake was a horrible smell, which only such a vile undead creature could bring with it; a reek, which Mason recognized as the very stench of the grave.

Armstrong recalled now how on the night of the suicide Washburn had called him to the house feigning some sort of emergency. He had always assumed that the man had made the call just moments before he decided to begin butchering himself, but now after many, post mortem encounters with the fiend, he realized he likely had made the call after he was already dead.

A month ago, Armstrong would have never believed such a thing possible; now he only wished it were not. It had taken a good deal of acting for the lawyer to convince Max Seiler that the chief's call to him had been the first Armstrong had heard of Washburn's death. In reality, after receiving Washburn's call he had hurried to the house and seen the carnage in the tub, but had fled the scene without taking any action.

Then he had made an anonymous call from a local pay phone to the police department. This had resulted in Chief Seiler hastening to the scene and eventually calling Armstrong, knowing the lawyer was handling Washburn's affairs. He had a feeling Chief Seiler had suspected him of being the person who had made the call, but the chief continued his pretext of ignorance during the entire investigation. Eventually, Seiler had no alternative but to declare the gruesome scene a suicide, although he had no idea what form of psychosis would drive a man to butcher himself so savagely.

Now back in Armstrong's office, the creature took one apprehensive and unsteady floating, twitching air-step after another like a newborn calf unsure of its footing. Armstrong was certain he could hear the thing's bones rattling against one another as the dreadful ghost-thing slowly made its way across the room. Then before it came into the light of the desk lamp it stopped, much to Armstrong's relief, as he did not want to have a better look at the ungodly hell-born demon.

It raised its right bony hand, pointing a long skeletal finger directly at Armstrong. Something appeared to move on its finger and Armstrong's stomach turned with revolution when he realized some sort of worm or maggot-like creature was crawling along the length of the gnarled and twisted digit.

Then speaking in a distorted multi-octave voice, the likes of which the lawyer had never previously imagined the creature said, "I've been monitoring your progress, Armstrong, and I see you have done exactly what I instructed you to do. Very good. Very good indeed... They are coming... She is coming...and so it can once again be as it was...good work, my minion...congratulations; you have earned yourself some additional time on this planet. Death will not be claiming you this day."

Armstrong sat silently, not wanting to even acknowledge the presence of the hideous specter. As the Washburn-thing hovered in and out of clarity in the dark shadows, Armstrong could see glimpses of its sagging flesh shining with some sort of thick slimy gelatinous fluid, which reminded him of transparent coagulated snot and it gave the creature a slick, wet appearance.

The lawyer suddenly realized with revulsion the countless worms and maggoty insects, which crawled freely in and out of the creature's festering wounds, must be leaving the disgusting snail trails as a slick medium to help them move about with ease. The very thought made him want to vomit.

"Don't bother trying to ignore me, Mason," Washburn said to the lawyer's downcast head. "You are wasting both your time and mine...But since I have an eternity...of damnation ahead of me, my time is meaningless...However, your time is still precious...

perhaps more so than you realize." Armstrong slowly lifted his eyes trying to avoid looking directly at the creature's jaws, which seemed to move in a way resembling those of a grinning hideous death's head. "Now...did you take care of that little problem...from last evening?"

The ghost was referring to the fiery death of Jack Moran the previous evening. "Um...yes..." Armstrong said reluctantly. "I spoke with chief of police Seiler, and he has decided to rule the death a suicide. For now, Moran's charred corpse has been listed as a 'John Doe'. The car had been reported stolen and even if they somehow were able to identify Moran's blackened remains, they would simply find that he was an ex-con, and they would never be able to tie him or his death to your property. I told Seiler since your estate was my responsibility, I would take care of cleaning up the site of the...the incident.

"Chief Seiler had a local towing company removed the car from the scene and today I had a landscaper out to the property, trimming the trees by the side of the road, smoothing the gravel and basically erasing all signs of trouble. As I am sure you already are aware, I went back into the house and cleaned up the mess Moran had made in your former bedroom, putting everything back in order. I replaced the broken jewelry box with a new one, and I returned of its contents to their proper place. That is to say, all except for Moran's severed finger. That particular item will never be found. So rest assured; when the Wright family arrives at the farm tomorrow for their tour, they will not notice a single thing out of place."

"They...had better not," the demanding specter moaned. "I'm relying on you...to make sure they fall completely in love...with the property...so they can't wait...to take possession...You must also be sure...to explain the contingencies of the will...so they understand they have little choice...but to move into the estate...as soon as possible."

Armstrong replied with a somewhat haughty tone, "I would make certain of that whether or not you were involved in the process. I am a lawyer after all; it is my legal and professional responsibility to make sure the Wrights have a thorough understanding of all the stipulations of your last will and testament. My integrity should never come under question."

The specter ignored the comment and replied from the shadows, "Just make sure...that you do, Armstrong...because I will be watching... and more importantly...they will be watching as well...And the only reason you are still alive and walking the earth...is because they still need you and your services... The day that particular need ceases to exist...so too will you... And the fate they likely have in mind for you...might make my agonizing death... seem like a pleasurable experience... However...if you keep them satisfied...with your performance...then great wealth and power could be yours...for the rest of your miserable earth-bound life... and I know how very important...that is to you."

The ghost began to float back toward the mirror and soon seemed to dissolve back into the glass. Just before the rippling, shimmering surface became still and the foul sulfurous stench began to slowly dissipate, Armstrong heard Washburn say one last thing, "Understand this, Armstrong...you don't ever want to let us down."

The lawyer sat at his desk with his head downcast, his hands trembling, his lower lip quivering, trying desperately not to burst into tears. He wished he had never met Emerson Washburn or taken him on as a client. He cursed himself for his own pitiful greed. He may have made a great deal of money from Washburn while he was alive, but now he was an unwilling servant to the awful spirit, or whatever the man had become since returning from the grave.

Armstrong thought back to all the money he had essentially stolen from Washburn by hiring his handpicked preferred contractors to do the work on Washburn's renovations and how he had falsified records skimming even more money from the gangster. He also recalled how the sicker and more demented Washburn became, the more he stole from the man. Now Armstrong realized he was not as clever as he had thought and was paying the ultimate price for his treachery. He was essentially dead Washburn's slave in the world of the living.

And he knew Washburn was not the only creature involved in this unholy alliance. The specter often spoke of "we" and "us" when discussing Armstrong's potential fate. As a result, Armstrong suspected there might be a sordid collection of dead spirits involved in the events taking place.

The lawyer had always justified his stealing from Washburn as something which was not wrong since Washburn, himself was actually a criminal. He constantly told himself that stealing from a thief was not actually stealing. Unfortunately, he refused to acknowledge that in the eyes of God, or morality in general or the cosmos, stealing was still stealing, regardless of the circumstances or trumped up justifications. He therefore eventually began to fear he might have crossed a line somewhere, and when his time to die finally did come, the universe might see fit so he too might be destined to become one of the same type of ungodly creatures, Washburn had become.

He also suspected that as bad as Washburn might have been in life and was still now in death, he might not be the worst of the worst. Armstrong was quite certain Washburn was not the top dog in this cadre of demons, but was simply another servant in some twisted unholy pecking order of the undead. This thought did little to ease his internal anguish since he suspected, when his time came to cross over, he would be at the bottom of that same food chain and would in turn be subjected to every torture Hell could imagine. But it was much too late to consider such a fate any longer; too much damage to his soul had already been done. His only chance for at least a temporary reprieve from such a fate was to say alive and find some way out of his predicament.

Chapter 8

When Jason walked into the bedroom, he could hear water running in the master bath as well as Sammy giggling and splashing merrily. Sammy was one of those kids who absolutely loved being in the tub. Before Sammy was born, Jason had all but forgotten how much fun it was bathing little ones and how much they enjoyed the splashing and playing. He still thought of Sammy as a baby even though at almost eighteen months old most people would consider him a toddler. He and Stephanie both assumed Sammy would be their last, although they still had not done anything in the realm of surgery to prevent any surprise pregnancies. Nor were they using any form of birth control. They just both had an unspoken feeling or perhaps knowledge there would be no more; as if they knew instinctively. As a result, neither of them was in a hurry to have the little fellow grow up and wanted to enjoy his being a baby for as long as they possibly could.

"Bubbles, bubbles, bubbles!" Sammy shouted as he slapped the surface of the tub trying to make the bubbles multiply as his father had taught him. Jason could smell the sweet, fresh scent of whatever bubble soap Stephanie had added to the water. It seemed that no matter how many years passed by every time he smelled bubble soap; it always seemed to bring back memories of his own childhood.

Stephanie quickly wet, shampooed and rinsed Sammy's dark brown hair then let him sit for a while in the shallow water while she stood and stretched out a kink in her back, which resulted from being bent over for too long. Then she hugged Jason and said, "Oh, honey, there is so much for us to think about."

"I realize that, baby. But I think we really should let all of this go until tomorrow," Jason replied. "Tonight we need to get a good night sleep, and I have just what the doctor ordered. Here you go, sweetie." He handed her the elliptical blue nighttime pain pill. "This should help you sleep like a baby and wake up with a clear head."

Stephanie replied, "I know I was the one who suggest we each take one, and those things always do knock me out. But sometimes I end up having very bad nightmares from them and occasionally I even wake up foggy in the brain as if the effect didn't completely wear off."

"Well," he suggested, "since we don't have a prescription for sleeping pills, I suppose it's either you take one of these or else you can take your chances naturally and possibly end up staying awake half the night thinking about the inheritance. If that happens, then you'll be exhausted all day tomorrow. For the record; I took mine earlier downstairs so I should be getting sleepy very soon."

"I suppose you're right," she agreed taking the pill from him, knowing within about forty-five minutes after taking it she would be out like a light and on her way to dreamland. She swallowed the pill using a glass of tap water from the bathroom sink, then fished Sammy from the bath, drying him with his favorite towel; the one with the rubber ducky pattern and built-in hoodie and simulated duck bill to keep his head warm. She loved how the oversized bath towel surrounded him, and it was clear Sammy did as well.

"Ducky towel!" Sammy exclaimed as he did every time Stephanie dried him with it.

As she snuggled Sammy in the towel she said to Jason, "Did you overhear what Mr. Armstrong and I were talking about just before I ended the call."

"No," Jason replied. "I was in with the kids and couldn't hear what you were saying."

"Well, it's really kind of strange," Stephanie said. "Mason had just suggested that tomorrow we should take the kids on that same mine tour. He even said he would reserve a set of complimentary tickets for us. Then just a few minutes later you brought up the tour to the kids. I don't know... it's just a funny coincidence."

Jason said, "Yeah. I suppose it is, but probably not really all that surprising. After all, the tunnel is the only tourist attraction Ashton has to offer. Plus, I'll bet being a local lawyer; he probably gets those tickets free to hand out to clients."

"Yeah. I'm sure you're right," Stephanie conceded.

Jason said, "I'm not at all surprised. But just give that magic pill a few minutes to take effect and by the time you finish getting ready for bed, you will be out like a light."

Once Sammy was thoroughly dried and dressed in his footy pajamas, Stephanie carried him to his bed and tucked him in. She stood over him singing his favorite lullaby as he drifted off to sleep. She could feel herself getting sleepy as well.

A few minutes earlier, Jason heard Cindy finish up in the shower and then go to her room. He was surprised to find that Jeremy had actually listened to him and was already in the bathroom. Jason went downstairs to do a final check to assure all the lights and appliances were turned off and all doors were locked.

As he walked past the large mirror in the foyer he thought for a moment, he saw something out of the corner of his eye; some sort of strange image briefly reflected in the glass. When he did a double take, looking once again the vision was gone. But for a second, he had been certain he had seen something. He recalled the similar sensation he had experienced that same morning at work in his boss's office.

He couldn't have said exactly what it was he had seen that time, but based on the quick glance he had a feeling it might have been something hideous and skeleton-thin. He thought perhaps it might have been the image of a man; one who seemed to have been looking out at him from the glass, as if it were a creature existing in some strange other world within the mirror itself.

"Wow! Maybe I shouldn't have taken that pill until I was in bed," he thought. "It is really screwing with my head already." Then he shook off the strange incident, turned off the remaining lights and went up to bed.

By the time he reached the kids' bathroom, he saw the door was open, and apparently Jeremy was already finished and in his room. Jason wondered just how clean the boy could have gotten with such a quick shower but decided to give him a pass this time. Tomorrow was going to be a very busy day for all of them, and right now sleep was what they needed more than anything else.

He stopped by both rooms to kiss the kids goodnight, then peeked into the nursery to check on Sammy. The boy was already sound asleep, and Stephanie was apparently was getting ready for bed. He walked into their bedroom and heard the familiar sounds of Stephanie washing her face and brushing her teeth. He changed into his pajamas and lay on the bed propped up on his pillow, his hands intertwined behind his head as he waited his turn in the bathroom.

After a few moments, Stephanie emerged and said, "Your turn." Then she gave Jason a peck on the lips and sighed, "Goodnight, honey. I'll see you in the morning."

Jason went into the bathroom to complete his own nightly ritual. Strangely, he found himself avoiding his reflection in the mirror as he brushed his teeth. It was as if he believed somewhere deep down in his subconscious, if he were to look directly into the reflective glass, it might result in a return of the hideous image he thought he had imagined downstairs. Part of him knew the idea was ridiculous, but still he could not bring himself to look into the mirror.

In a few minutes, he finished in the bathroom and turned out the light. As he looked across the bedroom, he realized his beautiful wife was already fast asleep. She was barely visible in the limited light from the lamp on the end table, as she was snuggled deep under her covers. Although it was spring, the evening had been a cool one. Jason originally thought he might want to discuss a few more ideas with her before they slept. But then he realized it was probably for the best that she was already asleep. Any conversation they might have had would likely have resulted in their both staying up later than they needed to. And besides, he too was starting to feel the effects of the nighttime pill, which meant he would very likely be asleep soon as well.

He crawled beneath the covers, turned out the light on the end table and quickly joined Stephanie in the world of restful dreams. But unknown to Jason, Stephanie would not be having a very restful sleep. Instead, her dreams would be haunted with horrible and terrifying images. Although she would likely blame the nightmares on the pill she had taken, they actually had their roots in some place much more sinister and menacing than simple over-the-counter pharmaceuticals.

During the night, Stephanie was bombarded with one horrendous nightmare after another. When she reached that place in the sleep cycle where dreams occur, she first encountered a young woman dressed in an early twentieth century evening gown, who looked quite a lot like her. The woman appeared to be mad with rage and was in the process of pulling two young boys, perhaps not more than four and six years old across a grass covered meadow. The two boys were kicking, screaming and pleading with the woman to let them go, but she would not relent.

Suddenly the image changed, and Stephanie was standing in a bedroom of an old house. The room was awash with light from candles and antique oil lamps. She looked up into the full-length dressing mirror, which stood in the bedroom suspended from a wooden frame. Instead of seeing her own reflection, she once again saw the familiar face of the same madwoman she had seen earlier. The woman was still dressed in an old fashioned evening gown, but the front of the gown was covered with small streaks of blood. Stephanie felt as though she was looking out through the crazy woman's eyes. Those eyes bore a wild animal-like look of savagery which she saw in the reflection, as the face stared back, smiling an insane smile.

After a moment, a man burst through the bedroom door. He was tall and wore an old-fashioned business suit. He carried a walking stick, with an ivory handle, which appeared to have been carved in the shape of a wolf's head. The man resembled her husband Jason, with his dark brown hair and wire-framed glasses, but he still seemed somehow different.

His eyes were filled with tears and wild with rage as he stormed across the room.

Then, with his breath hitching heavily in his chest, the man raised the cane high above his head and without a moment's hesitation slammed its ivory handle into the side of her skull.

In an instant, Stephanie found herself once again outside of the woman's body watching the scene from high above as if she was floating up near the ceiling. The angry man continued to squeeze the woman's throat ever tighter as her eyes bugged wildly out of her skull. Then surprisingly, the woman looked up directly at Stephanie, and as their eyes met, the woman smiled knowingly at Stephanie as if she were aware of Stephanie's presence.

The man sat weeping on the floor, cradling the woman in his arms. Then his eyes locked with Stephanie's in a knowing stare and she realized the man had also changed significantly and now appeared to be identical to Jason.

As Stephanie watched in terrorized silence, never allowing her eyes to leave the man's/Jason's strange gaze, he reached slowly into his suit jacket pocket and withdrew a long ivory handled straight razor.

Then, just as nonchalantly, he brought the razor up to his own throat and while still staring into Stephanie's eyes and giving her that strange half knowing smile, he slit his own throat from ear to ear.

Stephanie mercifully awoke with a start hovering in that strange state somewhere between asleep and awake not certain if she were still dreaming or was conscious. She looked around the bedroom surprised to find her blinds open and their room awash with moonlight. She was certain she had closed the blinds before going to bed. Stephanie heard a scratching, clawing sound coming from the foot of her bed. A cold chill seemed to start at the back of her skull and squirm like a slithering snake down to the base of her spine. She immediately understood something was not right. A foul smell had begun to permeate the room. The odor was like that of a dead putrefying animal.

At the bottom of her bed, she saw two skeletal hands creeping up apparently from the floor below. They were covered with withered grey flesh but were so bony in appearance as if to suggest the translucent skin was not actually there. The fingers gripped the covers of her bed as they slowly pulled themselves closer toward her. She could not move; neither could she let out the scream of terror, which wanted to erupt from deep within her tightening chest, from the very depths of her soul.

Stephanie sat bolt upright in her bed, awakening from the horrible nightmare, sweat beading on her brow. She thanked God that it had all just been a terrible dream. She looked toward the bottom of her bed, and although she could no longer remember why, she felt the need to do so. She experienced an unusual rush of relief at seeing the covers lying smooth at her feet. Then she began to feel foolish. What else had she thought she would see except for her covered feet? She had an almost certain sensation she might see something at the foot of her bed but for the life of her, she could not recall what that might be.

She turned to look at the glowing ghostly blue display of her digital alarm clock and saw it was only 2:15 AM. Stephanie was surprised at how bright the clock display seemed; much brighter than she remembered. She knew the glow was at least much more brilliant the previous clock she owned, which had been equipped with a red display but had broken a week earlier.

However, for some unknown reason the glow from the new clock appeared to be much too bright, more so than even the illumination she would have gotten from a lamp. She wondered why she had never noticed the way it washed the entire room with its eerie cobalt aura before. She decided, at some suitable time, she would have to do something about replacing it as well.

She could not recall what had actually awoken her, but realized she suddenly needed to use the bathroom. She twisted slowly in bed and placed her feet on the floor as she sat on the edge of the mattress for a moment, trying to get her bearings before standing up. The surface of the floor felt unexpectedly chilly on her bare feet as if the temperature along the floor had suddenly dropped thirty degrees, yet the air around her seemed to maintain its normal room temperature. It was only the floor, which had acquired the strange coldness. But because of the chill from the floor, combined with the haunting azure glow of the clock, Stephanie felt as though the entire room was beginning to cool.

As she was about to stand up, she felt something unusual in the icy air surrounding her feet. Icy cold tendrils seemed to slowly wrap themselves around her pale white ankles like some strange invasive plant or vine. She cautiously looked down at the floor seeing her feet take on a bluish grey appearance from the cerulean glow. The she realized with unbridled terror that some type of long bony fingers had appeared from beneath her bed and were now slithering like serpents, attempting to get a secure grip on her legs; perhaps wanting to pull her down, perhaps into some unseen portal under her bed, into world of the dead. Stephanie was overcome with terror and her heart felt like it had jumped into her throat.

"Mommy! Wake up!" Stephanie heard a distant voice calling to her from some faraway place. She groggily opened her eyes as the voice became louder and clearer and saw Cindy's pretty face next to her bed as the young girl shook her mother her vigorously, attempting to awaken her.

Stephanie was a bit confused and was trying desperately to find her way back from the world of nightmares. As she sat up and shook off the sleep and the effects of the nighttime cold pill she had taken, she saw Cindy was dress and ready to go.

"Honey?" Stephanie asked. "What...I mean who... I mean... how did you get ready to go...already?"

She heard Jason entering the room with little Sammy in his arms. She could hear the steady computerized tones of a video game in the distance and suspected Jeremy was downstairs playing one of his games. Jason surprisingly appeared to also be showered and dressed and ready as well. She must have had a strange expression on her face because Jason said, "Don't worry, Steph. I took care of them. You were sleeping so deeply, and I figured you needed to rest so I let you sleep a bit longer while we all got ready. Then I sent Cindy in to wake you up."

"Oh my Lord." She replied, "I was sleeping the sleep of the dead." Then a cold chill appeared on the back of her neck upon hearing herself uttering the expression, but she didn't understand why as the memories of her nightmares had faded.

Jason said, "I'll take the kids downstairs and make them breakfast while you are getting ready. I'll put a pot of boiling water on for tea for us as well. By the time you're finished, breakfast will be ready. Take your time. It's only about 7:15. We don't have to leave until around 9:30. The kids and I were just so excited about today we all woke up early."

"Ok...see you in a bit," Stephanie said as she stumbled into the bathroom to get ready for the busy day ahead. As she soaked under the hot cleansing shower, feeling herself come back to reality out from the fog of sleep, she had a strange apprehensive sensation growing deep inside of her, almost an intuition of some impending danger. Although she could recall nothing of the horrible dreams of the previous night, she was gripped by the uncertain and ominous feeling surrounding her.

Chapter 9

The four-year-old Dodge Grand Caravan followed the silver Cadillac along the winding two-lane country road. Jason and Stephanie Wright sat noticeably silent as if unsure of what to say. Or perhaps they were trying to come to grips with everything they had just learned. They appeared to be allowing the gravity of what they were told that morning in the Ashton lawyer's office to somehow sink in.

Slowly, Jason turned his head toward the passenger's seat, while simultaneously Stephanie turned to look at him. It was as if a type of telepathy, the kind that often seems to exist between older married couples, had suddenly found its way into their still relatively new marriage. They also seemed to share similar facial expressions. Stephanie's eyes were wide with a combination of shock, disbelief and an almost mad giddiness, while Jason's face resembled that of a small child with an all-you-can-eat pass for his favorite candy store.

He glanced back at the road for a moment; then as he looked once again at Stephanie, he silently mouthed a question, which he was certain, had to be on her mind as well. It was not so much a question as a statement, the very utterance of which was somehow more incomprehensible than an answer to any question might be. This was something he simply had to get out of his system but which he did not intend to allow the children to overhear. "Three...million!" his lips silently said as his eyes widened with ever dawning comprehension.

Stephanie slowly nodded her head in agreement as if trying to somehow wrap her own arms around the concept, but it was as if she too was unable to do so. She didn't reply because she truly had no idea what to say. Instead, she continued to stare at Jason with a small dream-like grin on her face; a look she feared might become a semi-permanent fixture until she was able to come to grips with everything.

The truth was Jason had nothing to worry about regarding any concern he might have about the kids overhearing their conversation as most of the time they didn't care to listen to "boring parents" talk anyway. And besides that, all three of them were busy talking at once in the back of the van. Jeremy and Cindy were animatedly discussing what they imagined the farm might look like or more importantly what adventures they would discover when they toured the coal mine later in the afternoon.

Little Sammy was spouting out a combination of both semi-recognizable words as well as garbled gibberish, his being caught up in the excitement of the day and doing his best to be included in the conversation. To anyone listening it would sound like wild and joyous chaos, which was precisely what it was.

The information that had thrown the couple into such a state of perplexity was what H. Mason Armstrong had told them during their morning meeting. He had read them the last will and testament of Stephanie's uncle, Emerson C. Washburn, in its entirety. The he proceeded to translate all of the legalese into plain understandable English. The bottom line was, the stranger, Stephanie's long-lost Uncle Emerson had accrued an estate worth over three million dollars. And he had left everything to Stephanie. They learned that the property had been given the name "Fallen Stones".

"Fallen Stones?" Stephanie had inquired. "What a strange name! Do you know why he called the property Fallen Stones?"

The lawyer hesitated for just a moment then replied with a cordial smile, "No. Not really. Mr. Washburn never explained that to me. I had asked him the very same question once and he refused to tell me, and then he changed the subject. Sometimes it was difficult to get certain answers from your uncle, especially toward the end. I assumed if he didn't want to discuss it then it was none of my business. Perhaps you will figure out why on your own eventually. Or you can always change it to something else." Both Jason and Stephanie found this mystery somewhat odd but not particularly troubling.

During the reading of the will, the children were out in the main office watching television while Jason, Stephanie and Armstrong were meeting in a side conference room. The kids didn't hear a word of the reading, and that was just fine with the couple. They had no idea what they would eventually tell their children but understood for the time being they would be telling them as little as possible.

The two also learned there were a few very important contingencies pertaining to the estate, each of which had the potential to affect their family to an even greater extent than the incredible value of the settlement itself. One such roadblock was the fact that most of the three million dollars was tied up in the property. The couple was told Washburn had purchased the land with the farmhouse and all the outbuildings relatively inexpensively because of its run-down condition. He had then proceeded to dump a mountain of money into outrageously expensive renovations and additions.

The lawyer explained how he believed Washburn had begun to lose his mind somewhat toward the end of his life and had begun to spend money with reckless abandon. Armstrong was quick to point out how he did his best to keep tabs on Washburn's excesses where it came to his finances but there was simply only so much he could do. As a result, the Washburn estate had only about three quarters of a million dollars available in liquid assets; the rest of the estate was tied up in the property.

Although such a sum was still quite substantial, especially to a couple with such an uncertain financial future as Jason and Stephanie had recently become, they quickly learned how most of those supposedly liquid assets were not very accessible either. There was stipulation in the will, which would, in essence tie up some of those funds as well. Washburn had insisted as part of acceptance of the terms of the will that his heir, Stephanie not be permitted to sell the property at any time during her lifetime. He also stipulated she could only leave the estate to her decedents when she in turn passed away. Also, as part of acceptance she must draw up her own will and specify that whoever inherited the property from her could likewise not sell it. The bottom line was she had a property worth over two million dollars, which she could not sell.

In addition, the lawyer explained how she would be responsible for paying the property taxes on the estate for the rest of her life and would in turn pass on that responsibility to her heirs when she died. Armstrong had assured her that Washburn had taken care of the tax and property maintenance issue by creating an investment fund, which would automatically pay the taxes as well as homeowner's insurance annually and would earn enough to cover those expenditures. Based on some quick calculations, the lawyer figured they would be able to keep about two hundred and fifty thousand dollars cash for their own personal use and still be able to forget about ever having to come up with money to pay for insurance or the taxes on the property. It would all happen automatically, behind the scenes, and money would perpetuate and would always be available for those purposes only.

At first, they were disappointed about the situation and had even considered refusing to accept the property; that was until they realized they were no worse off financially than they had been before and had in fact, a quarter of a million dollars to do with what they pleased. If they didn't like the area or the property, they could stay in Berks County and forget about the property or perhaps try to find some legal means to potentially circumvent the will and get permission to sell it later.

However, if the property were half as gorgeous as Armstrong had suggested, they would have a home and land the likes of which they would never have previously been able to afford. That is, if they were willing to relocate to Schuylkill County. They both understood because of Jason's current job situation they might have little if any choice in the matter.

Since Jason was about to lose his job and if he could not quickly find another, they would likely burn through the inherited two-hundred and fifty thousand dollars within a few years, and that was only if they stayed in their cramped little townhouse. Jason had been offered a promotion with a substantial raise plus relocation expenses if they were willing to move to the Ashton area. And now they had been given a completely remodeled property worth over two million dollars, to live in for as long as they chose to and never had to worry about coming up with the money to pay the taxes. It was starting to sound like a simple decision, a no-brainer, at least at first glance.

If only Stephanie didn't feel so much as if someone else was trying to take control of her future and like she had no say in the matter whatsoever. Everything was also happening so quickly. Two days ago, Jason had a secure job, she was a contented mother and part-time children's storywriter and they were both settled into their routine lifestyle. But in the matter of just twenty-four hours, so many important and potentially life-changing decisions had been thrust upon them. Maybe she was still feeling the residual effects of the previous night's pain pill, but everything around her was starting to take on an almost surrealistic feel.

"When will we get to the farm?" Jeremy asked from the back of the van, startling Stephanie from her thoughts. He was seated in one of the rear seats while Cindy and Sammy were both in the middle row.

"We should be there in a few minutes," Jason called back. "Mr. Armstrong said it was just a few miles outside of town. In the meantime, you should look out the window and check out the scenery. Enjoy the ride." Jason tried to sound convincing, but he understood when it came to anxious and excited kids there was no such thing as a short or enjoyable ride.

"All I can see outside is trees and woods," Jeremy replied.

Jason suggested, "Well, woods can be very interesting places to play, Jeremy. All sorts of animals live in the woods, like squirrels, raccoons, chipmunks, deer and the like."

"Yeah!" Jeremy replied. "And bears, and cougars and mountain lions."

Cindy said with fear, "I don't want to see any bears or mountain lions."

"You don't have to worry about that, honey," Jason explained. "Jeremy is just being goofy. There are no such animals to worry about in this part of the country. There are too many people living in the area for that. This is the coal region not the wilderness after all."

"Is there going to be a cold mind on our farm?" Cindy asked abruptly changing the subject as kids often do and getting the word "coal mine" completely wrong.

"Cold mind?" Jeremy laughed. "What the heck's a COLD MIND?"

"Jeremy. That's enough!" Jason scolded. He disliked whenever Jeremy made fun of Cindy. Since theirs was a blended family, he was always cognizant of any comments or behaviors, which might cause friction and affect the difficult enough task of making their new family work as a cohesive unit.

"It's called a coalmine Cindy. C-O-A-L-M-I-N-E," Stephanie explained. "It's a tunnel underground where they dig for coal."

"Whatever," Cindy said. "Is there going to be one of them under our farm?"

Jason said, "No, Cindy. Our farm will just be a house, maybe a barn or two and lots of land to play on." Jason suddenly realized he had just begun referring to the farm as their farm for the first time. This realization of his willingness to accept the idea of them owning the property felt somewhat strange to him. They had not even seen the property yet, but for some unknown reason he was already starting to think of it as their own; not just their possession but quite possibly their new home.

"Wow!" Jeremy exclaimed. "A coal mine under our land would be even cooler than a cave or something like that. It would make a really cool place to hang out."

Jason said, "First of all a coal mine is no place to hang out or play, it is way too dangerous. Besides, this is a farm, which means it is nowhere near any coal mines. The only hole you might find on a farm is maybe an old fashioned well, and chances are pretty good that there won't be any open wells on the property either."

Stephanie suddenly felt a chill skitter down her back at Jason's mention of a well. What was it about a well that made her feel so apprehensive? She couldn't recall what it might be, but she suddenly experienced a weird sort of momentary flashback where she saw a mental image of a woman who looked very similar to herself and who appeared to be dragging two young boys toward a well off in the distance. Before the image could solidify, it vanished.

"Steph? Steph? Earth to Steph!" Jason was calling from the driver's seat.

"Oh, dear," she replied startled. "I'm sorry, honey. I guess my mind went somewhere else for a moment."

Jason replied, "Not surprising after the day we've had so far."

Up ahead at a break in the trees, the Cadillac turned left onto a long driveway, which seemed to snake upward through the woods. Jason put on his turn signal to follow the lawyer. "Looks like we're here," Jason announced.

The two older children started shouting, "We're here! We're here." But, little Sammy said nothing. He was sitting hunched in his car seat staring out the side window toward a clearing along the side of the road, which Jason, Stephanie or the other children hadn't noticed. The youngster appeared to be in an almost trance-like state. At first glance, the area looked to be no different than the rest of the bushes lining the highway, but if one were to look closer he might notice how some of the tree branches had been recently trimmed and the gravel appeared to have been raked a bit too evenly. If one were then to investigate even closer, he might notice some leaves, branches and grass, which would appear to have been recently burned.

Sammy was too young to comprehend exactly what was wrong or even what he was seeing, but whatever it might be it did not seem to be something good. Sammy knew how good things looked and how good things made him feel. He understood nice things and happy things. He also knew about bad things and about sad things. But, he didn't really understand what he was seeing and could never hope to put it into words at his very young age. What he saw was neither good nor happy. He was seeing what looked like a cartoon or maybe a TV show, but it was playing outside, along the road and it was one he could see right through it like it was on a window. The show was of a man in a car that was on fire.

Sammy knew about fire and that fire was hot and fire was bad. Sammy knew to never touch hot things and especially to never touch fire. The man looked like he was hurting and like he was screaming but Sammy couldn't hear him, like somebody turned off the TV sound. It was all so very strange for Sammy. He felt sad and scared and had a strange feeling deep in his tummy. He didn't know why nobody one else in the car could see the bad, sad thing. He didn't know what to do, or how he should feel, so he just looked away from the bad, sad thing and became very quiet.

As the minivan followed up the long driveway, which seemed more like a road than a driveway, they noticed how dense the woods were along the way. When Stephanie had first heard the property referred to as a forty-acre farmette, she supposed it would all be open farmland but here were thick forests on both sides of the access road and she hadn't expected woods. Before she could finish the thought, their van emerged from the shade of the canopy of trees and out into an incredibly bright and open expanse of meadow and farmland. It was as if they had entered another dimension; a special oasis of sorts, removed from the rest of the world around them. A large rock about the size of a Volkswagen Beetle was positioned on the left side of the driveway, its polished face engraved with the name "Fallen Stones". Stephanie didn't understand the name and assumed at some time it might make sense. But for now she was too excited to care.

At the end of the driveway, she saw the Cadillac circle around to the left following the curve of the roadway as it approached the front of an incredible three-story farmhouse; although farmhouse barely describe the amazing spectacle before them. Jason hit the brakes, and they sat momentarily staring, their mouths agape, gawking at the structure looming in the distance. It was truly one of the most beautiful buildings either of them had ever seen. The words renovated or remodeled didn't begin to do justice to the unbelievable craftsmanship which had gone into the transformation.

Both Jason and Stephanie had seen their share of century-old farmhouses having been raised in rural Western Berks County, but never had they seen or even imagined anything close to what they now saw. If this had once been a farmhouse, it no longer could be referred to as one; this was an estate. The center of the structure appeared to be the original three-story brick building, but it was obvious that all of the windows had been replaced with new units, most likely no-maintenance, and it looked like the exterior woodwork had been covered with some sort of stucco to eliminate such work as well. It also appeared as if all of the original brick had been sandblasted and re-pointed to look like new. A large roof extended out over the front door entrance and covered part of the driveway for weather protection when guest arrived by car and which was capped with copper, reflecting like a jewel in the afternoon sunlight.

Where the roadway curved around to the front of the house Stephanie could see the blacktop road ended, giving way to an enormous circular-shaped pattern concrete driveway the likes of which she had only seen associated with luxurious mansions on television. The driveway wrapped around a large multi-tiered concrete fountain which stood at least ten feet high, with water flowing from the small top most bowl, down into lower bowls, each one getting larger with each tier until it finally ended in a large circular concrete pool perhaps twenty feet in diameter.

At the largest part of the circle, the driveway continued for another hundred feet or so where it fanned out to allow access to a massive four-bay, two-story garage attached to the left side of the original structure and which angled forward so the massive garage sat at about a forty-five degree angle to the main structure.

Between the house and the garage, a two story enclosed tinted glass breezeway served to connect the two. The structure was very modern looking with heavy brown metal framework holding the large glass panels in place. Stephanie could see sunshine coming through the glass indicating the back of the breezeway must also be constructed of glass. The sight was breathtaking.

The garage was constructed of brick and wood, which very closely matched that of the original structure. Its roof was obviously of slate construction, which Stephanie understood to be one of the most expensive roofs available. She had heard they were known to last for at least fifty years. The windows of the two-story garage matched those of the original structure and she could only imagine what potential the second floor of the garage had to offer. She immediately had a vision of a combination writing/art studio for creation of her children's books. Since she did both the writing and the illustrating, it would probably suite her needs perfectly. The thought caught her by surprise. It was as if she knew it would be perfect somehow even without seeing the space. It was as though it was meant for her.

Attached to the right side of the main house was something they found surprising. Washburn had constructed a two-story addition to the original structure with a matching window scheme to blend in with the main building and garage. It was covered in stucco, which made an incredibly stunning first impression. Its roof sloped upward to connect just below the peaked roof of the main building and like the garage roof was constructed of slate. Stephanie assumed the roof on the original structure had likewise been redone in slate, but it was much too high for her to see from inside of the van.

She could only imagine how many square feet of living space the structure offered, but she had to assume it must be in the three to four thousand square feet range; and she had not yet seen the back of the property. If Washburn had built out the back as well, the property must be enormous in size. Near the front of the house, she could see Armstrong exiting his Cadillac and waving them to come forward.

"Holy crap!" Jason said, his mouth hanging slack-jawed in amazement.

Stephanie replied, "You can say that again."

Cindy and Jeremy were looking wide-eyed out at the incredible structure and were shouting simultaneously, "Is that our house, Mom? That can't be our house, can it? We're rich. Holy cow, Mom, we're rich! Just look at that house!" Sammy had gotten over his earlier unhappy feelings and was now eagerly joining in with his excited siblings. "We wich! We wich!" he shouted imitating his brother and sister to the best of his ability, and not understanding what he was saying.

Trying to calm the kids down Stephanie said, "No, kids, we are not rich by any means. But you are right that this certainly is a nice house and yes, it is ours. But we have to check it out and see what it's like first, so it is very important that you all to calm down and relax. Ok?"

Jeremy, who knew several kids at school who he considered to be rich kids, but whose houses didn't begin to compare in size or grandeur to the house he now saw, understood this was a very special house indeed, and despite what his stepmother had said, they had just suddenly struck it rich. But, he also understood by his parent's expressions, they were not comfortable with their newfound financial situation and were obviously under a lot of stress dealing with all of the potential change. Jeremy decided since he was the oldest, he should try to help keep the two younger children in control.

Putting on an air of nonchalant disinterest, he said to Cindy, "Mom's right, Cindy; it's not that big of a deal. It's just a house, that's all. Nothing to get all worked up about." Cindy looked at him at first as if he were crazy, then not surprisingly, followed his lead and began to play it cool as well. Jeremy looked knowingly at his dad in the rearview mirror and gave him a wink. Jason acknowledged the gesture by winking back. Stephanie was grateful for the way he managed to calm Cindy and then Sammy as well. Stephanie was often so surprised how one minute Jeremy would act like a little kid then a moment later, he could seem so mature.

"Well, we had better get up there. Armstrong is waiting," Jason said as he slowly pulled the van off the blacktop, onto the beautifully sculpted concrete driveway, which was formed in a herringbone brick pattern and then drove around to the front entrance of the building. He and Stephanie exited the van and walked around to retrieve Sammy from his car seat. Cindy and Jeremy already had the sliding door open and were standing on the reddish brown driveway staring up at the house. Both of them resembled first-time tourists in New York City gawking up into the air looking at skyscrapers.

Stephanie walked over still holding Sammy on her hip and in the crook of her right arm taking Jason's right hand in her left. Armstrong waved his arm in a somewhat theatrical semi-circular gesture indicating the property and said, "So what do you think so far?"

"I...I...I honestly don't know what to say..." Stephanie explained quite sincerely.

Jason interjected, "It makes one heck of a first impression."

"Truer words were never spoken," the lawyer agreed, "but to be perfectly honest with you, you haven't seen anything yet. If you think it looks amazing from the outside, just wait until you see the inside. It is quite spectacular."

"Oh my goodness," Stephanie said, suddenly overwhelmed. "I just can't believe...this is actually ours...it's just so...so... beautiful." Then she began to cry. She didn't want to but simply could not stop herself.

"No cwy Mommy. No cwy," Sammy said gently brushing his mother's cheek fearing something might be wrong with her.

She smiled, let out a loving chuckle and kissed little Sammy on the top of his head. "Don't worry, baby boy. Mommy's fine. It's just that I'm so very happy." Sammy understood happy. Sammy liked being happy. He never cried when he was happy, so he didn't really understand why his mommy was crying because she was happy. But he knew mommies were different from little boys. He could see by her smile she was all right and that was enough to make him happy.

"Well," the lawyer said to Stephanie and Jason, "time's a' wasting as they say. What say we take your lovely family inside and show them their new home?" He said this to make a specific point. He planned to continue deliberately making similar statements all during the tour to reinforce the idea the property was theirs and to make them feel comfortable with ownership. He needed them to move into the house as soon as possible because Washburn had ordered him to make sure that was exactly what they did. The last thing he wanted was to make Washburn angry. So, he had to do whatever he could to convince them to love the house and want to take up immediate residency. However, he had to be careful not to be too overt or pushy in his suggestions. Subliminal subtlety was what the ghost Washburn had determined was required and what the specter had demanded.

Armstrong understood the sooner they came to grips with the fact that the property was theirs, the sooner they would begin to form an emotional bond with it and it would truly become theirs and then, they in turn would become one with the property. Once that bond was solidified, it would be time for its eager spiritual inhabitants to do whatever it was they needed to do.

Armstrong walked to the front door, inserted the key and prepared to escort the family inside.

Chapter 10

Jason heard Stephanie's breath catch in her throat as soon as she walked through the door. Still holding her hand, he followed. The front door opened to a modest sized entry foyer at the base of a long wide set of stairs, leading up to the second floor. Based on his wife's initial reaction, Jason had at first expected some type of grand and luxurious two-story entry hall but then recalling the structure had been a refurbished early twentieth century farmhouse, such a feature would not have been possible without completely changing the interior structure of the building itself. However, once he stepped through the door he understood why Stephanie had been caught by surprise.

The woodwork of the stairway leading upward was immaculate, having been completely restored to its original beauty and luster. An expensive looking carpet runner was meticulously installed down the center of the stairway leaving the restored wood stair treads exposed on the sides. Likewise, the entryway had an equally luxurious carpet, surrounded on two sides by the refinished oak flooring. As Jason stepped inside and turned to look at his wife he noticed, how the carpet continued down a long elegant hallway to the right of the stairs.

Stephanie had turned to face Jason and her back was to a wide entryway to what appeared to be an enormous living room. Stephanie must have backed toward the room because it was obvious she had not yet looked inside. At a quick glance, looking past Stephanie, Jason realized the room was probably double its original size because of the two-story addition they had noticed from outside, which Washburn had put on the right side of the house. Back when the building was originally constructed it was likely only ten or twelve feet deep, but now it appeared to be at least twenty-five feet in depth and was awash with bright light from its many windows.

"Wow!" Jason said surprised. "Look at the size of that living room!"

Stephanie turned as the group headed toward the room with Jason passing her to lead the way, when suddenly they both stopped dead in their tracks. "What the hell?" Jason said in a confused and slightly angry tone.

"Oh oh!" Cindy said from behind them

"Dad said a swear word," Jeremy chuckled.

Little Sammy unfortunately mimicked Jason's surprised expression as he often did in such situations, "Wat a heaw, wat a heaw."

"Quiet now, baby boy," Stephanie said to the baby as she tried to divert his attention.

Jason was unable to offer his customary apology for his unplanned outburst, and since Stephanie also had just seen what had shocked Jason so, she was simply speechless. It was not just because of the size and splendor of the room, but because of what they both saw across the room hanging over the hearth of a huge stone fireplace.

"Hey look," Jeremy said. "It's Mom and Dad in old peoples' clothes." Cindy stood with her mouth agape staring speechless.

What hung on the wall before them was an oil painting of a man and a woman in early nineteenth century formal attire. The portrait appeared to have been created to commemorate the couple's wedding as the woman was dressed in a long white gown while the man wore a suit complete with a top hat. The woman looked very much like Stephanie, enough to pass for her sister, and the man had dark brown hair and wire frame glasses similar to Jason's. He sported a substantial mustache while Jason was clean-shaven. Nonetheless, he looked quite a lot like Jason, again close enough to be a sibling. The man held a walking stick or cane of some sort in his hands with what appeared to be an ivory handle sculpted in the shape of a wolf's head.

Stephanie continued to stare in astonishment. They eyes of both of the subjects in the portrait seemed to stare out directly at them. It was one of those situations where no matter where one stood in the room, they eyes seemed to follow. The illusion gave Stephanie the creeps. A strange feeling welled deep in the pit of her stomach and for a moment, she actually felt as if she might become faint. Fortunately, she had not recalled anything of the dreams, which had plagued her the previous night or she most certainly might have collapsed.

"Wh...who...who are...those people?" Stephanie asked with a trembling voice, never taking her eyes from the portrait.

The lawyer replied looking somewhat confused, "Why, Stephanie...those are your great grandparents, Dwight and Marie Livingston. I'm terribly sorry...I just assumed you might have seen pictures of them sometime before."

"No....no...I...I...haven't," Stephanie stammered. "I never even knew their names. Livingston? That was their last name?"

"Yes. Dwight Charles Livingston and Marie Louise O'Hara Livingston. This portrait was created in honor of their wedding day."

Jason asked appearing perplexed, "I can understand why the woman, Marie might bear a family resemblance to Stephanie since she is her great-grandmother, but why in the world does Dwight look so much like me? I mean, he looks enough like me to be my own great-grandfather...that makes no sense at all."

"Could be purely coincidental," the lawyer suggested. "In fact, it probably is...that is, unless your ancestors also came from this area, Jason. Then anything might be possible. You see, when you start tracing back your family lineage, often strange things are discovered. For example, I have learned that I am related to the legendary chocolate manufacturer Milton Hershey seven different ways. Yet before researching my family tree, I had no idea we were even related."

"Are you suggesting Jason and I could be related?" Stephanie asked sounding quite upset. "I'm certain that isn't possible."

Armstrong realized he was beginning to upset Stephanie and said, "No, Stephanie, absolutely not. I am not suggesting any such thing. As I said, the similarity is likely just a coincidence." Then he said with an odd look in his eyes, "But even if you were to discover someday that the two of you were somehow distantly related it would have likely been so many generations in the past that it would be irrelevant by now."

"But we're not related... I'm sure of it," Stephanie insisted now becoming visibly upset.

Jason, being the engineer that he was began to analyze all of the facts and possible scenarios before him and asked, "But if we weren't somehow at least distantly related, why would this Dwight guy and I look so much alike?" Jason pointed at the man in the painting and looked as if he were starting to believe he might actually be a relative of the man in the photo, and thereby distantly related to Stephanie.

The attorney replied, "I wouldn't bother concerning myself with that if I were you two. As I said, it's probably just a coincidence. In fact, I will be more than happy to have that portrait taken down and replaced with something more decorative and more in line with your personal tastes. Just say the word. Maybe you could tuck it away in the attic until you get settled in and then decide later what you want to do with it." The attorney once again offered the subtle suggestion for the family to consider taking up residency on the property.

Attempting to draw their attention away from the living room and the upsetting painting, he directed them across the hall at the bottom of the stairway to an area of the house he knew was sure to win them over. "I have a great idea," Armstrong suggested. "Follow me over to that side of the property. I have something that will be sure to impress you both."

Jason turned and looked behind him, seeing a short hall leading off to the left of the staircase. It opened to what he perceived must have been the enclosed breezeway connecting the house to the large two-story garage. But even from his location, Jason could see it was not as much a breezeway as it was an incredibly spacious room of some sort. Pulling Stephanie by the hand, he led her away from the living room and its bothersome picture. Then with Jeremy and Cindy following behind them, they followed the lawyer into the substantial space.

What they saw was an unbelievable twenty-foot high peaked atrium-styled glass enclosed living area. The floor of the room appeared to be made of marble or granite and it was bright with afternoon sunshine but the smoked glass dulled the glare just enough to make it perfect. Still holding Sammy in her right arm, Stephanie nudged Jason forward further, deeper into the large and luxurious space.

It was something, the likes of which she could honestly say she had never seen before or for that matter, she had ever dared to imagine. The room was at least thirty or more feet wide and expanded outward about sixty feet to where it met the door to the garage. It was a masterpiece of modern, glass and metal design. Large trees, some of them exotic or tropical in appearance grew from enormous planters scattered about the room.

Several large rock and water features were visible, and Stephanie could hear the soothing sounds of water falling along the stones and could see several large koi splashing in ponds. Strategically placed track lights high above them, provided additional accents to the tops of the tall trees. There were several small modern-looking sofas and comfortable chairs as well as tables with lamps tastefully spread around the space as well. The purpose of the area was much more than simply a way to connect the main house to the garage; it was a veritable oasis, a place to relax and read or listen to music or just unwind.

"Holy cow! Look at the swimming pool!" Jeremy shouted from behind them.

Jason chuckled and corrected the boy, "No, Jeremy. It's not a swimming pool; it's an indoor fish pond."

"Not that, Dad. I know what a fish pond is," Jeremy said with frustration. "I mean out there." He pointed to an area outside the back of the atrium.

Stephanie and Jeremy turned and could indeed see a huge in-ground swimming pool adjacent to a spacious stone patio, surrounded by a decorative stone wall. Jason was certain he also saw what appeared to be a grand outdoor kitchen and grilling area. It was almost too much to imagine.

"I'll show you that later on when we go out back. Like everything else on your property, I promise you it is quite impressive," the lawyer said. "For now let's go see what the garage and its second floor have to offer."

As they approached an exquisite set of wooden doors leading to the garage Stephanie looked up and saw an expansive deck area jutting out into the space from the second floor. The doors to the garage were located in the shadows beneath the deck. Off to the right of the doors Stephanie could see a set of curved iron stairs leading up to the second floor. Armstrong noticed her admiring the stairs and said, "We'll take a quick look in the garage first, and then we'll come back through and head up to the loft."

"The loft," Stephanie repeated silently in her mind. That term matched perfectly with the original concept, which had popped into her mind outside in the driveway. She had imagined having a quiet place to do her writing and illustrations. "The loft," she mentally repeated yet again. It sounded so right to her. It sounded so perfect to her. She recalled various interpretations of artists' lofts she had seen depicted in movies. "The loft," she thought once again. The sound of the words in her mind brought an even larger smile to her face.

"Yes, I think you will love it," the lawyer interjected as if reading her thoughts. "It has its own bathroom and kitchen as well. You'll see shortly."

Before they could become sidetracked by the mysteries awaiting them on the second floor of the garage, Armstrong opened one of the garage entry doors and reached in to flip on a light switch. The area beyond the doorway was immediately flooded with bright halogen lights, recessed in the ceiling. The space was immaculate. The floor of the garage was made of some type of Epoxy-based membrane material like the types of floors Jason had seen used in high-end NASCAR racing garages. It was mostly white but was sprinkled with silver, blue and dark gray specks.

Not only was the garage equipped with four bays and four automatic garage door openers, but also it appeared to be about one and a half times the depth of a traditional garage. The floor of each bay tapered ever so slightly downward on all four sides and at the intersection of the slopes in the middle, Jason could see four separate drains. He imagined how this would be perfect for washing his cars inside, regardless of weather conditions.

As if reading Jason's thoughts, Armstrong said, "The garage is heated and completed insulated. So between that and those four floor drains, you will be able to wash your cars inside, all year round."

The back wall of the garage was lined with a stainless steel workbench and a full selection of both wall and floor-mounted black and silver cabinets with a diamond plate pattern on the fronts of the doors. Jason loved to tinker and work on cars but could scarcely afford even the cheapest of the no-name brand tools or tool chests he considered buying. It had always been his dream to someday be able to afford real top-quality tools and to have a shop of his own.

Once again, as if reading Jason's mind, the lawyer explained, "Those drawers and cabinets along the back of the garage are stocked full with virtually every top-of-the-line mechanic's tool you can imagine, in both English and metric varieties."

At the far end of the garage by the last bay, Jason noticed the room made a sharp right turn. Armstrong led the procession to the far end of the garage and as they turned Jason's breath caught in his throat when he saw something he had never expected. Behind the fourth bay of the garage was a complete woodworking shop with walls of hand tools, cabinets and virtually every power tool he could have imagined, including a floor mounted drill press, table saw, radial arm saw, lathe, router, everything. And in the center was a large custom made thick oak workbench complete with old-style woodworking vises. Looking up at the ceiling, he saw a built-in exhaust system for collecting sawdust as well as an overhead crane and mechanical hoist. He immediately knew this shop was not only his dream woodworking shop, but it went far beyond his wildest imaginings.

"There is an intercom system for communicating with the loft upstairs as well as the main house," the lawyer said pointing toward an area along the right wall. "In addition there is a telephone for making outside calls in case you don't want to bring your cell phone out to the shop when you work."

He reached into a space along the wall at the back of the garage from which the woodworking shop extended and pulled out a hidden pocket style door. "You can close these interconnected doors which all travel on that track in the ceiling, to separate the shop from the garage if you want to keep the dust from getting on your cars as well. This area back here is designated for woodworking, while the tool cabinets and workbenches out in the main garage area are designed for doing work on you cars; that is, if you like to tinker."

"Oh boy! Do I ever!" Jason said, genuinely flabbergasted. "This is beyond amazing. This shop has everything!"

The lawyer replied, "By the way, there is a door on the back right side of the woodworking shop which leads to an enclosed entryway. From there you can either go straight out to the back yard or you can turn right and take a set of back stairs up to the loft. Oh yes, I forgot to mention: all of the larger power tools are on wheels for easy mobility. And one more thing, if you didn't notice, the back of the woodworking shop is equipped with its own automatic garage door in the event you want to open it to enjoy the air on a pleasant day or if you need to get a larger project out of the shop and don't want to bring it out through the main garage.

"Unbelievable! This Washburn guy must have been a genius! He thought of everything!" Jason said.

The lawyer grimaced slightly at this then said, "Well these weren't exactly Mr. Washburn's ideas. You see, he wanted the best garage and shop money could buy, and he put me in charge of the project. I hired a team of designers who specialize in this sort of thing and they came up with some truly innovative ideas. As you will see as we continue the tour, there are many other elements of this house, which you will likewise find quite intriguing. In each case, as with the atrium connecting the two buildings, a specific design team was brought in so I could provide Mr. Washburn with the best of the best, which is exactly what he wanted."

"It's so sad that he passed away before he even had a chance to enjoy his house," Stephanie lamented. Hearing her say this caused Armstrong to perk up and remember how Washburn had instructed him the previous night.

As such, he chose to ignore Stephanie's comment and decided to avoid any further discussion where Washburn was concerned. He had deliberately not told the couple Washburn had committed suicide. This thought made Armstrong recall the details of the man's bloody death. He was suddenly hit with a vision of how the ravaged Washburn looked in the gore-splattered bathtub with his severed appendage bobbing to the top of the crimson water. The mental image immediately made Armstrong's stomach turn with revulsion, and his face transformed into to a grimace.

"Are you all right, Mason?" Stephanie asked the lawyer noticing the displeasure apparent on his face.

He replied, "Oh... um... yes... I'm fine... most certainly. Sorry. I just have a lot on my mind. You understand... There's always so much work to do, and so little time..."

Having successfully regained his composure and simultaneously deflected the subject away from that of the late Emerson C. Washburn, Armstrong suggested. "Let's all go back out into the atrium and check out the loft upstairs."

"Here, honey," Jason offered. "Let me take Sammy off your hands before we head up those stairs. I have a feeling you are going to want to look around." Stephanie couldn't help but notice how even Jason somehow seemed to know the loft was meant for her. Perhaps it was simply another coincidence, but she knew by the look in her husband's eyes, he was having many of the exact same thoughts she was having.

The group exited the garage through the door by which they had entered, turned left and walked up the stairs to the elevated deck. When they reached the top, Stephanie discovered a large spacious area tastefully decorated with potted plants and a variety of thick-cushioned patio furniture. The outside wall of the loft was lined with three large double-French door units with lacy curtains displayed behind the glass multi-paneled panes.

"These three doors can all be opened fully to allow for a spectacular view of not only the atrium but the outside as well," Armstrong said.

Stephanie turned and looked out toward the railing of the deck and for a moment was hit with a minor attack of vertigo. The view of the atrium area truly was amazing, and when she looked out into the expanse of the back yard, the feeling could only be described as overwhelming. She teetered slightly and Armstrong grabbed her right arm, helping her regain her footing.

"Easy there," Armstrong said. "It might take a while to get used to the view. You just have to be a little careful at first. After all, we can't have anything bad happen to our new homeowner now can we? At least not on her first day in her house, Heaven forbid." Then he chuckled strangely, and Stephanie got an odd and unsettling feeling, which she didn't believe came from the vertigo alone, but perhaps also from the odd way the lawyer had chuckled. If she didn't know better, she would have thought there might be a trace of madness in that laugh. Again, she forced herself to ignore the bizarre feeling and followed Jason and her kids into the loft area.

Like everything they had seen of the house so far, the loft space was phenomenal. The room was well lit from a wall of large windows across the back. The ceiling was awash with illumination from skylights and the area was decorated with scattered sofas and chairs in a style exactly suited to Stephanie's taste. "Wow, Steph!" Jason said. "It looks as if you decorated this place yourself."

The entire loft occupied an equal amount of square footage to that of the main part of the garage but the area of the loft above what would be the forth bay of the garage was dedicated to a small kitchen area as well as an additional room of some sort.

Armstrong said, "The kitchenette is state of the art has everything you will ever need from refrigerator to dishwasher to stove to microwave oven." Stephanie held back a laugh; the so-called kitchenette was actually larger than her present kitchen in their townhouse. If Armstrong considered this small, she couldn't wait to see the real kitchen in the main house. The lawyer continued, "That room next to the kitchenette is a small bedroom and has a full bath and shower as well. I don't know if Mr. Washburn planned on ever renting out the space at some time in the future, but it certainly would make a nice apartment or guest area someday."

Stephanie knew she would never be using the area for an apartment, as it would most definitely become her writing and art studio. The bathroom and bedroom would be handy for Sammy's afternoon nap time while she was doing her creative work and the kitchen would be perfect for preparing his snacks. She suspected she would be spending most of her days in the space. It was then she realized she had made the decision, if it could actually be considered a decision; they would be moving into the home as soon as possible.

The group left the loft and descended into the atrium, then across the space and back into the main farmhouse. The lawyer suggested they see the upstairs bedroom area first before touring the rest of the house. When they reached the top of the stairway, they could see a long hall leading back toward a closed door. On both the left and right sides of the hallway, there were three doors. Armstrong explained how on each side of the hall there were two bedrooms, which shared a bathroom located in between them. Access to either of the bathrooms could be accomplished from the main center doors in the hall. In addition, each of the bedrooms had access doors as well. He said the door at the far end of the hall led to a master bedroom suite which occupied the entire length of the back of the house over the expanded kitchen area downstairs. He explained how Washburn had added the back area to the original farmhouse as well.

Pointing behind them, Armstrong indicated a door at the front right side of the house, which led to a space above the stairway. "That's the door to the third floor of the farm house. It's the only area of the house, besides the basement, which has not yet been renovated. Although it's been insulated, it remains, as it originally was. The area is actually still pretty dismal looking. Mr. Washburn only used it as an attic for storing some of his personal items which he never found time to find a place for in the new home. I suspect with all the square footage available in this place you probably won't have much use for it either."

"The original basement or cellar as we old fogies call it, originally had a dirt floor and was only about six feet or so deep. When the renovation was done, the basement was dug further down for ten feet of head clearance and a cement slab was poured for the floor. In addition, the old stone walls paralleled on the inside by a cement block wall the sealed, so there is little chance of water seepage down there. It's dry and doesn't have that typical damp basement feel or smell. However, it too is just a basement with nothing exciting or thrilling done to it either.

"When we go down stairs, I'll show you a door on the left side of the hall under the stairs, which leads down to the cellar... I mean basement. Other than to gain access to your various utilities such as the water heater, the gas furnace and air conditioning units, I doubt you will have any need to use the basement either. Although I suppose you could add some shelves and store boxes and holiday decorations down there rather than in the attic as that might be more convenient. Now let's head down the hall and peek in each of the bedrooms. We will also check out the master bedroom, but I must preface that with a bit of an explanation before we enter. In the meantime, let's look at the other rooms."

Armstrong said he thought the couple would be pleasantly surprised by both the size of the assorted bedrooms as well as their tasteful decor. He explained how he had hired a "conservative" interior designer rather than "one of those weird post-modernistic wacko types". The first bedroom at the top right of the stairway appeared to be designed as a guest room with neutral, traditional colors and furniture; with very little or no personality whatsoever, but it was clean, very neat and orderly.

The real surprises came when they looked into the other three bedrooms, each of which was decorated as if planned and designed specifically for each one of their children. On the left side of the hall the bedroom farthest from the master bedroom was decorated with Jeremy obviously in mind. In fact, it looked in many ways just like his present bedroom but with a lot more living space as well as furniture, including a television, desk and desktop computer with a large flat-screen monitor.

"Woa!" Jeremy said. "I claim this room. This has got to be my room." There was no need for him to make such a statement however; as everyone knew instantly, it was meant for him.

The same was true of the bedroom on the right located just outside of the master bedroom. It looked as if it was ready for Cindy to move in immediately with many of the same decorations and styles she already had in her own bedroom back in Berks County.

"Mommy. This looks just like my room back home, only a lot cooler!" the girl exclaimed with a huge smile.

Even more unusual was the bedroom, directly across the hall from the room they already thought of as Cindy's room. It was designed and furnished to be the perfect room for a toddler and being situated right next to the master bedroom, it made the location excellent as well. In addition, it shared a bathroom with the room Jeremy had claimed which would be perfect for when Sammy got older.

"This is all so very strange," Stephanie said with a noticeable tremor in her voice. "This place was renovated as if it were designed just for us. But how could that possibly be? I never met Emerson Washburn so how could he possibly know so much about us? And even if he did, why would he design his own personal living space with us in mind? After all it was his house, not ours." She was suddenly beginning to feel a bit uncomfortable about how the tour was progressing.

Once again, she had the bizarre sensation that she was losing control of her own destiny. She felt as if their privacy had somehow been compromised. She started to wonder what type of man this Emerson Washburn might actually have been. Then she began to speculate about the integrity of his lawyer, Armstrong, as well.

How far would Washburn have gone to learn about Stephanie and her family? Armstrong had told them earlier Washburn had hired a private investigator to learn about them. Now she wondered if the so-called investigator might also have had the audacity to break into their home at some point and taken pictures of their living area so it could be studied. Would the obsessive old man actually hire someone as unsavory as to infringe upon their personal space? She suddenly felt violated, as if she had been left naked and exposed before the eyes of a stranger.

Chapter 11

The lawyer immediately recognized the discomfort not only apparent with Stephanie, but he could see it spreading to the rest of her family as well. He hadn't anticipated this sort of negative reaction. Now considering things in hindsight he realized perhaps he should have. Regardless of his miscalculation, he had to quickly take what was rapidly deteriorating in to a potentially bad situation and find a way to turn it around, to make it right. So, he did what he did best; and that was to talk persuasively, like a lawyer.

He said to the perplexed couple, "Look, Stephanie and Jason. It's not really all that strange, although I can see why it might seem that way to you at first glance.

"You see, as I mentioned earlier, your Uncle Emerson was never married and had no children of his own. I also must confess he led a somewhat unsavory life as a younger man. There is no need to discuss the details of that at this point, however; perhaps another day. Suffice to say, Emerson was probably searching for something that was missing in his life: the family he never had."

"When he left his former life, he decided to settle down and do his best to lead a normal life. He also wanted to learn more about his own relatives. He once told me, this interest was sparked a decade ago when his brother and sister-in-law, your mother and father, Stephanie; were killed in a car accident. He apparently had been estranged from them for many years and actually learned about their tragic deaths by seeing it on the front page of your local newspaper, while he was passing through Berks County on business. He felt the coincidence of him learning of their deaths was more than simple happenstance. He believed everything in life happened for a reason."

Stephanie and Jason both glanced at each other obviously finding it shocking how an uncle she had never known believed exactly as Stephanie did; everything in life happens for a reason.

The lawyer continued, "As I brought up briefly in our meeting this morning, Emerson then hired a private investigator to track down family members and to learn as much about them as he could. He also had the investigator attempt to trace back his family history. That was how he learned about you and your family. He also discovered a few other family members such as your brother Charles and maybe a distant cousin or two, but for some reason which still remains unknown to me, he was fascinated by you, Stephanie as well as Jason and the kids; hence the reason he left his estate to you.

"Knowing Mr. Washburn both professionally and to a degree personally as I did, I suspect the reason the house appears to have been decorated with your own tastes in mind is because that was exactly what Mr. Washburn wanted. I think he wanted in his own way to know what it was like to be part of a family again, part of your family."

Then Armstrong further explained, "Although he never told me so directly, I suspect before he became ill, Mr. Washburn hoped at some point in time he might have been able to introduce himself to you and perhaps even invite you up for a visit. I believe he may have wanted to make the house look as much like home as he possibly could for you both."

Not a single word of his last statement had been true. It was all a pack of lies the lawyer had dreamed up on the fly to win over the Wrights. Armstrong was operating in full damage-control mode and was making things up as he went along, based on either the positive or negative reactions of the couple.

He said, "I realize the behavior might be perceived as a bit eccentric, but that was Mr. Washburn's way. He was somewhat reclusive and as such didn't interact with many people other than myself. And when he got an idea stuck in his brain it seemed he would obsess about it and was unable to think of anything else."

"I suspect that was how this property was for him. It should be obvious to you, that he put more money into the property than the resale market in this area ever would tolerate. But, since he had no intention of the property ever being sold, as you know from the stipulation in the will, I suppose it didn't matter very much to him. Just so you are aware, neither he nor anyone else ever used any of these bedrooms and he kept their doors closed. His room, his personal space was that room behind the door at the end of the hall."

Then the lawyer realized he had better prepare the family for what they were about to see in the master bedroom. He assumed if they had been caught off guard by the unexpected familiarity of the decor in the other bedrooms, they might truly be shocked by what they would find in Washburn's private chambers.

"Once again," Armstrong insisted, "please allow me to point out that toward the end of his life, Mr. Washburn was getting increasingly eccentric by the day. I suppose he could very well have been suffering from Alzheimer's or some other form of dementia, but he often seemed so alert and lucid at times that I never knew for certain what his mental state might be.

"Oh, and in case you are wondering, Mr. Washburn refused to see a doctor." Then after a moment of planned hesitation, Armstrong said, "So, does that seem to make a bit more sense to you, now?" Armstrong asked. He could tell by their expressions he had been successful in his persuasive monologue.

Jason cautiously replied, "Well... um... yes... I suppose it does."

Looking a bit sad and perhaps even somewhat guilty, Stephanie said, "Yes. I think it makes perfect sense now. But you know I actually feel bad for my Uncle Emerson. We were only fifty or so miles away, and yet we had no idea he was here. It's so tragic that he had to die alone."

Armstrong liked how she had referred to the man as "Uncle Emerson". She was starting to accept the man as part of her family. He also found it all a bit amusing. The phrase conjured up an image of a kindly old uncle, rather than a notorious gangster and thug who ended up sick, rail thin and lying dead in a blood-spewed bathtub, reeking with the stench of his own self-mutilation.

This image made the lawyer wince as he suddenly recalled not only how Washburn had died, but also the horrid undead creature the man had since become. And here Armstrong was lying through his teeth to convince these people to move into the house when he suspected, no knew, something bad awaited them here. He was struggling to keep his own game face in place knowing he was about to put the innocent family directly in harm's way. He didn't know exactly what Washburn and the other as yet unseen entities inhabiting the house had in store for these people, but he knew his own soul would likely rot in Hell for the part he now played in convincing the Wrights to move into the house. Regardless of his discomfort, he had no choice but to continue with an assuring and convincing air.

"Well," the lawyer replied, "as I have often heard said, 'No matter how many people are with us at the end, we all truly die alone.' Perhaps that's an accurate statement. I really don't know." The lawyer was now completely satisfied to see he had successfully smoothed things over, at least for the time being. So, before Stephanie could offer a reply, he directed them into the master bedroom suite.

As Armstrong prepared to open the master bedroom door, he stopped and turned to the couple saying, "I have to warn you all about something. As I said earlier, Mr. Washburn was losing touch with reality toward the end of his life. And even though this master bedroom area is new and was added on as part of the restoration, and should, in fact appear modern, bright and cheery, it sadly does not.

"Mr. Washburn became completely obsessed with surrounding himself with any paintings, furniture, carpets; anything that was original to the property. So you may find yourself a bit shocked with the bedroom." Then he reached down and slowly opened the door to the master bedroom: Washburn's private sanctuary.

If either Stephanie or Jason were still feeling any residual apprehension at the oddly familiar decor throughout the rest of the house, they quickly forgot their anxiety when they saw the interior of Washburn's private space. It may have been a new addition to the property, but as the lawyer had warned, there was absolutely nothing modern about the interior design.

The room was about as far from their decorative tastes as it could possibly be. The space was large, and as Armstrong had said earlier, it occupied the entire width of the home and was at least twenty feet deep. However, there was very little light in the room due to a wall of heavy dark drapes, which covered every window in the room. There was a dank, musty and stale old sort of smell to the room as if the furniture and draperies were aged and antique. The funky, almost foul scent reminded Stephanie of the odor often found in old libraries, whose shelves were lined with ancient tomes.

Seeing the unpleasant and surprised expression on the couple's faces, Armstrong suggested, "As I said, Mr. Washburn was a bit odd. The good news is you will be happy to know that money has already been set-aside for you to redecorate this room to your own personal tastes. Mr. Washburn wanted to occupy this space in a manner that came as close as possible to the same state the bedroom would have been in, when your great-grandparents lived here. Although the Livingston's actual bedroom was never as grand or as large as this bedroom, the location of the original bedroom was right here.

"Once the addition was finished," the lawyer said, "he had it painted and wall papered to match the original design of the bedroom. Then he literally brought in this hideous original worn-out carpeting and the very furniture they used.

"I would recommend whenever you do redecorate this space that you take advantage of the windows Mr. Washburn had installed along the back wall." With that being said, the lawyer walked over and pulled back the drapes to flood the room with afternoon sunlight. The room looked even more dismal, if that was possible in the pristine light. Every single beam of sunlight flooding across the room was awash with billions of moving dust particles.

As the outside light continued to wash through the room, Stephanie saw her original impression was correct. The room was filled with antique furniture and thick old carpeting, which was thread bear and tattered. It looked like the room of an elderly pauper rather than a multimillionaire. She realized this was likely what the entire house had looked like when Washburn had taken ownership. It served to help her appreciate what an enormous feat the renovation was; even more then she previously realized.

The lawyer asked them to come over to the back wall where he stood so he could to show them the incredible view it provided of the rear of thc property through a panoramic wall of glass. In the center were two tall glass doors, which opened onto a massive second-story deck constructed of some type of plastic no maintenance composite material.

Stephanie walked toward the windows and looked out onto the vast expanse of land behind the property. She saw several outbuildings, none of which were run-down but instead all appeared to be as new and pristine as if they had just recently been built. One of the buildings in particular caught her attention; one which was far off to the right in the distance. It was strangely hexagonal in shape. She felt a similar strong attraction to the building as she had with the loft area. Somehow, she knew it as a building constructed for her to enjoy. She would make sure they learned more about that odd structure.

Directly below the deck, she caught a glimpse of the enormous in-ground swimming pool surrounded by concrete, patterned and colored to resemble stone. She also saw a large area next to the pool with a roof shading it. Inside she thought she had not only seen an outdoor grill but what she suspected might possibly be a complete outdoor kitchen. Still somewhat overwhelmed by all she had seen so far, she turned to re-examine the master bedroom.

Even with the light pouring in through the window wall, the room still had a very dark and depressing feel to it. The original furniture and period décor was overtly masculine with large heavy-looking walnut pieces and worn carpeting in shades of dark maroon, blue and gray patterns. The large bed was covered in thick blankets in various equally dark hues. Likewise, the wallpaper in the large room was of a strange pattern, indiscernible from where she stood, but Stephanie could tell it was just as gloomy and old-fashioned as the rest of the room.

A few old paintings hung on the wall, appearing to be mostly nighttime scenes and rural landscapes in thick, ornately carved or gilded wooden frames. Many dark colored statues and other eclectic antiques were scattered around the room. Large worn oak shelves, lined with rows of dusty old books covered one wall of the bedroom and gaudy antique lamps stood on paint chipped nightstands on both sides of the bed.

Despite the lawyer's explanation, Stephanie could not comprehend how or why someone would choose to sleep in the same room with such musty-smelling furnishings. She was not a lover of antiques and found the ancient, nauseating smells of the room almost overpowering. She suspected it would take a great deal of work to insure the foul scent was removed from the room forever. She imagined opening all of the windows to let in the fresh spring air, tearing off all of the wallpaper and ripping up the carpeting. She then would have to scrub the walls and floors with cleanser, but she was determined to make this room as different from how it now appeared as possible.

In the far corner off the room, she noticed a large full-length mirror, which was held in place inside of a heavy wooden frame. Stephanie saw the mirror and for some reason she could not explain, was drawn to it as if it was something she had seen before, although she could not recall where that might have been. "That mirror...looks very old." She said, "Is that one of the original pieces from the house as well?"

"Oh yes," Armstrong replied. "That mirror as well as all of the other pieces you will find in this room is original to the home. Your great-grandparents purchased that glass when they built the farmhouse. It was hand-made by a local craftsman at that time. That makes it over one hundred years old. Although I'm not a collector of antiques and personally have very little appreciation for most of the furniture in this room, I do have a certain fondness for that mirror. I think there's something very special about knowing when you look into it and see your own reflection, you are looking into the very same glass your ancestors looked into so many years ago. That just seems so very amazing to me."

Stephanie too found herself awestruck. Such an idea had never occurred to her before. This mirror was a part of history, and not just history but her family's history. Her great-grandmother and great-grandfather; the two people from the portrait in the living room had actually stood in front of that same mirror over a hundred years ago and looked into it just as she was now doing. Once again, she felt a slight pang of recognition as if she might have actually looked into this very same glass sometime before. She knew the feeling was unfounded, as she had never previously encountered the piece. However, had she been able to recall her horrible dreams of the previous night she would have known exactly why the mirror was so familiar and instead of feeling so good about it, she would have been overcome with terror.

Just then, Stephanie heard a high-pitched keening sound coming from behind her; a sound she immediately recognized as coming from little Sammy. He always made that particular sound when he was about to cry. But this time the noise was much stranger in tone than she had ever heard him utter before. She turned and saw Jason holding Sammy looking at the boy, confused and uncertain what might be wrong with him. The child was staring intently at the mirror with his mouth agape, his eyes rimmed with tears and a look of utter horror on his tiny face. Reacting quickly, Stephanie hurried to Jason, grabbed the boy from his perplexed father and held him tightly against her chest as she carried him from the room.

Jason followed quickly as did the other children and the lawyer. "Is the boy alright?" Armstrong asked.

"Yes... I'm sure he's ok...at least I think so," Jason said, a bit overwhelmed by the incident. "I think he might have been weirded out by the room...by the dark colors...and by the funky smells... He's a very perceptive little boy. He always seems to notice things that older kids or adults seem to pay little attention to."

Armstrong suddenly realized he might have a problem with the little boy. He pretended to be unfazed by the child's outburst however, and said with a tone of understanding, "Yes, I know exactly what you mean. I have several grandchildren and a few of them have quite vivid imaginations and tend to interpret things somewhat differently than we adults do. Things we tend to ignore or take for granted can suddenly appear quite frightening to a young sensitive mind."

Sammy buried his head in his mother's shoulder whimpering and stayed in that position until he heard the door to the bedroom close behind them. Then he slowly began to look about the brightly lit hallway, as the terror began to visibly fade from his innocent young face.

Although the child was too young to comprehend exactly what he had seen in the mirror Sammy knew it was not a good thing or a happy thing. He was simply too young to understand what he saw in the big shiny glass. He thought at first he had seen his mommy looking out at him. Then he knew the lady in the glass was not his mommy but a lady who looked like his mommy. That is, at first she looked like his mommy. But then she only looked a little bit like his mommy. She was wearing an old lady dress like he saw once on TV and in the big picture downstairs. But the lady was not an old lady; she was a young lady like his mommy and she was very pretty like his mommy.

But then she stopped being pretty. The lady's eyes got big and scary like she was mad at Sammy. Sammy didn't know why she was so mad at him. He wasn't being a bad boy. He was being a good boy. The big scary eyes looked right at Sammy. It made Sammy think the lady could see him; like she wanted him to know she could see him. Then she started to get all yucky and her skin changed to a bad color and her face got really skinny. Sammy thought of the bony faces he sometimes saw on kid's t-shirts. Sammy knew his brother, Germie, had a shirt with a bony face on it. He called it a skulk or something that sounded like that.

The lady's face had changed to a bony skulk face, and her teeth got black and some of them even fell out. At first, it didn't scare Sammy too much, but then her big eyes got bigger and blew up like balloon. Sammy liked balloons, but he didn't like the mirror lady's balloon eyes. He started to feel like crying when they got big because he knew what happened when balloons got too big. Balloons that got too big popped. When balloons popped, they scared him. He didn't want to see the balloon eyes get too big and pop.

Then he started to think about something else. He thought of what bad things might come out if the ugly balloon eyes popped. He thought for some reason maybe yucky bugs might live in those ugly balloon eyes. Sammy thought he could see all kinds of yucky wormy bugs moving inside of the big balloon eyes. He didn't want to see any yucky bugs or maybe even wormies come out of the scary balloon eyes. So he started to cry so Mommy would take him away from the stinky room and the big glass and the bad lady with the bony skulk face and balloon popping buggy eyes.

When Sammy heard the door close, he looked around and saw he was back in the nice hall, and there was no more scary glass or a bony skulk-face lady with buggy balloon eyes. He saw his daddy and brother and sister and that fat man they called Armsong. The bad things were gone, and he started feeling much better right away.

"Are you alright now, baby?" Stephanie asked Sammy. "All that bad stuff is gone now. Don't worry honey; Mommy won't let anything happen to you."

Sammy loved his mommy and loved her soft voice. He knew he was always ok when Mommy hugged him. Suddenly he seemed to lose all of his sad and scary feelings and smiled saying, "I ok

Mommy." But he still held more tightly than normal to his mother's neck as she moved aside to let the fat man, Armsong pass. Sammy didn't like the fat man. He didn't know why, but the fat man made him not feel so good in his tummy.

"Well then," the lawyer suggested, "Now that we appear to be all back to normal, let's go downstairs and look at the rest of the house."

Chapter 12

The remainder of the tour of the farmhouse was, for the most part, uneventful, although the couple did find themselves giving another furtive glance at the strange painting of Stephanie's two great-grandparents as they passed by the formal living room. And each time they looked at the portrait, those strange eyes seemed to already be following their every move.

Even though they had not discussed it, both Stephanie and Jason had already made up their minds the spooky painting would quickly find its way along with the mirror, which had frightened Sammy so badly, up into the attic where they would remain covered with tarps in storage until the couple could determine what best to do with them. They also assumed when the remodeled the master bedroom, most of the ugly old furnishings would either wind up in the trash, sold to an antique dealer or given away to charity. Although Washburn's will had specified the house or land could not be sold, Stephanie figured she would be able to get rid of those furnishings she did not want. She supposed she should clarify that particular idea with the lawyer but decided a little bit of ignorance in this case would be to her benefit.

Stephanie knew exactly which painting she would use to replace that horrible portrait in the living room. Shortly after she and Jason were married, they had attended a charity art auction and had purchased an original oil painting by a world-renowned Italian artist named Guido Borelli. It was a bit of an extravagance for them, as they really didn't have the spare cash for such a purchase. But Stephanie had fallen in love with the work and the proceeds from the sale went to help the charity as well.

Although not really an art enthusiast, Jason agreed with the purchase not only because he was impressed with the painting, but also because he wanted to make Stephanie happy. He was quite fascinated with the various Italian scenes Borelli rendered in his paintings. Since that time, the couple had become great fans of the artist's work and had acquired several of Borelli's signed prints. They had also gotten to know him personally through email correspondence. They had attended several of his art shows and met with him whenever possible when he toured the United States.

Stephanie had never felt there had been an appropriate location for her favorite Borelli piece in their small townhouse.

The painting was actually the only original work of art she had ever owned, and now she believed she could proudly display it properly in a place of honor, which she knew the painting deserved. It would hang prominently above the mantle of the fireplace in their new home. Satisfied with her decision, she followed the group as they progressed through the rest of the house.

They were all once again pleasantly surprised by both the size, and modern design of the eat-in kitchen, not to mention that of the adjacent formal dining room. In the kitchen, every appliance was state-of-the-art and although the space was quite large it was designed with functionality and efficiency in mind. The dining room was likewise large and would more than accommodate their needs with its tasteful decor and high-end, perhaps extravagant dining room furniture. There was a large opening between the dining room and the kitchen with a countertop for making it easy to pass various courses from one room to the other.

Stephanie was happy when Armstrong mentioned the door next to the hall entrance of the kitchen, which he said led to a first floor laundry. In her present townhouse she had a first floor laundry and was afraid, the laundry for this home might be down in the basement as was often the case with older homes. When she opened the door and saw the size of the area, she was even more pleasantly surprised. In addition to having a large capacity washer and dryer, it had an ironing board and utility table. It also had plenty of cabinet space and shelves as well as a countertop and double-bowl utility sink. On the left side of the room near the ceiling, she also noticed a laundry chute which would permit her kids to drop down their clothing, saving her the trouble of having to carry everything in baskets down the stairs. Unfortunately, she assumed she would still have to haul the finished clothing back up.

"The laundry chute is located in the hall just outside the master bedroom." The lawyer said, "I'm sorry. I forgot to point that out when we were upstairs. You may have already noticed it. And directly inside the master bedroom, off to the left is a small powered dumbwaiter in a closet; you know, a small elevator of sorts. This will come in handy so you don't have to carry all the clean laundry up the stairs when it is finished. Also, if anyone is ever feeling under the weather it can be used to send food and medicines upstairs to them as well. It can be used for pretty much anything you can think of. However, it does have something of a weight limit, and is not safe for human transportation, so I would not recommend letting the children ride in it. That might be very dangerous. It is equipped with an electronic safety locking device and a code which you can give only to whomever you choose."

They walked toward the back of the kitchen as Armstrong opened the rear door of the house revealing a second expansive composite deck, leading out and terracing down to the pattern concrete patio surrounding the luxurious in-ground pool. Stephanie realized, it was likely the pool had only been recently opened, probably in preparation for their visit as the water glistened with crystal-like clarity in the afternoon sunlight.

"Can we go in the pool? Can we, Mom?" Cindy asked, knowing full well they had not come prepared for swimming. In addition, May in Schuylkill County was not quite as warm as it was fifty miles further south, and most of the time, only the most daring swimmers chose to hit the water before the end of May or early June.

"Not today, honey," Stephanie said. "We have a lot of business to take care of first, and don't forget about our trip to the coal mine later today."

Cindy replied with disappointment, "Yeah. You're right. I guess we can't do everything in one day. But boy oh boy does that pool look good." Stephanie knew Cindy would want to use the pool as much as possible as she not only loved recreational swimming but also expressed an interest in eventually joining the swim team at her school when she got to junior high.

"Don't worry, Cindy," Jason said "We own this house now, so soon we will be able to swim in this pool anytime we want to."

"What's that over there?" Jeremy asked pointing off to a feature located in the shadows just below a part of the upper deck. It circled out around the far left side of the pool.

"Oh my gosh!" Jason exclaimed in unchecked surprise. "It's a... well I...I believe it's called...a grotto."

A twelve-foot high, man-made stone feature resembling a mountain stood before them. Because it was positioned under the master bedroom deck, they had not been able to see the spectacular feature from upstairs. From the top of the simulated mountain, a continuous waterfall flowed down along its surface ending in a large pool at its base. The pool was surrounded with assorted sizes of artificial stones made of some type of hard concrete-like material with a small opening at the front to allow access. Jason was reminded of the scenery he had enjoyed when the family had visited Universal Studios Islands Of Adventure in Florida before Sammy was born.

Jason walked over to the opening in the rocks and look down into the water in amazement. Although it was disguised to create the image of a natural setting by the man-made stone, the pool itself was actually an enormous Jacuzzi hot tub with built in lights and what looked like dozens of jets. Looking closer, Jason saw there were also speakers present in some of the simulated rocks, he assumed for enjoying music while relaxing.

It was unbelievable. Jason stood looking at the feature in amazement. "Wow. Now I'm the one who wants to get in the pool." He was already trying to figure out how he and Stephanie could find time to sneak away and be alone in the grotto. He knew it would be tough if not impossible with three kids, but he was determined to take full advantage of the pool for personal romantic purposes sometime. He had an image of Hugh Hefner's famed grotto at the Playboy mansion in California.

"And look at this," Stephanie said pointing. Off to the right of the deck down along the side of the pool was a complete stainless steel outdoor kitchen with a gable styled roof. "This outdoor kitchen looks like it has more features than our in-door kitchen back home has." She walked over toward it. "And look. Besides the gas grill and the refrigerator, there's a regular oven, a convection oven, a microwave and... Holy cow...look at the brick pizza oven for God's sake. This is amazing!"

Jason walked over to check out the area not really wanting to leave the grotto or the fantasy he was imagining. But as he approached the area, he was glad he had. "And look at that!" He said. "That's a full wet-bar, and it's stocked with all kinds of goodies as well. Wow!" Along the decorative brick back wall of the bar hung a long and tall mirror with several shelves, each of which was lined with many of the couple's favorite brands of liquor.

"I...am...just...speechless," Jason explained. Stephanie just stood shaking her head in amazement. He said, "This is all so unreal. It's almost too good to be true." If Jason had realized just how profound that statement would turn out to be, he might have stopped himself from uttering it.

The lawyer replied, "But true it is. And it's all yours; along with the forty acres and the outbuildings."

"That's right," Jason said, the realization suddenly hitting him. We haven't seen the outbuildings yet. What are they like?"

"Let's go take a look," Armstrong replied. "There are four of them spread around the property. Most are simply storage sheds or places to keep things that you may need when you are working out away from the house. But two of them are a bit more special. Let's all head over to the large barn over there in the distance beyond the pool. That barn is one of the buildings I need to show you. I think you will like what you see there."

The barn was a two-story structure completely resided with new wood, stained light brown and sealed with a thick semi-gloss finish. Jason didn't know what sort of finish it was, but he could tell by its appearance, it would be very low maintenance. When they walked through the small man-sized access door, which was part of the larger double barn door, Armstrong flipped on a light switch, illuminating the massive two-story structure with a flood of bright overhead lighting.

They could see the heavy thick timbers, which had been the structural part of the original barn. Each of the beams had not only been refinished but where they might have been weakened from many years of exposure to the elements, had been reinforced with a combination of wooden or pre-fabricated beams and decorative black steel plates guaranteeing both the integrity while maintaining the aesthetics of the building. It was all done in a way that complimented the interior, rather than looking like a repair job or an after-thought.

Where there was probably once a dirt floor, there was now a concrete slab covered with a similar Epoxy membrane to the one they had seen in the garage. And sitting on the floor in the distance was a top-of-the-line John Deere garden tractor with a large mowing deck as well as both a front loader and backhoe attachment sitting off to the side.

But the truly amazing thing, which completely flabbergasted Jason, was the site of a brand new cherry-red Ford F-150 pickup truck. It was the most gorgeous vehicle Jason had ever seen, pristine and without a single scratch. Then Jason saw a large chrome snowplow sitting against the sidewall. He assumed the device could easily be mounted to the front of the truck as necessary.

Armstrong said, "I see you noticed your new toys, Jason. Up here in the coal region, winters can get a bit rough so Mr. Washburn wanted to make sure he had everything he would need to keep the driveway clean, and he also wanted to have a powerful enough vehicle to get around in the winter weather. You will, of course, have the option of doing your own snow plowing if you would like, or I can recommend the name of a local handyman who formerly did some snow removal for Mr. Washburn. He also maintained the landscaping and other yard work as well.

"You might want to consider hiring him, as he works cheap and can guarantee to have your snow removed in time for you to head out to work, no matter what the weather conditions might be. He can also help to free up some spare time for you during the summer months so you can join your family in the pool instead of spending your time cutting grass and weeding. The choice will be yours. If you do choose to do the work yourself, well... as you can see, you will have everything you need to get the job done, right here."

Then the realization struck Jason exactly how much work might be involved in maintaining a property of this size. He was not one to avoid hard work, and he was young and strong. However, when he thought about it, the maintenance of such a large estate did seem a bit overwhelming. He recalled how during the past six months or so, things had been so stressful and hectic at work, that he scarcely had time to think when he finally got home at night. His present townhouse was essentially maintenance free and for that he was grateful.

He also assumed once he accepted his promotion with its many new responsibilities, things might get even busier for him. He decided it might be a good idea to have someone standing by to help if needed. With the money they got from the estate as well as his pay raise, he was certain he could afford the occasional use of the handyman's services.

Then he suddenly realized that he was not the only one whose responsibilities would increase with ownership of the property. Stephanie's would as well, perhaps even more so than his own. His goal had been for Stephanie to be able to have the time and energy to devote to her book writing. However, he knew if she were bogged down with the tasks of taking care of the kids as well as cleaning and maintaining such an enormous house, that goal might never be realized.

"Yes," Jason replied without any further thought, "I think I might want to have that gentleman's name." Then he surprised himself by asking, "Also, do you know of anyone you can recommend who is available maybe one or two days a week or so to help Stephanie take care of the house?" He looked over and winked at Stephanie who was staring at him as if he had completely lost his mind. She had never considered the idea of hiring a cleaning lady before. It was not as if she was opposed to such an idea, but it was simply not something they could have ever considered being able to afford before. Suddenly the realization of their newfound financial status hit home with her as well, and she too understood they actually could afford what was once considered an unimaginable luxury.

"Well...yes, in fact I do," the lawyer replied. "The handyman is a gentleman named Wilbur Franks. He is in his mid-fifties but still in very good shape and quite skilled, not only with yard work, but also with plumbing, electrical and general contracting needs. His wife, Constance had cleaned houses for a number of prominent local folks, and I am certain she would be happy to help you both out as well. I will email their contact information to this you evening. And if you would like, I can take the liberty of contacting them ahead of time on your behalf."

"Excellent," Jason replied, suddenly catching himself off guard. He was oddly surprised at how quickly he was adapting to their new lifestyle. He almost had to laugh to himself for the way he had just said "excellent", as if hiring such domestic help was common to him; something he had done all of his life. He stifled a chuckle.

As the group walked from the barn and back outside, Jason felt a pang of uncertainty for the first time, wondering what potential negative effects this new way of life might have on him and Stephanie, not to mention on their kids. Both Jeremy and Cindy were old enough to still remember what is was like to grow up in a household with constant financial struggles and would not be likely to be affected to any great degree, but Sammy was only seventeen months old. He would only remember this new life. He would grow up knowing nothing but affluence.

Jason thought about some of his fellow students during his school days that he considered well off, whose parents were doctors and lawyers and other such professionals. He remembered how these kids tended to look down on those students whose parents were not in their same economic strata. Although Jason and Stephanie didn't know each other in school and were several years apart, they had discussed how they each came from lower-middle working-class backgrounds and as such were not even considered for acceptance by the elite upper class cliques.

He made a mental note to be sure to speak to Stephanie about the subject and to try to do their best not only to keep themselves grounded, but also to not let their newfound prosperity affect their children negatively. He didn't want his sweet innocent and sensitive little Sammy to become some snobby obnoxious heartless teenager someday. Jason had no idea if they could be successful at handling such a responsibility, but he was determined to do his best.

Stephanie interrupted Jason's train of thought as he heard her ask the lawyer, "What is that strange shaped building over there". She pointed to the hexagonal outbuilding, which she had originally spotted from the master bedroom window. Again, she felt strangely drawn to the structure.

"Oh. That building is the spa," the lawyer said nonchalantly.

"The spa?" Stephanie questioned, looking over at Jason quizzically.

Jason said, "Why would this place need a spa? It has an atrium, several decks, a pool, a hot tub and a bar. It has plenty of places to chill and wind down. I would think the last thing it would need was a spa."

"You are probably right, Jason," Armstrong replied, "but Mr. Washburn liked his privacy and even though he lived here alone, and could find plenty of places to unwind, he still wanted to have a place far from the house, almost at the edge of the woods where he could go and be totally isolated. As it turned out, that building, in its original hexagonal shape, suited his needs perfectly. In case you are thinking of asking, no I have absolutely no idea why a building built one hundred years ago would have been constructed of such an unusual and impractical shape. It remains a mystery. And even more unusual, as far as we could determine from its structure and from historical records, the original purpose for the building may have been very similar to its current purpose."

Stephanie asked, "Do you mean to say it was originally built as a spa...by my great-grandparents?"

"Well, yes...sort of," the lawyer tried to explain. "I'm not sure, but I don't believe they referred to such places as spas back in the early 1900's. It was, however, not all that uncommon for people of great financial means to have places where they could go during the cold months to relax in large tubs of hot water, basking in the steam next to a hot fireplace. They believed it not only served to help their physical health and well-being, but their mental health as well, which, when you come to think of it, is why we use such facilities today. Also keep in mind: back when these outbuildings were originally constructed, there was only a farmhouse. There was no atrium or swimming pool, deck or outdoor hot tub. That building would have been the only place the master of the house had to get away to relax in private."

"Wow," Jason said. "I hadn't thought about that."

The lawyer replied, "Well then, let's head over to the spa. As it turns out, that was the other outbuilding I wanted to make sure you had the opportunity to see during our short visit today."

Then Armstrong suddenly recalled how the little boy, Sammy, had reacted to the mirror in Washburn's bedroom. What if he were truly as sensitive as Stephanie had suggested? Taking the young child into the building where such unspeakable horror had occurred and one completely surrounded with mirrors, would likely have severely negative results for the boy and in turn for Washburn's plans. Even Armstrong with all of his oratory skills might not be able to talk his way out of such a situation as he had done earlier at the house. The last thing he needed was for the little brat to get all weird on him again and starting bawling and carrying on. He suspected whatever so-called sensitivity the boy possessed, which caused him to wig-out in the master bedroom earlier, would likely be off the charts in the place where Washburn had committed suicide. And he definitely couldn't allow that to happen.

So, he offered an alternative suggestion instead. "Why don't you let the kids run around outside for a while? You know, let them get some fresh air. Children need to run around and play and work off built up energy. Maybe they could go over there in the field near the woods for a bit, while I show you and Jason the spa. I am sure it will be quite boring for them, and this way they can roam around and get used to the property. I assure you there is nothing that can hurt them out there."

"I don't know..." Stephanie said uncertainly. "What about the swimming pool? I don't want them going near the pool." Luckily, the group was far from the pool, practically near the back of the property, but as a mother, Stephanie still was nonetheless concerned.

Jason believed Stephanie was always a bit overprotective of the kids, and especially of Sammy, perhaps because he was the baby or perhaps because he was likely the last baby she would ever have. He also thought the lawyer was right and it might be good for the three kids to walk around a bit and have a little freedom. He asked the kids, "Jeremy? Cindy? If we let you take Sammy and play over there in the field for a while, will you promise to stay over there and not go back near the house? We really need you to stay far away from the pool? Do you understand?"

He had already determined that before they moved into the house he would have a fence installed around the pool and grotto area to make sure Sammy couldn't accidentally wander close, fall in and drown. So today was likely the only time they would have to be concerned about it.

Stephanie looked at Jason uncertainly. He winked at her again, and she reluctantly set Sammy down and told him. "Sammy. You take Jeremy's hand, do not let go of it and do whatever he tells you to do, alright?"

"Germie hand," Sammy said, incorrectly pronouncing Jeremy's name as he always did.

"And Jeremy. You are the big brother, so you are in charge. We'll keep the door to that building over there open so we can here you all playing outside," Stephanie instructed. "If Sammy gets away from you, or if you see something that bothers you, even for a second, just yell to us and we will come right out. Ok?"

"Ok, Mom," Jeremy replied. He was visibly proud of his being given some big brother responsibility. "Don't you worry, we'll be fine."

Cindy said, "Yeah, Mom. Don't worry. I'll help watch the little stinker too."

"Alright then," Stephanie said as the three headed off into the meadow a short distance from the spa, each holding one of Sammy's hands. Whether she liked it or not, she had to admit her kids were growing up, and there was little she could do about it. Stephanie was still a bit concerned about leaving them, but figured since the spa and barn were both between the pool and the meadow where the kids were playing, she was quite confident they were far enough from any danger. And she would be listening extra closely for any trouble.

"Well then, let's go inside," the lawyer suggested as he took them in to show them the very place where Emerson Washburn had butchered himself. However, he would never tell the couple of the horrible event, and he was quite confident no specters would appear in the spa or any other building on this day or for that matter any day in the near future until the time was right.

The unholy creatures wanted the couple to move in and to do so quickly. Armstrong was quite certain the beings had no desire to frighten the family away, since doing so was not in the spirits' best interests. The horrid creatures had a definite and specific future in store for the Wright family. And Armstrong was unhappily certain things were not likely to end well for the unsuspecting young family.

Chapter 13

"I know I must sound like a broken record," Jason insisted as he looked about the interior of the spa, "But this place is simply amazing. Just when I think I've seen everything, we walk through another door and discover something even more incredible."

"Yes, it truly is amazing," Armstrong replied. "As I mentioned earlier, Mr. Washburn put a phenomenal amount of money into the restoration of this property. Far more than he should have, in my opinion." The lawyer made sure to give Jason and Stephanie the impression that on more than one occasion he had tried to warn Washburn about how much money he was spending. And despite his best efforts, he had found his attempts to control the man utterly futile. Jason was uncertain if he completely believed Armstrong's story but thought he actually could sense the frustration the lawyer was feeling. If the man was not being honest with Jason, he was at least feigning sincerity and doing so very convincingly.

In reality, the lawyer was simply playing the role he was supposed to play, that of concerned solicitor. The fact was, he had truly loved the way Washburn had spent his money like there was no end to it, and Armstrong had even encouraged the spending at every opportunity. Whenever Armstrong hired another designer, architect, carpenter, plumber, electrician or other such contractor, it was more money in the bank for the lawyer; both in his role as attorney and project manager for Washburn, as well as lawyer for all of the subcontractors he hired and coerced to become his clients.

Armstrong also understood his current instructions and knew he had to keep the ruse going in order to win the trust of the new homeowners, especially Jason, who he sensed was not a big fan of lawyers. He had gotten that impression from Jason the very first time they met and understood he would have to be careful around the man in order not only to win his trust but to maintain it as well.

Jason, Stephanie and Armstrong were walking around the interior of the gorgeous hexagonal-shaped building admiring the craftsmanship of the unique structure. At the center of the space, the large expertly restored cast iron claw-foot bathtub stood like a porcelain-encased sentry, its lustrous white finish glimmering in the sunlight streaming through the small windows up high near the ceiling.

"You might be interested to know, that tub is actually the original bathtub which was installed in this very room by your great-grandparents almost one hundred years ago," the lawyer said. "In its day it was considered the latest thing in bathing comfort. However, back then it was just a solid piece of molded cast iron with no faucet or handles. During the renovation, I sent it out to a company that specializes in tub restorations, and not only had it refinished, but also had them add the appropriate modern plumbing fixtures. This is because back in the time when your ancestors originally used it, there was no plumbing in this building so I assume there was no need for faucets and such. In fact, I don't really know if such features even existed in typical tubs back then. I'm no historian by any means, so I can't say for sure. But I do know there were no fixtures in this one. Any water which was to be used for bathing during that time had to be carried in buckets from a nearby well and then heated in that fireplace over there."

Stephanie was once again taken aback by the mention of a well. 'The well," she thought to herself. "What is it about a well that has me so off balance?" She didn't know why the mere mention of a well on the property should make her feel so uncomfortable, but it obviously did. She asked the lawyer, "You mentioned a well, Mason. Do you know, is there still a well somewhere on the property?"

"Yes, as a matter of fact there is," Armstrong replied, "but not the type of well I was talking about. You see, the farmhouse is supplied with water via an underground well and a pump typically found in almost all rural homes. Farms like this one are much too far from town to take advantage of the local water utilities and therefore homeowners must dig wells to supply their water."

Stephanie understood this concept without Armstrong's needing to explain it, since she knew of many, many single homes on large sprawling lots in rural Berks County, which had their water supplied in this manner. She had naturally assumed the same thing would be true on their farm. She was also familiar with how septic systems and sand mounds functioned as well as all the other things that rural properties required.

"Yes, Mason. I'm very much aware of that type of well." She explained, "What I was referring to was the old style wells, you know, the open top wells like you often see in books where you have to put in a bucket on a rope and pull up your water."

"Oh, I see." The lawyer said, "When I mentioned water being carried to this building from a well, it was that exact type of well I was talking about. Such a well did exist on this property at one time."

Stephanie suddenly had a mental image of the well Armstrong described, but it was not some generic representation of what a well might look like. What she envisioned was precise, as if to suggest she had mysteriously been made aware of every detail of what the original well on the property had looked like. It was all so strange, yet for some reason she accepted it as one accepts the convoluted logic and images one encounters while having a dream.

What she saw in her mind's eye was a circular stone structure, perhaps four feet tall made of random sized fieldstones, held roughly together with a type of cement or mortar. The appearance of the wall was very rough and almost primitive in nature, as if to suggest its builder had given absolutely no thought to aesthetics, only functionality. There was no tall wooden structure or roof constructed over top of the well like those she had seen depicted in pictures or on television. Therefore, there was no cylindrical cross member with a rope, crank handle or bucket to function as a pulley for retrieving water either. This was simply a stone wall, which surrounded a cylindrical hole in the ground. And at the bottom of the black shaft with its slick, wet vertical walls was cold water.

She was suddenly filled with the realization that the well had existed on the property long before her grandparents had every purchased it and built their home. She had rapid visions of many other homes over many other centuries being built then falling to ruin, or being destroyed by fire or other natural calamity, only to be replaced by yet another building. And all during that time, since the beginning, whenever that happened to be, the well had been here.

The unexpected awareness of the well and its apparent history caused Stephanie to feel extremely uneasy. At first, she assumed it was because as a concerned mother, she felt its low-walled construction and open top was such that it did little to prevent a young child from climbing up and falling inside to his death. But there was more to her concern that just safety. She didn't understand why she seemed to know about the age of the well and had no idea why the fact that the well had existed for so many centuries bothered her. After all, if what she thought turned out to be true, so what? It was just an old well. Of course it was built to last, and if constructed properly might it not be expected to last for many hundreds of years?

"You...said the well did exist...at one time... Is the well still here?" Stephanie asked the lawyer with obvious concern. "I mean is it still on the property somewhere? I wouldn't want such a potentially dangerous thing around, you know, not with my young children."

Armstrong assured her, "Not to worry, Stephanie. County records show the well was filled in with dirt and stone more than fifty years ago. In fact, I would be hard pressed to even begin to try to find the location of where it originally stood. Apparently, the well had been on the property for several centuries. You see, your great-grandparents were not the first to build on this land."

"Yes, I know," Stephanie said without thinking.

The lawyer got a startled look and asked with surprise, "You know? I don't understand. What do you mean you know?" As a lawyer, he was accustomed to listening closely to people. He naturally focused on nuances in speech, as well as changes in timbre and tone. Most people tended to ignore such things, but this was one of the talents, which made him so good at what he did.

Stephanie realized her mistake and saw Armstrong looking at her with concern. Jason, too, was looking at her strangely. The truth was she honestly didn't know anything about the property. She thought at first she had just had some type of epiphany, some mysterious understanding and awakening, but it was likely more imagination than revelation.

"No... I don't mean I actually know," she corrected. "How could I possibly know? What I meant is I understand how such a thing would be possible. You know, how a well could last through many generations. I suppose I simply misspoke because I was distracted, thinking of my concern about the danger and my children."

Feeling more at ease, the lawyer said, "Well...you won't have to worry about your kids. I assure you this place is about as safe as you can get."

Stephanie no longer wanted to think about what she had just imagined. She needed to take her mind off the well and think about something else. Armstrong had been talking about the tub and heating water over the fire. Looking more closely at the large fireplace she began to think about what a hassle it must have been to carry in bucket after bucket of water. Then the water had to be heated over the fireplace and then dumped into the tub. She had to assume by the time someone got the tub filled and crawled inside the water temperature might be tepid at best. Next, she thought about attempting such a feat in the middle of winter and could not even imagine how it might have been accomplished at the turn of the twentieth century.

As if following the same train of Armstrong said "We can only assume they had servants to fetch the water and not only heat it but to keep refreshing it so it stayed warm. I'm quite certain that original fireplace got quite the workout in its day."

Stephanie said, "The fireplace certainly is quite beautiful."

The lawyer continued, "Yes, I must agree. However, the original was practically in ruins at the time Mr. Washburn bought the property, as was most of the building itself. During the restoration, we had the fireplace equipped to handle either wood or natural gas, whichever you so desire."

"Natural gas?" Jason asked. "I never thought to ask how the house was heated. I assumed either electric or oil heat."

"No. Neither of those," the lawyer said. "Water, sewer and cable TV are the only services the property does not have access to. However, since it has a well, sand mound and satellite TV service, you are set. It does however have electric and natural gas service provided by public utilities. The gas company ran a line along the roadway a few decades ago, and Mr. Washburn had them tap into it and run a line up to the main house.

"Then he had another gas line run out here from the main house along with the appropriate plumbing. As you will eventually learn, there is also plenty of loose wood available around the property for burning if you prefer and of course, if you choose to take the time to gather, split and cut it.

"However, you no longer need to rely on the fireplace for heating purposes. It is simply here for ambiance. The entire building is well-insulated, and the heat is controlled by that thermostat mounted over there along that wall." He pointed to the device.

As Stephanie and Jason's attention was diverted to the thermostat, Armstrong found himself involuntarily looking over at the sparkling bathtub, once again thinking about a time when the tub was not nearly so elegant. He thought about the hideous ruby red splattered sight he had been forced to witness when Washburn had practically ripped himself to pieces, turning the bathtub into an enormous caldron of bloody human debris; a veritable consommé of gore.

Prior to the Wright family's visit, Armstrong had made sure any residue from the melted candles, not to mention the bloody remnants from Washburn's suicide, had been appropriately cleaned up and the tub returned to its original luster. He doubted even a team of forensic investigators could find any trace evidence of the horror which had occurred there. Armstrong had actually hired both the aforementioned handyman Wilbur Franks and his wife Constance to do the cleanup.

Armstrong was quite certain Franks and his wife could be trusted to keep their mouths shut about the messy situation for as long as he needed them to. That was one of the reasons he had also recommended the couple to the Wrights. He was formulating a plan for the Franks to be his eyes and ears on the property, so he could be kept informed as to what might be transpiring in his absence.

The lawyer and Wilbur Franks had a history, a very convenient history. In addition to being people he occasionally hired for odd jobs, the Franks were also Armstrong's clients, of sort. Several years earlier, Wilbur Franks had been charged with a minor drunk and disorderly infraction after an evening of too much revelry and found himself spending the night in one of the two cells the Ashton jail had to offer. Armstrong had smoothed things over with Chief of Police, Max Seiler, and had managed to get Franks off with just a slap on the wrist. Although extremely grateful, Franks didn't have the money to pay Armstrong for his services, so the lawyer made sure he took advantage of this unpaid debt whenever he found it convenient. Yes, Armstrong knew the Franks would both stay quiet and would also be sure to keep him informed.

Armstrong had often fancied himself a bit of a chess player as far as the game of life was concerned, although in reality, he had never actually played the game of chess, nor did he even know the rules. It was simply a euphemism, which he liked to use, to describe how he applied his manipulative skills in his daily activities. He once heard someone say a good chess player always thinks five moves ahead of his opponent. That was how Armstrong thought. He suspected if he ever took the time to actually learn the game of chess, he would quickly become quite proficient at it.

He prided himself on how, as a lawyer, he had been able to outwit virtually every opponent he encountered by anticipating the next several moves they would most likely make. This skill always worked for him whenever he needed to outsmart the living. But now, although he was unsure, he prayed his skills would not fail him when trying to outmaneuver the dead. This had become especially important, given his current predicament. He had found himself trapped between the proverbial rock and a hard place as far as Emerson Washburn was concerned, and he could only hope his skills were such that he could find a way to get himself out from under the thumb of the vile specter.

As Stephanie looked about the inside of the spa, she observed how the triangular zigzag patterns of the woodwork and the various wall-size mirrors created an almost fun-house type of illusion. Several times, she felt as if someone was watching her, but when she turned in that particular direction she would see only her own reflection and sometimes that of Armstrong or Jason. Then she would sense the feeling from another direction and each time she looked, the result was always the same. No one was there, yet she felt as if she were being observed. It was all so very strange and creepy. She was thankful the large stone fireplace and the entrance to the building took up two of the six walls. She was not exactly sure exactly what she would do to change the interior decor of the building, but she was quite certain at some point, the mirrors would have to go.

Jason noticed Stephanie looking strangely at the mirrors and asked her, "What do you think of all these mirrors, Steph? Kind of kinky, don't you think?" He gave her a knowing wink. She knew, as always, Jason was thinking with the wrong head and was likely imagining some type of sexual fantasy scenario in which the two of them would share a hot bath surrounded by their own reflections. Unfortunately for Jason and his misguided imaginings, the mirrors made her feel anything but sexy. In fact, they were really starting to bother her. Jason was going to have to give up on this particular dream; as far as she was concerned, the mirrors were history.

"If I'm ever going to come out here for a bath, I'm going to have to lose a few pounds and tone up a bit," Stephanie joked, hoping to discourage her husband, as she looked around at the bothersome mirrors. She was imagining with discomfort seeing various views of herself naked and recalling how she had not yet gotten back in fighting shape since giving birth to Sammy.

The lawyer interjected, "Nonsense, Stephanie. Don't be so hard on yourself. Just imagine what an old fat fossil like me would look like standing here in my altogether." Then he hesitated for a moment, feigned embarrassment, chuckled and said, "On second thought, you might not want to do that." They all laughed at Armstrong's self-deprecating comment and whatever tension Stephanie was feeling began to disappear.

Stephanie genuinely liked Armstrong. The lawyer seemed so friendly and easy going, she couldn't help but trust him completely. She noticed how Jason even seemed to be warming up somewhat to the man. This was quite unusual for her husband as he was not a fan of lawyers in general. She didn't know why he felt that way, perhaps because of his divorce; she had met many men who had gone through messy divorces and suddenly found themselves hating lawyers. She didn't know if this was the case with Jason.

But she recalled how he often enjoyed telling whatever the latest hot lawyer joke might be, which he and his coworkers were sharing. One of his favorites had always been "Why do they bury lawyers ten feet underground instead of six? Because deep down they're good people." She felt a bit guilty about that joke when she looked over at the lawyer. He seemed to be sincere and to be doing everything in his power to make things easy for them.

However, if Stephanie actually knew what was going on behind the scenes in this sinister life-play and the complicit role her supposedly trustworthy lawyer had assumed in the deception, she would not feel so kindly toward the man. Although his participation might not be completely of his own free will, there was enough of his personal greed involved in the process to make him more than just a mere pawn.

H. Mason Armstrong was a skilled manipulator and was equally proficient at hiding his treachery, which currently lurked just below the surface of his amiable facade. Neither Stephanie nor even the normally suspicious Jason had been able to see the truth. However, young Sammy had seen it. The young boy with his special intuition had sensed something was not right with the lawyer. But he was much too young to know what it was, or to explain it in words even if he were able to understand. He simply knew there was something about the man he didn't like.

As they continued to walk around and study the room, they suddenly heard a frantic cry coming from outside. It was Jeremy shouting. "Mom! Dad! Come out here. Hurry!"

Reacting with the urgency born of parenthood, the couple raced immediately from the spa. Stephanie looked instinctively in the direction of the meadow while Jason looked back toward the swimming pool. They were expecting to find one of the kids injured or worse as parents always do, but were both surprised to see the three children standing in front of a cluster of low bushes along a wooded area near the back of the property hand in hand, their backs to the couple, resembling three cutout dolls of decreasing size joined in a line.

By the time Jason and Stephanie reached their children, they were both out of breath. Being an overweight and dangerously out of shape man, Armstrong had chosen to stay behind and was standing on the walkway outside of the spa. He shielded his eyes from the sun to try to see what was going on in the distance, not wanting to risk a heart attack by racing over to the scene. He had considered walking over to meet the group but decided instead to stay right where he was. Better safe than sorry.

The three kids were still standing holding each other's hands tightly and staring out into a small area of underbrush just outside of the woods. None of them appeared to be injured or in any danger. Jeremy and Cindy stood staring as if transfixed, a mixture of fear and disgust visible on their faces. Sammy however wore a completely different expression than the other two children. Although he too was staring into space, he did not look frightened or upset, he looked contented and at peace. It was as if he were seeing something completely different than his brother and sister were seeing.

Jason looked at Sammy and saw the boy's slightly smiling lips moving slowly. Although he could not hear what, if anything the boy might be saying, he could almost read the child's small lips. Sammy seemed to be repeating something over and over; a word that started with the letter "b". Jason knew Sammy's young vocabulary was very limited so he began to mentally race through a list of b-words he recalled which Sammy knew. He immediately recalled, "big", "boy", "bad" and a few others but was not sure which he might be saying. Regardless, Jason could not comprehend why Sammy looked so happy while Jeremy and Cindy looked so horrified.

"Jeremy! What's wrong?" Stephanie demanded, breaking Jason's concentration. He suddenly realized with a start, he had temporarily been in a bit of a trance himself trying to understand what was going on with his youngest son. It was not how Jason should have reacted in such a situation. He was usually great in emergencies, but this time he had dropped the ball. "Ball?" he thought for a moment, "Was Sammy saying 'ball'?" Jason was thankful Stephanie was too preoccupied with the kids to notice his faux pas, or he might have found himself in hot water with his normally understanding wife.

Stephanie scolded, "We said to call us if you had trouble. You don't look like you are in trouble so why in the world did you call us?"

The boy just lifted his trembling free hand still holding Sammy's with the other, and shakily pointed toward the woods not taking his eyes off the grassy area. "There's something horrible... out there, Dad... It's ugly and all bones like a skeleton... And there's flies... like... millions of flies around it." Cindy just stood stock-still holding Sammy's other hand, her eyes pleading for Jason to do something to relieve their fears. Sammy remained smiling, wearing his beatific expression, his lips repeating the unknown b-word. "Bones?" Jason wondered silently. "Could Sammy be saying bones? Did he know the word bones? And if so, why the hell would he look so happy?"

Putting the thought aside, Jason climbed up into the tall grassy area and pushed aside some of the bushes, not certain what he might find hiding behind them.

Chapter 14

As Jason made his way into the grassy area, he feared he might find some sick or injured woodland creature such as a rabid possum, frothing and snarling in the underbrush, mad with disease, just waiting to bite him and infect him with its dreaded malady. This thought slowed him down somewhat; making him more careful than he originally had planned and apparently slower than Stephanie had wanted him to be.

"What do you see?" she called impatiently, wondering how it might be that the kids had been able to see whatever it was from where they stood, yet Jason had to move aside tall grass to try to find it. Then she realized from the children's low vantage point they were likely to be able to see beneath the same clumps of tall grass, which blocked Jason's view and forced him to move them aside.

"Just give me a second!" Jason said with apparent growing frustration. He knew he was being overly cautious and perhaps a bit short with Stephanie, but he couldn't get the mental picture of the salivating rabid creature from his mind.

Much to his relief, what he found was not some wild infected beast of the forest, but was instead the skeletal remains of what was once a deer, perhaps only a young fawn. The carcass was no bigger than that of a large dog, and for a moment, Jason thought it might actually be a dog. But when he saw its cloven hooves and the white spots present on what little fur remained on its decaying form, he confirmed it was a fawn. The poor creature had been practically picked clean by scavengers and what little remained was rapidly being transformed into a maggot condominium by thousands of flies eager to find a nesting place for their offspring.

The stink from the rotting animal was appalling. And the continuous buzzing sounds from the swarm of insects surrounding the remains were hypnotic, so much so that Jason found himself involuntarily losing touch with reality. Within the space of less than a few seconds while Stephanie waited to see what Jason had found, something unimaginable happened to him.

It was like he was mentally transported to another plane of existence, where reality seemed move at a rate thousands of time faster than in his own world. He was aware of Stephanie and the kids standing still, unmoving as if frozen in place. He could see the hundreds of flies hanging virtually motionless in the air about him. He felt as if he were suddenly encapsulated inside of some sort of bubble in some inconceivable reality. While mere seconds passed in the real world, minutes seemed to crawl by in this place while hundreds of thoughts simultaneously raced through Jason's mind.

The carcass of the dead deer appeared to be staring up directly at Jason through its blackened hollow eye sockets, the tasty morsels long gone, obviously the meal of some woodland creature. The source of their loss was irrelevant. What mattered was they were gone. Staring back into the hideous empty openings, Jason thought, "The eyes; why do they always take the eyes first?" He became shocked and revolted as he surprisingly found himself thinking, "I wonder what the eyeballs might taste like? Would they taste salty like olives? Or are they sweet like cherries?" The incomprehensible thought was so unexpected and so repellent it made his stomach turn with repugnance.

He then suddenly began to feel like the world around him was spinning and he sensed an uncomfortable tightening in his chest. He feared he might pass out and drop face first into the putrid carnage, or maybe he would simply drop dead on the spot. He was reminded of something his boss, Walt Wilson, had once said to him about when death came to call. "Jason, my boy," Walt told him, "death always has its own timetable. It comes whenever it is good and ready and there is nothing you, I or anyone could do to stop it." For the briefest of moments, Jason actually thought death might have come for him and was mocking him though the hollowed out eye sockets of the decomposing fawn. Perhaps death had put this creature in the woods simply to lure him into the bushes where the grim reaper waited patiently with its icy fingers to claim him for one of its own.

Then he thought about the death of Stephanie's unknown Uncle Emerson. Jason recalled how Stephanie was often fond of saying "Everything happens for a reason." He wondered if that was true after all. His once logical mind, the mind of an engineer appeared to not function in the same manner in this strange place of convoluted thoughts. Jason tried to piece together the complex ideas he was having regarding Stephanie's proclamation that "Everything happens for a reason." He understood her uncle had died, and now because Washburn had died, Jason and Stephanie had the opportunity to live in luxury. He wondered if Washburn's death was not just something that had happened by chance, but perhaps the man had died specifically so they would get the property. It was like the chicken and the egg; which came first? Did they get the property because Washburn died or did he die so they could get the property? Did death set in motion a series of events, simply to get Jason to this particular spot and this particular place in time in order to take him?

If Jason did suddenly die right there and then, Stephanie would still have everything she could ever want in life, that is, except for her husband. What would possibly be the logic or reason for that? It made no sense, but life didn't always make sense, he understood. To Jason it seemed such an occurrence would be based less on logic and would be more like a sick twist of fate. Maybe that was how life and death worked. Maybe it all made sense to the grim reaper or to the universe, but perhaps it was not meant to be understood by a mere mortal man.

He recalled a line from his Sunday school days as a young boy, "The Lord giveth and the Lord taketh away". Maybe that was what was happening right now. But maybe in this case, it was "Death giveth and Death taketh away". Within one day, he had learned how a death had brought them riches, and now his own death might very possibly take it all away, at least from him.

Yesterday, after losing his job, he had no idea what he was going to do to make ends meet financially. Now their lives were as close to perfect as he could have ever imagined. "Everything happens for a reason," he heard his wife say in his mind once again. Then in the warped logic of the strange environment he thought, "The fawn died and now other creatures of nature can live. And Washburn died so we can live in comfort. Which came first the chicken or the egg? Now am I supposed to die so Stephanie and the kids can live?" It was all so perplexing and overwhelming. It made no sense, yet simultaneously it made complete sense. Jason was trying to think logically in a place of complete illogic. It was like trying to communicate sensibly with Lewis Carrol's Mad Hatter.

Jason suddenly recalled one of the hatter's insane statements from the book he had read as a child or perhaps it was from the movie he had seen on television. He didn't know why he remembered the quote at all not to mention why he thought of it at this most untimely moment. The hatter had said, "You're not the same as you were before. You were much more..."muchier". What did this childhood memory have to do with him and his current situation? He didn't understand, but still he couldn't get that single thought out of his mind. Was it true and he was not the same as he was before? Would he ever be the same as he was before? Could he, Stephanie or the kids ever be the same? Were they all much more...muchier?

Then he wondered if the dead fawn had sensed it was sick and perhaps knew it was dying. Did it perceive the end was near and as such leave the herd to eventually collapse and die? Maybe the herd sensed there was something wrong with the fawn and drove it away to die for the greater good of the herd. He supposed such things happened all the time in nature.

Or was it all much more simple than that (much less muchier)? Had Death just chosen to take a perfectly healthy creature and strike it down in the prime of life in order to lure Jason into the tall grass? But surely Death didn't lure anyone anywhere to take their lives or steal their souls. Death just happened, whenever and wherever it happened, and as Walt had said there was nothing any of us could do about it.

Then, his train of thought shifted gears once again. He contemplated about how little he knew about Emerson Washburn; how the man had lived, how he had died or for that matter, or what had happened to his body after his death. Had he been buried? Had he been cremated? For the briefest of moments, Jason had an image of a body, Washburn's dead rotting body lying in a field similar to the one where he now stood, perhaps the very spot where he now stood, staring up at him through blackened hollow eye sockets as nature's underground creatures slowly stripped the flesh from the dead man's remains and feasted on the salty or sweet tasting eyeballs. "The eyes, they always take the eyes first," he thought once again.

Jason stared at the remnants of the fawn with its skeletal ribs jutting from fur and flesh, most of which was gone. Ants and other bugs were stopped in their tracks where they had formerly been busy cleaning what residual skin there was off the bones as well. Through his mental haze Jason could see a pinkish collection of organs inside the torso of the creature. He wondered why those particular organs were still there. Weren't they tasty like the eyes? He would have suspected they too might have been the first to go. But maybe they didn't taste as salty or perhaps as sweet as the eyes did.

Or perhaps it was that the particular creatures, which were fond of those morsels, had not yet found the remains. Jason noted he had not seen any turkey vultures circling above. He knew those birds loved to feast on innards. He had seen two of them once in a tug-of-war over some poor creature's intestines. Perhaps the vultures would arrive later to dine on those fine specimens.

The stench of death and decay was thick and soupy in the air around the skeleton. Just when he thought he could take no more, Jason felt the fog, which had enshrouded his mind begin to lift and he sensed as if time was once again returning to normal. Through the renewed buzzing of insects he heard Stephanie call to him.

"Jason? Honey, are you alright?" Stephanie said to her husband who had been staring down into the grass for several seconds as if in a dream.

Jason had no understanding of what had just happened to him and no recollection of the many strange thoughts, which had passed through his mind. But he did actually feel as if he had physically gone somewhere else for a time, although he knew that was impossible. It seemed to Jason as if several hours had passed; but he suddenly realized only a few precious seconds and gone by. Slowly coming back to reality, he turned and looked over his shoulders and said to his wife, "Yeah....um yes...yes... I'm fine. This is just a bit upsetting, that's all."

He noticed Sammy was still staring off into the distance and wearing that strange smile. Jason wanted to have the boy taken as far away from this area as possible. He said with great effort, "Honey...why...why don't you...take the kids to the house... I'll be there in a minute or so."

"What is it?" she asked with noticeable concern. "What's back there, Jason?"

"Nothing... nothing really..." He said, "Just a small deer...a fawn I think...looks like it's been lying here...dead...for quite a while I suspect...not too much left of it." He was making a somewhat disgusted face. "Just take them back by the house... and we'll talk about it later... I'll be right there... I just want to look around here a bit first...just give me a minute."

Jason didn't turn again to look at his family because he suspected if he did he would see Jeremy and Cindy still wearing their looks of horror and revulsion, while Sammy smiled and stared off into space repeating that mysterious and illusive b-word.

Stephanie could see Jason was apparently upset by what he had found, and she assumed he needed the minute to regain his composure. Jason liked animals and probably felt bad about the dead fawn. He also likely didn't like the idea of being so close to its decaying remains. She bent down and picked up Sammy and took Cindy's hand leading them both back toward the barn. Jeremy stood for a moment looking at Jason as if unsure of what he should do.

Jason sensed his son behind him and said, his back still turned away from the boy, "Go ahead, Jeremy... Go on back with

them too... I need you to take care of your sister and brother...
Then I promise I'll be right there... OK?"

The boy hesitated for a moment, not wanting to leave his
father with the horrible dead thing. He also didn't like the strange
look in his father's eyes. Something was wrong with his dad, but
Jeremy didn't know what it might be. Nevertheless, he obediently
turned and followed behind his stepmother and siblings. His
father had just given him the task of watching over his family and
that was a very important job indeed, which made him feel good
and made him feel very important. It was a real grown-up type of
job. So, he did what his dad asked him to do. Yet, as he walked
away, he ventured a look back at this father, still uncomfortable
with the strange way his father stared down into the grass.

Jason was looking at the rotting carcass realizing an
important aspect of their new rural lifestyle; and that was dealing
with nature on a daily basis, up close and personal. He had been
accustomed to either living in a town or in a subdivision where
the roads were always plowed by the township and his electricity,
natural gas, water, phone and other such services were all
provided for him by utility companies.

He turned slightly and looked out across the property, their
property, and saw nothing but meadows, fields and woods for as
far as he could see.

"Oh my Lord," he said aloud. "What have we gotten ourselves
into? This place is huge!" He was starting to doubt if he could take
care of such a place.

Jason was an engineer and liked things to be neat, orderly
and in their proper place.

But nature was never neat and orderly; nature was often the
antithesis of order and the epitome of chaos. Nature was not
analytical, tame and structured; nature was wild, chaotic and
free.

He thought of how the forces nature didn't particularly care if
the dead fawn was rotting in the back part of the property; in fact,
the corpse was obviously serving the very needs of nature by
feeding many of nature's lesser creatures. But to Jason, the
decaying mass was a blight scarring his land, a disease-spreading
pestilence to be dealt with and removed from their land as soon as
possible.

Jason turned slowly, once more looking back toward the
woods. He was going to have to ask the lawyer just how far their
property extended beyond the meadow; how far into the woods
were his responsibility. He was hoping it ended just behind
where he stood so this clump of bushes and the woods beyond

were someone else's problem. But regardless of where his land ended, dealing with it was going to be a major adjustment for he and his family to make.

Chapter 15

Jason looked down into the weeds just a few feet ahead of where he stood and noticed sunlight reflecting off something dull and gray jutting out of a clump of wild grass. It was located right in front of the carcass of the dead fawn. He hunkered down, pushed the grass aside trying to stay as far away from the repulsive remains as possible and was surprised to discover something he never expected to see. What had caught his eye in the reflective light were actually two small rectangular-shaped stone signs of some sort.

Then he realized they were not exactly signs, but to his shock and dismay, they appeared to be small grave markers about eighteen inches tall, a foot wide and an inch or so thick. The stones were lying flat on their backs as if they had been knocked over or had fallen down.

"Fallen Stones!" Jason said, instantly realizing the significance of his statement. "I wonder of that's where Washburn came up with the name for this place. Maybe he was out here walking around and found them or something like that." But then he wondered if that were true, why hadn't Washburn at least stand the markers back up in position again. They were not that large or heavy.

Jason studied the tombstones more carefully. Near the center of the slightly arched tops of the stones, he saw two identical images carved inside of a circle. They were that of an angel or a cherub of some type, typically seen on grave markers of small children.

As he pushed aside more of the grass he could see an inscription, barely legible just below the image on the weathered face of the first stone. It read, "Matthew James Livingston, June 12, 1916 - December 19, 1922". The second one said "Charles Edward Livingston July 2, 1918 - December 19 1922".

"Livingston?" He said aloud and recalled the portrait of Stephanie's ancestors in the main house. "That was the name of Stephanie's great-grandparents. Yes, Livingston."

Jason calculated the ages of the boys as he read the inscription once again. Since the boys had been so young at the time of their passing, Matthew six and Charles four, he made the assumption they must have perished from some terminal childhood disease. He knew as most people did, the mortality rate for young children was extremely high at the early part of the twentieth century. He thought about his own children, especially Sammy and realized how lucky he was to have been born at a time when such deaths were few in this country. Then he reread the inscriptions and saw something he missed the first time. Both boys had died on the same day. He could not imagine what sort of tragedy could have occurred which might have resulted in the both boys' simultaneous deaths, except for perhaps a fire or some other similar disaster.

He looked down at the first stone once again and upon further examination, noticed another inscription just below the date. He hunkered down closer to get a better look at the writing, dusting dirt from the front of the stone. The message was carved in a different font than the previous notation, one that was more calligraphic in nature. When he read the inscription, he saw that it bore the cryptic and ominous phrase, "Taken From Us Too Soon, By The Hand Of Evil." At first, the strange inscription stunned Jason. Then he looked closer at the second stone, Charles' stone, and saw it too bore the exact same inscription, "Taken From Us Too Soon, By The Hand Of Evil."

"What the Hell!" Jason exclaimed, trying to make sense of the whole situation. He suddenly felt as if he needed to put some space between himself and the ominous grave markers. He tried to shuffle backward away from the stones, but because of his awkward position, he stumbled and fell flat on his backside, catching himself with his hands. As he did so, he felt something soft and cold beneath his right hand. Then he sensed something crawling between his fingers.

He looked down and saw his hand had sunken deep into one of the open cavities of the dead fawn's torso and was immersed in the pink gelatinous cluster of rotting internal organs decaying within the beast. He saw hundreds of white worm-like maggots crawling between his splayed fingers, their shiny flesh glistening in the afternoon sunlight.

"Oh Jesus!" he cried out, struggling to his feet. "Sweet mother of God!" He shook off as much of the vile gooey matter as was possible while trying desperately not to vomit. Stirring up the mass of entrails had caused a new wave of stench to rise up from the remains creating an invisible cloud of foul odor Jason swore he could almost taste. A swarm of insects flew up from the rotting carcass and encircled Jason's face as if he too were a dead thing, which they could use in place of the deer. He swatted at them with his left hand careful to keep his right hand as far away from himself as possible.

Not wanting to wipe the disgusting substance on his clothing, he looked around for some large leaves or perhaps a clump of grass or anything he could use to clean himself. As he struggled to wipe himself clean in the tall grass, he inadvertently uncovered a few other headstones. He could see they were quite old as well, much older that the first two he had found, but he did not take the time to examine them or read their inscriptions. He realized this was not just some random cluster of weeds but he was in fact, in some sort of family plot, a small private cemetery.

When his right hand appeared to be as clean as he could get it, he walked out of the grassy area and headed back toward the spa where Stephanie, Armstrong and the kids waited. He assumed they had chosen to wait for him there rather than go back to the main house. He held his right hand away from his body, not wanting to get it any closer to him than necessary. As he walked, he forced himself to regain his composure for the sake of the kids. He already knew he was going to have to do something about that graveyard situation and do so before they moved onto the property.

Jason recalled how often when he and the family would take weekend drives in rural Berks and Lancaster counties; they would see Amish and Mennonite farms with small fenced in family cemeteries. Stephanie had often commented how it "grossed her out" to think about trying to live a normal life on a farm while "all those dead people" were buried not very far away. It didn't seem to matter that the people were deceased loved ones; to Stephanie they were simply dead bodies. It was not that she was superstitious or would believe the property could be haunted by the souls of the departed. Nor did she think some night the dead might crawl from their graves to feast on the flesh of living as was often portrayed in movies. She just didn't like the idea of knowingly sharing her property with the dead. Jason decided he would not mention his discovery to Stephanie, unless he absolutely had to.

As he walked back toward his family, he began to wonder. "What if there were no actual bodies buried in the cemetery? What if it was not really a graveyard at all, but was merely a spot of ground, which the former owners designated to commemorate the deaths of their departed, loved ones? What if the actual bodies were buried somewhere else and this was just like a shrine?"

Jason realized he had only been rationalizing. He was trying to convince himself there were no bodies buried in the tiny cemetery, so it would make it easier for him to do what he suddenly realized he was going to have to do. The more he thought about it, the more he realized his idea that no one might actually buried there was a weak hope at best. Jason assumed it was like being part of a firing squad and believing your gun was the one without the live ammunition so you could appease your guilt and sleep at night knowing you had done nothing wrong. He wondered if he would sleep at night once he had done what he was planning on doing.

Yes, he felt quit certain those were not just markers but actual gravestones. And buried below the gravestones would be real rotting corpses. He thought again about the dead fawn staring up at him through its blackened eye sockets and wondered if the bodies in that family plot had been staring up at him from below the earth, through their own empty eye sockets as well. The thought sent a chill down his spine and this discomfort only served to make him more aware of the filthy condition of his right hand.

By the time Jason reached his waiting family, he had already formulated a plan of action. As an engineer, Jason was naturally a problem solver and after all, this situation was nothing more than a problem that needed a solution. Regardless of whether there were bodies buried in the cemetery or not, he would carry out his plan. In fact, he decided he didn't even want to know if there were really bodies buried there, as that knowledge would only serve to complicate matters.

Jason decided, when he officially accepted the new Ashton manager's position on Monday at his office in Lancaster, he knew he was going to be required to schedule several business trips up to the Ashton plant before making his official transfer and moving his family to their new home. In reality, it might actually take a few weeks for him to move his new office to Ashton, and he would likely commute for perhaps a month or two before the family moved. However, he suspected they would be spending most weekends at the new house so he would have to work fast. There would be numerous things to do and many plans to make both at work and at home.

During one of those business trips, one which he would be sure to make alone, Jason would allow for enough time to return to the property, locate and then remove every one of the headstones from the dilapidated graveyard. Although he had given it some consideration, he had made up his mind that he didn't want to deal with what he assumed would be the bureaucratic hassle of relocating any graves to a different location.

This was not just because of the red tape but also because of the potential cost involved. Jason had no idea what such an endeavor might entail or what it would cost him, but he had to guess that exhuming and relocating one-hundred-year-old, and older, bodies to a new location would likely be a big deal and an expensive one as well. He could almost visibly imagine their two hundred and fifty thousand dollars dwindling away to nothing. Plus he had no desire for Stephanie to even know the bodies had been there at one time. Relocated or not, that mere fact might not sit well with her.

He also had no idea how many bodies might buried in the family plot. He knew of at least two, the young Livingston boys. But he did see several other stones, which meant the potential for additional bodies. He wouldn't know for certain until he returned to the plot for a closer, more thorough examination.

Also, the more he thought about it, the more he realized the likelihood that absolutely no one but he was even aware the family plot was there. Surely, Washburn had known and perhaps that was why he named the property "Fallen Stones". But he must not have ever explained that to the lawyer. Since Stephanie was the only relative ever contacted about the property and since, the graveyard was hidden from view at the back of the property in an uncared for overgrown clump of weeds, the idea of him being the only one who was aware of the site became even more plausible.

If he simply removed each one of the headstones, however many there might be and destroyed them by smashing them into small pieces, he could easily dig a hole out along the back of the property and bury them. All he would need is a shovel and his five pound sledge hammer. He was certain there must be a wheelbarrow somewhere on the property if he chose to use that to save some time. Or he could even use the lawn tractor with its cart attached to help him with the job. And when he was done, no one would be the wiser. He could instruct the kids to stay away from the woods and high grassy area warning them of dangerous varmints and snakes. The grass would continue to grow wild and he could even use the site as a dumping ground for yard waste, thereby covering it with more layers of soil and debris. Yes, he especially liked that idea.

However, he didn't really like the idea of keeping all of this a secret from Stephanie. He was certain if she had known she would agree with his course of action. Up until this point in their marriage, they never lied or kept secrets from each other. But he truly felt he needed to keep this from her. He supposed he just didn't want her to have to deal with such a problem. She had so much on her mind already and the thought of being the messenger of yet another bit of stressful news was something he simply didn't want to do.

The house and the land were incredible, and he desperately wanted his family to be able to start their new life enjoying the property as soon as possible. The last thing any of them needed was to look out from a relaxing chaise lounge on their gorgeous patio or deck and know just a few hundred yards away, a century old family plot existed with unknown ancestors moldering away to nothing below the surface.

Jason was now certain he had made the right decision. And if there actually were bodies buried under the headstones, then they could stay there and fester for another hundred or even thousand years. But the headstones and any other indication that a cemetery ever existed would be gone forever. Before moving day, before they spent a single night in the house, all traces of the Livingston family plot would vanish, and Jason would make sure of that.

"Are you ok?" Stephanie asked as Jason approached them near the spa building. "You look upset."

Jason replied as casually as he possibly could, "Uh...yeah...I'm fine... It's just...you know me...I am not used to dealing with dead stuff...and nature...you know?"

She responded, "Yes. I know how you are about stuff like that." Then she gave an involuntary shudder. "Me too, I suppose." She would not have liked to even be standing on the same grassy area as the dead thing.

Then Sammy raised his hand and pointed back to toward the place where Jason had found the graves and stunned Jason by asking "Daddy...see...boys?"

Jason stood staring at his son uncomprehending. "Boys?" He thought to himself, Sammy had been saying 'boys' back near the woods. That was the mysterious b-word." He had been smiling and saying 'boys' over and over again. Jason wondered what boys Sammy was talking about; there were no boys back there. Then Jason realized with gut wrenching horror that there actually had been two boys back there besides Sammy and Jeremy, but those boys were buried deep in the earth and had been moldering to dust for almost one hundred years. Beads of sweat began to form on the back of Jason's neck and trickle down his back.

Stephanie said, "I have no idea what he is talking about. He's been smiling and talking about boys since we left that clearing. The only thing I can think of is being back there must have reminded him of some boys he must have seen somewhere, some other time, maybe at the playground. I really don't know."

But Jason thought he knew exactly what Sammy was talking about but could only hope to God he was mistaken. He understood how perceptive and sensitive Sammy was. Surly the boy couldn't have seen what Jason feared he had seen. Surely, he couldn't have seen those two boys, the long-dead Livingston boys.

The instant he had the thought, Jason realized just how ridiculous it sounded. He was obviously exhausted from their long and busy day and was on edge as well because of his discovery of the cemetery. His mind must be playing tricks on him, getting him to think impossible thoughts and believe they could actually be real. No. Sammy had not seen any long-dead boys. In fact, he had seen nothing. He was simply a happy little boy with a very active imagination. Jason knew the boy fantasized things all the time; things that never made sense to anyone but him. Jason thought back to the day Sammy was looking into space and saying "doggie". There was no dog present, it was all his imagination, but to Sammy it was as real as if the dog had actually been there.

Sammy looked a bit confused. He didn't know what was wrong with everybody. Why didn't his mommy or daddy or Germie or Dindy say "Hello" to his new friends? Why didn't they ask the little boys to come and play? His mommy always was nice to little boys and girls; his daddy was too. But they didn't say anything to the new little boys. Sammy wanted the boys to come down from the grass place where Daddy was to play, but they wouldn't. They just stood there looking at him smiling at him. So, Sammy smiled back. Sammy didn't know the boys, but he liked the boys. He tried to call to them, but he didn't know their names. He kept saying "boys, boys, boys" but no one could hear him, and the boys didn't come down to play. They just stood looking at him and smiling.

At first, they scared Sammy like that lady in the big glass in the house because they looked like they might be sad and looked a little sick. Their faces were very white, their lips blue and their eyes had dark rings around them. But then they smiled, and Sammy smiled back and he felt much better. Sammy knew good things and Sammy knew bad things. The boys seemed to be good and nice. That lady in the big glass was not nice.

Sammy looked back to see if the boys were still in the grass, but they were gone. He felt bad about not being able to play with the boys. Maybe some other time they would come back and play with Sammy.

Stephanie noticed Jason holding his right hand away from his body. "What's wrong with your hand? You seem to be holding it out weirdly. Did you get hurt?"

"No," Jason said feeling a bit weak and perplexed, "I...um...lost my footing back there and well...I slipped and...had to catch myself with my right hand... I figured with that dead deer and all the bugs and stuff, I had better keep it far away until I get a chance to wash it off." He wisely chose to spare her the details of how his fingers sunk down deep into the creature's cold rotting insect-infested entrails. Stephanie looked carefully at her husband and could see he was being bothered by more than finding the dead dear remains. But she chose to give him his space and not pursue the matter; at least not for today.

Armstrong interjected, "Inside the spa, near the tub is a cabinet with all sorts of cleaning supplies and towels. In fact, I believe I saw an unused bar of soap on a stand near the tub when we were inside." The lawyer knew for a fact there was a bar of soap on a stand because he had given specific instructions to have it put there. He also knew there was a small dark wooden cabinet about thirty inches high with a twelve-inch square top. A fresh, unused bar of soap sat in a ceramic dish atop the cabinet within reach from the tub, and behind it was a small vase filled with several wild flowers. The cabinet had a dowel-rod attached to the side from which hung a hand towel monogrammed with the letter "W". It originally stood for Washburn, but could just as easily now stand for Wright. He simply chose to feign ignorance to not appear as manipulative as he actually was being.

"That sounds good to me," Jason said glancing at the wristwatch, which he always wore on his left arm. "Steph. Why don't you, Mason and the kids work your way back to the house? I will be there in a minute and we can wrap this up for today. I suspect Mason has other business he has to attend to and we did promise the kids that coal mine tour. What do you think, Mason?"

The lawyer replied, "Yes, that's probably a good idea. As soon as you are finished freshening up, we can go out front and finish up our business."

Jason washed and dried his hands thoroughly in the spa tub using water as hot as he could stand it. Steam billowed into the air surrounding him. Suddenly Jason felt like someone was watching him. He looked around the room but could see nothing but his own reflection in large mirrors as well as the rising cloud of steam. Perhaps the movement of the steam reflecting in the mirrors had created the illusion of someone watching. However, even with this explanation the feeling was still unsettling.

He finished his business and left the building, stopping once to look behind him as if expecting to see someone, but of course, he remained alone. Jason closed the door tightly behind him and headed to meet his family back at the main farmhouse. Back inside the spa the surfaces of several of the mirrors rippled wildly as maniacal laughter echoed from deep within the glass walls.

Chapter 16

"It's official," Stephanie said, her face beaming with an ear-to-ear smile, as Jason walked into the kitchen where she, Armstrong and the kids stood waiting. "Look. Mason gave me the keys to the house. It's all ours now." She held out her hand palm up to display the two sets of jingling keys. Jason noticed each set was attached to a key ring with a gold fob emblazoned with a stylish "W". Like the monogrammed towel he had used in the spa building, he wondered with uncertainty was that "W" for Washburn or for Wright; or did it even matter?

Stephanie said, "He suggested we take a few days to let all of this sink in and then start planning our next course of action. This is all so exciting, I feel like I am becoming a bit scatterbrained."

"That's to be expected," the lawyer said. "And remember, during the time you are away from here, if there is absolutely anything you folks need from me do not hesitate to call me. That also goes for any time in the future. As I mentioned earlier, I hope you are satisfied with the job I've done so far and will consider using my services for all of your future legal needs."

"Um... Yes," Jason responded a bit distantly. He was preoccupied, still unable to get the distracting image of the small tombstones and the family graveyard out of his mind. Also the way Sammy had seemed to see something in the cemetery. Not to mention, that strange inscription 'Taken From Us Too Soon, By The Hand Of Evil'. That message troubled him terribly as it kept repeating inside his head. "I think we need some time to absorb everything that's happened in the past two days, and also I'm sure there'll be many, many things I'll need to take care of at work as well. I think after the next week or so, we should have a good plan in place."

He looked again at the keys in his wife's hands and inquired of Armstrong, "Are they the keys for the house as well as the rest of the outbuildings?"

"Actually," the lawyer explained, "all of the doors on the property, front back, side as well as all of the outbuildings are keyed exactly the same, so you only need a single key to get inside any of the buildings. The other keys on the rings are for the Ford pickup and the tractor in the barn. There are no keys needed for the garage as they work with the automatic garage door openers. The four remote openers for the garage are in the top drawer of that cabinet over there." He pointed to one of the base cabinets along the wall. Jason walked over, opened the top drawer and saw the four garage openers.

The lawyer continued, "That reminds me, I should have pointed out each of the garage doors also have keypads mounted to the sides of the doorframes with keyboards, which all use the same four digit number combination, 1-2-3-4 to open them. Now that I think about it, I should probably recommend you change the combination to something you will easily remember, and something that's not quite as simple for someone else to figure out. Right now, I am the only other person alone who knows the current combination, so as soon as you reprogram the openers the number will be safe, secure and exclusively known by you and your family alone. And of course, there is no need or reason for me to know the combination any longer as the house is now yours."

"Yes. You're right. Thanks, Mason," Jason responded. "That's a good idea." As he looked at the lawyer, he thought he saw a momentary dark expression pass across the man's face. He could not put into words what it was about the look that didn't sit well with him, probably because it had appeared and then disappeared so quickly as if Armstrong had inadvertently let down his guard. It was like the lawyer knew something Jason didn't, and the man was keeping that mysterious knowledge from them. For a moment, Jason thought he actually might have misinterpreted the look, but the expression had been so intense and gave him such an uneasy feeling, deep down in the pit of his stomach, that he was certain there was something to his suspicions.

Because of these strong sensations, an idea unexpectedly entered Jason's mind; something, which at first seemed to be a bit paranoid to him, but which was an idea he couldn't seem to shake. Although Stephanie now held what were supposed to be the only sets of keys to the property, he wondered if perhaps there might be another set; one which the lawyer had made especially for himself. If the man did have his own set of keys then he wouldn't care one bit if the garage door opener combinations were changed because he could still gain access to the property whenever he chose to.

Jason didn't know why he suddenly had this idea, as he was usually not so mistrustful of people, although he would be the first to admit he didn't particularly care for lawyers. And Armstrong hadn't really given Jason any reason to distrust him. But when he combined the gut feeling he was experiencing with the strange look he thought he had seen pass over the lawyer's face, he began to wonder if he might actually be correct. As such, his level of mistrust of the man was beginning to increase by the second.

If the lawyer had made his own set of keys, it would mean whenever the Wright family was away from the property, Armstrong would be free to enter the house and could do whatever he chose to. Jason had assumed the lawyer had already been given such free reign to an extent before the death of Stephanie's uncle, and likely even more so since then. Jason also had made the logical assumption the man might not readily want to relinquish such access even though he and Stephanie had taken possession of the property.

What if, in his role as ad hock caretaker, Armstrong had started treating the property as if it were his own, believing he could come and go as he pleased? Jason thought about the self-deprecating joke the lawyer had made in the spa building about how frightening it might be to see his large naked figure reflected in the mirrors. He suddenly started to wonder if the lawyer had helped himself to several relaxing baths in the huge claw-foot tub. The image, which under normal circumstances might be somewhat humorous, made Jason's stomach cramp with disgust. Had Jason known what unspeakable event had actually occurred inside that same spa only a month earlier, he would have collected his family and fled the property, never to return. But unfortunately, he didn't know and could only analyze what he saw before him. The more Jason thought about the lawyer, the more he became certain of his distrustful feelings.

Then he began to wonder, what if Armstrong had stolen paintings or jewelry or other such possessions from the property and had already sold them? In the living room, Jason had seen some paintings on the wall that even to his untrained eyes seemed to be quite valuable. Stephanie's uncle had been dead for over a month and that had given the lawyer plenty of time to steal a few valuable items. Jason recalled how that morning at the meeting the lawyer had given him a complete inventory of the estate accounting for virtually every item in the house. He hadn't looked at the list very carefully as he was overwhelmed by the value of the estate. However, he would be going over the accounting in detail as soon as possible. He suspected such documents could have been altered to hide certain thefts, but he didn't know and maybe never would know for sure. Since neither he and Stephanie had known anything about Washburn prior to his death, they had no idea about the extent of his possessions. As such, it would make any thievery relatively simple to hide.

Jason didn't want to appear ungrateful to the lawyer and even felt a bit guilty about his suspicions, especially since the man had seemed to be nothing but helpful to them during the entire settlement process. But perhaps Armstrong had been too helpful. Jason recalled how that same morning the lawyer had all the critical papers ready, explained everything, answered all of their questions and even arranged for the remaining two hundred and fifty thousand dollars cash from the estate to be wire transferred to Jason and Stephanie's personal bank account so it was immediately accessible to them. But then Jason wondered if the cash had truly been all the money that remained in the estate. What if the actual amount had been more? What if it had actually been five hundred thousand or even a million? Would the lawyer have the means to swindle the young, unknowing couple?

And how could they ever know the true value of the estate or the extent of the lawyer's thievery? Since Washburn was a solitary type of man, with no relatives, no friends and one who apparently had led somewhat shady former life; it was unlikely even the best forensic accountant could accurately inventory his holdings and determine if anything was missing.

There was definitely something in the lawyer's strange look, no matter how brief, which caused Jason to now distrust the man completely. He began to sincerely believe what a few moments ago was just a passing fanciful thought. It was as if he suddenly knew for certain Armstrong truly had made his own set of keys and had, in fact, been stealing from the estate. Jason also presumed the lawyer had been swindling Washburn and skimming money all during the restoration.

Since Jason had now convinced himself of Armstrong's nefarious intentions, he had made up his mind to solve this dilemma himself and as with the gravesite, to do so quickly. As soon as he returned home, he was going to start searching the Internet for an area locksmith and was going to have all the door locks changed and re-keyed. Or perhaps he would hire a locksmith from Berks County instead, just in case one of the local businessmen had connections with the lawyer. He realized just how paranoid these thoughts seemed, even to himself, but it was something he just felt he needed to do. In fact, he was going to make sure the locks were changed even before he took care of the cemetery situation.

He had also noticed another security issue while they were walking around the inside of the house. It was one, which he was certain Stephanie hadn't observed. The property did not have an alarm system of any kind, whatsoever. He had seen smoke alarms at strategic places around the house but he didn't see any burglar alarm type system or control panel of any kind. He decided to broach the subject with the lawyer and see how he handled the question.

"Mason?" Jason asked pretending not to sound suspicious, "I couldn't help but notice something that I found quite strange, especially when you consider the value of this property, and I was wondering if you could explain it to me. I assume you will have the answer, since after all, you were the project manager during the renovation." Jason couldn't suppress the almost accusatory tone in his voice. Stephanie watched with a bit of confusion, unsure of where Jason was up to with his strange line of questioning.

The lawyer replied with obvious guarded anticipation, "Yes, Jason. If I can answer your question, I will be happy to do so. What is it?"

Jason said, "I didn't see any alarm system anywhere in the property. No electronic keypad, no cameras, no window alarms, nothing. You had said Mr. Washburn had a bit of an unsavory past, which he had left behind to move here. I would suspect such a man might have enemies and might also want to have some type of early warning system in place to protect himself."

"You are absolutely correct, Jason. And quite observant I might add." The lawyer replied with a pleasant and complimentary air. "The property does not have any security system. Mr. Washburn didn't believe in security systems of any kind, especially those with cameras. He felt he had taken care of himself his entire life and had always done so without the benefit of electronics and he was not about to start now. You may have noticed the combination smoke and carbon monoxide alarms scattered about the property. Mr. Washburn hated them as well, but local building codes required them and there was nothing he could do to get around that. Believe me, I tried at his request to get a variance from the requirement, but to no avail. He also didn't like the keypads on the garage doors, but they came with the doors and had been installed before we were aware of them. Apparently he didn't care about them enough to ask me to have them removed."

"But even we have a security system in our little townhouse." Stephanie suggested, "And our entire house isn't worth as much as just the garage in this place."

The lawyer explained, "Perhaps so, Stephanie. But you have to keep something in mind. And I say this with no disrespect to your community. Your home is located only about ten or fifteen miles away from a major city, Reading. You live in a much more highly populated area than around here. And whether you like to admit it or not, the crime rate is significantly higher in your county than here as well."

"But still..." Jason interrupted, "With a property of this value... No security system? Seriously? I mean, I just don't get it."

"Well, you just had to know Mr. Washburn," the lawyer replied with a bit of frustration. "He was set in his ways and had no interest in such security. As I mentioned earlier, most of the modern and more luxurious renovations to the property were to a great extent the results of our designers. As you saw by Washburn's bedroom, his needs were simple and specific."

What Armstrong actually knew, however, was that the designs for the property and all of the modern lavish renovations were actually ordered by the unseen, unearthly occupants of the property and were specifically created to appeal to the Wright's own tastes. He also understood there was no need for a security system of any kind. The beings inhabiting the property were more than capable of keeping the home safe from any unwanted intruders, as was evident with the recent fiery demise of one Mr. John "Jack" Moran, whose charred remains were still a fresh and revolting memory in Armstrong's mind.

Once again, that same strange expression passed across Armstrong's face, and Jason didn't fail to miss it this time either. Although he was correct in not trusting the lawyer, the look, which bothered him so much, was not born of any thievery Armstrong may or may not have committed. The truth was, the lawyer had not taken a single thing from the home and never would. He would not have been permitted to do so. The look he wore was one of trepidation. The lawyer could not help but recall his encounters with the specter of the dead Washburn and felt genuine guilt, possibly for what might await the unsuspecting family.

Regaining his composure the lawyer suggested, "I know of a local security firm, which I am certain would be happy to provide you with an estimate to install such a system for you. That is, if you truly feel it is necessary." To Jason, the lawyer sounded almost insulted by the proposition.

Jason replied, "Thanks, Mason. But that won't be necessary. When we are ready, I am sure we can take care of that ourselves." Jason decided he needed to cut the cord with the attorney as soon as possible and handling the security system installation without Armstrong's assistant was as good a place to start as any.

"As you wish," the lawyer said. Then he held out an arm directing the family toward the front hallway. "As Jason supposed earlier, I have to be at another appointment shortly, so I must be on my way. I know you folks will want to be heading into town for your mine tour as well."

"Thanks, Mason," Jason said, sounding as sincere as possible, "You have been a great help, and we appreciate it. But I think we want to wait here for a little bit longer and talk in private about a few things before we lock up and head out. We will be contacting you sometime next week. That is, if we feel there is anything we need and cannot handle ourselves." Jason imagined another piece of the imaginary cord connecting him to Armstrong snapping as he suppressed a smile.

The lawyer could tell by the tone of Jason's voice he would likely never be hearing from the man again. Though he had tried his best to not let his internal anxiety about the hell-born specters, he obviously had not been successful. It was apparent Jason didn't trust him and had wanted him out of their lives as quickly as possible. He could do little else about that. Armstrong had done his legal duty to the estate, and he had carried out the demands of his evil tormentor Washburn as well. Although he feared for the Wright family, he now feared more for himself and prayed Washburn would leave him in peace. But somehow, he didn't think that particular prayer would be answered.

Chapter 17

The lawyer sat behind his massive oak desk as the sun began its slow decent over the western silt-covered mountainous horizon on that Sunday evening. The glorious spectacle was visible in all of its majestic amber and crimson splendor as he watched through his large office window. "Red at night, sailor's delight." H. Mason Armstrong said aloud. Then he thought "More like, red at night, lawyer in fright." He knew "in fright" was not a strong enough description for the terror, which held him in its grasp like the tightening grip of the tentacles from some powerful unseen creature, slowly crushing him, choking off his ability to breath.

He had not yet switched on any of the lights inside his office. The glow from his computer monitor reflected in his reading glasses as darkness began to engulf the room. He had been intently scouring the Internet non-stop since the afternoon of the previous day following his meeting with the Wrights. He had been searching for any shred of information to help him out of his unholy predicament. However, so far, his search had proven to be fruitless, as he simply could not find the answer he so desperately needed.

He was futilely trying to ascertain the nature, if not the very essence of the entity, which his evil tormentor, the once living Emerson Washburn had now become. Throughout his entire career Armstrong had lived by the philosophy knowledge was power; the more he understood his enemy, the easier it would be to defeat him. That way of thinking had never failed him in the courtroom and he was most certain it could only benefit him now. He was convinced the key to surviving the impossible situation he now found himself thrust into, was to learn all he could about his horrendous undead adversary.

He wondered what sort of strange netherworld could be capable of unleashing such a ghastly creature into his own unsuspecting and defenseless world. Then he thought, perhaps he should not think in terms of just a singular creature but should use the plural, creatures. This was largely because, although he had only been approached by the threatening specter of Washburn he knew there were others.

He suspected Washburn was also not the main driving force behind the confluence of events either, but he merely occupied what might be considered a lower rung on the spectral ladder, so to speak. The more he thought about it the more Armstrong believed this impression. He also understood in order to find a way to eventually protect himself from these beings or perhaps even destroy them; he would need to be aware of what manner of creatures they actually were.

The lawyer had been researching various occult and spiritual sites looking for information on ghosts, spirits, poltergeists, demons, zombies and even other such evil mythical entities like vampires and werewolves but could not quite find a category in which to place Washburn.

Armstrong found it fascinating how each individual type of mysterious being seemed to come with its own set of rules and guidelines. This perplexed him. He could not understand why humans insisted in assigning limits and rules to everything they could conceive, even those things born of their wildest imaginings. What was the point of creating fictional creatures of awesome evil with incredible power, then impeding their abilities with various rules and regulations? Armstrong supposed it was human nature that no matter how despicable, malevolent and deadly the creature might be, humans always needed to have some way to destroy it, in order for mankind to remain in his rightful place at the top of the food chain.

He thought about the legendary vampires and the list of conventions they were required to adhere to in order to remain immortal, such as not going out in the daylight, sleeping in their coffins, or in their native soil, being burned by holy water or a crucifix. And who was it that decided they should not be able to see their own reflections, or that they would be terrified of garlic? He wondered if it could have been the legendary Bram Stoker himself, or perhaps it had been someone much earlier in time. Although he had read Stoker's legendary tale back during his younger years, Armstrong could not recall anything specific about the book; other than the fact, he had fallen asleep every time he read a few pages. This spoke volumes of Armstrong's opinion of the writing, especially when he could read mountains of so-called boring legal documents for hours and never nod off.

The same sort of question regarding rules might be asked about werewolves and their ability to shape shift into half-man half-wolf creatures during a full moon. Why a full moon? And why was it they could only be killed by a silver bullet? He also noted how these two creatures as well as the latest horror movie craze, zombies, all shared one similar characteristic.

If a victim were bitten and not killed or eaten by any of these creatures, he would shortly find himself transformed into one of the creatures as well. Supposedly, none of these imaginary beings had the ability to reproduce through conventional means, so the fictional universe had chosen to give them the ability to procreate in another fashion. These renowned creatures may have all been entertaining, but they were still fictional as far as the lawyer knew. Then again, up until a month ago, he assumed beings such Washburn were the stuff of fiction as well. Now he was fighting for his very life and immortal soul in a battle with such creatures.

Armstrong wondered if Washburn had actually become a ghost, a specter, a poltergeist, a demon or some strange hybrid as of yet unidentified in modern literature. Armstrong had read that simple ghosts or specters could do nothing to bring physical harm to living beings but could cause their victims emotional distress, torment and mental anguish simply by their presence. Poltergeists on the other hand, when angered might be able to cause inanimate objects to move or maybe make things fly off shelves. He supposed if he found himself in the path of a flying plate or book he could possibly be harmed. Demons supposedly could not manifest themselves in our world but had to occupy a human host in order to carry out their sinister plans. "Rules, rules and more rules," he thought once again. The sheer numbers of rules were beginning to overwhelm him.

The lawyer noted how Washburn hadn't appeared to be corporal but ethereal. Armstrong had learned those two words from his recent Internet research; corporal being physical in nature and ethereal being spectral. He began to wonder if there were such things as demonic ghosts. He didn't know. But it did seem to make sense to him Washburn might fit into this particular category. The lawyer recalled how at first Washburn had appeared to Armstrong only in mirrors, but at their latest several encounters, the creature had actually left the confines of the looking glass and had floated across the room, never actually encountering things of this world.

Then he recalled how when the maggot-like insects had fallen to the floor, they had shriveled up and disincarnated in a puff of foul-smelling vapor. He wondered if he somehow were able to get Washburn to touch something physical during one of his manifestations, would the horrible specter likewise disappear? And what would happen if Armstrong reached out and tried to touch the creature himself?

This made the lawyer think the entity must truly be a ghost of some sort. And although Armstrong had never come into physical contact with the spirit, he suspected doing so would not produce the sensation of any form of solidity. He also suspected if he did try to touch Washburn, it might not do the spirit any harm either.

But if that were the case, then Armstrong doubted there was anything the creature could do to physically harm him. So far, the only thing Washburn had been able to do to was scare the living bejesus out of him, and it had done a first rate job of that.

Thus far, Armstrong had dutifully carried out all of Washburn's orders. At first, while Washburn was alive, the lawyer had done so to fulfill his legal duties. But then after the man had returned from the dead in whatever form he now existed, Armstrong had done so more out of fear. But, he had to ask himself, fear of what? What did he really think this denizen of the dead could do to him? Yes, it might be emotionally distressing to be accosted with the sights, smells and sounds from some horrid underworld, but could it truly do him any physical harm? If he could regain control of his psychological reactions to Washburn's appearance, could he then learn how to drive the creature back into its world of the damned?

He realized what the very crux of his unfortunate dilemma was. He simply didn't know what the full extent of Washburn's powers might be. He had to admit, a creature capable of returning from the dead in any form, was surely one to fear or be very cautious of at a minimum. Then he thought again about the man who had burned alive in his car two nights earlier. It had been ruled a suicide by local police; a second suicide on the same property in less than a month. Jack Moran had been that man's name. How had that happened? What had Washburn or the other heretofore-unseen creatures done to him? Had he simply perished in some freak accident coincidentally occurring near the property, or had his demise be orchestrated?

Armstrong wondered if the ghosts had actually been capable of killing the man or if they had simply driven him mad then he killed himself. Then again, as he had wondered earlier, perhaps they had somehow controlled the man's mind and commanded him to kill himself. These were thoughts, which had to be given great consideration, especially in light of his own volatile situation.

During the past month, he had seen so many events come together in order to direct the unsuspecting Wright family to the farmette. This started with Washburn's moving to Ashton and hiring Armstrong as his lawyer. Then there was the long decline of Washburn's health followed by his creating his last will and testament, leaving everything to the unknown niece Stephanie Wright. After that Washburn had committed suicide, and now the Wrights were in possession of the home and the land. Armstrong assumed this well-orchestrated sequence of events was not only what Washburn had wanted but what the mysterious others wanted as well. But of course, he had no understanding what the reason behind the orchestration might be.

Armstrong recalled how as he had walked the family around the property the previous day, he had started to wonder what would become of him now that he had done all he was ordered to do. This was a legitimate concern for the lawyer, especially if Washburn or the other unknown spirits determined they might no longer want or need to keep him alive. As a result, Armstrong had gone all Saturday night and all day Sunday without sleep, trying desperately to find some solution to his problem.

As he stared at the computer monitor, searching over another list in the seemingly endless lists of supernatural web sites something caught his eye. He saw a link to a website, which claimed to have knowledge about something called demonic ghosts. "Demonic ghosts!" he said aloud. This was exactly what he had been thinking about only a few moments earlier. Perhaps that was what he needed to learn more about; maybe that was the answer to what Washburn had become. After a bit of wary hesitation he clicked the link and was taken directly to the site.

Then with frustration Armstrong saw that the site, like virtually every other website he had investigated previously, was designed to look as creepy and sinister as possible, with dark gray and black backgrounds and plenty of Gothic style fonts for all the text. And of course, the lettering was not only blood red in color but also it appeared to drip blood down the screen. "Oh boy," the lawyer said sarcastically after having seen thousands of sites just like it during the past twenty-five or so hours. "That certainly is original."

He was all set to give up and back out of the site when he noticed a small icon located off to the left and toward the bottom of the screen. The icon seemed somehow familiar to him. He wasn't sure why the icon had caught his attention especially because it was so small, and it was not very easy to make out any of the details. But it did appear to represent some type of picture, like a portrait of some couple. He immediately thought of the painting "American Gothic" by Grant Wood but didn't think that was what the icon depicted, but he was uncertain.

He bent forward, looking closer to try to see what the picture was all about but to no avail. When he placed his cursor over top of the icon. A screen hint appeared with the caption "Click this icon... you don't want to miss this." Now his curiosity was aroused and he had to see where the link led. He figured, what did he have to lose? He had already spent a sleepless night and all day trying to find his answers; maybe his solution was only a click away. So, he pressed the left button on his mouse and the screen became awash with an image, which shocked the lawyer to the very core of his being, making the pit of his stomach feel as heavy as a lead weight.

On the computer monitor just inches from his face was the image of Dwight and Marie Livingston; the very same scene depicted in the painting from the living room of the Washburn farmhouse. "What the hell?" the lawyer said involuntarily. What he was seeing was impossible. He looked up at the top of the screen to see what the URL for the site might be but the bar, which typically displayed such information, was missing as was his back arrow and other navigational tool bars. The image took up the entire monitor screen.

Armstrong assumed he must have accidentally clicked somewhere on the screen he shouldn't have and had inadvertently thrown the picture into full screen mode. He pressed the escape key, which he found usually took displays out of full screen back to normal operation mode, but the picture did not reduce in size and his tool bars did not reappear. "Wonderful," he thought with disappointment, "...some kind of virus no doubt." As he was about to shut down his computer, he saw the picture begin to change.

The first thing he noticed was the eyes of the wolf's head cane on which Dwight Livingston rested his hands, began to glow a bright red, which increased in intensity until they became an iridescent almost blinding white. He lifted his hand to shield his eyes from the luminescence but the light disappeared as quickly as it had appeared. Then he noticed Dwight Livingston's fingers move ever so slightly on the head of the walking stick as if tapping slowly and impatiently.

The logical part of his mind told him it was obviously some sort of computer animation technique; geared to make the viewer feel uncomfortable and perhaps even frightened by the image. But he couldn't understand why the web designer had chosen this particular portrait and where in the world he might have gotten a digital image of it. Of all the paintings of all the couples in the world, especially those of famous couples throughout history, why had the Webmaster chosen this one? It was the very same painting currently hanging on the wall at the Washburn farmhouse. It made absolutely no sense to him, yet there it was.

Then as if providing him with the answer he truly didn't want to receive, the faces of both Dwight and Marie Livingston began to change. The normal pallor of their skin turned from a healthy pink to a dusky gray. Their flesh began to shrink back upon their skulls, wrinkle and gain a leathery appearance as if the couple were withering away to mummified corpses right before his eyes. Large dark circles surrounded their sunken eye sockets from which their red-rimmed orbs stared directly at Armstrong, as if boring a fissure into his very soul. They were both looking at him if not looking straight through him.

The corners of their shriveled mouths slowly curled up in slight, knowing, sinister smiles. Armstrong felt as if the two horrible creatures shared some sinister knowledge, which he did not, but it might be knowledge he was about to unfortunately discover. The image of the woman, Marie Livingston, began to fade and drift backward out of the screen appearing to shrink in size, while Dwight began to grow and become much, much clearer, and almost three-dimensional in appearance.

The lawyer backed away from the screen sinking deep into the leather upholstery of his desk chair as the likeness of Dwight Livingston continued to grow until its cracked and blackened lips filled the entire computer screen. Then as the lips slowly began to part they revealed a few blackened, cavity-riddled teeth. A thick blackish-red liquid the consistency of melted tar began to flow slowly from the spaces between the rotten teeth. Then dozens if not hundreds of glistening yellow-white maggots drizzled from inside the hideous thing's cavernous mouth, spilling over its lips and falling out of the monitor and onto Armstrong's computer keyboard where the wretched insects writhed as if in pain before eventually disappearing as if vaporized in gray-green puffs of foul smelling smoke.

The air around Armstrong was thick with the vile sickening sweet stench he recognized of as the reek of death. It was the same repulsive scent he had encountered upon finding a dead rat rotting in his basement once a long time ago. However, the passing of time had done nothing to allow his memory to erase that stinking and always-recognizable odor. And this foul smell had an additional element, the scent of burned flesh, which Armstrong assumed came from the disintegrating larvae.

Terrified with fear, Armstrong tried to reach cautiously over as he pressed the off button on his monitor. Then he reached down and pressed the power button on his computer, but the image did not disappear. Instead, the maggot-infested mouth on the screen opened wider and the lawyer could see even more blackened and yellowed rotted teeth, many missing in places looking like randomly scattered and skewed grave markers in a long ago abandoned cemetery.

Inside the pitch dark maw, the man's withered blackened tongue still covered with squirming clinging larvae moved slowly about, serpentine in appearance as it snaked itself along the tops of the rotting teeth, occasionally snagging its paper thin flesh on a sharpened edge of a particularly nasty bit of decayed enamel and causing a laceration on its surface. Instead of blood trickling down from the cuts, a thick sickening dark green puss-like sludge oozed hideously from the wounds. The disgusting stench emanating from the screen had gone beyond anything Armstrong had ever previously encountered.

Then the gaping mouth began to slowly close as the face of Dwight Livingston backed away, until his entire visage once again filled the screen. Marie likewise began to slowly emerge back into the foreground and eventually took her place by her husband's side. Armstrong noticed for the first time, deep hand prints on Marie's neck and a long open slit across Dwight's throat, extending practically from one ear to the other and hanging open like a second, much larger mouth.

Within a few seconds, the flesh began to reappear on both of the corpses and the image gradually returned to reflect that of the original painting. The lawyer felt a momentary bit of hope assuming what he had just witnessed was nothing more than a sophisticated computer simulation, dreamed up perhaps by some local teenager as a prank. He guessed he had triggered the program when he clicked the icon and now the image would remain frozen until he backed out of the screen and re-clicked the icon once again. Then he suspected it would replay once again looping through the exact scenario he had just witnessed. He assumed the smells and the burning maggots were probably his imagination because of his exhaustion from lack of sleep.

Now the couple were completely restored once again and standing in the posed position of the portrait, staring harmless out at him. He breathed a sigh of relief. It had all been some sort of software related gag. Then incredibly, the eyes of Charles Livingston began to focus then stare insanely at Armstrong as it started to move its lips then unbelievably spoke. "Hello, Mr. Armstrong...do you know who I am; who we are?"

The lawyer was beyond the ability to speak or move and as a result, he could only stare in horror at the sinister specter addressing him from within the monitor. His mouth hung slack-jawed as he was certain he had either completely lost his mind or was well on his way to doing so.

Then the image spoke again, "Yes...I can tell you know exactly who we are...and I suppose you are wondering both...what we are doing here…and what fate we might…have in store for you… Is that not correct?" The lawyer stared silently, realizing he was paralyzed and incapable of even the slightest movement as a steady stream of drool dripped down from his slack lips. Then the thing spoke again.

"Marie and I have come here via this mechanical box of yours to thank you personally…for the outstanding work you have done on our behalf…that is to say the role you have played in getting our descendants to agree to…come and live with us in our home."

The lawyer's tension began to relax ever so slightly, and for the first time, he hoped that perhaps he might somehow be favored by the specters and that no harm might come to him. After seeing what he had just seen, the lawyer was certain the two beings had the capability of doing real harm to him if they so chose to. They were obviously the 'others' Washburn had alluded to. Then the repugnant face from within the computer screen spoke again. "…oh yes…and in addition to offering you our eternal thanks and gratitude…we also came here to kill you."

Before the lawyer had a chance to react, Livingston's two translucent hands shot out from the screen, one on each side, pulling the surface of the screen along with them as if it had been transformed into some type of elastic rubber-like material. Perhaps it served as a barrier to keep the things in Armstrong's world from causing harm to the undead creatures. The hands quickly reached across the space on the lawyer's desk and then effortlessly passed through him and sunk deep into the center of the lawyer's chest leaving behind a silvery red puff of vapor in their wake.

Armstrong had but a moment to notice this when suddenly he felt a sharp pain in the center of his chest as his left arm became numb and he broke out in an icy cold sweat. He sensed an incredible pressure building in the center of his chest as if an elephant was straddling him, crushing him. He was unable to breath, and Armstrong looked down wide-eyed at the arms jutting from his upper body with the rubber-like monitor screen trailing behind them. Soon the image faded from his vision, and he was consumed in a vale of blackness.

His lifeless body slumped backward in a heap on his chair stone cold dead. His head slouched backward and off to the side as his slack-jawed mouth, and his tongue lolled out of the side resembling the head of a recently killed deer. The ghostly arms slowly retreated backward into the monitor.

Then, displayed on the screen, three people could be seen walking away in the distance; a man in a turn of the century finely tailored but worn suit, using a walking stick on one side, and a woman dressed in a white wedding gown yellowed with age on the other.

Between the couple, walking with his head down as if cowed and beaten was a heavy-set man dressed in a rumpled business suit. Then the man in the center turned, and Armstrong got one final look out at his earthly remains lying dead in his leather desk chair before he took in place with the others for eternity.

Chapter 18

The following Wednesday morning Jason walked slowly from the back of the luxurious house, past the in-ground swimming pool and out into the vast expanse of the property, heading toward the large barn off in the distance. He was in no hurry to deal with the task awaiting him; a responsibility he had been both anticipating and dreading since his discovery of the family plot the previous Saturday. The very idea of a cemetery on their land, no matter how small or seemingly insignificant enveloped him in discontentment. The property had been perfect. No, it had been more than perfect; it had been absolutely amazing. And Jason had determined he would be damned if he was going to let anything as distasteful as one hundred-year old insect riddled rotting corpses ruin the joy he had seen on his lovely wife's face. No, he certainly would not. Instead, he would deal with the problem as he had planned and would take care of it by the end of the day.

Just before he walked out the back door of the main house, Jason gave final instructions to a crew of workers, regarding the installation of a security system. Jason was a natural planner and in his role as senior engineer, he was often called upon to manage multiple complex projects, so juggling the few duties on his list for the day would likely not prove to be a challenge.

However, keeping all of the activities a secret from Stephanie might have been the hardest thing he ever had to do. And this was not just because it might be a challenge not having her find out, but because the very idea of deceiving her went against everything he believed in. In fact, she was unaware he was even at the property. She thought he was at the Ashton manufacturing facility at an important meeting concerning his promotion. It was not that Jason minded her knowing about the security system as they had both agreed it was something they wanted to have put in, but he didn't want her anywhere near the property until he took care of the unsavory problem festering beneath the earth at the back edge of their land. It simply worked out that this day, he could kill two birds with one stone so to speak.

Jason had located a security company in the southern Schuylkill County city of Yuengsville via the Internet on the Saturday evening they had arrived home, after meeting with the Ashton attorney. Jason had sent the company an email through their website, and was surprised when the owner of the company called him personally Sunday afternoon. Jason was happy they had been prompt in returning his call. Luckily, Stephanie had not been home at the time so he could make his plans without her knowledge.

After Jason had spoken with the security company owner, he had arranged to meet a team of their technicians at the Ashton house first thing Wednesday morning. Jason had agreed that at this late stage in the remodeling process, when almost all the work had been completed, the best and least invasive solution would be to install a wireless system.

As he walked back through the grass, which was moist with morning dew, he thought not only about the unpleasant task awaiting him in the tiny ancient cemetery, but he also thought back on the many events, which had transpired since he and Stephanie had taken possession of the property only five days earlier. So much had changed in their lives, practically overnight. And although coming to grips with everything was quite stressful at times, they had still managed to find time to take in some local sights and have fun with the kids that Saturday as well.

The children loved the steam locomotive ride, which the tour guide referred to as the 'Lokie'. The train took its passengers about a mile out around a mountain where they got an amazing scenic panoramic view of the town of Ashton and its surrounding area. Jason was also surprised at how much the kids enjoyed the Pennsylvania Coal Museum. He was afraid they might become bored, as they always tended to be with most museums. But they seemed to be genuinely fascinated by the various displays of coal mine photography as well as the displays of various tools of the mining trade, dating back over one hundred years.

Then Jason recalled how unusual their tour of the Miner's Tunnel coal mine attraction had been, and how he had been truly amazed at seeing the inside of a real coal mine. The tour had been both extremely interesting and unfortunately at one point quite discomforting if not terrifying for Jason. He thought about how he enjoyed studying the rough-hewn timbers, which held up the low ceilings of the main gangway as the mine-car tracks sloped steeply downward into blackness, leading over a mile into the very bowels of the earth. Everyone enjoyed riding in the special mine cars that took the tourists safely to the bottom of the mine. Since they arrived at the mine close to closing time, there were not many people on their tour, which allowed him many occasions to ask questions. Jason was naturally inquisitive so asking questions was typical of him. His tour guide was extremely knowledgeable of the mining industry and his authentic coal

region accented speech made his comments even more
interesting.

Jason was surprised when he found they were all permitted to
leave the mine cars when they reached the bottom of the tunnel
and they were actually permitted to walk around inside the mine.
Bright electric lights illuminated the area allowing for detailed
examination of the various tunnels. The walls and the ground
seemed to be covered with a film of moisture from water seeping
through soil, which surrounded them. Coal glittered like black
diamonds where the water slid along its surface sparkling in the
lights. Each of the tourists had been given jackets to wear on the
tour and when Jason felt how cold and damp it was so far below
the earth, he was grateful for the extra layer of warmth. He looked
at Jeremy and Cindy and had to suppress a chuckle as their
skinny little legs stuck out below their coats, which were much
too large for them.

The kids especially enjoyed the last part of the tour, when
while traveling by mine car about halfway up the slope, the guide
stopped the cars to give the tourists a demonstration of just how
dark it could be inside a mine when there were no lights.
Unfortunately, for Jason, that part of the tour turned
unexpectedly into a very bad experience, one which he had not
anticipated and one he would likely never forget.

Jason had been in what he considered very dark places before,
and wrongly assumed that one dark place was the same as
another. But he had never imagined darkness as inky black as
what he experienced that day in the mine. With the flick of a
switch mounted on a heavy wooden timber the group was plunged
instantly into a state of darkness, the likes of which Jason had
never imagined; the complete absence of all light.

The tour guide explained through the blackness, in his thick
coal region accent, "Dis is wat dey mean wen day say 'pitch
daarrk'. Wen ya can't ev'n see yer hend in fronta yer face." Jason
was astonished by just how dark it was that far below the earth,
and suddenly he was surprised to find himself thinking about the
small graveyard he had found on their property.

Why he thought of it at this time he didn't understand, but he
couldn't prevent an image from forming inside his mind, as clearly
as if he were watching it take place right before his eyes. He
imagined himself being one of the decaying bodies of the young
boys confined inside of their rotting wooden coffins far below the
surface of his land, unable to speak, unable to move, yet somehow
completely aware. He had a realization that the darkness he was
experiencing in the mine was likely the same level darkness

present in the grave, and he began to feel as if he had been buried alive. His pulse began to quicken, as did his breathing, which started to come in short, uncomfortable gasps. And then his heart began to race as he broke out in a cold sweat. He could feel an uncontrollable claustrophobic sensation engulf him from head to toe and feared if he had to stay in the blackness of the mine much longer, his heart would explode inside his chest.

Just then, he felt something small and cold crawl insect-link across the top of his hand and Jason was certain a rat had made its way onto the car and was just seconds away from biting him with its disease-ridden teeth. He knew rats often could be found in dark, damp places such as mines. Then he heard a tiny voice whisper, "Hold my hand, Daddy. I'm scared." With relief and feeling a bit foolish, Jason realized what he had felt was Cindy tiny hand. She needed him, which meant he had no time for his own ridiculous imaginings. He held her hand gently in his and felt his own irrational fears began to quickly fade away.

Nevertheless, he was extremely thankful when the lights returned and the tour concluded. Jason was certain the entire time from the moment the lights went out until they came back on again couldn't have been more than twenty or thirty seconds, but it felt like an eternity to him. "Eternity," he thought to himself and once again imagined the bodies buried in the ground on their property. Those decaying remains would be confined to earth for eternity. And once he destroyed their grave markers as he planned, there would be no more record of them having ever existed. They would spend time without end trapped beneath the cold damp ground, until they became one with the earth. "Ashes to ashes," Jason thought.

"Are you ok?" Stephanie asked as they exited the mine car into the fading afternoon light. "You look a little pale."

Jason replied, "Ah...um...yes. Sure, honey. I'm fine. It just got a bit weird down there when the lights went out. Cindy got a little scared, but she was ok when I held her hand."

"You're a good dad," Stephanie said, and meant it as she reached over and kissed Jason on the cheek. She could also tell something else was on his mind, but if he didn't want to discuss it at this time, she wasn't going to push the issue. Besides, with all that had happened to them in the past twenty-four hours he could be dwelling on any number of things. He was however, acting a bit strange as he seemed to have acted back at the house earlier when he was standing in the field looking down at the dead fawn.

But what truly bothered Jason, was the fact that he was not normally claustrophobic, nor was he prone to wild thoughts like those he had experienced in the mine. He had never experienced the strange out-of-body sensations like he had felt back in the family graveyard either. And he knew although he had done everything he could to hide his discomfort, he could tell Stephanie had seen he was troubled. Jason suspected his problem was caused by the blackness in the mine being so incredibly intense it didn't take very long for his senses to begin to feel like he too was buried alive. The rest of the images were likely a result of his involuntary panic.

Thinking about coal mines in general, he could not imagine how anyone trapped in a mine cave-in could possibly keep from going insane. He had read newspaper accounts of mine accidents and cave-ins where miners had perished after being essentially buried alive. He believed such a death must be one of the worst possible ways to die.

Jason returned to the present as he opened the door to the barn, switched on the light and entered. He saw the bright and shiny John Deer tractor right where they had left it Saturday. In addition to the backhoe attachment, Jason saw the trailer cart attachment. He hooked the trailer up to the tractor, assuming it would make the job of transporting the small headstones a bit easier. He also planned to hook up the backhoe attachment if necessary after he found a suitable location to dig the hole where he would bury the soon-to-be broken up grave markers.

If he couldn't figure out how to use it, he would simply have to dig a hole by hand. As a precaution, Jason found a shovel and a large sledgehammer near the back of the barn, which he placed in the trailer cart. He also found a canvas tarpaulin, which he felt would work well to prevent his cargo from scratching the paint on the bed of the trailer. He wanted to keep any evidence of his activities at a minimum. Jason started up the tractor and eased it slowly out of the barn.

Chapter 19

As he sat atop the tractor, acclimating himself with its operation Jason thought again, with no small degree of guilt about how he had deceived Stephanie by not telling her he was coming up to the property today. She believed he was at the Ashton plant working out the final details of his promotion and subsequent transfer. Jason thought back to the previous Sunday when he and Stephanie had made up their minds to relocate their family to Ashton and about how they had spent most of that day making plans for the following week.

In the meantime, he said they could start to get things ready for their move. There were certainly plenty to do. Jason figured they could spend the two days packing some of their lesser-needed items into boxes to get a head start on moving. They would also have to contact moving companies for estimates as well as get in touch with a realtor about selling their Berks County townhouse.

Stephanie suggested they buy paint and spend the weekend gutting and repainting the master bedroom. She already had an idea of what her color scheme would be. "We can take out all that old junk and tear up the old, worn out carpeting," she suggested. "Then we can strip the walls and give the whole room a fresh coat of paint. We will worry about getting new flooring later but I think we could accomplish quite a bit in two days. I wish the kids were finished with school; if they were, we could head up Thursday and have four days to work. But they are not done until next Wednesday."

"There's no hurry," Jason said. "We still have to sell this place."

"I know. But I simply can't wait to see the house again." Stephanie replied. "I'm ready to move in tomorrow."

Then Jason asked, "If we are gutting and painting the master bedroom, where are we supposed to sleep Saturday night?"

"Well, there is no way I would sleep in that musty dark bedroom anyway. The answer is simple." Stephanie explained. "I'll share a bed with Cindy, and you can sleep with Jeremy."

"Ugh!" Jason replied. "Jeremy snores and kicks his feet in his sleep. That's why I haven't slept in the same bed with him since he was small."

Stephanie said, "Well if that doesn't work out there are plenty of sofas and large chairs around the place. You could always sleep in one of those."

"Well I guess you're right," Jason conceded. "Thursday morning after Sammy wakes up and is ready we can head into the home center and pick out what supplies we will need. But to be honest with you, I think you may be a bit ambitious with your plans for the weekend. We'll be lucky to get the bedroom cleaned out, let alone prepared and painted."

She replied smiling with understanding, "Yeah. I know. You're probably right. But I still would like to have the paint and stuff ready. Just in case."

"No problem," Jason said. "We can do all of that Thursday. Right now I have to think about getting everything ready for my visit to the Ashton plant on Wednesday."

Then Stephanie asked, "I don't suppose there is any way Sammy and I could come up with you on Wednesday morning is there?"

Jason knew at some point Stephanie was going to ask to come along and as such, he already had his reply prepared.

"No," Jason answered, perhaps a bit too quickly. Then he tried to backpedal by explaining. "You know I would love to take you both with me, but I have to be at the plant early, which means I will be out the door before any of you even wake up. Plus, you have to get the two older kids off to school and someone has to be here when they come home. I'm sorry, honey, but it's just not possible. I have to take this trip alone." Jason could see by the trusting look in her eyes she was buying whatever trumped-up story he was selling, and that fact alone made him feel even guiltier about the deception. But he kept reminding himself it was something that had to be done for the happiness and welfare of his family.

She asked, "Won't it drive you crazy to be so close to the house on Wednesday but not be able to stop by?"

Jason said, "No. Not really. I will have so much to do to get ready not only for the job transfer but also learning about my new responsibilities in Ashton that by the end of the day, my brain will be so fried the house will be the last thing on my mind."

Stephanie was always amazed at the way Jason could compartmentalize his life and his responsibilities. He had a natural tendency to categorize everything, put it into its own appropriate mental box and deal with it when required. She supposed that was how he was able to handle multiple projects and responsibilities so effectively. Stephanie found it mind-boggling how he could be in Ashton on business, just a few miles from their new and incredible house, yet he would have no interest in stopping by whatsoever, because this was not part of his plan for the day. Likewise, when he and the family went up to the house for the weekend, she knew he wouldn't even think about his new job or would never consider going anywhere near the Ashton plant, no matter how excited he might be about his new promotion.

It was as if Jason's brain was equipped with some sort of bank of switches he could turn on and off at will. Stephanie however, was the exact opposite. There was no way she could have dealt with being so close to the property and not have at least done a quick drive-by and maybe stop to take a few pictures with her cell phone. But not Jason; it was simply not his way. Then she suddenly got an idea.

Stephanie suggested, "Well why don't you stay overnight at the house Wednesday night and head back first thing Thursday morning? You are off from work anyway." Although she was sure, the inflexible Jason would probably not be interested in staying because it was not part of his current itinerary, she suggested it nonetheless.

"That might be a good idea," Jason said with very little enthusiasm, "But no. I don't think I will. I want my first night in the house to be with all of you. That will make it much more special." The fact of the matter was, Jason was certain after dealing with his unpleasant graveyard task at the house, the last thing he would want to do was be alone in the unfamiliar environment. He felt a cold chill race down his spine and did his best to ignore it. He didn't believe in ghosts or spirits and was not worried about the owners of the graves seeking vengeance against him for disturbing their rest, but the idea of his desecrating a gravesite then staying alone in the house on the same night just seemed a bit too creepy, even for him.

To Stephanie, Jason's was behaving as she predicted he would. She admired the way he smoothed over his refusal by suggesting it would be better if he spent the first night in the house with her and the kids. But she knew how his mind worked and his rejection of her idea was born more of his inflexibility rather than any desire to create a special family moment. She felt like saying, "Sometimes Jason, you can be so stubborn about things," but instead she chose to respond to his comment by saying, "Sometimes you are so sweet." And the she kissed him. She understood, on occasion, not being completely honest could be a good thing. However, had she known about Jason's true plans for that Wednesday, she likely would have thought much differently.

Truth be told, Jason knew he would likely be able to handle most if not all of his promotion and transfer paperwork over the corporate Intranet and there would be no business-related reason for him to travel to Ashton on Wednesday. He suspected he might have to do so at some point in time but what he had to do at this stage in the process didn't require a personal visit. The memory of their discussion faded as Jason's tractor passed the spa building.

Jason looked over at the hexagonal shaped building recalling the strange feeling he had experienced the previous Saturday. He would have sworn someone had been watching him although he knew it was not possible. He experienced so many strange unexplainable feelings that day, so he had pushed the sensation aside. Yet, now as his tractor passed the odd structure, the hair on the back of his neck began to tingle. He pressed down on the gas pedal, eager to get to his business.

As he bounded along the meadow, getting closer to the site of the graves, Jason recalled his previous two days of work. On Monday, as planned, Jason went to work and told Walter he would accept the promotion. Walt then instructed the personnel department to immediately begin processing the paperwork, including the application for relocation expenses. Jason figured he might as well take advantage of the cash regardless of the windfall Stephanie had received. Since he understood he would have to continue working anyway, he might as well accept all the benefits he could get. Walt offered to have the Ashton personnel department put him in touch with some local realtors the company often used. But Jason explained it wouldn't be necessary.

He briefly told Walt how Stephanie had been willed a house in the Ashton area, and they would be moving into that property as soon as possible. He deliberately neglected to mention the size or the opulence of the property and decided instead to let Walt make his own assumptions. Walter lived in the far western side of Lancaster County, almost into York County and although they had been friends, he doubted once the man retired he would ever see Walt again, especially with them moving so far north. He decided the less said about their inheritance the better.

"What a great coincidence," Walt said. "Stephanie gets a house in Ashton, right when you need it. That's amazing." Then Walt said, "But you're still going to need a realtor to sell your current house, won't you?" Then he quipped, "Or did someone with a bag of cash walk in off the street and offer to buy your house sight unseen?"

"No such luck," Jason said. "We'll need to find a realtor and put the place on the market. But I plan to use a local Reading area realtor for that business, and I can contact them on my own."

Then Walt reminded him, "Well, just be sure to keep copies of your closing costs and moving expenses because your new promotion entitles you to a refund for most of those types of expenditures."

Jason agreed to do so then reminded Walt of something he had said on the previous Friday. "Walt. Last Friday you told me if I took the job in Ashton I could take off this Wednesday through Friday to get some of my personal stuff straightened out for the move. Does that offer still stand?"

"By all means," Walter agreed. "As I said. If you can just cover for me while the folks from Ashton are here today and tomorrow, that won't be a problem."

Jason said, "Thanks, Walt. I appreciate that. By the way, who is coming down from Ashton today anyway?"

"Well..." Walt replied thinking, "as far as I know...the man you are replacing, Jim Dodson, as well as two of his engineers...who, now that I think about it, I suppose will very shortly be your engineers. One guy by the name of Brian Josephs and another named Ken Jackson. Do you know either of those guys?"

Jason felt a strange feeling in the pit of his stomach. For the first time he realized the two engineers who would be arriving shortly were going to be his subordinates within a matter of a few weeks. He had met all of the Ashton engineers at one time or another. He had gone out for drinks and pizza with most of them at some point in time, but that was as their equals, now things would be very different. It would be very strange to meet them again knowing he was going to be their boss and especially since he was told they had no knowledge of his upcoming promotional offer especially if they didn't know about it, which he assumed was the case.

Jason knew, Brian Josephs to be a good, hard-working technical non-political type of manufacturing engineer, concerned only with doing the best job possible. Jason suspected no matter whom his boss might be Brian would always do a good job. He was the sort of man one simply gave minimal instructions, pointed in the right direction then let him loose to solve the problem.

Ken Jackson, however, would be a different situation entirely. He was the senior manufacturing engineer and was likely the one who Jim Dodson had been grooming to take his place. He wouldn't be happy to learn Jason had taken a job, which he believed to be rightfully his. As Jason recalled, in addition to being good at his job, Ken was also a very political sort of animal. He was a local boy, born and raised in Schuylkill County with many local friends in the area. He knew how the system at Ashton worked and how to get what he needed. If any of the Ashton engineers were to end up being a problem for him, it would likely be Ken.

Jason hoped once his promotion was announced, Ken might become angry enough to leave the company and seek employment elsewhere. But Jason also understood the economic conditions in the country, not to mention in the job-starved area in and around Schuylkill County. He would likely end up stuck with Ken and would have to find a way to deal with him. Jason decided if possible, since Walter was leading the tour, he would keep a low profile and try to avoid any interaction with the group for the present. It was all so strange and uncomfortable for him. He managed to keep himself busy and was able to avoid the group on Monday.

But on Tuesday, Jason was required to sit in on a meeting with Walt and the Ashton group to discuss various technical aspects of the many pieces of equipment on their list for transfer. It was a bit awkward for Jason as well as the other engineers, but they all did their best to focus on the job at hand and Jason avoided eye contact as much as possible. Jason did notice Jim Dodson look at him several times in an appraising fashion. He assumed Jim was aware by now of Jason's acceptance of the job and that Dodson might comparing Jason to his own choice for his replacement, wondering if Jason measured up to his expectations.

Jason left that image drift from his mind as the tractor pulled alongside the copse of tall grass and weeds where he had discovered the burial sites of the two young boys while visiting the property the previous Saturday. He positioned the tractor so the cart was directly in front of the thicket and the tractor itself was blocking any view of the area from the house. He was quite certain none of the workers could see him from any of the windows due to the position of the barn and the spa buildings, but he wanted to be sure if anyone decided to walk out to speak to him he could have his activities hidden from their approach. He had instructed them to call him on his cell if they needed to speak to him, but in his experience most people often tended do whatever they wanted, no matter what instructions they might have been given.

With great trepidation, Jason stepped from the tractor onto the grass then up over the tall grass and into the family graveyard.

Chapter 20

As Jason's feet touch ground on the burial site, he felt a strange sensation, the likes of which he hadn't experienced the first time he entered the same area on the previous Saturday. Although his experience that day wasn't quite clear in his memory, Jason recalled how it had been surreal and possibly disturbing for him. A similar feeling was now overtaking him. Yet it was different, unlike anything he had ever encountered before. His entire body felt as if it were straining to move against some sort of current or force, which seemed to turn the very air around him into a gelatinous substance.

Jason forced his head to look downward, not wanting to trip and fall during what had suddenly become a painstakingly slow progression, fearing that doing so might cause him to hover helplessly in the liquid atmosphere not being able to regain his footing. As he looked down, he saw the remains of the dead fawn, now all but completely gone, save for the blanched bones and a few random tufts of hair. He was uncertain why everything around him seemed so strange and surreal, but the rational part of his mind chalked it up to a combination of discomfort at the ghoulish task awaiting him and perhaps an active imagination, which he realized was apparently working overtime.

He was certain if he could just keep moving forward for another moment or so, everything would be fine, the strange almost hypnotic spell would pass and he would return to normal. However, for the moment, he was certain something was definitely wrong. Then, as if to accentuate that very fact, the temperature on the bright sunny morning seemed to have dropped over thirty degrees and the light faded all around him to a dull gray, sending icy chills throughout his body. He noticed a foul stench; deep, woodsy and feral, like that of a wild animal. There was also another underlying smell, perhaps that of decomposition. He felt as if this were not simply the result of the rotting carcass of the fawn, but was something else, something much worse; something coming up from deep within the very soil of this strange place. The feeling caused him to sense a terror deep down in the pit of his stomach.

Then as he had hoped, after a few seconds and a few more challenging steps forward, he was able to once again move normally as the light returned and the temperature rose around him to where it should have been on such a lovely spring morning. Likewise, the rancid stench had disappeared almost completely.

Jason was suddenly reminded of an experience from his childhood. He had always been terrified of funeral parlors and the idea of dead bodies being laid out for display inside. One day, one of his friends whose uncle was a mortician called Jason and asked him to meet him at his uncle's funeral home, the plan being they would meet there then head to a local park to hang out. Jason was about nine or ten years old at the time.

He recalled standing at the front door of the funeral home with his hand on the door, frightened beyond reason and unable to pull it open. It was as if some genetic primitive survival mechanism built into his brain would not permit him to pull the handle. After a few tense moments, when he finally gathered the courage to pull and the large wooden and leaded glass door slowly opened a few inches, his senses were accosted with the overpowering smell of funeral flowers.

One would normally think such an aroma might be pleasant and calming, but not for young Jason Wright. The odor, which was actually a combination of many different types of flowers that had spent the day filling the funeral home with their various blended scents, seemed to Jason to be a vile and revolting stench, which when he opened the door hit him like a baseball bat to the face. This repulsive stink caused his young stomach to turn over with revulsion. Instead of the aroma of pleasing flowers, Jason's senses had been bombarded with the smells of rotting, decaying vegetation. His mind was filled with the image of an unrecognizable pile of putrid sludge, infested with worms and other crawling insects. To Jason, the rotting mass was representative of the same type of decomposition that would eventually overtake the current resident of the funeral parlor once he or she was put deep into the ground.

At first the young boy felt as if he might pass out from the offensive wall of reek, then he thought he might vomit. Instead, he stood staring into the darkness of the interior of the funeral parlor while the invisible barrier of fumes surrounded his face and blocked his entry, terrifying him to the very core of his young soul.

Jason had been certain if he tried to pass through that transparent wall of noxious vapors, the air might have felt thick and perhaps liquidy or gelatinous. Young Jason knew if he tried to enter the funeral parlor, the festering floral putrefaction would surround him like an invisible nest of living, deadly vines as it suffocating tendrils wrapped tightly about him in a final grip of death.

He imagined long, thin, serpentine fingers of unseen stench, crawling up into his nostrils, their slimy essence stealing slowly into his skull and penetrating his brain, while still other crept downward into his throat, eventually cutting off his air supply before slithering further down into his stomach, where they would begin to devour him from the inside out.

Overcome with terror, the young boy immediately turned and fled from the horrifying house of the dead, forgetting completely about his friend and not even caring if he ever saw him or the dreaded funeral parlor again. He recalled how when he had been running madly from the building he could have sworn he heard a voice inside his head calling him to come back and face his fate. But he refused to even turn around as he fled in terror.

Jason suddenly found himself alert and surprised that he had not run from this latest strange sensation but had somehow been able to rise to the challenge and make it past the strange barrier, that is to say, if there actually had been such an obstruction. Now safely on the other side, he was unsure of what, if anything he had just encountered.

He turned slowly and he looked behind him. It honestly felt to Jason as if he really had passed through some type of invisible barrier in which the air was thick and impossibly semi-solid and almost pliable. Now safely on the opposite side of the strange passage, Jason began to wonder if he would ever be able to return through it with the tombstones or if he might never again be able to penetrate the blockade. Suppose he had passed into some sort of alternative dimension? Suppose he was no longer in his own world?

He had a momentary attack of anxiety, imagining himself trapped behind the barrier like an animal in a cage unable to get back to his world. And if he were trapped, would he ever be found? He wondered what someone on the opposite side of the transparent wall would see, if anything. Might they see him trapped on the other side or would they see nothing? He could see the tractor and trailer right where he had left them. He began to be overcome by panic. He questioned if he might spend the rest of his life, or perhaps eternity, in some strange alternate dimension where he would be able to look though the invisible wall and see his family living their lives on the other side but they would never be able to see or hear him.

He couldn't wait any longer. He had to find out immediately. Jason reached his hand in the direction of the place where he believed the obstruction had been, expecting his fingers to sink deep into what he suddenly thought of as the gelat-mosphere and feel the icy cold encompass his hand. However, he was pleasantly surprised to find nothing. Whatever that previous sensation had been, real or imagined, it was now completely gone.

Jason shook his head as if trying to clear away the residual cobwebs of some strange disorienting dream. He felt as if he had just had a bizarre hallucination, one so detailed, so authentic it seemed to be completely real. But he knew such things could never actually occur. It was obviously some sort of strange spell or perhaps a type of seizure. He would have to be careful and watch for any other signs of such peculiar activity, as it might mean the onset of a serious medical condition.

He walked cautiously forward and after finding what he was looking for, knelt to examine the two small gravestones once again. As he had seen five days earlier, the first stone read "Matthew James Livingston, June 12, 1916 - December 19, 1922". And the second inscription said Charles Edward Livingston July 2, 1918 - December 19 1922". Then he reread the identical cryptic addendum carved into each small stone, "Taken From Us Too Soon, By The Hand Of Evil."

"Boy one and boy two," Jason spoke aloud. Then he said, "I suppose if you had lived, you two would have been great uncles to my wife, Stephanie. I wonder why it was you both died so young and on the same day; and also what this strange inscription might mean."

He looked about and found a few other gravestones, six of them. They were so thin, old and worn that none of the inscriptions could even be read. It seemed to Jason, that perhaps several hundred years had pass since the time the last person was buried in the plot, and the time almost a hundred years earlier when the two boys had been laid to rest in the graveyard. He realized it was more than likely the occupants of the other graves were not even related to Stephanie's family but were put here by previous owners of the land.

As he recalled from his conversation with the lawyer on the previous Saturday, the Livingstons had purchased the farm from someone else and were likely the first of her relatives to own the property. Whatever the case, the inhabitants were unidentifiable.

"Well. I suppose no harm, no foul." Jason said, "If I can't tell who these stones belong to then I suppose they don't belong to anyone." Then he thought of the old adage about the tree falling in the forest with no one there to hear it and thought "If a body is buried in the field and no one knows it is buried there, is it really there?" Then after a moment's hesitation he said, "Nope. Not as far as I am concerned it isn't."

He bent down and picked up one of the unreadable headstone finding it to not be as heavy as he might have expected and easily carried it over to the tractor, placing it gently down on the tarp he had laid across the bed of the truck. Each time he passed by the grassy edge of the cemetery, he expected to encounter the strange barrier, but for whatever reason, it never returned. In several trips, Jason had picked up the remaining illegible stones as well as the Livingston boys' markers, and placed them in the trailer. Once he was confident all of the stones had been removed, he looked around him and discovered something he had not seen earlier.

The remnants of what appeared to be a low stone wall surrounded the gravesite. After a closer examination, he decided it was hardly a wall in any normal sense of the word, although at one time it might have been. It was actually just a rectangular border of a few carefully placed stones, now spaced far apart, which he assumed were put there at the time of the boys' burial to separate the site from the rest of the area near the edge of the forest. Obviously, during the past several centuries, most of the stones had somehow disappeared, leaving only a few remaining, enough to indicate the former presence of the wall. Perhaps the wall's original purpose was to protect the site from disturbance of any future farming which might take place or perhaps it might have simply been a makeshift way for some grieving relatives to mark the location of their family plot. Regardless of the reason for the wall's existence, Jason decided it would be best to remove these stones as well. He had no desire for the area to even slightly resemble its original purpose.

Then he had a strange thought. Why had the two boys been the only members of the Livingston family to be buried in the cemetery alongside the graves of strangers? Where were their parents laid to rest? Shouldn't they also have been buried here in the family graveyard? It all seemed so very strange to Jason. Then with a pain in the pit of his stomach, Jason realized he was going to have to look around the rest of the property to make sure this was the only burial site present. The thought of a second or even third site was something he didn't want to consider.

After placing the last of the stones in the back of the trailer, and covering them with the tarpaulin to shield them from the potentially curious eyes of the security system installers, Jason decided he would drive along the back perimeter of the property to see if he could both find a suitable place to breakup and discard the headstones. He also needed to see if he could locate any other burial plots; he hoped against hope that he would find no more.

He climbed into the seat of the tractor and looked across the expanse of the field preparing to head off to the left. Then he would eventually make a complete circle of the property and finally returned to this point of origin. With any luck, by that time he would have successfully disposed of the tombstones in a safe and unidentifiable location.

He drove slowly along the periphery of the field looking over toward the woods, which surrounded the property on his right. After a few hundred feet, he stopped the tractor seeing something in the distance he hoped he was only imagining. "What the hell is HE doing here?" Jason said angrily to himself.

Far off in the distance from where the tractor sat idling Jason saw the shape of a man in a business suit, standing near the back of the property up on a slight rise similar to the one where he had found the grave markers. He was certain even from this distance it was that lawyer, H. Mason Armstrong; his rotund shape unmistakable. Jason suddenly became furious at the sight of the man. He had suspected the lawyer was going to be trouble from the very beginning. Armstrong had no right to be roaming around their property yet there he was, just as Jason had feared might happen.

Oddly, the lawyer didn't wave to him or acknowledge him in any way; he only stood, stock still, staring at Jason as if in some strange trance-like state. "Well. I suppose now I'll have to go over there, and set this guy straight about a few things," Jason said to himself. "I was hoping to avoid any such confrontation with the guy, but I guess he has left me little choice. Pushy damned lawyers. It looks like it's time for a 'come to Jesus' meeting, my fat little friend."

Not wanting the lawyer to see the cargo he carried in the back of the trailer, Jason got down from the tractor and strode purposefully toward the site where the lawyer stood. "Armstrong!" Jason shouted and he walked. "What the hell are you doing here? I didn't ask you to come out here!" The closer he got to the man the angrier he became. Not paying attention to where he was walking, Jason stumbled over a hole in the field and fell face first. Luckily as the ground came flying up to meet him, he was able to twist and roll to deflect most of the impact. The result was he didn't receive any serious injury, just a bit of embarrassment and perhaps a bruised ego. He imagined the lawyer chuckling to himself over his clumsiness. This only served to further fuel his rage.

As Jason slowly got back to his feet, he looked over to the place where the lawyer had stood and was surprised to see he was no longer there. "What the hell!" he said. "Where did he go?" Jason could see a large expanse of the field to the left of the lawyer as well as a substantial distance before it ended at the adjoining woodlands. He doubted that Armstrong, with his unhealthy bulk, could have possibly run or even walked fast enough to reach either the house or the woods so quickly; so where had the man gone?

With the lawyer now apparently out of the picture, Jason turned and walked back to the tractor, making a mental note of the location of the place where the lawyer had been. He started the engine and continued along the property for a few hundred yards until he came to the spot where he had seen Armstrong standing. This appeared to be as good a spot as any for getting rid of the stones. It was not visible from the house since its view was blocked by one of the outbuildings.

Jason walked over to the place where he had seen the lawyer standing, a bit more slowly this time being careful not to fall and risk further potential injury or embarrassment. His temper had begun to subside and he was once again able to think more clearly. Fortunately, he had changed from his office clothing into work clothing before the security team had arrived. He would have been hard-pressed to explain to Stephanie how he had gotten field dirt and grass stains on his good pants. When he reached the place where Armstrong had stood, he was surprised to not find a single trace the man had ever been there. No grass was trampled or disturbed in any way. Jason thought, surly a man of Armstrong's weight and size would have had to make shoe impressions in the dew-moist morning grass, yet not a single blade of grass was disturbed. He had no idea how such a thing could possibly be. And where had the man gone?

Looking about the area for any trace of the attorney, Jason saw something dark reflecting in the morning sunlight. As he approached, he discovered two objects. He could tell immediately by their shapes they were more gravestones. Both of the markers had fallen down and were lying on their backs in the moist soil. "Damn!" Jason said aloud in frustration. "Not another graveyard!" For the second time that day he was reminded of the name "Fallen Stones".

He then realized he had not actually found another graveyard but had only found two additional grave markers. These two appeared to be alone out in this isolated area of the yard, far removed from what one might think of as the official family burial location. This seemed almost as if to indicate a purposeful shunning of the inhabitants of these graves; like someone had deliberately segregated them from the others. He recalled hearing stories of how many years ago suicide victims were often buried away from church cemeteries so that would not be permitted to lie in hallowed ground. Perhaps this was the case for these people buried below this soil.

Jason also continued to speculate about the lawyer. What had Armstrong been doing hanging around his property, not to mention that particular area? It would really put a kink in his plan to keep the existence of the graves secret if Armstrong knew about them. There was always the risk he might say something to Stephanie. Maybe the lawyer would try to extort money from Jason in order to keep his secret. Jason decided sometime soon he would have to speak to the lawyer in private and make sure he had no choice but to forget anything he knew about the headstones. He would likely have to bring up attorney-client privilege and maybe threaten to file a complaint with the bar association or some similar professional ethics board if necessary.

Whatever the outcome, the lawyer was at least gone for the moment. Jason decided he might as well get rid of these stones along with the others all at the same time. He knelt down to read the inscription on the first marker and was shocked to read the name which although well-worn was still legible. The caption read: "Dwight Charles Livingston July 23, 1890 – December 19, 1922. Devoted Husband, Loving Father, Tragically Taken In The Prime Of Life"

"Dwight Livingston?" Jason said aloud. "That was the name Armstrong used for Stephanie's great grandfather when he showed us that wedding portrait." He recalled how Livingston had been the man who built the original farmhouse for his family and how much he so strongly resembled Jason. Then Jason thought of Livingston's wife, the one who look like Stephanie. Her name had been Margaret or Mildred or something like that.

"Marie!" Jason shouted in recollection. Then he knelt down to study the inscription on the other tombstone sensing it had to be Marie's but not being even close to prepared for what he would find carved on it. He read it aloud, "Marie Louise O'Hara Livingston June 6, 1892 – December 19, 1922... May Her Wretched Soul Rot...In The Bowels Of Hell...For Eternity" He stared dumfounded as an icy chill ran down the middle of his back. Suddenly the cool morning seemed unseasonably cold as if a sudden breeze had arisen, though Jason was oblivious to its effect.

Chapter 21

Recovering somewhat from the strange sensation, Jason noticed that both Dwight and Marie Livingston died in the same year 1922. "Now wait a second!" He said realizing for the first time that not only had they both died in the same year, but on the exact same day. "Whoa, hold your horses!" he blurted out suddenly remembering yet another piece to the strange puzzle.

Without hesitation, he walked over to the cart, pulled back the tarp and re-read the inscriptions on the two boys' headstones. One said "Matthew James Livingston, June 12, 1916 - December 19, 1922". And the other said Charles Edward Livingston July 2, 1918 - December 19 1922". Then he read the identical chilling message on each stone, "Taken From Us Too Soon, By The Hand Of Evil."

Not only had both boys died on the same day, but the parents had died as well. An entire family wiped out in one tragic event. But then he realized that assumption couldn't have been correct. Even if both parents and two children had somehow died in some horrible catastrophe, the whole family could not have been killed. A brother or sister of the boys must have survived in order to carry on the family lineage. He recalled Stephanie mentioning she had a grandmother named Sarah. Perhaps the surviving child had been a girl. Otherwise Stephanie never would have been born. Still, the entire situation was quite disturbing. "Four dead on the same day." He said aloud, "And what's with these strange messages?"

He was now unconsciously thinking and speaking aloud. "The boys' stones talked about their being 'taken by the hand of evil' and Marie's stone accused her of being wicked enough for her to 'rot in Hell for eternity'. And Dwight's said he too was 'tragically taken in the prime of life'. What could all this mean? What in the world could have happened to them?" Jason suddenly comprehended there was a real mystery existing within Stephanie's family, the knowledge of which might bring great distress to his wife not to mention would cast a dark pall over the joy she now felt from receiving the inheritance.

Jason also understood he was definitely going to have to talk to Armstrong about keeping his big fat lawyer mouth shut. He was first going to have the man disclose everything he knew about the family history. Then he was going to swear him to secrecy. But before that, he was going to have to make sure these stones were all destroyed and buried and would never be seen again. He walked about ten feet to the left of the place where he found the Livingston parents' stones; not wanting to inadvertently disturb any possible resting place and grabbing a pointed shovel began to dig a hole.

He was surprised at the soft, almost sand-like quality of the soil. This surely was fertile farmland. He was accustomed to the primarily clay soil of his townhouse development. He had heard somewhere that sometimes when builders plan subdivisions they scrape off all the prime topsoil until they get to the virtually worthless clay base level below. Then they come back and spread a measly foot or less of low-grade topsoil after all the houses have been constructed and then quickly hydro seed the lawns to make the properties look green and lush, when in reality they are sitting on infertile mounds of clay with a light veneer of topsoil. The developer then sells of the remaining tonnage of good topsoil for a substantial profit.

This was not the case with their land however. The soil was dark, rich, and his spade cut through it, like a knife through butter. Within a few minutes he had a substantial hole dug, a hole more than adequate to bury the remains of the soon to be crushed headstones. "Remains?" he thought for a moment, then felt the return of the chill he had felt earlier.

Not wanting to take time to dwell on his discomfort, Jason put on a pair of safety glasses then walked over to the cart and retrieved two of the tombstones whose names could not be identified. He placed them on the ground and suspended between Dwight and Marie's fallen stones. Next he grabbed the sledge hammer from the back of the cart and raising it high above his head, prepared to bring it down on the stones.

For a moment, he seemed to freeze in place, the sledgehammer hanging motionless in the air above him. The entire hesitation lasted no more than a second or two, but in that brief period, Jason had a horrifying vision, which seemed to go on for an incredibly long time. The daydream started with Jason seeing himself completing the swing of the hammer and the small and fragile tombstone breaking into a thousand pieces as the sledgehammer fell to the ground.

Then the sky began to darken and the wind whipped into a frenzy of blowing dirt, grass and other such debris. Jason stood terrified among the flying maelstrom, his arms hanging limply down at his sides, helpless to do anything. Then the ground at his feet started to move and undulate, as to his horror, he saw bony fleshless fingers working their way up from beneath the earth below.

Soon two sets of skeletal hands were reaching up from the ground and had grabbed Jason by the ankles. He still was unable to move or resist as the bony claws gripped him ever tighter. He looked down and saw the tops of two skulls rising from the shifting soil, both almost hairless save for a few remaining patches of flesh and white thinned follicles, which blew wildly in the torrential wind. Soon both skulls were out of the ground and looking up at Jason through eyeless sockets, yet he knew they were still somehow seeing him.

Dirt fell like sand from the tops of the skeletal heads as they rose further. Jason could now see their mouths and jaws, which were rapidly opening, and closing like sets of chattering teeth, but there was nothing comical about those mouths. They had seemed to be hungry for something or someone and Jason was certain he was the subject of their cannibalistic desires.

Worms crawled from the hollow eye sockets and at one point Jason saw a long slithering snake try to work its way past the snapping jaws. Razor sharp teeth severed the snake's head and a sickening green goop poured from its decapitated body, which fell back inside the skeleton's mouth. Then Jason saw the two heads once again slowly begin to sink back down into the earth and felt an even stronger tugging on his ankles.

He looked at his feet and saw they were beginning to follow the sinking skulls down into the soft earth. He realized he was being pulled into the ground by the impossibly reanimated undead remains of Dwight and Marie Livingston. Soon he would be joining them deep in the cold earth where he would spend eternity among the rotting corpses.

The sledgehammer came down with a crash easily shattering the gravestones into several smaller pieces. Jason stopped for a moment looking around and then down at his feet certain something bad was about to happen. He could not recall the waking nightmare he had just experienced, but by the cold sensation he felt flowing throughout his body and the way the hair on the back of his neck stood on end, he knew something must be wrong. Jason looked all around him as if anticipating something to happen but nothing did. The sun continued to shine, the air was still and he could hear birds chirping in the nearby trees. So, he reluctantly and with a degree of caution continued with his work.

He repeated the smashing process for the remainder of the stones, including those of the two boys. Then he leaned both

Dwight and Marie's tombstones on the accumulated pile of broken markers and proceeded to break them up beyond recognition as well. When they were all shattered to bits, he shoveled the broken pieces into the large hole he had dug. The he covered them with soil, refilling the hole.

As he stepped back to check out his work, he couldn't help but notice how the mound of dirt looked uncomfortably like a freshly dug grave. Fortunately, he had planned ahead, and had kept the upper layer of topsoil, which he had removed in clumps that were held together by weeds and plants. He tamped down the mound with the back of the shovel then replaced the clumps of weedy soil on top. Jason was pleased with his work. Even from his close proximity, he found it difficult to see where he had buried the stones. He suspected, by the time he and his family moved onto the property, more weeds and grass would spring up making it completely indiscernible from the rest of the ground. Maybe if he did a good enough job, he wouldn't be able to find the spot himself, although he somehow suspected he might never be fortunate enough to forget its location.

With his work finished, he wiped the sweat from his brow, brushed the dust from his jeans and prepared to clean and return all the equipment to the barn. Then he planned to go into the house, shower and change into office clothes, in preparation for his return trip home. First, he would complete the planned circle of the property just to make certain there were no more stones anywhere.

He realized he would have some time to kill so he decided taking a trip to see H. Mason Armstrong might be in order. It was time he and the lawyer set some ground rules about the property. Just thinking about the man, made Jason's anger begin to rise once more. He hoped he could control his temper when he spoke to the lawyer face to face.

As he placed the last tool in the cart and was getting ready to start the tractor, his cell phone rang. He looked down at the caller ID and saw it was Stephanie. He took a moment to compose himself and to be ready for any questions she might have regarding his supposed business trip. Then he pressed the answer button.

"Hey, Steph," Jason said. "What's up?"

She replied with a troubled tone in her voice. "Oh, Jason. I'm so sorry to bother you at work, but I had to call you."

"Is everything alright, you sound worried?" Jason asked.

"Yes...well no...not exactly," Stephanie replied. Then she hesitated for a moment and noted, "Jason, it sounds like you are outside."

Thinking quickly, Jason said, surprising himself with how easily he could come up with a lie, "Um...well, yes...I am. I was walking through the shop when I felt my phone vibrate. It was much too noisy in there, so I walked outside so I could hear you better. Plus I suspect the cell reception is much better out here than inside. Anyway, that's not important. What's the matter?"

She said without preamble, "I had an upsetting call this morning...from Mason Armstrong's office."

Jason thought silently, "Oh, great. That damned lawyer called to rat me out already, before I even had a chance to talk to him." Then with a tone of frustration Jason asked, "Well...what did he want? I thought everything we had to do with him was taken care of." Jason thought about how less than an hour earlier he had seen the man standing staring at him from the spot where he found the Livingston's headstones. He was trying to prepare himself for whatever was to come next. He suspected, depending upon what Armstrong had told her, he might have to come clean about where he actually was and perhaps even what he was doing.

"It wasn't Mason that called Jason." Stephanie explained, "It was his secretary, a woman named Mrs. Flannery."

"Mrs. Flannery? His secretary? What? I don't understand." He as a bit confused as he was unaware the lawyer had a secretary. "What...what did she want?" he questioned.

Stephanie hesitated for a moment then exclaimed, her voice breaking, "He's dead, Jason. Mason's dead."

Struck with shock and disbelief, Jason asked, "Dead? What do you mean he's dead? I just...." He stopped himself just short of blurting out how he just saw the lawyer that very morning, but luckily, he managed to catch himself. "I...just...can't believe it...I mean when, how...what happened?"

"Mrs. Flannery said he must have been working late on Sunday evening, and he apparently had a massive heart attack. She found him in his office dead in his chair, when she reported for work Monday morning. It must have been horrible. His computer was still turned on. She could hardly talk about it," Stephanie explained.

Jason stood shocked unable to reply at first. He would have sworn under oath in a court of law that he had seen the lawyer standing in his field, but now he knew it was impossible. Who had it been? Who had been standing out there staring at him? He was certain it was Armstrong. But then again, he had been certain he had walked through a strange gelatinous transparent barrier earlier when approaching the graveyard. But then he later found it had not actually been there. And now that he thought about it, hadn't he been feeling a bit strange and perhaps out of sorts all morning? Maybe he was coming down with some sort of spring flu or something. The more the thought, the more he was beginning to believe it must be so.

"Jason? Honey, are you still there?" Stephanie asked from the cell phone. Jason realized he had been standing for a few moments and had not said a word.

"Um...yes...I'm...I'm...h...h...here..." he stammered. "I'm sorry, Steph... This just all caught me...you know...by surprise, is all. "

She replied, "I know exactly what you mean. I probably wouldn't have even bothered you and would have waited until you got home but...well, I guess I needed to hear your voice and know everything was ok...you know what I mean? I guess it's just all so disturbing for me."

He understood completely. She was fifty miles away and alone with the baby trying to deal with all of the latest life changing events. Then to have her stress compounded with the news of the lawyer's death. He knew what she needed. She needed her husband. He looked down at his watch and saw that it was almost 1:00 pm. He said, "Look, Steph. I'm almost finished here. I'm going to wrap things up and head right home a little early. Whatever is left can wait until another day. I should be home by two thirty or so."

"Oh, Jason, you are so sweet. But I really didn't mean to mess up your work schedule today. Look, why don't you just finish your day, and I will see you around five. I'll be ok, I'm sure."

He replied, "I'm sure you would be fine, but I think I really want to come home to be with you. Also, to be honest, I have not been feeling like myself all morning. I feel like I might be coming down with some sort of flu or bug or something. My head is feeling really heavy and strange, you know, like right before you get sick. I may just be tired or stressed and need to rest. There has been an awful lot going on in the past week. Anyway, I'm going to head home shortly and if I still feel this bad tomorrow we'll cancel our shopping plans and just take it easy for a day."

"Ok, I suppose. Just please be careful driving home, especially if you're not feeling well," she encouraged.

"Don't worry, Steph. I promise I will and I'll tell you what. I'll give you a few calls along the way so you'll know I'm fine. Deal?"

"Deal," she said reluctantly. "Love you."

"I love you too, sweetheart. And I'll see you shortly," Jason replied.

Jason quickly completed his circle of the property but didn't find any more graveyards or tombstones. Then he put his yard equipment away in the barn and walked back to the house where he informed the security company workers he had to leave on a family emergency. The owner had stopped back to check on their progress and was still there when Jason returned to the house. He said they were on schedule and would have the system completed by the end of the day.

They agreed they would stop back on Saturday afternoon to show Jason and Stephanie how the system functioned and give them a brief training session. Jason had already planned on telling Stephanie he had contacted the firm and gave them access to the house, but he would not say that he had been present. Then he thought of something else.

"And Bob?" Jason asked the owner of the security company. "Could you or whichever of your workers comes back on Saturday for the training not mention I was here today? I wanted this to be a surprise and if I told my wife I was up here today without her, surprise or not, she would have a fit. She is dying to come up here to see the house again. So unless you want me be spending more time in the doghouse than in this house, I would appreciate you not saying anything."

"Not a problem, Mr. Wright," Bob said. "In fact, I will be sending someone up on Saturday who isn't even here today, so he won't have any prior knowledge of today's events whatsoever. We have a gentleman who specializes in customer training. In fact, he is out doing several training sessions today. "

"That will be perfect," Jason said with satisfaction. "Thank you so much for everything, for getting here so quickly and for doing such an excellent job."

Bob replied, "It was our pleasure. And thank you for your business. If you don't mind, I would like to leave you a few brochures with information about all the security based services we offer."

"Absolutely," Jason said, "And for now, just leave the security system inactive. We will activate it on Saturday when your man arrives for the training." Although Jason still wanted the house protected by the system at some point soon, he felt now that Armstrong was out of the picture that was one less problem he had to contend with. The lawyer would likely be too busy knocking on the pearly gates to have time to prowl around their property any longer.

Jason got in his car, which he had left parked in the driveway in front of one of the garage bays and looped around the fountain to head down the driveway and home. As he passed the front of the house, he thought he saw someone at the end of the field near the woods, but when he stopped the car and looked in that direction again, no one was there. The chill returned to creep with icy claws once again down Jason's back and his stomach began to knot. He could see plainly that no one was there, but for a moment, just for the briefest of moments, he thought he had impossibly seen the dead lawyer standing and watching him from the place where he had buried the broken gravestones. The man seemed to have been staring vacantly with lost and mournful eyes.

Chapter 22

On a bright sunny morning near the end of June, Stephanie woke up feeling especially contented. The sun was streaming in though the wall of windows in the master bedroom and the day had showed potential of being a good one. The recently redecorated room was bright and pleasant in direct contrast to the dark conditions, which had originally defined the space. Likewise, gone were the gloomy antique furnishings, replaced with a brand new bedroom ensemble.

She looked over at the clock on her nightstand. Since moving to the new house, she had replaced her former alarm clock with its overly bright eerie blue glow and had purchased one with a more subdued crimson display. She couldn't recall what it was about the blue lighting that bothered her so much, but she knew she had to get rid of it.

Looking at the display, she saw it was still quite early, only 7:30. Jason had already left for work but by the lack of sound in the house, she could tell the kids were still sleeping. Jeremy and Sammy's rooms were windowless, as any windows would have only looked out into the atrium. She and Jason were considering a modification to add such windows at some point in the future. She looked at the clock again and sighed, knowing it wouldn't be long until Sammy began to stir and then the other kids would surely follow.

After lying in bed and basking in the glorious silence for a few heavenly moments longer, Stephanie decided to get up and shower so she would be ready when it came time to corral the kids and get them ready to go. She wanted to make a trip into Ashton to the grocery store. They had made a family shopping trip about two weeks earlier, but it was way past time to make another, as the cupboards were getting bare. Jason had kept them in staples by making quick stops periodically on his way home from work. His plant was only about a quarter of a mile from the local supermarket.

And although she did appreciate him stopping and getting whatever they required, he had been working long hours and many weekends trying to get up to speed in his new job and Stephanie hated to ask him. Plus, she really wanted to get out and explore the area at a slower and more relaxed pace. Although there was not much in the line of shopping in town, there were a few scattered stores and restaurants, which she had never taken the opportunity to investigate. She knew Jeremy might complain a bit at first but once she told them they would be going out for breakfast at Maggie's Restaurant before heading down to the supermarket; she assumed he would come around.

Jeremy had eaten there once on a father and son outing with Jason shortly after they moved into the house and had come home praising the pancakes, sausage and hash browns he enjoyed for breakfast. Since that time they had never found the opportunity to return, so it looked like today might be as good a time as any. Neither she nor Cindy had ever had the pleasure of dining at Maggie's and although she was not normally a big breakfast eater, she looked forward to checking out the place.

Then she planned to drive around town for a bit to get a feel for the local color before heading to the grocery store located at the lower end of town. She decided to make it her last stop so she wouldn't have to worry about the perishable items spoiling before getting them into her refrigerator. She figured she could get everything done and be home by lunch. The day looked like a promising one weather-wise, so she and the kids would likely want to spend the afternoon in the pool.

She had finally started working on her children's book again, but lately found it difficult to find the time. She did what she could when she was able, but with Jason's schedule, it was often difficult to be alone long enough to do so. The important thing was she was making progress.

An hour or so later the kids were all awake, dressed and loaded into the van, and they were heading to Ashton for breakfast. As they approached the town, Stephanie realized something she knew Jason had once told her but she hadn't paid much attention to previously, which was that Ashton had something of an unusual appearance.

The town itself was situated along the side of a continuously climbing hill. The main street in town was known as Centre Street and ran from it eastern end at the bottom of the hill to its far western end at the top for a distance of about a mile or so. At the western side, located at the crest of the hill was Maggie's Restaurant, which occupied a corner building formed from what were once two wood-framed row houses. The town was made up of hundreds of similar two and three story structures ranging from eleven to twenty feet wide; left over remnants from the turn of the twentieth century days when coal companies built the original structures to accommodate their employees, most of whom were European immigrants. Stephanie learned they had once been called "company houses" for that very reason.

As they stood in front of the restaurant, Stephanie noticed for the first time a sign at the intersection of Centre Street and another perpendicular road reading "Cantrania 3". She had heard of that town before. In fact it had made national news because of a mine fire which had been burning beneath it since the nineteen sixties. She had forgotten it was so close to Ashton. As she recalled, the entire town had to be demolished because of the unsafe conditions the fire had caused. Stephanie had read one article about a boy who fell into a sinkhole in his back yard and would have died had he not been able to grab onto some tree roots and pull himself free. This was the first time the fire made the news in a big way and put the town in to the national spotlight. She believed she had read that later, other homes became uninhabitable due to lethal mine gas. She decided if they had time today, maybe she and the kids would take a trip to Cantrania to see what the place looked like now.

On the large front window of the building where they stood was a sign whose letters were worn but still legible, spelling out "MAGGIE'S RESTAURANT". Inside the restaurant, a group of apparently regular patrons sat eating breakfast while engaging in boisterous conversations. In Ashton, it was typical for conversations not only to take place among people at adjacent tables, but apparently shouting across the entire restaurant was acceptable as well. This was a tightly knit community of people, who had known each other for many years. Stephanie could feel the closeness of familiarity in the air.

"We haven't opened up the back room yet this morning," a woman said from Stephanie's left, apparently seeing her looking that way with interest. The attractive woman was standing behind a counter surrounded by stools all occupied with patrons. "But it looks like we might have to soon." She wore a dark tan shirt with the name Mary Ann embroidered over the left pocket. She appeared to be in her late forties and was in good shape.

"Please follow me." The woman said cheerfully, "I think we still have a booth or two available over on this side." Stephanie and family followed Mary Ann to an empty booth near the back part of the front dining area. "There you go," the woman said. "This should be just fine."

"Maggie?" Stephanie asked, "What a neat idea. You named the restaurant after her?"

"Well not exactly," Mary Ann replied. "It's sort of a long story, but I can give you the two minute condensed version if you'd like." Stephanie had a feeling this was a game of sorts, which Mary Ann might have liked to play with new customers.

Stephanie replied, "Sure, why not?"

Mary Ann took a deep breath and in a series of quick sentences, she told her story in a concise manner, which obviously had evolved into its current format from answering that particular, question hundreds of times before. "The original owner of this restaurant was a woman of Irish decent named Maggie Maloney during the 1940's. My mother, Jeanie Wilkins started working here in 1960 when I was five years old. In 1975, Maggie decided to retire and my mom scrapped together the money to buy the restaurant from Maggie, who gave my mom a great deal on the place. I started working here in 1983, and found myself pregnant with my daughter. Then Maggie Maloney passed away before my baby was born and at my Mom's suggestion, I named my daughter Maggie. My mom got sick in 1995, passed away and left the restaurant to me. Now Maggie is learning the trade and will be taking over the business whenever I get around to retiring. So eventually, Maggie's will be Maggie's once again." Mary Ann took a much needed breath and said "Wow. That was pretty quick. I should have timed it. I think I may have set a new record."

Stephanie looked at her smiling with amusement. "That certainly was a great story. I can't wait to tell my husband; I'll bet he's never heard it before."

"Well, if he eats here very often, he's bound to hear it sooner or later," Mary Ann replied.

Just then, a pretty, young waitress about twenty-five years old approached shaking her head and smiling. Even before Stephanie saw the name "Maggie" on her uniform, she knew the girl had to be Mary Ann's daughter. She looked like a younger version of the woman. "Mom! Don't tell me you're boring these nice folks with your story."

"That's quite alright," Stephanie said. "We asked to hear it and loved it."

Maggie replied, "Well maybe the first hundred and fifty times, but after that it gets a bit old." Then she immediately got down to business, "Can I get you folks something to drink while you decide what you would like for breakfast?"

"Sure," Stephanie said nodding at Cindy and Jeremy. "What'll it be kids?"

"Coke," they said simultaneously.

"Not for breakfast!" Stephanie chastised. "Make it two glasses of milk."

"Chocolate milk?" Cindy asked. Stephanie conceded and said, "Yes, two glasses of chocolate milk."

"Got it," Maggie said smiling at the kids.

Stephanie said, "I'll have a cup of hot tea and can I have a small cup of chocolate milk for little Sammy?"

"Choka mook," Sammy said.

"What a little sweetie pie!" Maggie replied. "And what beautiful big eyes! That one is destined to be a big hit with the ladies someday."

The thought of Sammy growing up suddenly filled her with a momentary rush of melancholy.

"Is everything ok?" Maggie asked, apparently confused by the obvious change in Stephanie's expression.

"Um...yes...everything's fine," Stephanie replied. "I guess I'm still waking up slowly."

Maggie said cheerfully, "Well. I guarantee a good, healthy breakfast is just what the doctor ordered to take care of that. I'll be back in a jiffy with your drinks."

A few minutes later, Maggie returned with the drinks. "Are you ready to order now?"

After Stephanie and the kids placed their orders Maggie inquired, "Are you folks just passing through town today? I don't recall seeing you here before. I'm pretty good with faces."

"Actually, no," Stephanie replied. "We moved to the area a month or so ago and are still getting settled. We're living outside of town. I hope to drive around a bit before heading down to the grocery store."

Maggie said, "Well there ain't too much to see around here. There's a mall up in Franksville and another one down in Yuengsville, but other than that, not much around other than the essentials. But I think you'll like it here. The folks around here are nice enough. I'll be back soon with your order." And with that, the busy woman turned and left to get their breakfasts.

Stephanie looked about the restaurant and realized what Maggie had said was true. The people in the room all seemed to know one another and there was a genuine feeling of the relaxed family-like atmosphere which only small town living could bring.

Soon Maggie returned with their order; plates overflowing with pancakes, eggs, sausage and hash browns. Jeremy and Cindy's eyes grew wide with anticipation.

Maggie looked at Jeremy as if recognizing him and asked. "You look familiar. Were you ever in here before? Remember I said I'm pretty good with faces."

"Once." Jeremy said over a mouth full of pancakes. "With my Dad."

"Jeremy, don't talk with your mouth full." Stephanie scolded.

"Um -K" Jeremy said, his mouth still full of food. Stephanie chose to ignore him, not missing the irony.

"My husband, Jason brought Jeremy in maybe a month ago. He works down town at Technofacture International."

"Jason. Jason." Maggie said as if trying to recall. "That's right. I do remember now. Your husband comes in here often. Now I see where the little one gets his good looks."

This statement bothered Stephanie. She knew it was offered only as a compliment, but it was troublesome to think of another woman eyeing up her husband in that way. Plus, she had no idea Jason ate at Maggie's so often. It was starting to sound as if he was a regular. No wonder he headed out for work so early. She trusted Jason, but having been through one divorce, she was always on the alert for other women, especially younger and attractive women.

"So," Maggie asked, "where do you folks live?"

"Um... yes..." Stephanie said, recovering from her momentary discomfort. "We live out in Ashton, RD. In a property, I inherited from my uncle Emerson Washburn. It's called 'Fallen Stones'"

Maggie's mouth visibly dropped open and she stammered, "Fall... you mean... the old Livingston place?"

"Why yes." Stephanie replied. "You seem to be familiar with our property."

"Um... yes... I mean no..." The girl didn't seem to know what she meant. "You see... that place... not the place it is now... but how it was before, all run down and abandoned... it sort of... sort of had a reputation around here."

"Reputation?" Stephanie asked curiously. "What sort of reputation?"

Maggie hesitated for a moment then said, "Well it's sort of silly now that I think about it. But back when the place was in ruins, before your uncle bought the place and fixed it up, kids used to drive out there and hang out. You know..." She hesitated, looking cautiously over at the two older kids.

"Yes I think I know exactly what you mean." Stephanie said suppressing a smile, assuming the girl was likely talking about whatever sort of mischief teenage kids got up to when left alone in an abandoned property nowadays. Stephanie was thinking in terms of sex and beer but what Maggie was referring to was something much more sinister.

But for whatever reason, Maggie chose not to share that information. Instead the waitress looked oddly at Stephanie and said, "Well, um... I've got to get back to work now. This place is really busy. Nice meeting you." And before Stephanie had a chance to reply, the girl turned and left, almost as if fleeing. Stephanie watched her and saw her head directly for her mother. She watched Maggie whisper something to Mary Ann and the woman's face took on an expression similar to the troubled one her daughter had just worn. Stephanie had a strange feeling there might be something about her property these local people knew, but she didn't. She began to wonder what that might be.

As Stephanie and the kids ate their breakfast, she occasionally watched Maggie going from booth to booth taking and filling orders. She thought she might be imagining things, but it appeared as if in addition to doing her duties, Maggie seemed to be saying something to each of the patrons and occasionally looking over in their direction, almost as if she were talking about Stephanie and her kids. She was not normally prone to such feelings of paranoia, but this all seemed a bit peculiar to her. When she and the kids had finished eating, Stephanie stood up and began to slowly walk the children up to the main counter to pay for their meals. She hadn't been aware of something at first but now she most certainly was. All of the busy chatter in the restaurant had abruptly stopped as soon as she stood up. She felt as if she was walking through some sort of gauntlet of staring eyeballs and the distance to the cash register suddenly seemed miles away.

She and her children gradually made their way to the counter. It was so quiet; Stephanie was certain she would have been able to hear the proverbial pin dropping and she knew that every eye in the restaurant was focused on her. She could feel those same eyes boring holes in her back. She had considered turning and confronting the people, shouting something at them but decided against it. She simply wanted to pay her bill and get out.

The two older kids noticed the bizarre feeling, which had taken over the restaurant as well. "What the heck are they looking at?" Jeremy whispered to Cindy.

"Beats me." Cindy said. "They look like a bunch of weirdos or something. Mommy why are they looking at us that way?"

"Shush." Stephanie said, "Let's just get pay for our food and get out of here."

They approached the cash register where Mary Ann waited with their bill in hand. Gone was her pleasant demeanor and in its place was a look of uncertainty and possibly distrust. Stephanie resisted turning to look back at the restaurant patrons, certain they would all be watching her. She handed Mary Ann a twenty-dollar bill and abruptly said, "Keep the change". Then she led her children out of the restaurant and into a pleasant morning light, which at that particular moment never looked better to her.

After the unpleasant incident at the restaurant, she no longer had any interest in checking out the rest of the town. In fact, she had no desire to even go to the grocery store but she knew she had to restock the pantry so they had little choice. Stephanie couldn't shake the strange and unpleasant feeling she had experienced in the restaurant and even when they were shopping at the supermarket, she felt as if people were staring at them. She knew that wasn't possible since they had just left the restaurant a few minutes earlier and the people in the supermarket wouldn't know them or know anything about them.

Stephanie decided the entire experience had been one best forgotten. Obviously the locals thought of her and her family as rich outsiders, interlopers who had moved into a once-abandoned place which they had fond memories from their youth. Likely, they resented the opulence of the renovated farmhouse and were jealous of Stephanie's good fortune. She didn't need to associate with small-minded people like that. She had her family and she had her property. That was enough for her.

Chapter 23

Stephanie sat relaxing on the sofa out on the deck overlooking the atrium outside the loft. Sammy was inside taking his afternoon nap in the small bedroom next to the kitchenette. She looked out across the expanse of the atrium into the back yard. In the distance, she could see the first signs of autumn approaching in the slightly changing colors of the leaves. She could not believe it was the first week in September already. The idea was almost impossible to grasp. The two older children were already settled into their new school. It seemed like only yesterday they had learned of her inheritance, but that was four months earlier and now she was comfortably relaxing in her luxurious home as if she had lived in the place her entire life.

Inside the loft, far behind her, a decorative mirror hung in the center of the back wall. It occupied a space next to the kitchenette between the small bedroom where Sammy slept and the bathroom. It was quiet inside the loft, just as Stephanie liked it. Not only did she want to make sure nothing disturbed her son's rest, but she enjoyed this quiet time herself; a time to relax and reflect.

In the silence of the large loft space where the only light needed was the natural sunlight filtering down through the skylights and in through the many windows, the surface of the decorative mirror began to shimmer, then ripple in concentric circles emanating from the center of the glass and noiselessly working their way outward. Soon an image, faint and faded at first, then becoming clearer began to take shape inside the rippling mirror. It was the face of Marie Livingston, long dead great-grandmother of Stephanie Wright. The visage appeared to be staring intently out toward the deck and at the woman reclining there, whom she knew, was her descendent and who resembled Marie enough to be her sister.

For the past several months, Marie Livingston and the others had chosen by design to stay quiet and out of sight. They had no desire to make their presence known and to do anything to frighten the Wright family into leaving. They had waited almost a century for the correct family to become available and now the long wait was almost over and the time for action would soon be upon them.

They had plans for the family; plans which needed to be carried out in the timeframe required. They wanted to give the family time to become acclimated to their new home and lifestyle. The inhabitants of the land of the dead had been carefully watching and monitoring the Wright's progress, all the while being careful to remain unseen. Although normally time would be an irrelevant concept to creatures such as they, the spirits had a deadline in mind and needed to adhere precisely to it. And that meant the first phase of the plan would to begin shortly. That was why Marie had appeared at that location and at that exact time; to plant the first of many seeds, which would eventually put the wheels of fate in motion once again.

As Marie looked out at the woman on the deck and saw how similar, they both were in appearance; her hatred and envy toward the woman grew. She cursed Stephanie for being alive and for having all of the things the dead still remember from their own lives on earth, but could no longer experience; such as the touch of a loved one, the joy in a sunset or simply the feeling of being alive.

On more than one occasion, during particularly frustrating and angry times, Marie had been tempted to reach out to Stephanie and take control of her mind, then force her to slowly kill herself in some incredibly horrible fashion. Marie knew she had that power, but that was not in her master's plan. Doing so would have brought Marie severe consequences and great suffering. She had forced herself to hold her anger and stick to the timetable as her husband had demanded. Eternity was a very long time to suffer his wrath to any worse degree than she was already being forced to endure.

She and her cohorts also discovered how it had proven to be more of a challenge than anticipated to remain unseen by that infernal small child, Samuel, who seemed to have been constantly milling about. Prior to the Wrights moving onto the property they had been able to come and go as they pleased, the living for the most part never being any the wiser. But that little boy had some sort of natural ability to sense their presence and see them whenever they appeared. Marie discovered this the very first day the family had visited the property and the boy had seen her watching them from the large mirror in Washburn's master bedroom.

As a result, they had to learn to be extra careful. The young boy was getting older, and his vocabulary and understanding was increasing daily. In the beginning, he not only couldn't comprehend the meaning of their appearances but even if he had understood, he did not have the vocabulary necessary to express his sightings. Marie recalled how the boy almost had revealed the presence of the other two; those damned boys, when he had seen them at their gravesite. Fortunately no one understood what he was talking about, as he could not make himself clear to his family. That was several months ago. Now, however, he might be more capable of doing so.

The spirit wished she could see the boys herself; wished they were accessible to her, then she would fix them so they could never cause her problems again. But they were on some other plane of existence; separate from her own and she could never quite locate them, although she could sense their occasional presence. She didn't know if they could see her and Dwight from where they existed. She suspected it might be possible, however, since she could see the humans in their world, but they could not see her. Even after almost one hundred earth years, she was still new to the spirit world and unable to understand everything about her reality.

She cursed the heavens for her rotten luck. It would not be fair if she could not find the boys while they could see her, if that was the case. But one thing she learned quickly after death was that nothing in this afterlife was any fairer than in life had been when she was alive. Marie was in constant turmoil worrying about what would happen if the boys continued to manifest themselves to the small child. Eventually he would find a way to let his parents know what was going on.

Fortunately, Samuel was the only member of the Wright family with this ability. And as such, she and Dwight had devised a way to control Samuel and what his visions showed to him, since they were not able to be in command of their two former sons' comings and goings. And they had done so without the use of violence, much to Marie's chagrin.

Many times, Marie had wished she had the ability to float a pillow over the boy's head as he lay sleeping in his daybed and smother the very life out of him, putting the brat out of their way forever. But she unfortunately didn't possess such power. And even if she had, she knew Dwight would never tolerate such an act, as it would cause so much heartache and chaos in the family it might drive them apart and eventually away. If she were responsible for that, there certainly would be hell to pay and she felt she was already paying quite enough hell already. Besides, she knew they needed the three of them, Jason, Stephanie and Samuel to complete Dwight's plan. If anything should happen to the boy, it might take several more centuries until they once again found the right combination of souls.

Out on the deck, Stephanie was thinking about how today had been another quite productive day of putting the final touches on her illustrations. Things had been going extremely well with her latest children's book over the past few months; so much, that Stephanie believed she might be able to declare the work finished at last.

She understood when it came to writing or art or any creative endeavor, it was very difficult to say for sure when a work was completed.

Her practice had been, once she determined a book was completed she would set the book aside for a few weeks, maybe as long as a month. During that time, she would begin a new project, perhaps another book or maybe something completely different. She had been thinking more about researching her ancestry lately; perhaps she would begin that project next. It might make for a good change of pace; one sufficiently different enough to allow her to clear her mind.

Then in a month, she would sit down with a fresh set of eyes and an open mind, and then begin the process of re-reading, editing and critiquing her work.

Although Stephanie had been thinking about beginning a genealogical investigation, the idea had not actually been her own. Since the day she first learned of Emerson Washburn, Stephanie's mind had been receiving occasional subtle suggestions from the creatures of the dead to begin her research. It was critical to their plans. But even more important was for Stephanie to believe the idea was her own.

As she looked out at the cool September afternoon, Stephanie shook her head in disbelief, trying to come to grips with how the entire summer had passed by so quickly. And so much had happened during those months as well. Jason had taken the new job, and they had sold their own home and moved into the Ashton estate. They had done some limited remodeling, especially in the master bedroom and had sold of most of the antique furnishings and pictures for a substantial profit, which helped to make up most of the cost of their painting and cleanup of the bedroom. They had kept the tall mirror from Washburn's bedroom as well as the portrait of her great grandparents from the living room, but had stored them up in the attic along with a few other items they thought they might want to keep. Stephanie liked the mirror but decided to hide it away because of the way it had seemed to bother Sammy. That particular incident had been so strange. She wondered what it was about the mirror. Perhaps when Sammy was a little older she would bring it down from storage and try once again.

However, neither she nor Jason cared for the portrait. The thing bothered them both to no end. First, because of how the subject's eyes seemed to follow everyone anywhere they might move throughout a room. And secondly, because of how much her great grandparents looked like she and Jason. Stephanie thought again about her idea to do a family tree and realized now she had to make sure to include Jason's side of the family as well. After all, that side of the family was not only important to Jeremy but to Sammy as well.

Chapter 24

Stephanie heard a rattling sound from down below and immediately recognized it as being Mrs. Franks, Connie, dusting the furniture in the atrium area. Stephanie was so very grateful to Jason for suggesting they hire Connie to help her with maintaining their new home. She realized that without the woman's assistance, she might never have been able to finish her book. If she were to be perfectly honest with herself, it was more like she was helping Connie, who was doing the lion's share of the housework.

And Connie's husband, Wilbur had become a great asset to Jason as well, helping him with the yard work and other such duties. With his new job and growing responsibilities, Jason often had to go into work very early and stay late into the evening. Like Connie, Wilbur had assumed most of Jason's chores as well. And although Jason was enjoying his new position, it was causing a great deal of stress for both he and Stephanie. His came in the form of overworking and hers in the form of loneliness. She found herself spending far too much time by herself, especially now that the two older kids were settled in their new school.

She found the time alone to be something of a double-edged sword. From a writing perspective, it was a blessing because it allowed her time to think, to work and to illustrate her projects. But from the standpoint of a wife and mother, it simply meant she had far too much time in solitude; too much time to miss her husband and far too much time to imagine. Being a creative person, her imagination found itself in high gear, particularly during the alone times and not necessarily always in a constructive or positive way. She had often found herself imagining things about Jason she knew he would never do, could never do, but still the ideas came nonetheless. She simply had too much quiet time.

Stephanie found this situation to be quite ironic, since prior to meeting Jason when she was a single working mother she would have given her eye teeth for one tenth of the time she now had available. Now she would give something equivalent just to have less free time. She silently scolded herself for being so ungrateful and thought "Be careful what you wish for, you just might get it."

To break things up, she often would take Sammy out on trips to the town Ashton and the surrounding communities to become familiar with the area, but there was not much to see. The place was not a booming metropolis of specialty stories and custom boutiques. Most of the people she met during their trips were all very friendly and seemed to be honest hardworking folk, but the blatantly poor economic conditions of the county only served to depress Stephanie.

She missed being only twenty minutes from the bustling and trendy shopping district in Wyomissing or the cultural opportunities of downtown Reading. All of that was a good hour or more away now. She had considered returning to Berks County for some day trips but chose not to. If Ashton was to be their new home, then she had to find ways to make it their home. And she understood running back to what was comfortable or familiar was not the answer.

Being a caring person by nature it made Stephanie feel bad and frequently guilty to live in such splendor while so many people in Schuylkill County were financially suffering. Yet she knew there was little she could do to help anyone even if she was so inclined, as all of their wealth was tied up in the house. Jason had been right about one thing, with their inheritance and Jason's promotion, they truly were living like a king and queen among peasants when they compared their home and land with the meager wood-framed dwellings owned by most of the people in the community. Even the local business owners, doctors, lawyers and politicians did not have homes, which could be considered in the same league as theirs.

But neither the presumed wealth nor the prestige it brought with it mattered to Stephanie. She really missed Jason and missed the way their life had been just a few months ago. Yes, it was true that back then every day had been a struggle financially but they were happy. Now she had no more money problems, was living in a mansion and plenty of time to work on her books, but her husband was seldom around to offer the type of emotional support she needed. Stephanie didn't consider herself to be high-maintenance, emotionally speaking, but that was how she was beginning to feel.

And to make matters worse, their love life was suffering as well. There was a time, not all that long ago, when Jason couldn't seem to keep his hands off of her; but now that had changed too. By the time he finally got home from work, Jason was exhausted, mentally stressed, and it seemed that lately sex was the furthest thing from his mind. Stephanie had done all she could think of to keep herself in shape and to keep Jason interested, but nothing seemed to work lately. The various self-help stories she read in various women's magazines about rejuvenating their love life had proven useless as well.

For the briefest of moments during one of her dreary days of solitude, when her mind chose to wander to one of those places it had no business going, she began to feel the slightest stab of concern or perhaps suspicion about Jason. She had even started to imagine that Jason might not be working as much as he claimed, but might instead be involved with another woman, perhaps someone at work. She didn't believe it was possible for someone as devoted as Jason to become caught up in such a thing. But she also knew it had happened to her before with her first husband, Bill, and that time she had been caught her completely by surprise. "Once Bitten, Twice Shy" she recalled the title of the song she had once heard by the band Great White.

Maybe it could be happening to her again. She hated when she had those sorts of thoughts and tried to force them from her mind. She blamed them on too much spare time; too much time to think and to imagine the worst. Maybe it was also from her reading too many articles in too many women's magazines. But hadn't Jason also seemed somewhat different lately? Didn't he seem distant, distracted and even short tempered with the kids? Had she been imagining that too?

"It's time," the dark sinister voice said to Marie Livingston as she stared angrily out at the contemplating Stephanie from inside her world, inside the mirror. The voice had not been so much spoken as it had simply appeared in what she still thought of as her mind, as the voice always did. There was no need for speech or for such traditional types of communications in the foul place she now resided. She didn't understand how she and the others communicated, they just did. They of course, no longer had physical brains or organs with which to generate speech or for that matter to hear the speech if generated, yet somehow they could understand and differentiate each other's thoughts as if they had been spoken aloud. And as such, she knew this latest communication had come from her husband.

"Time?" she questioned. "Time for what?" she wondered absently. She had been so intently staring at her descendent that she had not heard him approach. Although, truth be told, he could and often did approach silently, whether she was actively listening for him or not.

The 'voice' now took on a more angry tone and it seemed to reverberate deep within her as it shouted, "Why do you question me, woman?"

Marie knew she had inadvertently done something she should never have done; she had questioned the Master. "No...no...my husband. I am not questioning you," she quickly replied. "You just caught me off guard.... I am so sorry."

She knew she was never to question him. In life, he had been her husband, her friend, her lover, but now in death he had taken on a new roll. Marie did not understand how everything had changed, but she was certain the unforgivable acts, which brought them both to the world of the undead had somehow cursed them both. Perhaps in this hell or purgatory, the universe had chosen to assign new roles for them; Marie, the submissive servant and Dwight, the heartless and unforgiving master. Although she didn't feel the roles were justified in this or any other version of an afterlife, it was clear this was her fate and although perplexing and unexplainable, she had to do all she could do to keep her horrible existence bearable. She only hoped this was an interim step in her journey into the afterlife and not her final destination.

Whatever force had caused this to happen to her; it was how things now were and how she supposed they would be for some time. Dwight's role apparently was to do with her as he chose and to make her suffer whenever he the mood hit him. She understood she likely deserved such a fate, especially after the most heinous acts she had committed while on earth. But he had done something almost as bad, hadn't he? Often she wondered why Dwight was in the role of master while she was a mere slave. She could only hope after they were finished with the Wright family things would change and perhaps they could move on to whatever else awaited them and could hopefully do so separately. They had waited almost one hundred years for this, and she hoped the end was in sight.

"Now you know what you must do," he commanded, "You must start putting the wheels into motion. But be sure to take it slowly. It must be gradual. They cannot suspect anything. Do everything as I have explained, and all will happen according to my plan. But the final act must take place at the prescribed time."

Not wanting to anger him further, Marie said, "As you wish, my husband." And she hated every word of the thought she was transmitting to him. She despised the horrible creature her husband had become. She thought she could not possibly hate him more than when he was alive but realized what he had since become was so much worse. And what she had turned into was a pathetic cowering creature. As if that was bad enough, she feared there might be no redemption for her, no escape and no end, ever.

After a moment, Marie sensed her husband's presence moving away, although he was never completely gone from her, and might never be. Now she had to do what Dwight had ordered and start a carefully orchestrated series of events in motion which like a snowball rolling down a hill would continue to grow and progress until its final climax on the designated date; December 19th; the anniversary of the deaths of their two sons and the day they had died as well.

From inside the mirror the creature, which had once been Marie Livingston, began to focus all of her concentration toward Stephanie Wright and extending her gnarled index finger out of the mirror sending out the tiniest wisp of sparkling white illumination in the direction of the unsuspecting woman. When the light reached Stephanie, it hung above her head spinning in a circular pattern resembling a small wreath, before settling down atop her head like Christ's own crown of thorns. Then the lights slowly began to seep in through the pores of Stephanie's scalp, tingling, working their way deep inside of her mind, where they were to become the first seeds of doubt, what would fester, grow and eventually become the seeds of destruction.

Stephanie's eyes opened wide, and they seemed to take on a new, intense look of suspicion and anger. Only a moment earlier she had been criticizing herself for thinking such horrible and distrustful thought about Jason. Now, however she was suddenly thinking these thoughts again and these ideas were becoming more real and potentially truer to her than ever. She found her mind drifting back toward something, or more accurately someone. There had been a young female accountant in the financial department of the building where Jason now worked. She recalled him mentioning her once at dinner. At the time, it had seemed innocent enough; him just mentioning a coworker.

She recalled how she hadn't wanted to allow her own insecurities to make her feel jealous and did her best to try to suppress those emotions. But she knew her husband, and knew if he was taking the time to mention someone, it was for a reason. Perhaps it was simply his way of showing respect for her professional skills or perhaps it was more. God, she hated thinking that way, but it seemed lately, the less she saw of Jason on an intimate level, the more they seemed to become distant. A thought came into her mind "If he's not getting it at home, he's getting it somewhere else." She had no idea where that thought had come from, but it planted itself deep in her subconscious, and although she might forget about it superficially, it would remain and fester, never allowing her to completely forget.

She suddenly began to wonder if she might have been wrong about not being more concerned about this woman, this potential interloper. "What was that woman's name?" she thought to herself. "Jo- something. Joanne? No that wasn't it... Jolene! Yes, her name was Jolene.... Jolene Roberts. That was it."

Stephanie had only met the woman once during a visit to the office, and she had been in her estimation a "knockout". In fact, she was drop dead gorgeous, divorced and definitely looking for a pair of male slippers to put under her bed. Now Stephanie began to wonder if the woman might be setting her sights on Jason and was only keeping her distance temporarily, to bide her time until the moment was right. Stephanie could recall the feelings of personal insecurity she felt in the presence of such a confident and beautiful woman. She was certain if Jolene Roberts chose to sink her claws into Jason, it would take everything he had to resist her advances.

She decided she would begin to pay more attention to the way her husband behaved and would monitor his comings and goings more carefully. She would also try to find out more about this Jolene Roberts and find out what her intentions might be in regards to Jason. She trusted Jason, she believed in him, but she also knew how seductive some women could be. She would not allow some bimbo to ruin her marriage and break up her new family.

From behind Stephanie, another small burst of sparking light flew, encircling her head once again before settling down and sinking in through the top of her skull. Then she suddenly and abruptly changed her train of thought; this one not one relating to Jason. If fact, she had completely forgotten about Jason, Jolene, her suspicions and all or misgivings. Those things had receded into her subconscious, but they would continue to gnaw at the fibers of her brain and eventually gain a life of their own.

Stephanie suddenly felt an uncontrollable urge to go up into the attic of the main house and find a box. She could not recall seeing the box before during any of the times they had hauled junk up to the attic, but for some reason she could now see it a plain a day. It was a brown cardboard box with the initials LFH written on the front and top of it. And just as she mysteriously knew about the box, she also somehow knew what the initials meant. They stood for Livingston Family History.

The box contained the records of the genealogical research Emerson Washburn had commissioned several years ago from the private investigator. She could not understand how she knew this but she was quite certain. She had to find the box, and had to do so immediately.

"Connie?" Stephanie called to the woman dusting the atrium below. "Can you please come up here for a moment." She decided she would ask the Franks woman to wait and listen for Sammy while she went to the main house and found the box. A few minutes earlier, she wasn't sure what she would do with all of the idle time suddenly available to her, now she felt as though there weren't enough hours in the day to do what she needed to do.

Back in the shadows of the loft, the rippling mirror returned to its natural state and deep in the world on the other side of the glass could be heard an evil and sinister laugh. "It has begun," the voice said.

Chapter 25

Jason drove down though the hillside town of Ashton, heading back home after a late day meeting with the factory manager, Tom McClellan. Tom had been nothing but complimentary of the way Jason had transitioned into his new position as well as the manner in which he was rapidly reorganizing and restructuring the manufacturing engineering department. Tom always felt the now retired Jim Dodson had been good man and a responsible leader, but he was rooted in old methods and techniques, lacking the ability to change. He believed Jason was the "breath of fresh air" the company needed to help it continue to grow and prosper long into the future.

Jason loved his new position as well as his new responsibilities. At first, everything he attempted seemed to be a monumental task and something to be feared; but he rose to meet every challenge head on and did whatever it took to surpass any obstacle. Initially that meant long hours and an incredible amount of stress, but then the pressure gradually began to ease with each passing day as he became more acclimated to his new role.

It had been a tough couple of months, and he had been working far too many hours, feeling like he would never be able to get back to the point when he would once again have a more normal work schedule. He also knew the long hours away from home were beginning to take their toll on Stephanie as well. She had been very understanding and tolerant of his need to make a good impression in his new job, but he sensed her patience beginning to wane a bit more each day.

Now, however, he had decided things would be different. Beginning the following week, he was determined to start bringing things back to normal both at work as well as at home. This meant he would be putting in fewer hours on the job and spending more time at home with his family. The kids were all growing like weeds, and the past summer had gone by in a blur. He had decided it was time to slow down a bit and make things right with them. He had discussed this with Tom McClellan at their meeting that afternoon, and Tom agreed with Jason wholeheartedly.

In fact, it was McClellan who had actually raised the subject, telling Jason he appreciated all the hard work and additional effort he had been putting into the job, but it was time for him to slow down before he burned out. Tom, who was in his fifties and on his third wife, warned Jason of the pitfalls of putting too much into his job and not enough into his family. This observation and encouragement from Tom helped Jason to see the impending error of his ways.

Jason stopped on his trip through town and picked up a bouquet of flowers for Stephanie at local florist, and now he was trying to think of something interesting his family could do over the weekend. He knew he had to try to make things right before Stephanie's patience wore too thin. He had noticed she had become a bit distant and sometime short of temper whenever he was home. He tried to explain his need to be successful at his new position and the importance of the money in their lives. They had paid off some bills with the two hundred and fifty thousand dollars, made some money on the sale of the antiques and had invested a bit then put the rest of the money into a college fund for the kids. So his salary was still their main source of income.

Maybe it was time to consider taking some of that money and planning a trip to Florida or some other warm location over the Christmas holiday. By that time, Jeremy and Cindy would be off from school for their holiday break and he had not used much of his vacation yet, so it sounded like a good idea to him. He decided to discuss it with Stephanie after dinner while the kids were out of earshot.

Jason turned onto their access road as the sun began to set in the distance, looking at the breathtaking view of their home in the distance. It was truly a remarkable sight and with the help of Wilbur Franks; the grounds surrounding the property were immaculate. He regretted not having much time over the summer to make use of their swimming pool, although the kids and Stephanie had used it extensively. What he regretted most, however was not having found time to be alone with Stephanie for any adult quality time. He recalled how he had joked about him and Stephanie finding a way to be alone in the hot tub grotto or in the spa. But neither had happened. It was not like them to go so long without intimacy. And it certainly was not like him. The realization of how little attention he had been paying to his wonderful wife suddenly made him ache with guilt. It was as if he had just awoken from a coma to realize several months had mysteriously slipped away.

He pulled his car into the garage and as he walked out into the atrium, he could hear the kids playing in the family room. He and Stephanie had decided there was little need for a formal living room in their lives so they had immediately converted the first floor front room of the house into a family room with plenty of comfortable sofas and chairs for reading or watching TV. They also added cabinets for the kids' movies and video games. Because of its size, it made the perfect family space.

"Hey, kids. What's up?" Jason said enthusiastically as he crossed the foyer. Looking to his left, he could see Stephanie in the kitchen making dinner. He held the flowers behind his back. She didn't seem to see him or else for some reason, she wasn't acknowledging his arrival. "Great!" Jason thought. "I'm in trouble again!"

"Hi, Dad," Jeremy said, raising his left hand in a cursory wave, not taking his eyes off the movie he and Cindy were watching on their new big-screen TV. She too gave a brief wave obviously just as engrossed in the movie as Jeremy was.

Sammy, who had been sitting on the floor stacking blocks, stopped and ran toward Jason, hugging his leg and shouting "Daddy! Daddy! Daddy!" Jason loved how excited Sammy still got whenever he came home and was in no hurry to have him outgrow this part of his young life.

"Hey, stinker," Jason said, picking the toddler up with his free arm and giving him a big kiss on the cheek as Sammy squeezed his neck tightly. "Aggggh..." Jason said with a comical mock chocking sound as he stuck his tongue out the side of his mouth, pretending to be gagging from the strength of his young son's hug. Sammy gave a great belly laugh as he always did when Jason played these games with him.

Then he sat Sammy back down on the floor and said, "Ok, buddy. I want you to go back and play with your blocks now for a bit before supper. I need to go out and talk to Mommy for a little while. I promise I will come back in, and I'll call the three of you when it's time for dinner." Sammy looked a bit disappointed but went back to his playing. The other two were still sitting entranced by the movie and likely didn't hear a word he said to them.

Walking down the hallway toward the kitchen, being careful to keep the flowers hidden behind his back, Jason could see Stephanie, still busy at work. She glanced up at him as she was setting the table for dinner.

When Stephanie's eyes met his, Jason saw something or perhaps he just imagined he saw something for the briefest of moments, which caught him completely off guard. In the matter of a millisecond, as if time itself had slowed to a crawl, he saw the look in Stephanie's eyes go through a series of impossible changes. He knew it was unfathomable for so many changes to occur so rapidly, but Jason was certain he had seen it.

First she looked at him as if she had no idea who he was, as if he were a total stranger, someone she had never seen before who had broken into their home and was about to accost her. He assumed maybe she had not heard him come in and did not expect to see him home so early. Next, he saw the look change as a glint of recognition entered her eyes realizing she was looking at her husband. He expected to see the look change to pleasant surprise at his early arrival home but that was not what happened. Instead, her look changed to one of anger bordering on hatred or perhaps even insane rage as if she had just encountered someone she detested rather than loved. Had all these looks not occurred so rapidly, Jason would have physically stepped backward after being confronted with such a look. But he scarcely had time to think, let alone to react.

Then the hostile glare disappeared just as quickly as it had appeared and was replaced with a calm then somewhat aloof look as she returned to setting the table. "I see you are home early for a change," she said coolly. "To what do we owe this honor?"

Jason was still mentally reeling from the many intense emotions he had just witnessed crossing his wife's face, and stammered, "Um...ah...yes... Sorry... I suppose I deserved that...I was able to get out early today. And look what I brought you." He held out the flowers.

Stephanie ignored them and instead said sarcastically, "Well then. I suppose we should all be thanking the heavens above that you have chosen to grace us with your wonderful presence."

Jason hesitated for a moment, being sure to choose his words carefully. It didn't take a rocket scientist to know Stephanie was in a foul mood and likely looking for an argument. As such, he said with extreme caution, "Look, Steph. I understand your frustration with me as well as with the responsibilities of this new job. And believe me when I say I am so very grateful for your patience during the past few months. I honestly could not have done this without you and without your help, honey."

Stephanie didn't reply, but Jason believed he saw the cloud of anger begin to slowly fade from her troubled face. He said, "Look. Just so you know; I spoke with Tom McClellan today and told him I needed to back to a normal schedule." Jason decided to act as if the idea was his and not Tom's. "I told him the extra hours were taking its toll on my family and I was in danger of burning out. I figured the worst that could happen was he might fire me, but I didn't care anymore. I decided I simply couldn't expect you and the kids to put up with this any longer. And I told him so."

Stephanie now looked at Jason as if she were seeing a side of him she had never seen before. The Jason she knew was a hard working dedicated professional and a good corporate soldier who did whatever was necessary to succeed at his job. But the idea of him standing up to the plant manager and essentially demanding to have more time for his family was something she had never expected. Stephanie never doubted how important she and the kids were to Jason, but she also knew how critical his success on the job was to their financial future. However, just because she understood, didn't mean she couldn't still become frustrated and angry about it.

Now she suddenly felt very much ashamed at the way she had just spoken to Jason, recognizing she had been out of line and he certainly deserved better. If she were being honest with herself, she would realize she didn't even have any idea why she had behaved in that way toward him. She didn't know what had come over her. It had almost been like someone else had put a bunch of strange ideas into her head. Jason had been working his fingers to the bone for the past several months to make a better life for her and the kids and here she was treating him as if he were someone who cared nothing for his family. And now he had just proven it by putting his family ahead of his job.

"Look...Jason...I'm...I'm...really sorry about..." she stammered as her eyes welled up with tears.

Jason moved the flowers to the countertop and reached out, taking Stephanie in his arms. "No, baby, you have nothing to be sorry about. I am the one who should be sorry. I guess I got all caught up in this promotion thing and temporarily lost sight of what really matters." He looked into her eyes and said, "I'm so very sorry, and I promise to do my best to make it up to you and the kids." They embraced again, and as Stephanie rested her head on Jason's chest, she was certain everything was going to be right.

In the attic of the farmhouse, the surface of the antique full-length mirror began to shimmer and ripple as the residents of the netherworld beyond the glass silently howled with frustration at the turn of events taking place in the kitchen below. The had been gradually and subtly planting seeds of doubt in Stephanie's mind in order to drive a wedge between the couple which would make it much easier for them to complete their plan. And although this brief setback was no more than a bump in the proverbial road, it still provided more aggravation than they wanted to endure.

They would rethink their strategy, and as they got closer to the predetermined time, they would double their efforts if necessary. They would get their way eventually and there was no force, in Heaven or on Earth capable of stopping them.

Downstairs in the kitchen, Stephanie backed away from Jason and dabbed at her eyes with a napkin. Jason decided to change the subject and asked, "So how's the book coming? Is it done?"

"Yes. I just finished it this afternoon," Stephanie replied. "Well, as much as it can be finished. I emailed Sean, my publisher, today and told him I would send him the rough draft in a month."

"In a month?" Jason asked. "If it's finished, why not send it now?"

Stephanie remembered Jason was unfamiliar with her writing methodology. "Well," she said. "Here is how this works. I finish the book then set it aside for a few weeks, maybe a month. During that time, I do something else...something new. Then I come back and look at it one last time and make any improvements before sending it on to the publisher."

"Oh, yeah," Jason said contemplating, "I think I understand your logic. Let it rest for a few weeks then take a last fresh look at it. That's a great idea. I sort of do the same thing with reports at work. I write them one day, then let them sit overnight and look at them again the next morning before submitting them. Makes sense to me." Then he thought for a moment and asked, "So what are you going to work on in the meantime? Are you going to start another kids' book or do something different?"

"I was thinking of something really different," Stephanie replied. "Ever since we learned about this house I have been thinking about doing some research into my family tree. You remember I mentioned that to you a few times?" Jason nodded and Stephanie said, "Mason Armstrong had told us my Uncle Emerson hired a private investigator to do a good deal of research for him. I believe it's all in a box I located today up in the attic. I didn't take much time to check it out, but I suspect I should be able to find all sorts of stuff in it. Depending upon how much I learn, I was thinking of organizing everything into a nice understandable document. You know, into book form. And then maybe using one of those on line print-on-demand places, I could make a few copies for us, the kids and Chuck and his family. It might make for a nice Christmas gift for them. And it will serve to take my mind away from my kids' book for a while too. It's just what the doctor ordered."

Jason replied enthusiastically, "Steph. That's a great idea. Wow. I never would have thought of that."

"To be perfectly honest with you," she said, "I can't believe I thought of it either. I have no idea where the idea came from. It just seemed to pop into my head." She turned and looked at the timer on the oven then told Jason, "Honey, could you go and tell the kids to wash their hands and get ready for dinner?"

"You bet," he replied, happy to find things quickly returning to normal once again.

Upstairs in the attic a quiet guttural burst of laughter could be heard coming from deep within the old mirror. Dwight Livingston's ghostly voice said, "Well. It looks like some of the suggestions you gave to the woman have taken root after all. Now we simply have to wait for her to come to us and read what she needs to read. Then she will be ours, once and for all."

Chapter 26

Stephanie sat with her legs crossed on the worn wooden plank attic floor. A large brown cardboard storage box sat on the floor next to her. She was positioned in a way that permitted her to benefit most from the meager lighting coming from the single bare bulb suspended from the fixture high above her head. The attic was every bit as grimy and disordered as Stephanie had remembered from the last time she was there several months earlier. And if she were to be perfectly honest about it, the place gave her the creeps. She was starting to think; perhaps she shouldn't have come up to the dreary room alone in the first place. But she had wanted to get her project underway and in order to do so she needed to locate the box containing the private investigator's research material.

Now that the box was so near, she couldn't wait to gather some of the documents and then return to her loft to begin her work. She had a natural dislike for attics in general and this one, in particular, seemed much less hospitable than most, it being filled with many of the unsold antique items they had removed from Washburn's bedroom as well as many other mysterious unopened boxes and crates. They had assumed these containers had been stored there, most likely by Washburn, prior to Stephanie's taking possession of the property.

She realized she would need to have Jason carry the large box to her loft workspace later when he got home from work, as it was both too awkward and too heavy for her to manage on her own. In the meantime, she was briefly looking through some of the photos and notes to see what she might want to take with her immediately.

Fortunately, young Sammy had gone down for a nap in the loft bedroom a half hour earlier, and Connie Franks had been nice enough to agree to watch over the boy once more while she dusted loft area. This permitted Stephanie a brief time whereby she could venture up into the attic in search of the needed documentation. Fortunately, Sammy had taken to both Connie and Wilbur Franks as did the other kids, and couple had become their surrogate grandparents. So, Stephanie felt confident if Sammy awoke early, he would be quite comfortable finding Connie watching over him instead of her.

Stephanie couldn't help but notice that Sammy seemed to be sleeping a lot lately during the day. It didn't cause her a concern as of yet, but she had made a mental note to watch his sleep patterns more closely for possible signs of trouble.

Upon examination of the box, Stephanie was surprised by how disorganized everything inside was. Absolutely nothing was in any proper arrangement whatsoever. She had naturally assumed a highly paid private investigator would have done a more systematic job of keeping things organized. Then she realized perhaps the investigator actually had done so. Maybe he had submitted all of his findings to Emerson Washburn in a nice, neat and orderly package. However, if Washburn had been as mentally unstable as she suspected he might have been near the end of his life, it was very possible he had actually been the one who and muddled up the files.

No matter what the cause, Stephanie knew she would have a big job ahead of her. But rather than become frustrated with the potentially daunting task, she found herself becoming excited over the challenge. As she thumbed through the top most layers of documents, she discovered a large stack of assorted photos, wrapped in a thick rubber band. Being an illustrator, she realized the importance of visual media and decided rather than submerge herself into a stack of textual documentation at this early stage, she would start with something more in her comfort zone.

She thought of the old adage of a picture being worth a thousand words. Stephanie decided she would study the pictures and learn what she could from them. If nothing else, they might give her a first look at some of her ancestors and help her to get a good feel for a past with which she was completely unfamiliar.

She also wondered if there would be any dates and identifiers written on the backs of the pictures, something to help her determine when the photos were taken and perhaps who was present in the shots. She recalled how when she was a little girl she would help her mother put pictures into their photo albums. Her mother would always write the date and the names of the people in the photos on the backs of each picture. She assumed her mother must have learned that practice from her own mother and hoped the tradition had started even further back in her lineage. Or maybe the private investigator had made personal notations on the back of the pictures. If so, then it might go a long way to help her quickly get things reorganized.

Stephanie turned over the first picture on the top of the stack. It was a photo of two young boys perhaps ages four and two years old. She was amazed at how much the two boys not only looked alike but also bore a striking resemblance to her own little Sammy. She held the card up to the light to see if she could read the caption on the back, which was written in an elaborate, flowing cursive hand. The light was unfortunately too poor in the attic to allow her to see much but as best as she could discern the inscription read "Matthew James Livingston age 5, Charles Edward Livingston age 3", followed by the date, "July 20, 1921".

"Matthew and Charles Livingston" she said aloud, realizing they could very well be the sons of her great grandparents, and most likely were. These two might have grown up to become her unknown great uncles. Stephanie knew she was going to love this project because of how even this simple bit of previously unknown information thrilled her to no end. She knew the Livingstons had other children because if she was correct, her grandmother had been the sister of these two boys and had originally been from Schuylkill County. However, she didn't know how many other children, if any, the Livingstons may have had. She knew back in the early part of the twentieth century people tried to have big families because often illness or some other tragedy would result in an early death for young children. Plus, if the place were operated as a family farm, Livingston would have wanted many children to help with the chores, especially boys.

Stephanie felt a chill run down her spine, and she suddenly sensed she were being watched, observed from somewhere by someone. She slowly turned and looked about the attic but could see nothing out of the ordinary lurking in the dark shadows. She saw the portrait of Dwight and Marie standing along the back wall of the attic wrapped tightly in its protective tarp and tied securely. She suspected at some point in her research she might once again have to unwrap the portrait to study it in more detail.

Then, whether having been a trick of the poor lighting, or maybe a breeze entering the attic through a crack or simply her own overactive imagination, Stephanie thought for the briefest of moments, she had seen the surface of the canvas tarpaulin covering the portrait, rustle ever so slightly. When she looked at it more intently, the movement did not return, that is to say if it had ever been there in the first place. She would have sworn, however, she had actually seen it move.

She assumed by the strange feelings she was starting to experience, she may already have stayed too long in the eerie space. Stephanie decided to take the large stack of pictures from the attic and out to the loft where she could begin cataloging them in a better lighted and less gloomy setting. She wished she could take everything with her immediately and avoid another trip up to the dismal garret but realized the best thing to do was start small with the pictures and build from there. Besides, she was going to send Jason up for the box later, which meant she could avoid the spooky attic from then on.

Stephanie reached down and closed the lid of the box, setting her stack of photos on top of it. She carefully stood up on legs, which had all but fallen asleep, and then bending over, she pushed the large box across the dusty attic floor, getting it as close to the door as possible, while leaving drag marks in the dust. This would make it easier for Jason to find it when she asked him to bring it to her studio that evening. Upon seeing the drag marks, she brushed off the seat of her jeans while still in a bent over position, seeing a light cloud of dust was billowing behind her.

She thought back to how uncharacteristically angry she had gotten with Jason, and she had been so grateful he was finally putting his family first, ahead of his job responsibilities. She recalled the long summer days and evenings she had spent alone with the kids while Jason worked long hours. Then she felt ashamed at how she had begun to suspect perhaps he had not been working but might have become involved with another woman. How could she have thought such a thing? Jason would never consider cheating on her, would he? No, she was certain he never would.

Standing up straighter, slightly out of breath she saw stars flashing in front of her eyes as often happened when she got up too fast from a bent position. Then surprisingly, she thought she saw something out of the corner of her eye; something moving along the shadowed back wall of the room. She knew there could be nothing back there except for the wrapped portrait of the Livingstons and a few pieces of furniture from Washburn's bedroom, including that century-old dressing mirror.

Assuming she had been mistaken or that the illusion had resulted from her standing up too quickly, Stephanie picked up the stack of photos, switched off the light, closed the attic door and went back to her loft studio.

Chapter 27

The cold November winds howled outside as Stephanie intently scrutinized the ever-increasing mountains of documents and photos, making annotations in the margins of the typed pages of certain items she felt were of significance. She would occasionally stop and enter some information on her laptop computer. Then she would return to the pile of documents, which had spread to cover the entire area that had once been her desktop. Likewise, her drawing board, once used to create beautiful illustrations now was covered with a large piece of butcher paper containing what appeared to be a hand-scribbled version of a family tree, with long, thick lines resembling a flow chart and script which was erratic and barely legible.

The children's book she had set down over a month earlier, lay somewhere under the pile of documents completely forgotten. Stephanie's goal had been to put it out of her mind for a short while then get back to finalize it. But she had no idea when she put the book down that she would become so obsessed with her new project. The previous week had been the time she had originally designated to revisit the book for a final proofing before sending it on to her publisher. But last week and come and last week had gone as did this week and she never even thought about the book. Nor would she look at it any time soon. The fact was she could scarcely even remember writing the book in the first place. That was how absorbed she had become in her latest endeavor.

She was currently dressed in a pair of baggy gray sweat pants, which were stained with paint, coffee, food and God only knew what else. Her shirt was an oversized pink sweatshirt sporting similar stains to those on the pants, and on her feet were a tattered pair of threadbare bedroom slippers. This had been her standard work outfit for the past week or more and even she was starting to notice its pungent aroma, as it was beginning to get a bit ripe and was in desperate need of spending some quality time in the washing machine. But even so, her condition didn't seem to matter to her. Stephanie's hair looked as if it hadn't been combed since she got up that morning, or even the previous morning. That was because it hadn't been. And if asked, she would not have been able to tell anyone the last time she had bathed or showered either. She likewise hadn't worn makeup or cosmetics of any kind in weeks. Her eyes, which were sunken behind dark circles, had the wild gaze of intensity bordering on mania; the types of looks one might see in the eyes of a homeless woman, muttering to herself while pushing a shopping cart full of worthless trash down the street.

Over the past month or so, since beginning her research, Stephanie had become so incredibly obsessed with her work that it had reached a level approaching psychosis. The family history was all she thought about morning noon and night, twenty-four hours a day, seven days a week. And what was worse, it was all she cared to think about.

On those rare occasions when she left her loft long enough to speak with family members, it had been in short, clipped and often barely intelligible half-sentences, and the topic always seemed to contain names or snippets of information about one of her recently discovered ancestors. She spoke of them as if she knew them personally, as if they were friends or acquaintances she had known all of her life. She also discussed them as if everyone else in the family should know these former strangers as well. Each week she seemed to decline steadily becoming further absorbed into the world of her family's past.

Stephanie spent almost every available waking moment in her loft, which had been transformed from its original neat and efficient workspace to something resembling a disaster area after a hurricane. She not only spent all of her available time on the project but also used most of the time she should have been spending with her family, buried deep in her work.

She seemed to be driven by some strange force, one far beyond her ability to control. And she was likewise too frenzied to eat, since it was apparent to all; in addition to her strange behavior, she had lost well over fifteen or more pounds during the past six weeks.

To say her family was concerned about Stephanie was an understatement. However, Jason was at a loss to determine how best to deal with it. The family was still new to the area, and Jason was unfamiliar with most people outside of his immediate work environment. He also didn't feel close enough to any of them to share such intimate concerns about his wife.

Over the summer, the couple had taken the kids to a local pediatrician for colds, as well as for their school registration requirements, but they had not found a doctor for their own needs. Neither had they joined any of the many local churches, so as of yet there was no spiritual advisor Jason could turn to. He sensed he was putting off the inevitable by not calling for some type of professional help, but he so wanted to find a solution to this problem on his own without seeking outside intervention.

He had called Stephanie's brother Chuck the previous week, and briefly explained about his concerns. Both Jason and Stephanie had been so busy over the past several months they had unfortunately not kept in touch with Chuck and his family. Jason was surprised by the cold vibe he sensed coming over the phone line from his traditionally jovial brother-in-law's uncharacteristically icy voice. Whether his hostile attitude was the result of their unplanned lack of contact or if it came from Chuck's feeling slighted by Stephanie receiving Washburn's inheritance, Jason didn't know. But the bottom line was Chuck provided no support for Jason, and as a result, their call was short and abrupt. Jason knew sometime in the future he would have to work on mending that particular broken paling in the family fence but for the moment, he had too many other more important problems to solve. Jason hoped perhaps someday soon Chuck would come around of his own accord.

With Stephanie as indisposed as she had become, the majority of the house cleaning was now being handled exclusively by Mrs. Franks. Jason had changed the woman's work status from one or two days a week to five days. She even occasionally stopped by on Saturdays as well. Connie was responsible for cleaning the entire house except for the loft area, which was a place Stephanie now insisted everyone including all of the family members avoid. The only exception to this rule was Sammy, and that was simply because he took his naps regularly in the loft bedroom while Stephanie worked and the rest of the time he just sat quietly staring at the television in an almost catatonic state.

Stephanie had thought by now Sammy would have outgrown the need for a nap, but for some unknown reason his time asleep seemed to have actually increased, rather than decreased. Had she been more aware and in a normal, more focused frame of mind, Stephanie would have become much more concerned by this change in his daily routine and would have found it to be at best, a bit peculiar. However, she was not thinking properly. She was simply thankful the boy was quiet and not bothering her. If she had taken the time to find out why Sammy was behaving as he was, she would have been both ashamed by her lack of concern and horrified by the reason for his lethargy.

At Jason's further request, Connie Franks had also taken over the responsibility of preparing dinners for the family, as well as school lunches for the two oldest children. On Friday night when Connie had to leave early, Jason would often order pizza or Chinese food from local restaurants and have it delivered in time for dinner. If there were not a sufficient amount of leftovers, he would also order out on the weekends. This had been going on for more than a month, and Jason didn't know how much longer he could allow it to continue. He tried to be as supportive of Stephanie as she had been of him over the past summer, and he really wanted to be, but her strange absent-minded behaviors were really beginning to concern him.

In the loft, Sammy sat on the floor in what had become his usual manner, staring at some mind-numbing children's video which Stephanie had left playing in the DVD player. He had most likely watched the video more than a hundred times, yet he still sat as if mesmerized. The fact was, he was not aware of the program and even if the TV had been turned off and its screen black, he would not have noticed the difference. The young boy's mind was elsewhere, a million miles away in a magical land where every young child's imagination would love to travel. Although he was staring at the screen with his glazed eyes open, his mind was in a wonderful place of candy cane trees and lollypop flowers; a place of vibrant colors, amazingly pleasant smells and a never-ending array of delicious tastes.

However, below the surface of this idyllic landscape, evil lurked. The incredible land of wonderful childhood pleasures was a lie, a falsehood, a sham, projected into the young boy's mind by the ghastly beings that inhabited the property. And deep in the back of his young mind, Sammy could sense the underlying presence of the evil, but try as he might, he could not escape the grasp of their control. Whenever he started to become aware things in the magical world might not be quite as he thought, he would be confronted with some other amazing wonder and would in turn be conveniently distracted once again, forgetting his concerns.

It had taken the creatures some time and quite a bit of thought to determine a way to render the boy unable to remain a problem for them. This was especially difficult since they needed to do so without taking his life. But they had finally come up with the appropriate distraction. They created a hallucination; an imaginary place where the boy could be sent every day in order to be out of their way and out of Stephanie's as well so that she could complete the work which they had arranged for her. When he napped, his mind also traveled to that same special place of childhood wonders. This was the reason he seemed to nap for such long periods; he had no need or desire to wake up and leave the miraculous land.

This diversion had been created to be a strictly temporary situation in order that by the time the two older children got home from school and Jason returned from work, Sammy would always revert back to his normal persona, never remembering a single thing about the fantasy world of amazing daydreams. But when he and Stephanie were alone, he either slept for hours on end or spent his time awake staring at the television screen like a mindless zombie, while she toiled relentlessly, cataloging and documenting all day long.

In the beginning of her project, before the current level of intensity had set in, Stephanie often felt guilty about not spending enough time with her family and using all of her time to concentrate on her research. But now, if someone were able to get through to her and was actually able to solicit a normal intelligible response from her, Stephanie would not have even recalled those same earlier guilty feelings. The project had become the most important thing in her life, the only thing in her life. It was as if everything else became second to finding out the mystery of her lineage. Sometimes the need to know was so overpowering, she felt as if she might not be in control of her own actions. It was as if she were being driven to work more, and to learn more; like she were a marionette and someone else was working her strings.

To a casual observer, it would have appeared as if Stephanie had actually switched roles with Jason and had taken his previous workaholic traits to an even greater extreme. He was no longer spending long hours on the job and was home every evening and on weekends. But then again, he had to be, since Stephanie had all but abandoned her family. However, if anyone at his job were to ask Jason about his new work schedule, he would simply say he was spending more time with the family. He would never tell them that he was substituting for his wife, or that something was becoming so very wrong with her and that he had to be home as much as possible. The truth was Jason had absolutely no idea where Stephanie's mind was of late. It seemed to him at times as if she were becoming someone else entirely.

Now hard at work in the loft, Stephanie looked closely at the screen of her computer where she had typed a version of the almost completed family tree, compiled from her scribbled notes on the butcher paper hanging over her drawing board. When she began the project she only had a few names listed; her own, Jason's, the kids', her parents, Jason's parents, her brother Charles, her Uncle Emerson and her great grandparents, Marie and Charles Livingston.

However, during the past several weeks, she had been quite successful at completing her side of the family tree. The private investigator Washburn hired had done an incredible job of compiling his data. She learned from the report, the investigator had been a man named Jake Malone. His name sounded more like that of a gangster than a private investigator, but she supposed with Emerson Washburn paying the bill, anything might be possible.

With the hopes of supplementing Malone's investigation, Stephanie signed up for several different genealogy web sites. Although they were chocked full of great information, she never learned anything above and beyond what she had found in the large box of photos and documents, which Malone had compiled. She suspected he too must have utilized the same web sites she had found.

She looked carefully at her family tree on the computer screen, examining it for what must have been the thousandth time. Her side of the tree started at the top with the Livingstons and ended with her present family. It also displayed the dates of birth and death for those who had passed away; at least those whose dates could be confirmed.

She likewise had completed most of Jason's family tree back to his grandparents, and although she had identified his great-grandmother, she was unable to find anything about who his great-grandfather might be. This was causing a particular degree of frustration for her. It was like she had a puzzle waiting to be completed but the final piece was missing. She knew this single missing bit of information was the thing that was bothering her the most. But for the moment, she decided to put that particular missing link out of her mind and go back to reviewing her own side of the family tree.

Chapter 28

During her research, she discovered the Livingstons, Dwight Charles Livingston and Marie Louise O'Hara Livingston, had produced three offspring, two boys and a girl. The family tree notations for the parents read as follows:

Dwight Charles Livingston born July 23, 1890
died December 19, 1922
Marie Louise O'Hara Livingston born June 6, 1892 died
December 19, 1922.

Stephanie was troubled by the fact that both of her great-grandparents died on the exact same day. Nor was she able to miss the connection between their deaths and the deaths of their two sons as she reread the next entry on the tree just below that of the Livingston parents.

Matthew James Livingston born June 12, 1916
died December 19, 1922
Charles Edward Livingston born July 2, 1918
died December 19, 1922
Sarah Louise Livingston born August 15, 1920
died October 16, 1975

Stephanie wondered what might have happened to cause the deaths of four family members on the same day. She was particularly bothered by the fact that December 19, the day they all died was the very same day little Sammy had been born, only it had been eighty-eight years earlier. She hated coincidences, and they never failed to cause her discomfort. Yet over the past six months her life had seemed to become a series of never ending coincidences, and this was yet another one to add to the list.

Sarah Livingston, the only child to survive, had been the grandmother she had never known. Sarah passed away the year before Stephanie was born. She realized as she read the entry how close her family lineage had come to ending on that fateful day in 1922 when four of the five members of the Livingston family somehow perished leaving her grandmother, Sarah, an orphan at two years old. Whatever tragedy had befallen the Livingston family must have somehow spared the toddler.

"Unbelievable!" Stephanie thought to herself. "She was only as old as my own little Sammy." Then she realized she had stumbled upon yet another coincidence. A cold chill raced down her spine as she shivered thinking about the young child Sarah. She could not imagine her own baby boy growing up without his family. How horrible that must have been for her grandmother.

Stephanie had recently made an additional notation to the section on Sarah Livingston, when she had found a note among the piles of paperwork explaining how Dwight Livingston's younger sister, Amelia Livingston Miller had taken young Sarah to live with her and her family in Ashton, eventually adopting the child and raising her as her own daughter. The girl had taken the surname Miller, and the family had moved sometime later to the suburbs of Berks County.

Continuing to follow the family tree downward, Stephanie read the next entry; the one indicating when her grandmother married her grandfather.

Sarah Louise (Livingston) Miller married
Stephen Edward Washburn June 8, 1943.
Stephen Edward Washburn died May 15, 1968.
The couple had two sons.

This was how the Washburn name entered the picture. The next entry on the tree showed the births and deaths of her father, her mother as well as her uncle Emerson.

Emerson Charles Washburn born August 7, 1945
Died April 12, 2012
Nathan Edward Washburn born September 3, 1948
Died July 20, 1994
Marie Stephanie Jacobs Born August 18, 1949
Died July 20, 1994 - wife of Nathan.

There it was again; another coincidence. Stephanie couldn't help but notice the strange twist of fate in how the Livingston family not only lost four relatives in one day, but then many years later, her own parents died when struck by a drunk driver, resulting in a second listing on the family tree of multiple deaths occurring on the same day.

Once again, she wondered about the original Livingston family tragedy and what might have happened. She found herself both wanting to know and at the same time not wanting to know. She somehow understood the answers to her questions could be answers she might not really want to learn. She followed the chart further downward finding the listing for both herself and her brother Charles under her parent's names.

Charles David Washburn born Feb. 17, 1973
Stephanie Sage Washburn June 12, 1976

Stephanie had originally had the word "Died" with a blank space next to their names, but no matter how many times Stephanie looked at the entries, it bothered her to see that empty space next to the word "Died". So, she chose to eliminate it instead. She understood the idea was silly, superstitious and maybe even a little paranoid, but she felt better with it gone. She had the same opinions about cemetery headstones, which often had the name of a living person along with their date of birth and a blank for date of death. Although Stephanie knew she, like everyone else would die someday, the idea of having a spot waiting like a hotel reservation gave her the creeps.

She looked again at her brother Chuck's name above hers. "Charles" had been part of the male family members' names since Dwight and perhaps earlier. If they had been aware of Dwight Charles and the rest of the family lineage she might have understood, but she suspected her grandmother may have had little knowledge of her own history, yet somehow the name Charles had nonetheless traveled down three generations. It was yet another coincidence, and once again one, which did not make her feel comfortable whatsoever.

Stephanie hadn't been able to find anything about her family earlier than her great grandparents so she was unsure how far back the naming tradition may have existed. She looked at the next entry.

Stephanie Sage Washburn married
William Joseph Sanders on June 2, 1998
Cindy Marie Sanders Born December 12, 2001
Stephanie and William divorce March 22, 2003

She hated having this entry in her family tree because of the bad memories it dredged up, but she knew if this were to be an accurate historic representation, she had to post the bad right up there with the good. This was especially true since someday Cindy might want to conduct her own research and trace her father's genealogy back several generations, since his family history was hers as well.

Then she looked at the final piece of her side of the tree, her marriage to Jason and the birth of their son, Samuel.

Stephanie Sage Washburn Sanders married
Jason John Wright (born May 22, 1974) on May 16, 2009
Stepson Jeremy John Wright born October 21, 1999
Son, Samuel Jason Wright born to Stephanie and Jason
December 19, 2010

She hesitated again for a moment seeing Sammy's birth date. How strange it made her feel, realizing the date of his birth matched the date of the Livingston family tragedy. That was how she how she had begun to think of the mysterious event, the Livingston family tragedy. She had no idea what catastrophic series of situations might have resulted in the deaths, but understood they likely had been bad ones.

Stephanie got comfort from knowing her side of the tree was finally completed and Jason's side was on the way to being finished as well. She knew he was starting to lose patience with her and the amount of time she was putting into her project but it had become very important to her. Perhaps she would agree that she might have been a bit out of sorts at times and may be even somewhat scatterbrained, but it was only because she had been so intently focused on completing her work. Jason simply had to learn to understand that. And besides, Jason had no right to complain since she tolerated his absence all summer long, while he was busy settling into his new job.

One might argue that Jason's work brought in an income whereas hers was just a research project, a hobby of sorts. But she knew it was much more than that. It was her family, and it was her family history. And it had been her relative who had died and left them the inheritance, so in Stephanie's mind her work was equally as valuable as Jason's if not more so. Besides, she was not just working on her own lineage, but Jason's as well. And since her family tree was complete, she was now trying to find the final frustrating piece of his side of the family. She was sure when he saw the completed work he would be very happy and would better understand why she had such a desperate need to finish it.

She moved her view over to Jason's side of the family tree and starting with Jeremy's birth, traveled back through Jason's first marriage and then continued to work backward in time.

Jeremy John Wright born October 21, 1999
Jason John Wright married

Sarah Cynthia Jones June 4, 1996
Couple divorced April 13, 2006
Jason John Wright born May 22, 1974
Cheryl Elizabeth Wright born July 25, 1976
died July 25, 1986

There were several other strange coincidences. Sarah Jones Wright, Jason's first wife, had the middle name Cynthia and Stephanie had named her own daughter Cynthia. His ex also had the first name Sarah, which was Stephanie's grandmother's first name. Perhaps this coincidence was just another random happenstance and didn't really possess any particular significance whatsoever, but she couldn't help but make note of it.

Then Stephanie thought for a moment about Jason's sister Cheryl. She died when Jason was just twelve years old and she was ten. She apparently had some rare form of bone cancer and fought the valiant fight for several years until finally succumbing to the disease on her tenth birthday. Then she thought of another coincidence, it was her friend, whose name was also Cheryl who helped she and Jason get together. Jason often talked about his sister and recounted many fond memories for Cindy and Jeremy. He tried to stress the importance of family and having siblings. This was especially important in the blended family situation they had created. She followed the tree back further.

Edmund Walter Wright born September 8, 1946
died January 3, 2005
Married to Linda Celia Jensen born March 15, 1947
died February 26, 2007

From discussions with Jason after they had met, Stephanie learned that his father, Edmund, had died the year before Jason and Sarah were divorced. He had a massive heart attack at home and was gone before the ambulance arrived. Jason had been visiting at the time and had seen everything. It was quite traumatic for him and the stress probably did little to help them deal with their troubled marriage. His mother had been suffering with dementia prior to his father's passing and had to be placed in an assisted living facility where she eventually simply faded and died, lost in that incomprehensible world of confusion the disease often brings with it.

Stephanie followed the family tree back to the last few entries she had been able to locate for Jason's family.

Walter Stephen Wright born November 29, 1919
died April 11, 1973
Married on June 21, 1944 to Elizabeth Jane Jefferson
born May 22, 1921, died July 2, 1982

This is where Stephanie had hit a dead end. She could find nothing more about the Wright side of the family. She found no information on Walter Wright's parents whatsoever. She suspected his father might have been an immigrant and perhaps had a completely different name upon his arrival. He might have taken the name Wright upon landing in the United States to make him sound more American, as so many immigrants did in those days. She could only guess, as there were literally no records and no information about him whatsoever.

She had a little bit more luck with the grandmother, Elizabeth Jane Jefferson in that she was able to identify Elizabeth's mother, but was unable to identify her father.

Agatha Jane Jefferson born August 3, 1897, died 19??

That was pretty much the end of it. She had no idea when Agatha died, who her husband was, if she had one. Stephanie suspected Jefferson might be her married name as the concept of having children out of wedlock in that day and age was virtually unheard of. But if there was a Mr. Jefferson, there was not a trace of it recorded anywhere.

Stephanie looked across the room and saw Sammy sitting slack-jawed staring at the television, a steady stream of drool dripping from his lip. She could smell the foul stench of his soiled diaper. She suspected the boy might end up with a severe rash if she didn't tend to him soon. She knew she should go to him, she knew she was doing her son a great disservice by ignoring him, but she also knew she was almost finished with her work. She was so close. She just needed to find out the final piece of the puzzle.

The problem was, she had been through every single bit of information in the box from the investigator, Malone, and had exhausted all of her Internet resources as well, yet the death of the Livingston family members remained a mystery, as did the identity of Jason's great-grandfather. She knew she could not rest until she solved this final part of the story.

Stephanie looked one last time into the empty box. She had no idea what prompted her to do so. It was one of those strange feeling she sometimes had, an obsessive compulsive type of situation, which suggested if she just looked one more time maybe there just might be something she missed; the final piece to her puzzle. She knew it was an exercise in futility as the box had been empty when she checked only a few moments earlier. But she could not stop herself from looking inside the box one last time nonetheless.

However, instead of seeing an empty box, she found an old, tattered yellowed envelope lying in the bottom. She could not believe her eyes. Stephanie was certain the box had been empty, yet there it was. She reached down into the box and withdrew the envelope, hoping against hope to find the final answer. She found much more than she had bargained for.

Chapter 29

Stephanie sat staring at the strange envelope she held in her quaking hands. Where had it come from? She was certain it hadn't been in the box previously. She was reminded of that day almost half a year ago when she held another envelope in similar shaking hands; the day she received notice of her inheritance. But somehow, she knew the information in this envelope was not going to be a letter notifying her of impending good fortune but would be one leading to nothing but tragedy and sorrow. Still, she had to open the envelope. She had to know what was inside.

The envelope was actually a brand new manila envelope; the same type she had been using to catalog her discoveries since the start of the project. She had personally purchased the box of envelopes at a local stationary supply store. But none of that prior knowledge seemed to matter to Stephanie. Because when she looked at the envelope, it appeared to her to be old, yellowed and tattered, as if to suggest it might have come directly from one of her ancestors. And in a true and very horrifying sense, it actually had. That is to say, the illusion of the aged envelope had been planted in her mind. The entities inhabiting her home and controlling her thoughts needed her to finish the story and wanted her to discover the horrible truth. Stephanie had to believe she was finding this secret for herself in order for the evil creatures to complete the final portion of their unholy scheme.

Stephanie slowly slid open the top flap of what she saw as a brittle envelope, carefully and gingerly folding it backward in order to withdraw its contents. What she found was a letter, several pages long, which appeared to be written in longhand in an elaborate calligraphic style. Like the envelope, the paper appeared to be an ancient and fragile type of yellowed stationary stock, likely expensive in its time and was personalized with a watermark in the shape of a stylized "L", which she assumed, must stand for Livingston.

As Stephanie stared down at what was actually several blank sheets of modern typing paper, she began to read the contents of the mysterious ancient document; written in words only she could see.

From the personal journal of Marie Louise O'Hara Livingston Nov. 16, 1922.

Stephanie was caught off guard for a moment. "Today's date is November 16, 2012," she said aloud in amazement. "It is exactly ninety years to the day, from when this entry was made." Her heart thudded with both anxious anticipation as well as an unexplainable sense of impending dread. She nonetheless read on, driven by a thirst for knowledge, which demanded to be quenched.

Dwight must think me some sort of fool. He believes I am unaware of what he had been doing behind my back, and with whom. While I stay at home raising his three children, he is out gallivanting with his whore; that immoral sow, that depraved vixen who goes by the name of Agatha Jefferson.

Stephanie was stopped in her tracks. That name, Agatha Jefferson. Stephanie suddenly realized where she had seen that name before. She went back to her computer screen and reexamined Jason's side of the family tree. Her stomach sank with revulsion. She was right. She wished to God she was mistaken but she was correct. Agatha Jane Jefferson had been the name of Jason's great-grandmother, the one for whom she could not locate a husband. Could this be the same Agatha Jefferson that Marie Livingston had written about? She didn't like the direction this letter was heading; no, not in the slightest. Her stomach felt as if it might heave at any moment.

He claims to be working late, to be busy conducting his business dealings far into the evening, but I am no fool. I know better. The Devil's business is what he is up to I say. Spreading his demon seed about the county with his harlot is the only business in which he participates. Sharing a bed with that jezebel. That is his supposed important business.

"Oh my God!" Stephanie said aloud in bewildered amazement. "What in the world was going on? Was Jason's great-grandmother sleeping with my great-grandfather? Is that what Marie is saying? Could that have actually been possible?"

Stephanie suddenly recalled how the lawyer. Mason Armstrong had mentioned, since both sides of their family had been from Schuylkill County there might be a chance they were distantly related several generations back. She thought he was just trying to be funny or clever, but perhaps he had unknowingly been right. Or maybe he had seen the letter she now held in her hands and he had known about everything. She was uncharacteristically grateful the lawyer was now dead. She knew how terrible such a thought was for her to have, but at least she wouldn't have to face him in her shame.

She never counted on discovering something as unsavory as an extramarital love affair, let alone a love triangle involving ancestors from both sides of their families. She hadn't believed such things happened back in the early 1900's. But then she realized such types of illicit relationships were going on since the dawn of time. Although disgusted by what she read, she was driven to learn more. She looked down at the blank paper and continued to read the message Marie Livingston wanted her to read.

But I am not the fool Dwight makes me out to be. I have heard the women in the marketplace speaking in hushed whispers as I walk by. They all laugh at me behind my back. They enjoy my pain because we are wealthy and they are but the wives of poor coal miners. They seem to take pleasure from what has happened as if it somehow brings me down to their low social level. I have overheard snippets of their conversations... bits and pieces... enough for me to be able to piece together the sordid mess. I have found out about her, Agatha, about what she has been doing with my husband... and about their bastard daughter as well.

"Bastard daughter?" Stephanie exclaimed. This story was getting worse by the minute. Now she wondered if the daughter about whom Marie was speaking was some other daughter or could it actually have been Elizabeth Jane Jefferson, Jason's grandmother. Could her grandmother, who had survived the Livingston tragedy and Jason's grandmother have been half-sisters? It seemed impossible, or at least it was impossible for Stephanie to comprehend.

Oh yes. I have learned the horrible truth and I would be dishonest if I didn't say that the knowledge has vexed me to the point where I am struggling with my own sanity. Each day that I am forced to reside in this house with that ungodly fornicator, knowing that his illegitimate offspring lives in town, just a few miles away, knowing that others in the community have been aware of his indiscretions and are ridiculing me behind my back, the more I feel myself losing touch with reality. And why would that seem so strange? Why should I want to try to live a normal life, bearing the burden of this knowledge? Why should I not just let my mind go? Why not just stop fighting this inevitable creeping madness? I suppose should speak to someone. Maybe I could talk to our minister, but what in the world would I say to him? After all, he too is a man. He would most certainly side with Dwight and blame me for not providing for my husband's manly needs. Oh dear God, I am beside myself with anguish.

Stephanie's eyes welled up with tears. The language Marie used in her journal was so heartfelt and so incredibly painful to read, that she felt as if she, Stephanie, were feeling the very same pain and sorrow Marie had endured. Stephanie suddenly was reminded of how several months earlier Jason had been working so many late nights and she had briefly wondered whether or not he might have been having an affair; perhaps with someone at work. Although she had put the idea all but completely out of her mind, she now recalled the pain she felt in the pit of her stomach at the very thought of him cheating on her. Had it been true, she might have suffered with the exact same feelings Marie expressed in her letter.

My heart has been broken and now I can feel my mind is rapidly on its way to shattering as well. I know I must do something but I know not what that might be. I am not proud to say I have actually considered killing both Dwight and his harlot. I have had fantasies of slitting their throats with a butcher knife and listening to their final breath bubble and gurgle from there open wounds. I have dreamt of watching the light leave their eyes as they slipped away in death. I have even imagined kidnapping and drowning their little bastard, Elizabeth Jane, in the river like a sick kitten; and perhaps someday I will.

"Elizabeth Jane?" Stephanie exclaimed horrified. It was as if reading the name of the child in Marie's letter made it official. The "bastard" girl Marie referred to was Jason's grandmother. Stephanie and Jason really were related. And although any relation might be considered distant, it was still too close for Stephanie to feel comfortable. To make matters worse, Jason's great-grandmother had been a shameless slut, not only throwing herself at Dwight, a married man, but allowing herself to bare his illegitimate child as well. Then the woman had the audacity to parade the little girl around town proudly like there was nothing wrong and as if she had every right to do so. She shamelessly allowed all of the women in Ashton to see the result of her immoral actions.

Stephanie was becoming furious as she thought of the shame and humiliation Marie must have felt at being subjected to such an outrage. Marie was obviously a proper woman; a woman of high breeding while Agatha was likely nothing more than a common tramp. What other sort of woman would allow herself to behave in such an unacceptable manner? And to think that this slut, this whore was Jason's great-grandmother! Stephanie was starting to realize that had she been Marie; she too might have wanted to seek revenge for the injustice. She too might want to drown the illegitimate child in a river as Marie had suggested. With extreme uncertainty, Stephanie read the next section of Marie's journal entry.

Drowning seems like a fitting end for such an immoral blemish on a righteous society. Miraculously, I have somehow managed to hold onto enough of my shattered mind to prevent myself from turning my murderous thoughts into foul deeds. I can still comprehend that if I were to take such an action, I would likely spend the rest of my life in prison. Perhaps someday, when my mind has become completely lost... I can only hope then I will be able to act without any such moral or rational considerations.

But for now, I have to think of my children... Dwight's children... my two sons and daughter. My Sarah Louise is the spitting image of me. She is my sweetheart and my joy. She is my precious own little girl for certain, so much like me that I now prefer to imagine she was conceived without the benefit of Dwight's accursed seed. She looks nothing like her father. She acts nothing like her father. In fact, she IS nothing like her father. She is like me and only like me.

"My grandmother," Stephanie said quietly. "My grandmother looked just like her mother." Stephanie thought back to how she, herself had resembled Marie in the portrait which had originally hung in the living room and which now was stored in the attic. "We all must look similar. We must all look like Marie." Stephanie recalled her own mother and how much they resembled each other as well. Stephanie read further.

My boys on the other hand, Matthew and Charles, they are so very much like their father. In fact, they look and act so much like their father that it sometimes frightens me. It is almost as if they are not just his sons but copies of himself. And now, since learning of Dwight's sinful treachery, I have begun to wonder what will become of these two boys when they grow to be men.

Do they have more than appearance in common with Dwight? Will they too someday grow up to break the heart of the women they profess to love? Will they lay with wanton women and father bastards like Dwight has done? Will they subject their wives to shame and humiliation as I have been subjected? I suspect they probably will. They both are so much like their father. They idolize him, imitate him and want to be just like him. I would have to assume their fate will lie on a similar accursed path as their father's.

Stephanie was once again taken aback. What was Marie saying? If she originally didn't like the tone of the journal, she liked it even less now. Once again her stomach turned, but this time in anticipation of what sort of unspeakable direction the journal entry might take.

I must do something to punish Dwight for what he is done to me, but what that will be I still do not yet know. I can barely find the strength and presence of mind to write this account, let alone to plan my revenge. My mind wanders constantly, never able to stay on one subject for very long. I seem to think in short random bursts and from the reactions of those with whom I have interacted of late, I suspect my speech might also have become just as erratic. I see how they look at me and how they all talk about me when they think I am not noticing. It is like they all know I am going mad and as if they are all in it together against me; all waiting for the madness to take control.

Perhaps I already am mad, and if so then all the better. Because if I truly am insane then these horrible thoughts of revenge and violence I have been having are not my fault. If I can't stop these thoughts and if I can't control them, how can they be my fault? Maybe I am a danger, not only to others but also to myself. Maybe I should be locked away

*somewhere, in a place where I cannot act on my
unspeakable thoughts.*

*But what if I were to act on them, would it be my fault? Of
course not. The blame would lie entirely at Dwight's feet. He
is the guilty party here, not I. I am quite certain people
would all say he was the one responsible, not me. He is the
one who had lain with the harlot. He is the one who
fathered the bastard child. He is the one whose activities
would have been responsible for driving me mad. How could
that possibly be considered my fault? Who would blame
me? No one, I suspect. They would say Dwight brought all of
it upon himself by his immoral actions. They might even
honor me for my courage in the face of such adversity.*

*They might try to lock me up or even hang me for my
actions, but what would I care? My life as I once knew it is
over, so what would be the difference? It would still be
better than living with the shame of what has happened to
me, and being helpless to strike back. I'm certain if I am
locked up, I would miss my lovely little Sarah, but God help
me... I believe I would not miss the boys. No, not one bit. I
would not miss seeing their father's face reflected in theirs,
his eyes in their eyes, his sinful actions in their future
actions. I know that is a most horrible and un-motherly
thing to say, but the more I think of it the more sense it
begins to make to me. Those two are more his boys than
mine.*

A cold chill ran from the base of Stephanie's skull to the
bottom of her spine, and her stomach clenched to read such
insane ravings. Marie may have believed she was losing her mind,
but Stephanie was certain the woman's mind was long gone by
the time the letter was written. She could not imagine thinking
such evil thoughts about her little Sammy. True he did look
exactly like Jason, he too idolized his father and in many ways
acted just like Jason, but he was his own special person. Sammy
was the result of both her and Jason's love. She could not imagine
herself thinking as Marie had thought, but then again neither had
she gone through the mental anguish which Marie had suffered.
Perhaps such trauma caused one to think irrationally and allowed
irrational ideas to seem rational. Stephanie hoped she would
never have to find out for herself. She read on.

I know such a statement might sound cruel, especially since the boys sprang forth from my own womb, but they are just so much like him; like that horrible lecherous father of theirs. I know I shouldn't think like that. They are not just his boys but they are my boys too. I love them. But they are also his boys as well and he loves them too. And God forgive me, but I hate him so. And I want to hurt him in a way he will never forget.

I must think further on this. My mind is swimming in a river of befuddlement. I am beyond confused. I am unsure of which of my thoughts are real and which are fantasies. I know what I want to do but that is in direct conflict with what my mind is telling me I should do. I think I now know how to hurt Dwight. I know now how to break his heart as he has broken mine. But I can't do it. Can I? Yet I know I must do it. I will do it, but not today. Not this month. Another time. God help me I need to rest. I need to think clearly. I hate what Dwight has done to me. And I hate the rambling wretch he has caused me to become.

That was where the letter ended. Stephanie looked off into the distance as if in a trance, thinking about what he had just read. She set the papers down on the floor next to her and once again, it was no longer the aged stationary adorned with calligraphy but was a stack of new printer paper completely blank.

Stephanie reviewed the newly typed family tree and compared the names once again with those she read in the letter. As strange as it might seem to her, it was true that Dwight Livingston was not only her great-grandfather but was Jason's illegitimate great-grandfather as well. They shared a common ancestor, and although distantly related, they were essentially cousins.

In Marie's letter, she had said how much her boys looked like Dwight and her daughter looked like her. Maybe Dwight's illegitimate daughter carried whatever genes might be responsible for this similarity and passed it down through Jason's lineage as well. Stephanie remembered again how much she and Jason resembled the portrait of Marie and Dwight. Then she began to recall how often people commented on how they both made such a perfect couple, how good they looked together, or how much they looked as if they were meant to be together. Some people even went so far as to say they looked more like brother and sister than husband and wife. And now she had discovered the reason why; they actually were related!

She began to ponder if she would have discovered this information early on in their relationship; would she still have gotten involved with him?

She assumed she would not have, under fear of potential birth defects in their offspring. But Sammy was not deformed or didn't suffer any mental deficiencies. He was a perfectly normal child. Then she realized something she had never thought about previously. Sammy was not exactly a perfectly normal child, was he? No. He was special, very special. She recalled how he was overly sensitive to things that for most children went unnoticed. Stephanie recalled how he had reacted when he had seen the mirror in Washburn's bedroom so many months ago and how he had appeared to react much differently to their other kids when he stood staring out into the field where the dear carcass lay rotting. They had been revolted, disgusted and frightened by the event, but not Sammy. He had been smiling and repeating the work boys, repeatedly.

"Boys?" Stephanie said. "He had been saying boys. What had he been seeing?" She thought once again of Marie's journal entries about her two boys and about how those two boys as well as Dwight and Marie had all died on the exact same day. And how that day was December 19, which was also Sammy's birthday.

She had to find out what happened back then. She had to learn what tragedy had befallen the Livingstons of that December day in 1922 when Dwight, Marie, Matthew and Charles all perished. And she had to learn once and for all what the mysterious horrible family secret was that caused her parents to essentially destroy their own family historical records.

From inside the mirror Marie watched unseen from her world of the dead. She was becoming anxious with anticipation, seeing the plan finally beginning to take shape. Now there was just one more thing Stephanie had to see today.

Stephanie looked once again into the envelope, which she thought was empty and was surprised to find a folded piece of yellowed newspaper buried deep near the bottom of the envelope. It was strange that she had not seen it before when she had found Marie's letter, not to mention the fact that she had never noticed the envelope in the box in the first place. But like the letter, it seemed today was the day that this article was to make its presence known.

To any other onlooker, the "article" from the newspaper would have looked like a clipping from the previous day's daily newspaper, freshly printed in modern newsprint, probably an advertisement or some general uneventful local news. But to

Stephanie, like the letter it appeared ancient, yellowed and tattered.

The front-page article was dated December 21, 1922 and was from the Ashton Daily News. The headline screamed in bold letters "Murder-Suicide Claims The Lives Of Four Family Members".

Chapter 30

"Murder suicide?" Stephanie exclaimed. "Oh my Lord!" She looked back to make sure she had not alarmed Sammy with her outburst but saw he was still sitting lethargically staring at the television screen. She didn't even notice that the screen was completely blank. Instead, she refocused on her documents and began to read the details of the story as reported in the mysterious article. She had been familiar with modern day big city newspaper style, short and to the point with little flourish. The article from the box read more like a pulp fiction story than a newspaper article. Perhaps it was because that style of writing was something accepted in small town turn-of-the-century newspapers or maybe it was because nothing so horrendous had ever occurred in the area before. Either way she was surprised by the tone of the narrative writing style.

The bodies of four local family members were discovered in the early afternoon hours on their small farm located just a few miles outside of Ashton. Although Ashton constables are investigating the occurrence, unofficial reports suggest the unpleasant incident might possibly have been a case of murder-suicide.

An unidentified informant close to local authorities told the Ashton Daily News the bodies of Dwight and Marie Livingston, ages 32 and 30 respectively, were found on the floor of their bedroom. Mrs. Livingston appeared to have been strangled to death by her husband, who was found with an apparent self-inflicted fatal knife wound across his throat. Two separate knives were found at the scene, one was a kitchen knife, lying apparently unused on the bedroom floor. While the other blade was an ivory handled straight razor, apparently belonging to Mr. Livingston, which was found covered with Mr. Livingston's blood lying next to his dead body.

"Ivory handled straight razor?" Stephanie exclaimed, recalling the antique razor Jason had found in a cigar box in one of the dresser drawers in the master bedroom. He had been quite surprised to find the implement in such good condition and assumed Emerson Washburn had used it. Jason now used that razor to shave daily. Stephanie wondered if Jason's razor could have possibly been the same blade described in the newspaper article. She hoped to God it was not.

Stephanie thought about the journal entry she had just read from Marie Livingston and how the woman had said she wanted to slit Dwight's throat with a kitchen knife. But according to what the article read, Dwight may have actually slit his own throat. Although disturbed by the facts unfolding before her eyes, Stephanie wanted to know more.

Mr. Livingston was found on the floor in a seated position, his back resting against a wall cradling his dead wife's body in his lap. She was said to have been found dressed in an evening gown and covered with Mr. Livingston's blood, which had flowed down from her husband's mortal wound.

For some unknown reason this scene seemed strangely familiar to Stephanie. It was as if she had seen it played out before, perhaps in a movie. In reality, she had seen this and much more in the series of nightmares she had experienced the night before their first visit to the property months earlier. But as before, she never was able to recall having the dreams.

Sometime later, police discovered the bodies of the Livingston's two sons, Matthew age six and Charles age four near an open well on the property. Cause of death was presumed to be drowning.

Details are unsubstantiated at this time, and it is unknown if the drowning was accidental or if either Mr. or Mrs. Livingston may have killed the two boys in a fit of madness by drowning them in the frigid well water. Until more evidence has been gathered, sources said all the police can do at this time is speculate based on what they have seen.

Our source close to the authorities said the police are considering the possibility that Mrs. Livingston may have drowned her sons as her arms were covered with small scratches of the type one would receive from a struggling child. It was further suggested that Mr. Livingston might have returned home, found the boys then confronted his wife in their bedroom where he apparently strangled her for her part in the foul deed.

The Livingston bedroom door was found broken and dangling from a single remaining hinge, indicating the husband must have broken it down. If the above scenario were accurate then one could speculate that Mr. Livingston, overcome with remorse for his own vile actions in the murder of his wife, may have slashed his own throat with his straight razor eventually succumbing to his wound and dying with her corpse in his arms.

"Oh my God!" Stephanie said as the tears welled up in her eyes and began to stream down her cheeks. Her breath was coming in short hitching bursts and a buzzing began to ring inside her head making her feel as if she might pass out. Her worst fears had been realized. No. This was far beyond her wildest imaginings. Her great-grandmother, Marie Livingston must have lost her mind upon learning of her husband's treachery and killed her own two sons in some misguided attempt to get revenge against him. Why or how the woman could do such a thing made no sense to Stephanie and although she knew nothing about insanity, she had to assume Marie had not been in control of her faculties and wasn't completely aware of what she had been doing.

The bodies of the Livingston parents were discovered in the early afternoon by Mrs. Amelia Miller, sister to Dwight Livingston. Mrs. Miller said she had been returning the Livingston's youngest child, daughter Sarah Louise Livingston, age two, who had been spending the night with the Miller family. Mrs. Miller then sent her carriage driver to the town of Ashton for help. While awaiting arrival of the authorities, she looked about the area for the boys and sadly found their dead bodies next to a well at the back of the property.

Mrs. Miller, a resident of the town of Ashton was stricken with grief over the tragedy and provided only one comment. She said, "This... this is so incredibly horrible... so unthinkable. Thank God I had Sarah with me or she might have been part of this awful tragedy as well." Mrs. Miller has assumed temporary custody of her niece.

"Oh my heavens!" Stephanie cried aloud. "This is unbelievable!" Then she began to think again about all of the things she had learned about her family, about Jason's family and was quite certain the newspaper had gotten the story correct.

Stephanie sat for a moment in silence trying to absorb all she had discovered. From inside the mirror hanging on the back wall of the loft, Marie Livingston stared out with wild and insane eyes, which glowed madly with her sick pleasure. She had accomplished what she needed to accomplish. She had gotten Stephanie to learn the facts of the family tragedy, but that was still not enough. She needed the woman to feel her pain; to experience the events as if she had lived them herself. This was not only important but it was essential for the next part of the plan to evolve as necessary.

From inside her mirror world, Marie waved one of her gnarled fingers and from the tip of her yellow-brown split nails, a series of sparkling white tiny iridescent lights flew, traveling across the loft area and encircling Stephanie's head. Within a moment, the lights began to sink down through her scalp and enter the top of her skull, implanting themselves deep within her brain.

Stephanie went into a trance-like state, not unlike that of her son Samuel, who still sat mouth agape staring at the blank TV screen. Stephanie too was now staring out into space, unaware of her surroundings, watching a scene like a movie unfold within her mind.

She was no longer sitting in her loft but was sitting in the formal living room of the farmhouse. She thought of it as her parlor. It was traditionally a place to meet and entertain guests, decorated in a fine style fashionable during that time period. However, today she was not entertaining anyone in her formal room; she was alone and was contemplating her plans for later that day.

It was early morning on December 19th, 1922, and Marie had arranged for her sister-in-law Amelia Miller to come and take her daughter Sarah to stay with her and her husband overnight. Marie not only wanted to have Sarah out of the way, but she also wanted to have provisions in place for the child's future care. She knew her actions, which would soon follow, would force Amelia to take the steps necessary to provide this care.

Amelia loved little Sarah. And as of yet her own marriage had not produced any children, so she treasured any time she could have alone with the child. Marie knew no matter how Amelia might feel about her personally now, or how she was likely to feel about her in the near future, she would be more than willing take Sarah under her wing and love her like one of her own, in the event such a need arose. And Marie was quite certain the need would indeed arise after tonight.

Marie and Amelia had not always gotten along very well and on occasion, Amelia seemed to act very strange and distant around Marie; perhaps even more so in recent weeks. Marie had to admit her behavior and mannerisms had become a bit eccentric due to the strain she had been feeling from recent developments. She suspected Amelia noticed those erratic behaviors and she might simply be reacting to them. Then again, Dwight was her only brother and perhaps Amelia sensed the strain in their marriage and was distancing herself from Marie in order to be loyal to her brother. As they say, blood is thicker than water.

Amelia arrived by carriage about 9:15 am and entered the house where Marie sat waiting with Sarah and her small travel case. When Marie opened the front door for Amelia, little Sarah ran to greet her, hugging her legs.

"Hello, Marie," Amelia said, lightly grasping her sister-in-law in an obligatory but not heart-felt embrace. "I trust all is well with Dwight and the boys."

Marie couldn't help but notice how any well wish for her was blatantly missing from the statement. Whether intentional or not, it was obvious to Marie.

"All is as well as can be expected, I suppose," Marie replied cryptically. She didn't intend to discuss any of the marital problems she was having, with her husband's sister of all people. Besides, Marie suspected if half the town of Ashton knew of Dwight's philandering, then it was likely Amelia did as well.

"And so where are Dwight and the boys today?" Amelia said with an unusual tone in her voice, or perhaps Marie only imagined it.

Marie replied, "They are all fine. Dwight is away for the day on business and should be arriving later this evening. The boys are out in the fields playing and doing whatever it is boys do in such situations."

"Those boys are adorable," Amelia said. "They remind me so much of their father when he was a boy."

This statement caused Marie to twitch slightly as if she had been stung or bitten by an insect. "Yes..." Marie said trying to regain her composure. "I had been thinking the very same thing. The boys adore their father and I wouldn't be at all surprised if they grew up to be just like him."

When Amelia heard Marie say this, the look in the woman's eyes did not match the look of pride, which such a statement should have invoked. Instead, it appeared as if Marie might be disappointed at the idea of her boys growing up to be like their father. She could not comprehend this, as she loved her brother and was proud of the way he provided so handsomely for his wife and children. Her own husband did his best to earn a living but he would never be as successful as Dwight. In Amelia's opinion, Marie should not only be proud of her husband but should worship the ground he walked on. Marie never shared that sentiment, and especially not of late.

"Well then," Amelia said after a few moments of awkward silence, realizing she had nothing else to say to her sister-in-law. "I suppose we should be on our way." With that Amelia and Sarah entered the carriage and the driver headed down the lane to being the trip back to Ashton. "We will see you tomorrow late morning then. Say hello to Dwight and the boys for me. Sorry I missed them."

Marie replied, "I certainly will." But in her heart, she knew by the time Amelia returned with Sarah, the boys would be dead and hopefully their father would be as well. Her own future would be uncertain but she suspected the rest of her life would be either spent rotting away in prison or dangling from a rope; that would be up to the courts.

The scene in Stephanie's mind suddenly changed to dusk, later that same day. She was now inside the body of Marie Livingston and was staggering out toward the back of the property, where a large open well stood looking like a small stone edifice sprouting from the ground. It was round and constructed of large fieldstones and stood about three feet high.

As she approached the well, each of Marie's hands held tightly to the tiny hands of her sons, Matthew, age six and Charles age four. The boys seemed to sense something was very wrong as they were struggling to break her tight grasp.

"Mommy. Stop," Matthew said. "Where are you taking us Mommy? Please. Mommy, we're afraid. You look so angry Mommy. What did we do? Please stop Mommy. We'll be good. We promise. We won't be bad boys anymore."

Charles didn't speak, he just cried, probably egged on by the obvious terror in Matthew's pleading voice. This begging was futile as it fell upon deaf ears. Marie was too far-gone for rational thought or to succumb to the pleas of the terrified boys; Dwight's boys, as she now thought of them. She had a plan and a mission, and no force in Heaven or Hell could stop her.

Young Charles held a small stuffed bear in his free hand. It was his favorite toy, given to him by Dwight. Marie ignored their cries for help and continued to drag the boys onward. She kept repeating in her mind and mumbling incoherently, "Just like your father. You look like him. You act like him. Someday you will end up being whoremongers just like him. Not if I can help it. Oh no. Not if I can help it."

Dwight had constructed a cover for the well out of timber to prevent any young children from accidentally falling into it. The trap door of this cover was always kept closed and secured with a lock, the key for which he kept high in a cabinet in the kitchen. The depth of the well was such that a man or even young teenager could have successfully climbed out. In fact, a fully-grown adult could lean into the well and with a bit of stretching could touch the top surface of the water. However, small children would never have been able to escape its depth, nor scale its slippery sides. Marie had come out earlier in the day with the key and opened the top of the well.

When she reached the side of the well she stopped for a moment, then without a word of explanation, she lifted the smallest boy, Charles by one hand over the side of the well and dropped him screaming into the icy water below. As he flew through the air, he dropped his stuffed bear onto the frozen meadow near the well. Then Marie bent and using both hands lifted Matthew. He fought, scratched and clawed at her arms in a futile attempt to get free of her grasp, but his only freedom came during those few seconds as he was hurled through the air seeing the icy blackness of the well below rapidly approaching.

Marie stood at the top of the well looking down at the boys and began screaming maniacally as tears streamed down her cheeks. "He made me do this. Your father made me do this. You are both so much like your father. Just like your whore-loving worthless father. You will never get the chance to do to anyone what he did to me." From below, she heard the boys' cries and pleas for help but stood above watching them bob in the icy water below, without an ounce of sympathy for them. If she had a last minute change of heart she could have reached in and saved one if not both of them, but she was too far-gone for that. The boys soon came together and hugged each other in and final attempt to get warm before eventually succumbing to the frigid December temperatures and drowning in each other's arms. "Just like your father." She said breathlessly, "The both of you. Just like your father. And soon he will be just like you. Dead. Just like the both of you."

Dwight Livingston slowly made his way up the long dirt and gravel roadway, which led to his house from the main road. His model T Ford chugged and sputtered nosily up the frozen drive, occasionally slipping and sliding as plumes of smoke and steam billowed around it in the cold night air. Dwight was one of the first people in the area able to afford a motor vehicle and as such was probably prouder of this possession than just about anything else he owned. As he approached the house, he saw some activity out in the back of his property near the well. In the bright moonlight, he could see a woman in a white nightgown staring down into his well.

Marie turned hearing her husband's car approaching in the distance and decided she had better head back to the house. She glanced over and saw Dwight leaving his Model T and start walking across the meadow toward her. She hurried away, trampling Charles' stuffed toy into the slush and mud as she did. When she was about a third of the way to the house, Dwight had made it about half the distance to the well. He saw Marie storming back toward the house. At first, he was going to call out to her to let her know he was home, but suddenly he realized something felt very wrong.

Dwight got a strange sensation in the pit of his stomach and looking out at the direction from where Marie had come he noticed the top cover of the well was removed. Only he or Marie knew where the key for the well was kept. Then he looked back at Marie and saw she didn't have a bucket or any means of carrying water. So why was she at the well if not to get water? As he approached the well, he saw something on the ground smashed into the wet snow covered soil. In an instant, he recognized the object as the stuffed bear he had recently brought home for little Charles.

"Oh my God, no!" he screamed silently in his mind and using his walking stick for support, began to hurry toward the well, hoping not to find what he somehow knew he would find.

When he got to the well, he bent down and picked up Charles' toy then headed straight for the opening. The boys knew not to play near the well; he had told them so and they knew they were forbidden to play there. The boys always obeyed their father's requests. There was absolutely no way they would have come this close to the well without either he or Marie bringing them here. And he was quite certain they would be terrified to come near. He had done a good job of making them fearful of the dangers.

With dread building deep in the pit of his stomach, Dwight peered unwillingly down over the side of the well where he saw his two beloved sons entwined in a last embrace of death, bobbing in the frigid, but not yet frozen water below. Without hesitation, he leaned as far as he could into the well and with his long arms was able to grab onto the water-soaked coats of both boys. Pulling with all of his might, he lifted their cold, still bodies from their icy tomb and laid them as gently as possible on the frozen meadow. Their ice glazed bodies seemed to glow iridescent light blue in the moonlight making them look like angels.

Dwight fell to his knees near his dead sons and began to scream and cry his heart out. Near the house, Marie turned upon hearing Dwight's wails and stood for a moment with pleasure, watching him fall to pieces over the bodies of his boys. She walked into the house, through the kitchen and along the way picked up a long butcher's knife. She would be ready. When Dwight came for her, she would be ready. Then she walked slowly up to the master bedroom.

Chapter 31

Stephanie continued to stare out into space in her hypnotic state, watching the events of that horrible night play out on the movie screen of her mind. She was now inside the mind of her great-grandfather, Dwight Livingston, seeing the scene from his perspective and reliving the thoughts and feelings he experienced.

Dwight slowly tried to stand up on wobbly legs, looking back toward the farmhouse. He saw Marie looking out at him for just a moment as she approached the kitchen door, just before she quickly turned to enter the house. He wanted to call to her, but his voice caught in his throat when he saw her face: that horrible expression. He would have sworn in the rising moonlight he had seen her smiling at him. But it was not her typical smile, not the one he known and had fallen in love with so many years ago. It appeared more like a hideously bizarre grin; one that radiated some twisted sort of rapture, which bordered the realm of insanity. What was wrong with his wife, and what in the name of God had happened to his boys tonight? Had she found the boys dead in the well and lost her mind with grief? God knew he was barely able to hold onto his on sanity over it. But why in the world had she been wearing such an unsettlingly hideous expression at such an unimaginable time?

Dwight had assumed at first some type of terrible yet innocent accident must have occurred. He had given Marie the benefit of the doubt because she was his wife and the mother of his children. He assumed she might have mistakenly left the top of the well open. He thought perhaps the boys had disobeyed his orders and had accidentally fallen into the opening. Perhaps Charles had fallen in and Matthew had climbed in to try to save him. Although it wasn't far down to the surface of the water, Dwight knew the sides were too steep and too slippery with ice for them to have had a chance to get out. The frigid water surly had taken them quickly. Although it was an unspeakable tragedy, he was certain it surely had to have been an accident. Perhaps Marie had heard their cries for help and had come to the well in a futile attempt to try to rescue them. He wanted to believe that was so; he needed to believe it. But he couldn't because deep down inside, he already knew the truth.

After seeing the insane look on his wife's face as she glared madly out at him from the kitchen doorway, he had no choice but to accept the truth. If she was innocent then why, when she had finally seen him, hadn't she come out to be with him? Why didn't she let him console her and she him in this time of devastating sorrow? Why instead would she look at him with that mad look then turn and quickly enter the house? None of it made any sense to him. He was bewildered, heartsick and confused.

But Dwight was also starting to comprehend. He realized this and began to accept his original assessment of a possible accident had likely been wrong. Maybe some other series of events had taken place; something beyond his previous imaginings; something unthinkable. Could it be that the unimaginable thoughts, which were now forming in his mind might actually have taken place? He couldn't believe such a thing possible. Could it really be that something so vile, born of unbridled evil had actually occurred? And could it be that his own wife; the boys' own mother had been deliberately responsible? He could scarcely allow the question formulate in his baffled mind. He tried to force the thought away but it continued to push its way to the forefront of his thoughts and he had no choice but to accept it.

Once he was able to acknowledge the idea, it went in an instant from a mere thought to a reality. Marie had actually murdered her own sons, his sons.

With a growing anger, Dwight began to make his way through the meadow grass, which was wet with snow. He trudged back toward the farmhouse, stumbling clumsily along the uneven ground, using his walking stick for support. When he got closer to the house, he saw the dark upstairs bedroom, his and Marie's bedroom, begin to come alive with the bright glow from several lanterns. He saw Marie's shape passing behind the sheer curtains covering the windows as she moved about lighting one lantern after another. Under other circumstances, he might have found that image alluring and sensual, but now it seemed sinister and surreal.

By the time he reached the backdoor of the house, the bedroom appeared to be ablaze with light. He saw the silhouette of his wife standing at the window apparently looking down at him. He could not make out her facial features in the shadows but assumed she still wore that mad grin he had seen just a few minutes earlier.

Surprisingly, he began to recall other unusual events, which had taken place over the previous month or more. He remembered how strangely Marie had been acting, how distant and how cold she had been toward him. Now that he had taken the time to think further about it, he realized she must have been in the throes of some sort of mental decline brought on by something, but what that might be he had no idea. Or perhaps he was not being completely honest with himself. Perhaps he really did know exactly what would have driven her to such madness and that he was likely responsible.

He was uncertain if this idea was a real possibility or if it was simply the result of his own guilty conscience. Might it be possible that she had somehow learned about his mistress, Agatha and his illegitimate daughter? He had always been concerned such a day might come, but he never thought finding out would have driven Marie to the point of insanity and murder. He mentally cursed the gossiping old biddies of Ashton, those who were likely responsible for Marie learning his secret.

But then again, he hadn't really been discrete, had he? In fact, he had been quite arrogant and flagrant about his indiscretions. He had allowed himself to be seen in public with the mother as well as his child. Now in hindsight he realized just how foolish he had been. At the time, he had felt so confident about what he was doing, almost as if it had been his right as a successful businessman to have a mistress and a second family; but he now felt the hard, cold truth. He was just a broken and sorrowful fool. Marie was always a strong and forthright woman. He should have realized she would never have tolerated his philandering.

Dwight was not necessarily proud of what he had done by any means, but it had made him feel special at the time. He did love the woman Agatha as well as their daughter, yet at the same time he believed he still loved Marie and was certain he loved his other children as well. He realized she might not be able to believe he did still love her, but it was the truth. Could that really be what had happened? But if he were being honest with himself, what else could have driven his wife past the brink of sanity?

Marie knew everything there was to know about Dwight, his strengths as well as his weaknesses. Therefore, she knew how to hurt him. She knew where to strike the blow that would bring him to his knees. She understood how much Dwight loved his two boys and how much they idolized him as well. But could she really have murdered her own flesh and blood as some sick attempt at seeking retribution against him?

Suddenly Dwight thought about their youngest child, their daughter little Sarah. "Oh my God!" he thought, stopping in his tracks. Where was Sarah? What had happened to Sarah? Had Marie killed her too? Surely, Marie couldn't have thrown Sarah into the well, could she? Sarah was so much like her mother that killing her would be like Marie killing herself. But then Dwight realized he was still thinking somewhat rationally, and that was not the way to think if he were trying to follow Marie's train of thought. Since, for Marie Livingston, the days of thinking rationally were gone forever.

He turned and looked back toward the well trying to decide if he had missed finding his daughter's body floating in the bottom because of his shock and confusion. Reflected in the moonlight, he could see the glistening wet bodies of his two dead sons, Matthew and Charles. For a moment, he almost forgot about Marie and considered returning to the well to look for Sarah, but he realized such a move would be futile. If Sarah were truly in the well, it was far too late for anyone to do anything to help her. She would likely have been the first to be thrown in. His heart broke with sorrow and his gut clenched with revolution.

Then he began to fill with a raging fury the likes of which he had never known before. He was going to get the truth from his wife. If was going to find out what had happened to his children if he had to beat her to death to get the answers he needed.

Dwight plowed through the kitchen door and as it flew open it slammed against the inside wall shattering several of the windowpanes. The broken shards tinkled to the floor, sounding like tiny musical instruments as they rained down on its surface. In the back of Dwight's mind, the sound reminded him of the high-pitched melodic laughter of children; his children; his now dead children. Marie would surely pay for what she had done. Dwight realized he was no longer just considering the possibility his wife had killed their children; he was now certain of it. He swore by all that was holy he would make her suffer while she was on earth and cursed her soul and prayed he might find some way to make her pay for her foul deeds in her own special hell.

Stephanie squirmed slightly in her seat, a disturbed expression forming on her face, as the scene played out in her mind. She knew what was coming next in the series of events, but was unable to do anything to stop the steady progression of the living movie flashing across her mind.

At first, she had seen all that Marie had seen. In fact, she had become Marie. Then things had changed and she had become Dwight. Now she seemed to have become separated from both of them and seeing things from the perspective of a spectator, watching the events unfold. And somehow, the situation seemed even more terrifying from this latest perspective. She understood the madness, which possessed Marie as well as the fury, which encompassed Dwight from sampling their emotions first hand. She understood bringing together two people who were operating under extreme emotions would be a recipe for disaster. And of course, she already knew what exactly the disaster was which would follow.

Stephanie found herself floating in the bedroom of her farmhouse. The room was as it appeared in the original house; much smaller than the present day master bedroom but she was still able to recognize it. The room was filled with many of the same antique furnishings, which she and Jason had sold at auction; the ones which Emerson Washburn had chosen to live with. But in the image she was watching, the furniture looked brand new. The room was bright with illumination with an amber glow from a mixture of candles and oil lanterns. Stephanie was surprised by how bright the space appeared.

Across the room she saw Marie, dressed in a night gown, which was wet and splotched with mud and what appeared to be smears of blood. She stood before a full-length mirror, the same one which was now stored in the attic of the farmhouse. But as with the other furnishings, this version of the mirror appeared new. In Marie's reflection Stephanie could the woman was looking down at her own hands, which were covered with deep scratches. The blood in the gashes seemed to have dried and was no longer flowing. The front of her white gown was stained with even larger smears of blood, which must have come from the gouges obtained during her struggling with the boys. Marie was looking into the dressing mirror, and seeing a face, which she apparently did not recognized as her own. Her hair was a mess and her cheeks glistened with the tears yet her face wore an unexplainable expression of ecstasy.

To Stephanie's surprise, Marie picked up a large hairbrush and began delicately stroking her long tresses, never taking her eyes from the eyes of the woman in the mirror. It was like she was locked in a gaze with a person she had never met before, but with whom she was completely fascinated. The bizarre look of calm and the insane, inappropriate smile never left her face, even when the door to the bedroom exploded behind her.

Chapter 32

In a shower of splinters and shattered wood, Dwight Livingston burst through the bedroom door. His business suit, which once hung neatly from his muscular frame, now was in disarray. He still held tightly to his walking stick, with its wolf's-head ivory handle, but now he gripped it less like a means of support and more like a weapon. In the bright light of the oil lamps, Stephanie was amazed at just how much Dwight Livingston resembled Jason, with his dark brown hair and wire-framed glasses, although she had never seen Jason wearing such a look of anger. And she was equally perplexed by how much Marie looked like herself. It was as if she were watching a movie drama in which she and Jason were actors, playing the roles of the Livingstons.

Dwight's eyes brimmed with tears and were wild with rage as he stormed into the room. His breath hitched heavily in his chest, as he struggled to ask the question he obviously wished he would never have to ask, "What the hell did you do, Marie? What in the name of God did you do to our boys?"

Marie slowly turned away from the mirror, looked directly into her husband's eyes. Her calm and relaxed demeanor took him by surprise. His wife smiled and replied, "Me? I did nothing my husband. It was all of your doing."

"M...m...my...my doing?" Dwight stammered, scarcely able to form the words. Then his anger returned. "Of what do you speak, woman? Was it not you who killed our children?"

She hesitated for a moment then admitted with no apparent signs of regret, "Yes, Dwight. I carried out the deed which needed to be done... I was the one who drowned our boys in the well, but it was entirely your fault... It was all because of you... You see, my husband, I had no choice... The boys... well... they were so, so much like you... They worshiped the ground you walked on... They even looked like miniature versions of you... I had no doubt that if I didn't take some sort of action...if I allowed them to grow into men...they each would surely have become the same kind of unfaithful whoremongers just like you have become."

"But...but..." Dwight exclaimed, still unable to completely take control of the situation, "Buy why, Marie? Why would you murder our two innocent babies?"

"Not our babies, Dwight. YOUR babies," she shot back. "They may have come from inside of me but they were the result of your rotten demon seed; the fruit of your damnable loins. And what do you care, anyway? You'll just go out and find one of your trollops and make another baby, or maybe two or three more. For all I know you may already have a dozen other little bastards running about, besides that little bitch I learned about. Oh yes, Dwight, those boys were more yours than mine, and because they were, they needed to die, just like you must die."

With that, Marie pulled the butcher knife from behind her back and held it in front of her, determined to stab her husband to death; to allow him to join what she now thought of in her broken mind as his demon spawn offspring. At last she would get the final bit of her revenge. Holding tightly onto the handle, she thrust the knife at his stomach.

But Marie was not prepared for Dwight's quick reaction. He was much faster than she had anticipated. Before she had a chance to strike, he slammed the ivory wolf's head handle of his walking stick into the side of her skull. Marie collapsed to the floor in a heap, falling down directly in front of the mirror. The knife skittered across the floor out of reach.

Within a second, Dwight was on top of her. He reached down and wrapped his strong hands tightly around her throat squeezing with all of his might. His eyes blazed like fiery embers in his skull glowing with a level of insanity, seeming to surpass even that of his mad wife. The furious Dwight continued to grip Marie's throat ever tighter as her eyes bugged wildly from her skull. Stephanie could see blood begin to trickle down the woman's neck where Dwight's fingernails dug deep furrows into the flesh of her throat. He throttled her back and forth as her head bobbed helplessly to and fro, until eventually with a sharp crack, Stephanie heard the woman's neck break. A moment later the woman who was Stephanie's great grandmother, Marie Louise O'Hara Livingston collapsed to the floor in a dead heap.

Dwight sat on the floor weeping and cradling the dead woman in his trembling arms. With the madness now completely gone from her lifeless eyes, Marie looked even more like Stephanie than she previously had. In fact, it was almost as if she had actually become a doppelganger of Stephanie. As Dwight sat sobbing, Marie's corpse shifted slightly and her arm flopped down, hitting the floor with a sickening thud.

As Stephanie watched in terrorized silence, Dwight reached slowly into his suit jacket pocket and withdrew a long ivory handled straight razor. Now seeing the razor, she realized it actually was the very same razor Jason had found. This realization repulsed Stephanie to no end as chills of disgust and revulsion raced down her spine. She knew what this razor was going to be used for from the newspaper article she had found and wanted to turn away in horror, but was forced to watch the terrible tableau unfold in front of her.

However, unknown to Stephanie as she watched in horror, not only was the razor the exact one used by Dwight almost a century earlier to commit his atrocious act, but it was also used by Emerson Washburn to butcher himself earlier that same year.

It was the same razor, which set in motion the series of events, which would eventually bring her and her family to the property. It was the cursed talisman which allowed Marie and Dwight Livingston to venture beyond the confines of their own place of eternal damnation to begin planning for their one chance to escape from the confines of their torturous hell.

Dwight slowly and calmly lifted the straight razor to his left arm and made several deep horizontal cuts across his wrist. Blood pumped from the wounds and streamed onto the body of his dead wife. It trickled along the length of her arm and eventually began to puddle on the floorboards. Some of the blood beaded on the surface of the floor while the rest of it seeped down into the cracks between the boards.

A moment later, Dwight brought the bloody razor up to his throat and sliced a gaping wound from just below his left ear and continued it over across to his right. It was as though he was unable to feel the pain of the blade. With his head raised and his throat extended, the incision split open up like a cavernous fleshy mouth, exposing all of its musculature inside and allowing blood to pour down his arms and the front of his suit, drenching his dead wife's face and torso with gore. From her point of observation, Stephanie bellowed a silent scream, as she could not stand to see any more.

Within a split second, Stephanie found herself standing in the field behind their property. It was early in the morning on an overcast winter's day and a heavy fog seemed to enshroud everything around her. She saw a woman standing on a rectangular area of the property behind a low wall of stones. She was dressed in a long heavy black woolen coat and wore a matching dark fashionable hat and scarf.

The area looked quite familiar to her, as if she had seen it before and not just because it was part of her property but also because she believed something significant might have happened there which she could not immediately recall. Stephanie turned to her left and saw the familiar hexagonal shape of the spa building in the distance and understood she was standing at the back of her property near the spot where her children had stood staring on the first day they had come to see the house. She wondered how she had gotten outside and why she was at the back of her land.

She looked again at the spa building, noticing how much different it looked, realizing she was looking at the building, as it appeared when it had first been constructed ninety years earlier. Stephanie heard a sniffling sound and saw the woman, standing behind the low wall was crying. She turned slightly in Stephanie's direction and Stephanie immediately recognized the woman as Amelia Miller, Dwight's sister. From behind the Amelia's legs, a small girl dressed in winter coat and hat stepped forward slightly and looked down at something on the ground behind the wall.

Stephanie stepped closer and noticed behind the wall was a small cemetery; a family plot similar to those she had seen on occasions while driving past family farms in rural Pennsylvania. As she approached the two figures, she recognized the young girl as Sarah Livingston. Stephanie followed their gaze downward and saw two small gravestones marking what appeared to be two fresh graves. She also noticed other small gravestones scattered about the place, but their inscriptions had been weathered away by time and the elements making them illegible.

Focusing on the two newer stones Stephanie read the inscriptions "Matthew James Livingston, June 12, 1916 - December 19, 1922" on the first and the second one said "Charles Edward Livingston July 2, 1918 - December 19 1922". She realized she was looking at the grave markers for the boys she had just seen murdered. Each of the stones also had an identical inscription below the dates. Stephanie could barely make them out through the morning fog, but looking closer, she could see they read "Taken From Us Too Soon, By The Hand Of Evil."

Then Amelia spoke, as if addressing the dead boys, "Poor little Matthew and Charles. That miserable witch did this to you and all because of the misdeeds of my own brother. He was so very wrong in what he did and he should have been made to pay for his indiscretions. But there was no reason why you two innocents should have suffered for his mistakes, and most certainly not with your young lives. Although I couldn't have stopped your father and his sinful ways, I was aware of what he was doing. Perhaps I too am guilty; perhaps I should have tried harder to dissuade him. But I did not and I will be sorry for the rest of my days for what happened to you." Then the woman wept openly. Little Sarah clung to her leg, but said nothing.

"But don't you worry, boys," Amelia sobbed, "I promise you with all my heart, I will take good care of your little sister, Sarah, and will raise her as one of my own children. I can only hope you boys have found peace on the other side."

Sarah raised her head slightly as if looking at something else in the graveyard. Stephanie followed her gaze and could see two shapes forming in the morning mist. Her breath caught in her throat as she realized what she and Sarah were seeing appear before them were the images of Matthew and Charles Livingston. Amelia did not seem to see the manifestation, as she showed no signs of reacting in any way.

The boys stood side-by-side, still dressed in their nightclothes, holding hands looking directly at their little sister. Their pajamas appeared to be sodden. The boys were pail as milk, their skin a dusky blue-gray and their large hypnotic staring eyes were sunk deep in their heads, surrounded by dark circles. They seemed to still be covered in a thin skin of ice, which gave their mottled flesh the slightest blue glow. The little child, Sarah, looked out at them with a beatific smile and silently mouthed the word "boys".

Stephanie suddenly flashed back to the first day they had come to the property and recalled that same expression on Sammy's face as he stood in front of what she now believed was this same plot of ground, only almost one hundred years later, wearing that very same expression and mouthing that same word, "boys". Sammy was special, both Stephanie and Jason knew that but they previously had no idea why. But now Stephanie could see her own grandmother as a two-year-old, looking like a miniature version of Marie Livingston, seeing with the same sight beyond normal sight. Now she knew where the gift had originated. Sammy was part of she and Jason, and they were both descendants of Dwight Livingston. This special sight which Sammy seemed to have must be a genetic predisposition handed down through the generations.

Neither she, nor her daughter Cindy had never shown signs of having such a gift and to the best of her knowledge neither had Jason or Jeremy. It must have taken the combining of their similar, but different genetic makeup to allow some recessive gene, which controlled such a sight to come forward in Sammy. Then Stephanie was distracted suddenly hearing Amelia's voice in her head.

Amelia was looking off in the distance to the far left, unaware of the two ghosts watching her. , "Over there is where we put the bodies of your parents." She was silently speaking in her mind to the two boys buried beneath her feat. "I am sorry that I forced you to lie in the same ground with strangers, but I could not allow those two heathens to be buried on the same hallowed ground where you now rest. To bury them here would be a blasphemy to God and an injustice to you both as well. You are better off finding your way to paradise together without your parents" Then speaking to herself she said, "I sincerely doubt they will ever be joining the boys in Heaven. I suspect they will be spending their eternity subjected to the tortures of Hell, at least that is my personal wish for them."

Then the two boys turned slowly together and looked directly at Stephanie. Their dead eyes, now gray with the film of lifelessness seemed to stare a hole in her. The larger of the boys, Matthew on the left raised his hand and pointed in a direction away from their present location and opened his mouth as if to shout. Stephanie felt a vibration building inside of her head and a howl steadily increasing in volume. It seemed to build as if reaching a crescendo and Stephanie feared her eardrums might shatter from the unearthly cry. The banshee shriek was unlike anything she had ever heard uttered from any living creature. Then again, she knew these two entities floating before here were anything but alive. Matthew's gaping maw surrounded by purple-blue colored lips continued to howl until Stephanie thought she might lose her mind.

Then suddenly the noise stopped and Stephanie was no longer standing in the family graveyard but was in another plot of unmarked ground where she could see two other fresh graves with carved headstones. She looked back in the direction where she assumed she had come from. The spa building was now off to her right in the distance and she could no longer see the small graveyard with its low stone wall as it had been engulfed by the morning fog. Fortunately she could likewise neither see nor hear the two dead boys. Then Stephanie's concentration was interrupted by more of Amelia's thoughts.

"I ordered special gravestones for them," Amelia thought. Stephanie was surprised to find that not only had she been transported miraculously to this new location, but so had Amelia and Sarah. Amelia was rambling and apparently speaking to no one in particular. "I have to admit I was a bit generous with Dwight's inscription by having it say 'Devoted Husband, Loving Father, Tragically Taken In The Prime Of Life'. I know he was anything but a devoted husband; however he was a loving father and was also my brother so I chose to be kind and forgiving on his final message.

287

"But in the case of that murdering witch, Marie's grave, I wanted to make sure the world would know exactly what type of horrid creature she was. That's why I had her inscription read, 'May Her Wretched Soul Rot In The Bowels Of Hell For Eternity'

"And believe me, I pray by all that is holy, to the Father, the Son and the Holy Ghost, that Marie's soul does just that. In fact if I could have but one wish it would be that both Marie and Dwight Livingston are forced to share eternity in damnation together, miserable in each other's company until the end of time. I would ask that Dwight be given dominion over her and she would spend her time as his slave. I know that's not the Christian thing to wish but those two lovely little boys are dead because of the sins of both of their parents. They deserve some type of retribution for their suffering."

Looking down at the graves, Stephanie saw something she couldn't at first quite comprehend. Something appeared to be slowly rising up from each of the freshly dug graves. She looked over at Sarah and saw she too was staring down at the earth, mouth agape with a look of terror on her face. As before, Amelia did not seem to see anything.

Before their shocked eyes, images of Dwight and Marie Livingston slowly began to rise up from the mounds of dirt covering the graves. They were dressed exactly as they had been on the night of the murder-suicide, Marie with her blood stained white night gown and Dwight with his rumpled business suit soaked with gore. Marie held her head at an odd angle as if something was not quite right with her neck and the front of Dwight's dress shirt was saturated with blood which seemed to still occasionally trickle from the gaping wound in his neck.

Stephanie was so shocked by what she had just seen and heard she suddenly found herself once again awake in her loft workspace, feeling as if she had just risen from a disturbing dream. Although she could not recall all of the details of what she had just experienced, she remembered the majority of what she learned. Dwight Livingston had fathered a child out of wedlock, a child that would grow up to be Jason's grandmother. Marie had learned of Dwight's indiscretion and had lost her mind, killing her two sons, but for some reason sending her daughter, Stephanie's grandmother away in order that she could survive. Then Dwight had killed Marie and in a fit of anger and then had taken his own life. And it was quite possible the family had actually been buried somewhere on her property.

This was her family's tragic secret and their shame. And she realized this past was not just her family's history but Jason's as well. Both of their families had directly or indirectly played a part in this tragedy. It was a shared disgrace, a shared transgression. And now almost a century later, she and Jason, had come together, both the products of dishonored families; related families. When they met, they had believed themselves to be strangers but that had not exactly been the case. True, they had not known each other and had been strangers in that sense of the word, but they did share a common ancestry. And perhaps at the base level, the primitive animal level, it was possible this shared DNA may have allowed them to feel comfortable with each other from the beginning and might have been what brought them together.

And as such, their union now completed the family circle of blood. But for what reason had they come to meet and eventually become married? Had it truly been by chance or had it somehow been orchestrated? Had whatever unnamed force of the universe, which had caused so many coincidences over the past months, also been responsible for bringing them together.

And why had they been brought to this home? This was the very same home where everything apparently had started. She suddenly believed more than ever, there was some force, some unseen element, which was directing her destiny. And she believed she could do nothing to stop it.

Stephanie had felt from the beginning something was wrong with all of what seemed like apparent good fortune. She always had to work hard for anything she had ever gotten in her life. She should have realized if something seemed too good to be true, it probably was. And now her family members were all here together, forced to live on the very same property where her great-grandparents and family had died so violently.

She had to go and wait for Jason to come home. She had to let him know what she had discovered. She had no idea what they would do next but she knew the bodies of her ancestors were buried somewhere on the property and she needed to find out where. She was sure when Jason learned the whole story, he would think of some way to deal with it. He always had been able to think of some solution in the past; she only hoped he could now.

Stephanie finally began to feel as if she was returning to normal, as if she had awoken from some strange dream or hypnosis. However, she was not actually as normal as she had believed. She took the blank sheet of typing paper in her hands but she nonetheless still saw the hand-written letter from Marie. Likewise, the newspaper article from a recent local newspaper also looked to Stephanie to be the aged story from the Ashton Daily News. Stephanie placed them both back into what to her, appeared to be an old and tattered envelope. Then she tucked the envelope delicately under her arm and walked over to where Sammy sat staring at the blank television screen. Apparently, the DVD had run out some time earlier, but Sammy didn't seem to notice.

Stephanie bent down and picked up her son and began cleaning him up in preparation for heading back to the main house. As she did so, she caught a glimpse of Sammy in the wall mirror and was shocked at just how much he was beginning to look just like Jason, as he grew older. He always had looked like his father, but now as he was beginning to lose his baby looks and take on more of a "big boy" appearance, the resemblance to Jason was becoming more obvious and more pronounced. Although Stephanie could not recall the two boys from her earlier daydream, she thought about the picture of the two Livingston boys she had found earlier and decided to check sometime to see just how closely they might actually resemble her little Sammy. She suspected the similarity would be amazing.

"Oh, Sammy," she said with an odd tone, not quite sounding like herself and as if noticing Sammy's resemblance to Jason for the first time, "You are so much like your father." Then she walked back toward the main part of the house.

Inside the mirror, there was a hideous rumble of merriment as the creatures from the world of the damned, cheered over what they had accomplished; understanding their time of being trapped between worlds would soon end. They would finally find their way out, and in their place, Stephanie and Jason Wright would remain to serve out their sentence.

Chapter 33

Jason looked at Stephanie as if he were trying to make sense of the ramblings of a crazy woman. He had just returned home from work and was hanging up his jacket in the foyer closet seeing the kids playing in the family room. He gave them his customary greeting and could see Connie Franks in the kitchen preparing dinner.

He assumed Stephanie was still in her loft working on her infernal project as usual, but was surprised to see her sitting at the dining room table, paging through a thin document, which she held in trembling hands. She fidgeted in her seat, looking as if she was unable to get comfortable, like she was extremely anxious. She briefly looked up from her page and catching his eye, she frantically signaled him with her gesturing hand to come into the dining room. He sat on the chair next to her, which she had pulled out for him and he could see by her disheveled condition and her less than desirable aroma that yet another day had passed without her benefiting from proper hygiene.

"Jason! Jason!" she said in a whispered voice fraught with agitation, much more so than he had ever seen her before. "Jason! You have to see this... it's unbelievable! ... Just wait 'till you see this!" Her eyes were bulging wide with excitement, perhaps appearing worse by her gaunt and haggard looking face. She seemed to have aged five or more years, the sight of her made Jason think of photos he had seen of World War II death camp survivors. This entire situation was getting way out of control and he knew he would have to take some drastic action very soon.

Several months ago, Jason might have become caught up in her excitement. In fact, he had been very supportive and enthusiastic in the beginning, before things got so strange. But after seeing her in her current mental and physical condition, he was far too concerned about her health and well-being to share in her fervor.

"Steph?" he asked with apprehension. "What in the world is going on with you? Didn't you get a shower again today? You look as if you didn't bother to clean up in days. What's wrong, Steph? Please tell me. I want to help you."

"Nothing's wrong, yet in a way everything's wrong. Don't you see, Jason?" Stephanie replied with a frantic dismissive quality to her voice. "I don't need any help. Not from you. Not from anybody. You don't have to worry about me. I'm fine. In fact, I am better than I have been in a long time. But that doesn't matter...all that matters is this...look...look at this."

Stephanie showed Jason the printed copy of the family tree she had developed. Jason had to lean back a bit to escape the rank smell of Stephanie's foul breath. He wondered with great displeasure when she had last brushed her teeth. Trying desperately to maintain his focus, he reluctantly looked at the document she passed to him.

It appeared to be the very same copy, which she had asked him to look at almost every night for the past several weeks. Each time she showed it to him he had done his best to be supportive. Whenever she would add a name or a date or some other insignificant tidbit of information she would show it to him acting as if she had discovered some rare and priceless treasure. He always tried to react with feigned enthusiasm, although he was honestly sick and tired of hearing about it. What had started out as a harmless little past-time project, had somehow evolved into a full-fledged obsession bordering on mania.

Jason glanced briefly at the document, not actually paying any attention to it, and with unplanned sarcasm born of his months of frustration, he asked sardonically, "Ok, honey. What new incredible historical fact did you discover that has gotten you so excited? Leave me guess...your grandfather was once a physician's assistant...no...no... Your great-grandmother had a long lost cousin named Bertha who knew someone who knew someone who once knew Abe Lincoln. I can hardly wait to hear the news." He hated hearing the cynicism in his own voice but it had been an exhausting week both at work and at home and he was stressed to the point of breaking. The last thing he wanted to do was to sit and listen to the wild ramblings of his fixated wife.

Stephanie's reaction to Jason's sarcasm was not what he had expected. He had assumed she was so caught up in her own world the comment would pass right by her unnoticed. Fortunately, the kids were too engrossed in the blaring television to pay attention to them. But Connie Franks was keeping an eye on the escalating situation with furtive glances from the kitchen. Stephanie noticed the woman paying what she felt was far too much attention to them so she stood abruptly, grabbing Jason by the wrist.

"Jason, come with me!" she said in a commanding tone, which caught him so by surprise there was little he could think to do but to follow her. She led him out into the hallway, past the family room and finally up the stairs and down the hall to the master bedroom. Once inside, Stephanie shut the door and directed Jason to sit on the edge of the bed.

He sat quietly, looking attentively holding the family tree document while Stephanie paced back and forth impatiently. He could see something building up inside of her. She held a manila envelope in her left hand while repeatedly opening and closing her right hand in a fist. A change seemed to have come over Stephanie almost as if she were neither her normal self, nor her maniacal self, but another person entirely.

Her response came in the form of a concise and coherent tirade directed angrily at Jason through clenched teeth. "Don't you dare speak to me in such a condescending manner, acting as if you are trying to humor a rambling mad woman. I may be a bit involved in this research project, but I am most certainly not insane. In case you haven't noticed, I've been working myself ragged trying to find the final piece of this historical puzzle and I finally found it today. And for your information, Mr. Condescension, the missing link, the thing that has been causing me so much frustration, ended up coming from your side of the family tree...not mine. So why don't you keep your snide sarcastic comments to yourself and shut up for a minute, listen to what I have to tell you."

Jason was taken aback by Stephanie's reproach. She had never reacted in such a way before and he was unsure if she were simply overwhelmed by something she discovered, or she had finally gone over the edge. There was a fire burning in her eyes, the likes of which he had never previously seen. He cautiously replied, "Look... Steph... I'm...I'm...sorry...I shouldn't have been so smart about all of this... I know how important it is to you...please...forgive me...and please show me what you found out."

For a moment, Stephanie stood glaring at Jason with a wild rage that seemed to bore a hole through him. He was genuinely concerned that for the first time in their marriage she might be inclined as to pick up a sharp implement and plunge it into his throat. She had never even remotely made him feel that way before, and he had no idea what might happen next. Fortunately, after the brief moment of uncertainty he could see her anger fade and become replaced once again by her excitement about her discovery. Jason, again felt more comfortable as he watched her fury dissipate.

"Well," she began, pointing to the first of two typed sheets of paper he held. "Remember how I told you how my great grandmother and grandfather, Marie and Dwight, as well as their two sons, Matthew and Charles all died on the same day?"

"Yes, I do," Jason replied, adding, "We assumed something like a fire or illness or some other such tragedy must have killed them." Jason thought uneasily about the day several weeks earlier when Stephanie discovered actual documents, which led her to that particular discovery. At that time, when she had told him, he acted like it was the very first time he had learned about the coincidence of the four family members' deaths on the same day. Jason couldn't let on that he was already aware of it, not to mention the graveyard, the headstones and the probably significant of the name, "Fallen Stones". He had done his best to appear surprised when she had told him her news. He couldn't risk Stephanie learning about what he had found or how he had destroyed and buried the headstones so many months previously.

Back then, he felt he was doing what was best for Stephanie and face his family at the time, but now that she had become so involved with her family history, he was certain she would be furious with him if she knew he destroyed the headstones. In hindsight he realized perhaps he should have simply left the stones lie where they were. Chances were no one would have found them anyway and then he could now pretend to discover them and end up looking like a hero to Stephanie. At that time, however, he truly believed Stephanie would have been bothered, knowing about the graves. But back then his wife was a different person than the rambling, confused woman he now saw standing before him.

For a moment, he considered digging up the pieces and spreading them around in the tall grass. If he did that, then he could act as if he stumbled upon one of the fragments. Stephanie would assume they had gotten broken over the years quite naturally or, at the very least, by some vandal. They could then look for the rest of the pieces together eventually completing their reconstruction. Maybe he would still want to do this in the spring after the ground had thawed. But he needed to give the idea more consideration. He could wait and see what Stephanie's frame of mind was by then. Living with her in her current level of agitation made spring seemed like it was years away.

He said with a degree of hesitation, "Well...did you finally learn what happened?" He tried his best to sound as if he too wanted to learn the truth, but he most certainly didn't. He recalled how back when he had found the gravestones he experienced many strange sensations and even had suffered hallucinations. No other such events had happened since that time and he didn't want to open any doors, which might lead to a potential reoccurrence. But he somehow knew even before Stephanie told him what she learned, the story would be a bad one and might change the entire dynamic of their lives together forever.

"It's much worse than what we could have ever imagined." She said. Then she began to tell him about Maria murdering her two sons.

"Oh my God... what are you saying?" Jason interrupted. "How could you possibly know this? How...how did you come by such information?"

Jason felt a tightening in the pit of his stomach. All of the strange messages he had seen carved on the tombstones now started to make some bizarre sense to him. "Taken from us by the hand of evil" he thought to himself. That had been the message on both of the young boys' grave markers." At the time, the statement had seemed so mysterious and cryptic. Now it made perfect sense. The "hand of evil" was Marie Livingston's own hand. She had murdered the two boys.

Jason exclaimed, "Oh my word. This is all so horrible! But... what..."

Stephanie stopped him midsentence. "Wait. There's more... much more." Then she continued with the tale telling Jason of Dwight's murder of Marie.

"Oh my Lord!" Jason said but was unable to say another word as he stared at his wife with his mouth agape.

"There's still more," Stephanie said and told him of Dwight's suicide.

"Unbelievable!" Jason exclaimed. "I can't imagine such a thing." But now many things suddenly began to make sense to him. The way the two boys' headstones were located separate from their parents; the fact that Dwight and Marie were segregated from the official cemetery and most of all, the cryptic inscriptions on their tombstones. It was all so clear to Jason now. He was overcome with sadness for his poor wife, having to discover such a horrible secret.

Chapter 34

"Oh, baby... Oh my God. I'm so, so sorry," Jason said, as tears began to well up in his eyes. He reached out to take Stephanie in his arms but she resisted. She surprised him by being neither upset nor overwhelmed by the information. Instead, she wore the excited look of someone who had made a miraculous discovery.

"Jason, look at me. I'm fine. And in case you didn't notice, I'm not a baby, and there is no reason to treat me like one," she replied stepping away from him. He was a bit surprised by the reaction as he had often used that particular term of endearment towards her previously, but he decided to let her unexpected comment pass for the moment. Then Stephanie began to pace rapidly back and forth, gathering her thoughts, before finally turning to Jason to tell him the rest of the story. "There's more, Jason. And I'm sure you're not going to like what I have to tell you."

Jason slumped back sitting on the edge of the bed. He didn't know how much worse this story could possibly get. After all, what could surpass a family murder and suicide? Stephanie's strangely calm demeanor unnerved him and since he was unable to read her, he braced himself for whatever news she was about to deliver.

"What more could there be?" he said. "That was some of most horrible news you could have discovered and it's a major black mark on your family history. No wonder you had such difficulty finding out the truth. I would imagine no one wanted this type of news to come to see the light of day. Your family probably did their best to bury it." An involuntary shudder ran down his spine upon hearing his own words. "Bury it?" Why had he chosen that particular phrase? He realized suddenly, if there had been a family conspiracy to hide the truth, he too had become a major part of it. He thought once again, about his own burying of the shattered tombstones; the fallen stones. Stephanie spoke up and interrupted his train of thought.

"You don't know the half of it, Jason," she replied with more than a pinch of anger in her voice; her eyes staring intently at him. "Members of your very own family played a major role in causing the deaths of my ancestors as well!"

"What? My family?" Jason exclaimed questioning. "What in the world would my family have to do with your family, let alone be involved in this mess? You just said that the tragedy was a murder and suicide involving your great grandparents. What does that have to do with my relatives?"

Stephanie interrupted him, "Jason, just listen." Then she proceeded to tell him about the affair.

"Whaaa.... what? What are you talking about? That's... that's just ridiculous!... It's... it's not...not possible." He stammered as he rose to his feet.

Jason was pacing back and forth next to the bed, as if trying to absorb what Stephanie had just told him. Then he realized his problem was much greater than that. It was not that he was trying to come to grips with the news; it was that he was genuinely concerned about his wife's mental state. Obviously, she had suffered some sort of psychotic break and had been hallucinating. How else could she have come up with such a crazy story? He heard Stephanie answering his question.

She said, "Yes. Not only is it possible, but it's also completely true. Agatha Jefferson was Dwight's mistress. She eventually became pregnant with your grandmother and then had her baby out of wedlock. Marie Livingston found out about the affair and about Dwight's illegitimate daughter and the knowledge eventually drove her insane. Then in order to get back at Dwight she drowned her two sons."

"But... but... why would she kill her own sons? That makes no sense whatsoever." Jason said with a weak and confused voice.

"Dwight loved his boys incredibly. And in Marie's damaged mind it must have seemed logical that by her killing them she would be killing Dwight emotionally... or something along those lines I would suppose."

Jason stood by the side of the bed, shaking his head in disbelief and looking down at the floor imagining the two dead bodies. "I... I just can't get my arms around all of this, Steph. I can't believe such a thing is possible. And if it were true, that would mean we are distantly related."

"I know it's hard for you to accept, Jason." Stephanie said. "But it's true and we have to learn to deal with it."

"But how did you find out all of this?" Jason asked, his engineer's mind looking to find a solution to their situation. He would want to see the evidence of this tale and would need to corroborate all the facts before he would allow himself to get too upset over it. After all, it could just be a big misunderstanding; a mistake. He knew nothing as important as this could simply be accepted on someone's word alone. He tried again to get an answer from Stephanie. "Where did you get this information?"

She explained, "I found out about the affair from an excerpt from Marie's personal diary, written in her own handwriting. And then I learned about the murders and suicide from a newspaper article from 1922." She held up the manila envelope. "I have them both right in here."

Jason reached to grab the envelope from Stephanie's hand wanting to see the proof first hand but she quickly pulled it away from him. "Easy, Jason. This stuff is almost one hundred years old. It is very brittle and fragile. I will be happy to let you read it but you have to calm down first. I can't have you damaging the documents."

With frustration and a great deal of self-control, Jason took a deep breath and stood still for a moment, allowing himself to become calm. "Alright Steph. I'm ok now. I just want to read the letter and the article."

"Very well." Stephanie said as she carefully opened the manila envelope and slowly withdrew the three blank sheets of crisp white printer paper. She delicately sat them down on the side of the bed, one next to the other as if she were handling century-old documents from the national archives. Jason watched her with complete disbelief. Then she reached into the envelope once again and withdrew the newspaper article and gingerly set it next to the blank sheets of paper. "There you go Jason. Read them and know the truth, but be very careful, I haven't had time to laminate them or protect them yet."

Jason looked at Stephanie with confusion for a moment. Then he looked back down at the blank papers and the recent newspaper article. One again he turned to look at Stephanie. At first he thought this might be some sort of strange joke on her part, but she had never been prone to doing such things before. Then Jason realized by the look in her eyes she was not joking. Stephanie really did believe these papers were ninety-year-old hand-written notes from Marie Livingston and the newspaper article was from 1922, not 2012.

He was not certain what he should do next. He was beyond confused, having never had any previous experience dealing with a situation such as this. Jason was both worried sick about his wife's mental state, but at the same time relieved to discover that all she had just told him was most likely untrue; just a figment of some delusional fantasy she was experiencing. He didn't know if he should try to explain to her that she was imagining everything or simply play along with her. If he tried to tell her the truth she would likely become angry and perhaps he might push her further over the brink of insanity. But if he said nothing he might be helping to fuel her delusions.

"Well?" Stephanie said, "Look at them, Jason. See for yourself what Marie wrote and you will understand that I am telling you the truth."

"Um...ok...just...just give me a minute," Jason said as he turned and bent over the bed. In that instant, he decided it would be best to play along for a while until he could figure out how he should handle Stephanie's situation. He knew now he was going to have to seek professional help. He was going to have to find a psychiatrist, psychologist or counselor of some sort. He didn't know how he would get Stephanie to talk to them, but things as gone way too far.

He pretended to peruse the documents, his hand clasped behind his back as if he were being careful not to touch them. As he did, he tried to estimate just how much time it would take to read a hand written document of this supposed length so Stephanie would believe he was actually reading something. He knew if he went too fast or too slow, she would sense something was not right and might become agitated. When he got to the end of the final blank sheet, he turned slowly to look at Stephanie.

She was standing next to him, observing him and nodding with a look of I-told-you-so on her face. "See, Jason. You see know what I was talking about. Now read the newspaper article."

So he did. It was a lot easier to pretend with the newspaper article, as it was an actual printed document. It was just not the particular story Stephanie thought it was however. The article was about a local woman who had written a historical book and had donated a copy to the Ashton Public library. Jason could sense Stephanie standing behind him, watching.

"See?" she questioned again. "Murder-suicide. Marie killed the boys and Dwight killed her then himself; all because of his affair with YOUR great grandmother."

Jason thought for a moment about how he should proceed. He assumed any newspaper article printed in that day and age would have only dealt with the facts of the case and would not have gone into anything such as an affair or illegitimate child.

After reading the article Jason stood quietly shaking his head. "Yes, Steph, you're right." he said, trying to sound convincing. "It just so awful; I'm certain the newspaper would not have lied."

"Of course they wouldn't have. They reported the facts as they were discovered."

Jason decided to take a chance based on his assumption about the newspaper. "But the article didn't say anything about any affair or any illegitimate child."

Stephanie said, "Of course not! They would never print such a thing! But you can plainly see it in Marie's journal entry. She knew about the baby and about your great-grandmother. You can tell by her writing the news was slowly driving her crazy. It was that affair which caused her to lose her mind and eventually kill her boys."

Jason had to be extra careful how he proceeded from that point on out. "But, Steph. Look. Just because Marie suspected something, doesn't mean it actually happened. She may have imagined the whole thing. Just because she put her feelings down on paper, that doesn't mean its factual information. It may have been real in her mind but still not true."

"It most certainly was true, Jason," Stephanie retorted. She could not understand why Jason was in denial and having such difficulty accepting facts, which were right in front of his face. She had known he might not react well to hearing the news but to try to pretend the facts were mere hallucinations was ridiculous. "Didn't you read what she wrote about how she heard all of the local women gossiping about Dwight and Agatha? The truth is spelled out on those pages in her own words and in her own handwriting? What more proof could you possibly want?"

But there was nothing spelled out on those blank pages. Whatever Stephanie believed she had read was all in her own mind. He had no idea how those thoughts had found their way into her head, but he knew they were nothing but fantasies. He was doing his best to restrain his anger but he wanted to shove the pages in her face and scream, "These are blank pages! There is no letter from Marie!" But he knew he couldn't be the one to do something so terrible to the woman he loved with all of his heart. When he spoke of Marie's hallucinations, he was actually speaking about Stephanie's but he could not bring himself to confront her directly about it.

"Look, Steph," Jason said. "I am willing to accept what you told me about the murder and suicide, but the rest I cannot accept without more solid evidence. He wondered to himself if it were possible to do a blood test and determine if he and Stephanie were distantly related. He believed it could be done. That would surely provide proof, assuming he really wanted to know the truth.

Behind the couple in the shadows, the mirror above their dresser began to ripple slightly and a thin, bony finger covered with gray shriveled flesh extended and pointed directly at Stephanie.

Suddenly Stephanie said, "Well then. Maybe we will have to arrange to have a blood test to see if any of this is true. That should be proof positive.

Jason was shocked to hear her repeat the very same thought he was just having but had not spoken aloud. What in the world had made her think of a blood test? It was almost as if she could read his mind or like someone else was putting the ideas in her mind. Jason suddenly felt as if someone was watching him or more accurately, watching the both of them. He quickly turned around and thought he saw some slight movement in the shadows behind him near the mirror on the dresser. But if it had been there it was now gone. Everything looked as it had been. He decided it would be best if he could continue to humor Stephanie until he could figure out at better way to deal with everything.

"Well then...maybe we should," he said, appearing to agree with her idea. "Or maybe we can have our DNA tested. One of those tests should confirm or deny your assumptions about all of this." He looked down again at the blank sheets of paper and still feeling as if he needed to protect her obviously fragile mind. "It's just that I can't simply believe what someone wrote in a journal almost a hundred years ago, and I don't know of any other way to resolve this once and for all."

"Neither do I," she replied. "We can schedule something sometime soon." But they would never have the blood test. Unknown to them at that time, they were about to enter a very unpleasant phase of their marriage and would not be communicating civilly enough in the upcoming month to agree on anything.

"For now," she said, "I have to go back to the loft now and type Marie's journal entry into my genealogical document and scan the newspaper article as well. This is probably one of the most important discoveries of my entire project."

Jason was curious about what Stephanie would end up typing from the blank sheets. He realized once she had finished, he would be able to, at the very least, read what Stephanie believed she had seen in the imagined journal entries. Once he could see exactly what she had fantasized, he might be better able to counter any argument she might come up with. But with only blank sheets in front of him, he had no idea what to do.

"But what about dinner?" Jason tried to say, wanting to do anything he could do to keep her from going back to the loft. Once he had thought the loft as a great relaxing place for Stephanie's creativity. Now however, he saw it as part of the growing problem whittling away at his wife's sanity.

Stephanie replied dismissively, "I'm not hungry. There's too much work to be done. Much, too much work to be done."

And with that, she carefully picked up the papers and gingerly tucked them back into the manila envelope, which she placed under her arm as she headed for the door. When she had passed through the doorway, she turned and looked back at Jason with kind concern saying, "Look, Jason. I know this might make things a bit weird, us being related and all... But I want you to know it doesn't have to change a thing between...well between us. No matter what our lineage, we are not Dwight and Marie Livingston, we are us. All of this is...well it's just history, water under the bridge. You and I can still be the same. Right?"

Jason gave his best, most convincing smile to his deranged wife nodding his head and replying,
"Um...ahh...yeah...ahh...yes...you...you bet, Steph. You and I are fine, and our family is fine as well... You're right... Why don't you go back to your work... I'll see you later at bedtime."

But Jason knew things were not fine. Things were so far away from fine that he wondered if they could ever be fine again. His lovely wife had suffered some sort of mental breakdown and he had to do something about it, but what that might be. He just didn't know.

Chapter 35

It was late Wednesday afternoon of December 19. It was young Samuel Wright's second birthday and just a week before Christmas, but one would never know it by looking around the Wright home. There was no Christmas tree, no decorations and nothing to suggest the upcoming holiday. Likewise, there were no plans to celebrate Sammy's birthday; no balloons, gifts or birthday cake could be found. A rift had developed between Stephanie and Jason since their discussion about the family secret and since that day, the couple had found it difficult, if not impossible to have any sort of civil conversation. They spoke when they needed to for issues concerning the kids, but other than that, the couple had started to drift further apart each day. Almost all communication had broken down to a point of non-existence.

Stephanie sat at her computer, carefully reviewing and editing her almost completed document. It was far more than a simply a document, however; it was an actual book, a detailed history of both sides of her and Jason's families starting at the present and going back to their great grandparents. The work was not only made up of text but was a combination of text, photos and charts, complete with scanned images of many of their family members dating back almost one hundred years. It had taken her months of dedicated time and energy to compile everything, and she was probably more proud of it than of anything she had ever previously done.

And it was not a typical family history laden with facts and statistics but was an emotional account of the tragedy, which had befallen the Livingston clan. It read like a novel, its story being told with all of the passion required to allow the reader to experience exactly what had happened on that eventful day. It also explained how a series of coincidental events eventually led Stephanie to inherit the property and discover the tragic family secret. Stephanie had made a point of not glossing over any of the unpleasant details, and as a result, to some it might have read more like a narrative work of fiction than a historical account.

Stephanie knew that, in Jason's opinion, it actually was nothing more than a work of fiction. He would not accept the fact that his great-grandmother had played such a crucial role in almost destroying Stephanie's side of the family. But whether he believed her account or not was of no consequence to Stephanie, because she knew everything in it was completely factual, and that was all that really mattered. That is to say the facts had been real enough in Stephanie's mind; however, she hadn't been the one controlling the presentation of those facts.

Her book included the image of Dwight and Marie's wedding photo. It was not quite as clear as she would have preferred since she was required to photograph the large portrait with her digital camera then put that particular image onto the computer. The original portrait was no longer stored in the attic but now hung proudly on the wall in Stephanie's loft. It didn't bother her any more how the couples' eyes seemed to follow her wherever she moved in the room. In fact, now the strange eyes made her feel assured, as if her great-grandparents were watching over her and guiding her in the project. Little did she know that was exactly what they were doing; that and so much more.

From deep inside the mirror, the ghost of Marie Livingston watched unseen, occasionally sending out her particles of mind control to keep Sammy locked in his world of imagination and to keep Stephanie focused on her work. But there was much more involved in Marie's actions than just controlling the day-to-day activities of her two descendants. She was gradually instilling a new reality in Stephanie's brain; the reality which would be required for completion of the final phase of their unholy plan.

The book also contained the text of the newspaper article from December 20, 1922, as well as from the journal entry Marie had written. Before Jason and Stephanie had stopped speaking, he had asked to read her transcript of Marie's journal. He told Stephanie it was to refresh his memory. As she watched him read the document, it almost seemed to Stephanie as if it was the first time he had actually seen the words.

Later in the family history book, Stephanie embellished on Marie's original writings by describing in detail the events of that dreadful night.

When Jason read her account of the Amelia Miller incident, he was shocked to discover the areas Stephanie described had matched exactly to the places where he had found the fallen tombstones. Then his stomach sank when he saw she had even included sketches depicting the actual grave markers he had seen, complete with the inscriptions exactly as they had been carved. Jason had no idea how she could have possibly been able to create such an accurate rendering having never seen the stones herself; stones which he had personally smashed to pieces and buried.

Jason believed something strange was going on; some unidentifiable source was feeding his wife a mixture of small amounts of factual information along with a larger amount of absolute lies. By doing so, this person had convinced Stephanie everything was true.

In Stephanie's mind, Jason was still refusing to believe what she told him. Just a week earlier, he even had the nerve to lie outright and claim the original papers she had shown him containing Marie's journal entry were not brittle old parchment written in Marie's hand but were actually blank sheets of modern printer paper. She couldn't believe he would lie so blatantly and make such an outlandish claim.

Since that time however, things had become increasingly strained between them.

Stephanie was standing at her computer screen looking closely at the various scanned pictures of her ancestors now on display.

Sammy sat on the floor staring at the same video he had been watching daily for several months. His face still wore the same look of ecstasy as was now commonplace, while his mind wandered through the fictional landscape of amazing childhood pleasures.

There was a foul stench of urine and feces permeating the room because the boy was unknowingly sitting in a pile of his own filth, which was leaking from a gap in the side of his saturated diaper. Stephanie's complete immersion into her historical project had delayed the start of young Sammy's potty training by several months, which was just fine with her. It was much less trouble to simply slap a diaper or training pants on the boy and then plop him down in front of the television. She usually remembered to check on him periodically and change him as necessary, but even that responsibility had fallen by the wayside. Today she was far too preoccupied with her thoughts to notice or even care about her own son's hygienic needs. She knew she would have to make sure he was presentable by dinnertime as she did every evening, although she suspected Jason would not be home for dinner again tonight.

There was also an additional odor barely noticeable but nonetheless present lurking just below the surface. Unknown to Stephanie, this foul stench was the reek of death, signaling the approach of the heinous creatures that were the architects of the scheme, which they were about to make real.

So many mysterious and correlated things had happened over the previous several weeks. She had finally completed the family tree and discovered the secret of the Livingston family tragedy. She had told Jason everything and had even shown him the supporting documents but he didn't seem to be able to accept the truth.

There were also a number of other things, which Jason had done, that Stephanie found confusing. For example, shortly after she had shown him Marie's journal, Jason brought some man, a stranger home for dinner. He claimed the man was a friend of his and said the friend was a doctor of some sort. Stephanie had never heard Jason mention the man before and she had an odd feeling there was another reason for the man's visit. She felt as if the so-called friend had been studying her a bit to intently, perhaps being more of a doctor than he was Jason's friend. For a time she suspected maybe, Jason's so-called friend was more interested in her than Jason.

This was not to suggest the man had attempted to hit on her or do anything of a sexual nature, but he seemed to ask her a lot of personal questions; questions about her feelings and emotions. She felt many of the questions were inappropriate and quite intimate in nature. On more than one occasion during the dinner, Stephanie had looked over at Jason, attempting to convey her displeasure with unspoken visual cues, but he didn't seem to notice. Then she began to suspect perhaps he understood exactly what she was trying to do but was ignoring her. Stephanie had found it all very unsettling

The man also seemed to be far too interested in learning about her research. Perhaps that was simply the nature of the man's overly curious personality; perhaps it was something else entirely. The bizarre evening made Stephanie feel a bit uneasy as if to suggest Jason and his friend might have been working together toward some sort of hidden agenda relating to her.

She realized the idea seemed a bit paranoid but what else was she supposed to think? Jason had shown up at dinner with a stranger who he claimed was and old friend. Then the so-called friend began delving into Stephanie's personal feelings and then when she turned to her husband for support he ignored her, allowing the stranger to continue his inquiries. How did that expression go? It's only paranoia if everyone isn't really out to get you.

However, one positive thing, which had occurred during the previous weeks was that her brother Chuck had started to visit them on weekends. She was happy to reconnect with him, as they had temporarily lost contact since the family had moved. Stephanie had begun to worry that Chuck might have resented her good fortune in receiving the inheritance, but now that they had gotten together, several times she knew he held no hard feelings about it. Although she had to admit, much like Jason and his doctor friend, Chuck had been acting a bit odd around her.

Sometimes he had had seemed a bit too quick with his compliments and encouragements, especially in regard to her project. Like everyone else, he seemed to be weighing his words at times when speaking to her. Chuck was usually more direct when he spoke; he was her brother after all. And Stephanie was not oblivious to the subtle changes in the way he acted around her. This made Stephanie begin to wonder if her brother might also be involved, in whatever strangeness it was Jason was up to.

Yet, other times Chuck seemed to be genuinely supportive. Once when she felt exceptionally trusting, Stephanie had even shown him Marie's letter, not the transcript but the original letter and he had appeared quite surprised when he studied the document. But when she noticed the way he looked at her and how the look was so similar to the way Jason had looked at her, she was momentarily afraid he might not believe what he had read any more than Jason had. But instead, he told her she was doing great and important work for the family and couldn't wait to have his own personal copy of the book. He said he was anxious to see the project finished so she could take some time to get some much-needed rest.

Stephanie was unaware that Jason had already debriefed her brother about her deteriorating condition. Jason had told him about the alleged ancient documents and the message they supposedly contained. Since he had been prepared, Chuck was able to pull off a relatively convincing performance while pretending to read them. He had then surprised Stephanie by volunteering to take Jeremy and Cindy back home with him on occasions for sleepovers on weekends when she needed time to work. She always kept Sammy home during these outings, however, since he was not yet potty trained.

The kids presently were off school for their Christmas break and Chuck's company was on a holiday shutdown. Earlier that morning he had stopped by to pick up the two older children for another overnight visit; a special middle-of-the-week excursion. He planned to bring them back the afternoon of the next day. And Stephanie was certainly grateful for the time alone to finish her work.

Despite the fact it was Sammy's birthday, Stephanie had allowed the kids to go with Chuck. Had she been thinking rationally she might not have permitted it. And if she were asked, she might not have been able to explain why she let the other two children leave. The reason was not something tangible or concrete; it was more like a subconscious, uncontrollable need to be alone with Sammy. And since Jason was at the office and was likely going to be working late once again, she and Sammy would be alone together.

Recently, at the end of each day, when Stephanie took Sammy to the main house to be with the other kids and to have dinner, Jason was nowhere to be found. Connie Franks always had dinner ready and Stephanie had begun to try to spend time with the two older kids again after dinner. But Jason wouldn't arrive home until much later at night. Connie had the week off for Christmas so tonight Stephanie would have to fend for herself for dinner. She would throw something together for her and Sammy. Suddenly she had a fleeting idea cross her mind. The phrase "the last supper" suddenly appeared in her mind along with an image of the famous painting by Leonardo da Vinci, but she had no idea why. She put the thought aside and instead once again wondered about how things had become so bad between her and Jason.

On several occasions, Stephanie had confronted Jason, and each interaction had ended badly.

Now Stephanie sat at her desk tapping her pencil irritably at the recollection of those encounters. Recounting the various arguments she and Jason had, Stephanie realized he really didn't care at all about her project. All this time he had been humoring her, acting as if he was interested when in fact he was not.

And now that she thought more about it, she began to wonder about Jason's doctor friend again. Had he really been a friend or had Jason brought him around to study her? She could tell by the way Jason looked at her he sometimes thought she was a bit off. Maybe it was more than that. Maybe he was thinking about accusing her of being mentally unstable. Then she began to wonder if he might be gathering witnesses to testify against her. Could he be trying to find a way to have her declared insane? Could he be working a scheme to have her deemed incompetent and then have her institutionalized so he could take control of her fortune?

In the back of the loft, the presence of Marie Livingston inside the mirror was smiling a rotten-toothed grin of pleasure. Yes, the plan was almost complete. Stephanie was ripe for exploitation. She was starting to believe exactly what they wanted her to believe. And today was the day it all had to come to its inevitable climax. It was the ninetieth anniversary of that terrible night. And if things went according to plan, as she and Dwight would make sure they would, then before midnight, they would be free of their

Purgatory and Jason and Stephanie Wright would take their places among the damned for eternity.

Chapter 36

Stephanie sat stewing in frustration at her memories, growing angrier and more irrational by the second. She recalled how Jason had tried to convince her they were almost cash broke, but she knew that was impossible. She was sure they were really wealthy, and she was certain they had more money in the bank then what Jason had told her; perhaps more than they could ever possibly spend. After all, they lived in a mansion and had Mrs. Franks to cook and clean as well as her husband Wilbur to do yard work. Common people couldn't afford such a luxury so they most certainly had to be rich. She didn't understand why Jason would lie to her about it.

She tried to recall exactly how much money the lawyer H. Mason Armstrong said she had inherited. The estate document was somewhere in the loft, but the area was so disorganized and such a mess, she had no idea how or it she would ever be able to locate it. Jason had said the cash in the estate was only about three-quarters of a million dollars but she was certain the figure was much, much higher than that. She was not sure of the exact amount but she believed it had to be at least several million in cash. Yes. That made perfect sense to her. She even thought she could recall the lawyer telling her there was at least ten million dollars in cash available to her. And now the more she thought about it, that figure was probably more like twenty million dollars, maybe more.

In the mirror across the room the image of the deceased, H. Mason Armstrong appeared in the pulsating liquefied glass. Stephanie couldn't see his visage in the shadows and as such had no notion of his presence. Had she seen him standing and looking out at her from his world, she would have been stricken with horror at the gaping hole in his chest cavity from which Dwight Livingston had plucked his heart. Wormlike creatures crawled freely from the massive wound, dribbling down the front of his suit coat and creeping up his chest and onto his gray mottled face where they burrowed deep into the thin flesh of his cheeks. He had once been a prestigious lawyer, a respected pillar of the community of Ashton. Now he was just a walking buffet for foul creatures of the netherworld. But he also had an assignment to carry out for the Livingstons.

The ghost of Armstrong was focusing and sending thoughts from his world out into Stephanie's already confused mind. He was giving her false memories of their meeting, convincing her she had inherited great sums of money, and Jason was trying to steal it from her, lying to her for his own selfish gains.

"Yes, that explains it!" she suddenly said aloud. That was what Jason was up to. If he could get enough people, especially those with credentials, to say she had lost her mind he might be able to take control of her twenty-five million dollars. But she couldn't understand why he would do such a thing. They had joint bank accounts, so Jason already had access to all of her money to spend as he chose. So what could be the reason for his treachery? Didn't he love her anymore? Would he do such a horrible thing just to control her money?

Stephanie had always heard how coming into money often changed people. Maybe the idea of getting his hands on her thirty million dollars was enough to make Jason betray her. Then she realized he actually might be inclined to do so if the amount of money was as high as she somehow knew it had to be. Yes, he might do it for thirty-five million dollars.

In the mirror all of the specters of the homestead now stood together; both Dwight and Marie Livingston, the lawyer H. Mason Armstrong, Emerson Washburn and the charred remains of Jack Moran. They were all apparently connected now and as such, all had something to gain from what would occur this night and each of them was doing their best to help control Stephanie's delusion so she would do what they needed her to do.

Suddenly another realization hit Stephanie. It was instantly all too clear to her. She knew why Jason wanted to have her declared insane and wanted her money. It wasn't just for the money alone but it was for another woman. She suddenly understood Jason was obviously having an affair just like his illegitimate grandfather Dwight Livingston had done. Perhaps it was with someone at work; most likely that woman from the accounting group who had been practically throwing herself at Jason all the time. Stephanie couldn't recall her name but didn't care. Yes. That had to be it.

"Oh my God no!" Stephanie said aloud with the realization. Sammy still sat silently staring at the blank TV screen, lost in the fabricated world of illusion; sitting in his urine-soaked, waste-filled, foul-smelling diaper. Sammy couldn't hear what his mother was saying, not while he was busy in his special place. Stephanie was now certain Jason was probably screwing that home-wrecking slut from the office, maybe right now in fact. Stephanie imagined them going at it like two rutting beasts on the top of his office desk. She knew now why he was plotting to have her declared insane. He and his bimbo would steal her forty million dollars. Jason must have been planning this for months, slowly putting his list of witnesses together. He had probably been banging that bimbo since back when he first took the job. Brainless tramps like that always go after the bosses who seem to be on the fast track to success, hoping no doubt to be the trophy wife. Stephanie had suspected as much earlier, but now she was certain.

Inside the mirror, all the hideous specters were concentrating, pooling their thoughts and projecting them out at Stephanie. She was theirs now, and with the thoughts they were planting in her mind, she would do whatever they wished.

Then as if experiencing and epiphany, Stephanie suddenly realized something else. "Oh my, Lord, no. She must be pregnant." Stephanie was overcome with panic as she paced manically back and forth in the loft, trying to determine what she would do next. Nothing seemed to make sense to her yet at the same time everything made perfect sense. She understood now how Marie Livingston felt when she learned about Dwight's bastard daughter. Jason was Dwight's illegitimate descendant and like his great-grandfather Dwight before him, Jason had apparently found his own cheap little whore to impregnate.

Behind her in darkness, the specters continued to send volley after volley of thoughts out to Stephanie. Tonight was the night when it all had to happen as it had happened before so many years ago.

Stephanie began to think of Jason as no so much Jason but as a modern incarnation of Dwight Livingston. She also began to see herself as a later day version of Marie Livingston. Stephanie now was convinced Jason had wronged her. He had cheated on her with his harlot and had sired his own bastard child. And like Dwight before him, Jason was going to have to pay for his sins. She knew what Marie had done to get her revenge and now she too had been wronged. So now, she suddenly knew exactly what she had to do.

She looked over at Sammy sitting on the floor in his soiled diaper, watching the blank television screen. She suddenly realized why she had sent the two older kids away with her brother Chuck. The glass in the mirror began to pulsate more rapidly than ever as the specters began to press hard against the surface of the mirror, preparing to make their way out into the world of the living. They continued to send their vile force of thoughts out from their world toward Stephanie.

As Stephanie looked down at little Sammy, she couldn't help but notice how much he looked like Jason. She also realized just how much he looked similar to the portrait of Dwight Livingston not to mention the photo she had seen of Charles and Matthew Livingston, the two murdered boys. He looked more like them then he looked like his own half-brother, Jeremy. Sammy definitely had the Livingston family features, which meant he had the Livingston family blood, the blood of adulterous whoremongers. Why hadn't she noticed it before?

"He looks just like his father," Stephanie said with a flat monotones voice, which no longer sounded like her own. This was because she was speaking in the voice of Marie Livingston who had been slowly feeding her poisonous ideas into Marie's consciousness in tiny installments over the past several months. She had not taken over Stephanie, but enough of her thoughts were present so that she could begin to control Stephanie's will.

Stephanie looked down at Sammy and said in Marie's voice, "He loves his father. He idolizes him. Someday he will probably grow up to be just like Jason; and just like Dwight. Yes, I suppose someday he will likely find a whore of his own to impregnate and will break his loving wife's heart. It is the Livingston way; the Livingston destiny."

Suddenly Stephanie knew exactly how she would get even with Jason. It became clear and she knew what she had to do. She looked at the calendar hanging on the far wall, then looked down at the hypnotized form of her son and with an ironic smile, said, "Happy Birthday Sammy." Her voice was the voice of a mad woman.

Across the loft, the mirror on the wall was now vibrating wildly and practically rattling off its hooks. Soon a long slender grey withered hand with yellowed split fingernails eased from the glass. Next, another followed and soon the hideous head of Marie Livingston with its wild greasy hair slid out from the liquefied glass.

The fluid surface of the mirror began to slowly ooze from the confines of its frame, and cling to the surfaces around it; walls, floor and ceiling. It formed a thin translucent film of mercurial liquid, which flowed outward like a hand with many wide splayed fingers spreading in every direction.

Then the unspeakable creatures of the netherworld began to crawl forth from their land of the damned along the silvery surface always careful not to touch any objects of the world of the living. Soon they would be able to do so, but not yet. First came Marie Livingston, who crept out of the rippling glass and onto the left side of the mirror. She still was dressed the blood-splattered dressing gown she had worn the night she died. Her gray-filmed eyes still held the same look of insanity. As she clung to the sidewall on the glistening pool of mercury, her movements appeared jerky and erratic. Stephanie didn't notice her as she was still in a trance, staring out into space.

A moment later, the charred remains of Jack Moran likewise crawled from the pulsating glass, moving upward and clinging to the ceiling like a giant blackened, fleshless spider. Following him was H. Mason Armstrong and Emerson Washburn, both creeping out of portal and taking their positions along the wall, clinging like insects while staring with hatred at Stephanie. It was clear they were all focusing their attentions in her direction assisting Marie, as they were able.

Finally, two gnarled hands emerged from the mirror, one gripping each side. A moment later the form of Dwight Livingston, master of the cadre of the damned leapt out of the darkness and stood upright in front of the mirror, floating inches above the surface of the floor. Then likewise, the remaining specters flew from their perches and hovered behind their master. Marie and Washburn stood directly behind Dwight while Armstrong and Moran took their place in the rear. They said nothing but remained standing and looking at Stephanie, who seemed to be lost in her own world and who was apparently getting angrier and more agitated by the second. Stephanie's ravings were also becoming louder as she paced wildly back and forth, waving her arms and screaming epithets about Jason and his many women.

Sammy sat staring and the blank TV screen. After a few moments, his glassy eyes began to flitter in a sign of his waking. It was not yet time for him to awaken, however. Perhaps the energy required to maintain the intensity of Stephanie's mania caused the creatures to no longer be able to support the boy's illusion. Whatever the cause, Sammy soon found himself awake and sitting in front of a black television screen.

He could hear his mother yelling and sounding very angry. Sammy didn't like when Mommy was mad. Lately, Sammy noticed his Mommy and Daddy were mad at each other lots of times. He didn't know why they yelled so much but it didn't like it. When they did that, it made his tummy hurt. He liked how it was when Mommy and Daddy hugged and kissed. That was better than mad and yelling.

Sammy turned to look at his Mommy to see what might be wrong and stopped suddenly. He saw something bad; something really bad. Sammy knew bad stuff for sure. He was two and knew lots of words now. He could say a lot of them but could understand even more words than he could say. He knew them in his head but couldn't always say them with his mouth.

He looked and saw people, bad people, standing near the kitchen in the room; Mommy's special room that she called "the loff". He could tell these were bad people as soon as he saw them. They were really, really scary. They were scarier than any scary thing he had ever seen. The scary man in the front looked sort of like Daddy but not just like Daddy. He remembered that scary man from the picture Mommy kept up there in the loff. The man had really scary eyes with dark rings around them. It made Sammy feel like the man's eyes were looking out from black holes. And the scary man had a big cut across his neck that Sammy thought looked really yucky.

There was a lady behind him who Sammy didn't like either. He remembered her from the first day they came to the new house. She was the scary lady in the glass who had made him cry by looking at him with her spooky eyes. And right next to her he saw that other man he didn't like. Sammy remembered his name was Armsong or something like that. Sammy didn't like Armsong before, and he didn't like him even more now. He was really scary and yucky now and Sammy didn't like that one bit. Sammy didn't want Armsong to see him so he closed his eyes, but when he opened them again, Armsong was still there.

The men in the back row scared Sammy the most. He didn't know them, but the one man looked like the burned up guy he saw in the fire car a long time ago when they came to see the house. He looked all burned and his face was like a skull face. Sammy knew what a skull face was. He used to think a skull face was called a skulk face, but now that he was two, he knew the right word. And that word was skull.

The bunch of bad scary people made Sammy's belly hurt worse than hearing Mommy yelling really loud. Why was she yelling so loud? Sammy didn't like it one bit. He wanted to cry and he felt like he was going to cry really bad when he saw something that made him forget about crying.

Between Sammy and the scary people, he saw two shapes start to become real where there wasn't anybody before. It was like a magic show; one time nobody was there, then two shapes started to be there. Sammy knew what two meant. He could count to two in his head and say it with his mouth. His mommy liked when he said, "one, two". It would make her smile instead of yelling and being mad. She would call him her "little geen-us"; whatever that meant. Sammy was pretty sure it meant he was good and was smart. Mommy liked when he was smart. Sammy wondered if saying "one, two" would make Mommy smile now. He didn't think so. He didn't think anything he did would make Mommy smile today.

When the two shapes stopped doing the magic thing and became people that he could see, Sammy recognized them. "Boys," he thought. Then he moved his mouth and silently said "boys" with his mouth. These were the same boys Sammy saw in the field that day a long time ago. Sammy forgot about the boys because he never saw them after that one time; but now the boys were back and maybe they came back to play with him.

Sammy liked these boys; they weren't scary like those bad people back behind the boys. They didn't even look as scary as they did when Sammy saw them before. They didn't look sick or tired anymore. Something was different. Now they looked very nice and clean and they had a bright light all around them. It was bright yellow and Sammy couldn't look right at it or it hurt his eyes. Sammy knew all about bright stuff and he knew some of his colors too. He had crayons and markers. He liked to draw stuff with his markers but most of the time he got lots of marker juice colors on his hands and face. But none of his colors were as bright like the yellow light around the boys. The light made Sammy feel good in his tummy and made him not want to cry. The boys were wearing suits like Daddy wore to church but they were all white and shiny with the bright light.

Then Sammy was surprised to hear some words inside his head. He was pretty sure the boys were saying the words because it sounded like two boys talking together and saying the same words. But the boys' mouths were not moving. Sammy never knew people could say words inside his head without making their mouths move or without saying the words. But that was what the boys were doing. They were putting words in his head without talking. Sammy thought that was pretty cool. He liked this game, and he tried to see if he could make words in their heads too.

Sammy thought the words "Hi, boys," in his head. The two boys smiled at Sammy, and then he heard two voices say, "Hello, Samuel."

"Samuel?" the little boy thought. Who was Samuel? Then he realized "Samuel" sounded like it might be fancy way to say Sammy. "I'm Sammy," he thought, "not Samuel."

The boys did not reply to his correction but instead said together, "Sammy. You have to listen carefully to us. Do not be afraid."

Sammy wasn't afraid any more at all, especially of these boys; not even a little. They were nice boys. Sammy knew nice stuff. He had been afraid of the scary people, but now he couldn't see them because of the bright light and that was ok with him. In fact, he had just about forgotten about the scary people. He thought, "I not scared... you good boys."

"Yes, Sammy," the boys replied. "We are good boys. And we are here to help you. Those bad people want to hurt you and your mommy and daddy. They are making your mommy think bad things, and they are going to make her do something really bad to you."

Sammy thought this was silly. His mommy loved him and would never do anything bad to him. The boys must be mixed up. Mommies were good not bad. Sammy loved his mommy so much it sometimes made him feel like crying. She would never do anything bad to him.

"You are right, Sammy," he heard the boys say. Your mommy is good. But those bad people are making her not be good. We cannot stop the bad people. We can see them, but they cannot see us. But we cannot hurt them or stop them. Only your daddy and mommy can make the bad people go away. You have to get your Daddy to come home right away."

"Daddy, help," Sammy thought as he silently formed the words with his mouth. "Daddy, help," he mouthed and thought again.

"Yes. That's right, Sammy. Can you say the words 'Daddy help'?" the boys asked. Sammy knew he could say those words and many more. He was two. He knew lots of words now. "Daddy help," Sammy said quietly.

The boys said in Sammy's head. "That's really good Sammy. Do you know how to say 'please'?"

Sammy thought for a moment and mouthed the word please, but it came out sounding like "peaze".

"Good, Sammy," the boys said. The turned and looked toward the place on the floor where Stephanie's purse lay. It was overturned on its side, and her smart phone was visible.

Sammy heard a scraping sound and saw the boys moving their hands as they made more magic happen. Mommy's phone started sliding across the floor and soon stopped right in front of him. The front of the phone lit up, and Sammy could see all the little pictures on the screen. Sammy knew a lot about Mommy's phone because she sometimes let him play with it. She had some fun stuff on her phone. Sammy liked the cat that said stuff back to him. He could say a word and the cat would say it back in his silly cat voice. And sometime the cat farted. Sammy loved that. The cat farts always made him laugh.

Sometimes he pushed the picture of Daddy by mistake and then he heard his Daddy talking on the phone. When he did that, Mommy took the phone away and said "No". Sammy didn't like to hear "no". He liked to say "no" lots of times but didn't like to hear it. He was thinking now about that time he pushed his daddy's picture on Mommy's phone.

"You must call your daddy, Sammy. You must say 'Daddy help please' until your Daddy comes home. Can you do that, Sammy? Can you do that?"

"No," Sammy thought. "Mommy said 'no touch.' Sammy no touch Mommy's phone. Sammy no call Daddy. Sammy no push Daddy's picture."

Then the boys said, "But, Sammy, it is alright this time to call Daddy. Only Daddy can help you and Mommy. Only Daddy can make the bad people go away. Daddy must come home. You must call Daddy, Sammy. It's alright to do it this one time. You're two years old today. You're a big boy, Sammy. And big boys are allowed to call daddies."

The cadre of the undead floated slowly across the room toward the large rear windows, which were currently hidden by a wall of closed curtains. They paid little attention to Sammy, as he no longer posed a threat to them. They could not see the ethereal forms of the two Livingston boys but the boys were definitely aware of their every move.

They told Sammy, "You must do it, Sammy. You must get your Daddy to come home. If not you will die. Do you know what it means to be dead?" Their questioned made Sammy feel very scared in his tummy. Sammy knew about dead stuff. He knew about not being alive. He had squashed bugs and made them dead. He saw the dead deer in the field with all the bugs. If that was being dead, he didn't want to be dead. He didn't want bugs and birds eating him up a little bit every day. Dead stuff was yucky, and Sammy hated yucky stuff.

He looked down at the lighted face of his mommy's cell phone and saw the little picture of his daddy. The boys were telling him in his head to call his daddy. His mommy was screaming and shouting all kinds of bad stuff; a lot of words he didn't know and had never heard her say before. Sammy didn't know what to do. He didn't want to be a bad boy, but he really wanted his daddy to come home. He took a deep breath, sighed then reached down and pressed Daddy's picture on his mommy's phone.

He could hear the phone begin to ring as he waited to hear his Daddy's voice. He knew what he would say: "Help Daddy peaze." If he did that, Daddy would come home and help him to not be dead and help Mommy too. Daddy could make the bad people go away. The boys told him so.

Across the room, Dwight Livingston lifted his withered arm and pointed it at the back wall of the loft. The drapes flew open revealing a panoramic view of the rear of the property through the wall of windows. The yard was awash with moonlight. Dwight approached the windows and began saying something silently while looking out into the yard.

The ground, near the back of the property began to tremble. Suddenly in an area about five feet around, the ground began to rise up as if a force from somewhere down below was burrowing, pushing the dirt outward. Within a few moments, a large round hole was present in the ground and soon it began to fill with icy December water from some unknown underground source. The dirt around the hole began to mold itself into a shape resembling a cylindrical structure of field stone and mortar, while maintaining the texture and color of soil. The well, which had claimed the lives of Matthew and Charles Livingston almost a century earlier, had returned, and it waited for its next victim and for the final phase of the creatures' evil plan.

Chapter 37

Jason was at his office desk deeply engrossed in a series of charts and spreadsheets, the results of the same project he had originally been assigned during his time at the Lancaster division of his company. Since that time, all manufacturing at the facility had ceased and rumors of an impending sale of the building and closing of the facility were rampant throughout the company. None of these stories were of any surprise to Jason however, as he had recognized the warning signs many months earlier. In fact, since taking the job in Ashton and moving his family north, he had never had any need or desire to return to the Lancaster facility. He felt it was better to cut all ties with the people at that plant from the beginning, and so he allowed his engineers to handle the equipment movement to the Ashton factory and likewise kept his email correspondence with the Lancaster facility to a bare necessary minimum.

Now almost seven months later he was in the implementation phase of the project and unfortunately things were not progressing as closely to plan, as either he or his managers would have liked. Because of the special nature and complexity of the parts being run across the machine, it was becoming a challenge to make the numbers he had forecasted in the justification phase of the project. Likewise, the upfront work to get the Computer Numerical Control (CNC) programs written for the multifaceted machine tool, as well as development time for those programs, were taking a lot more time and manpower than he had originally estimated.

The result was he had been getting a lot of heat lately from his new manager, Bill Bostwick, who was not nearly as laid back or understanding as Tom McClellan had been. Unfortunately, with all the negative press the project had been getting around the plant of late, it was apparent to all that the project was not the immediate success they had hoped it would be. Jason was sure the project would eventually be a winner and would give them everything they expected from it. But the ramp up time was longer than they had anticipated due to a steep learning curve. This excuse however did nothing to fight back the fecal storm brewing in the executive offices. And as Jason well knew, crap rolled downhill. So, every time the defecation hit the ventilation, Jason found himself covered in it. As a result, he had been forced to

abandon much of his free time once again and return to his
schedule of working long days and even weekends.

He missed his family so much. He worried about Stephanie.
He hated the long hours, and if he were to be perfectly honest
with himself, he was really starting to hate his job. Part of him
wished he could get fired so he would be forced to take the
initiative to either find another job or start his own consulting
company. Jason often wondered if he would have been better off
had he chosen to be fired from the Lancaster facility. He had
allowed Stephanie's inheritance to cloud his judgment; hell, they
both had. Now in hindsight, he was questioning the logic of their
decisions, which seemed to have been way off base. Not for the
first time, Jason had the strange feeling that many of the
decisions they thought they had made on their own were actually
being made for them by someone else, or at least somehow
remotely manipulated. Each time he had these thoughts he
recognized just how bizarre they were, yet he still had the feelings
stirring deep in his gut nonetheless.

Suddenly Jason was startled by a vibration, than a ringing of
his cell phone in his shirt pocket. It was almost 8:30 at night.
Surely, any call he might receive on his personal cell had to come
from home. And that could only mean something was wrong. He
quickly looked at the digital display and saw the call was from
Stephanie's cell; he could also tell by her special ringtone and her
picture displayed prominently on his smartphone. Jason looked
down at the picture of a happy, smiling Stephanie and was
shocked by just how much her appearance, not to mention her
mental state had changed for the worst during the past several
months.

Jason was a bit apprehensive about answering the call. In
fact, he couldn't remember the last time Stephanie had even
bothered to call him when he was working late. He suspected it
had to have been many weeks. Usually, back when she did call, it
was to bug him to come home and she often would dump a major
guilt trip on him. The calls usually ended with her yelling at him
or crying or just hanging up. And during those calls, Jason
couldn't help but remember the happier times before the
promotion, before Ashton and before the inheritance. They had
little in the line of material possessions back then, but they were
so happy simply having each other. Now things seemed to be
getting worse between them daily.

Jason wasn't sure why Stephanie had chosen to call him this
time, but he suspected she must have had a good reason for doing
so tonight. As the phone rang again, Jason suddenly began to

worry more about some possible family emergency with his kids. He knew Jeremy and Cindy were staying with their Uncle Chuck overnight so he assumed things were ok with them. Otherwise, he would have heard directly from his brother-in-law. Jason was not thrilled with the idea of the kids being away on Sammy's birthday but here he was working late again so what right did he have to stop them? Also, Chuck was well aware of Stephanie's problems and knew to call Jason first in the event of an emergency. So putting all apprehension aside he pressed the button to answer the call.

Jason cautiously asked, "Hello? Steph? Honey? Is everything OK?"

He listened carefully and thought he could hear breathing on the other end of the phone, as well as strange indistinguishable noises in the background.

"Steph? Is that you, honey? Is everything all right?" Still the breathing continued and the strange noises seemed to be increasing in volume, sounding like a woman shouting about something. The strange quality of the voice made Jason's stomach constrict like some primitive warning sign of impending danger.

Then he relaxed somewhat when Jason realized what must have happened. Sammy was a very bright and precocious child who never ceased to be amazed by both of their cell phones. Although he couldn't yet understand numbers and letters, he did like to press the buttons on Stephanie's smart phone. Stephanie had the numbers in her phone associated with pictures so Sammy could easily call Jason and had accidentally done so on more than one occasion. Stephanie was in the habit of leaving her cell lying around where he could easily get to it as well.

Jason assumed Sammy had either deliberately or accidentally called him again. Perhaps the background noises were simply one of his cartoon shows. They were always so loud and the dialogue sounding like people were shouting all the time. He often wondered why cartoon voices all seemed to have that same noisy and irritating quality. He listened for the young boys breathing on the other end.

"Sammy? Hey, baby boy. Is that you, sweetie? Are you calling Daddy again?" Jason said with the hopes Sammy might respond. Then Jason heard something that made his stomach knot up all over again. His little boy, his precious Sammy said in a small voice, one obviously filled with fear, "Daddy... help... peaze."

"Sammy! What's wrong, honey?" Jason said terrified but trying desperately to sound calm as he stood at his desk and began putting on his winter coat.

"Sammy? Please put Mommy on the phone," Jason pleaded. "Can you please get Mommy, sweetie?

Again Sammy said, "Peaze... Daddy... Help" and then the boy started to whimper. That sound of terror in his young son's voice drove a spike of pain deep into his very soul. It was then that Jason again heard the shouting in the background and realized for the first time the voice he was hearing was not that of some animation voice-over, but it was Stephanie's. She sounded like a madwoman shouting and screaming at the top of her lungs. Keeping the phone in the crook of his neck, Jason finished putting on his coat as he hurried out through the main office area. Those of his staff who were working late watched him leave with concern, seeing the expression on his face and assuming something bad must have happened at home.

He skipped the elevator and as Jason ran down the stairs taking them two at a time, he could hear Stephanie shouting words like "whoremonger", "bastard child" and threats like "he'll die for this" and other equally horrifying phrases the likes of which he had never heard his beautiful wife utter before.

Jason realized it must have finally happened. Stephanie's mind must have broken, and now his son was alone in the house trapped with a raving lunatic. He didn't know for sure, but it was very possible Stephanie might be a real threat to both herself and Sammy. He had to get home as soon as possible. He jumped into this new Ford pickup truck and sped out of the parking lot. He knew he could be home in less than ten minutes, but he hoped with all of his heart that would be time enough. The last thing he heard before the phone went dead was the voice of his little boy crying "No, Mommy. No peaze."

Chapter 38

Stephanie walked barefoot across the frozen field between the garage and the strange hexagonal spa building toward the menacing well, which had appeared near the back of the property. In her spellbound state, she was oblivious to the frigid conditions around her, including how her feet ached from the ice covered grass. The area was illuminated brightly by the motion activated security lighting which Jason had installed giving the icy ground an otherworldly appearance. Under her right arm she carried her small son, Sammy who was kicking and screaming fiercely, trying in vain to escape. He had no idea what fate awaited him, but he knew the woman carrying him was not acting anything like his mother.

Behind the newly reawakened version of the deadly well located on a slightly raised area of frozen meadow, bordering the forest, Stephanie could see the assembly of the undead beings all lined up as if waiting to participate in a very special ceremony; which was exactly why they were there. In her present state, it didn't faze Stephanie that she was staring at five dead beings. Stephanie seemed to not comprehend the fact that the demonic spirits had risen up from the bowels of Hell itself and were planning some horrible fate for her and her family. It was as if she knew what they were, but didn't really grasp the significance of their being there. In fact, it seemed quite natural and acceptable to her, as if it were something she somehow always knew it was some event in which she was destined to partake.

Focusing on the creatures she, of course, recognized Dwight and Marie Livingston as well as her former lawyer, H. Mason Armstrong. She also recognized Emerson Washburn from photos she had found during her research, although in his emaciated condition she was barely able to do so. She had no idea who the fifth being was, but she assumed it might be another relative of hers, whom she simply didn't recognize. She suspected she wouldn't have been able to identify the relative anyway. The wretched thing was barely more than charred flesh pinched tightly over blackened bones.

The five waited for her along the back of the property as the menacing icy well glowed in the bright security lights. Some of the water had bubbled up over the top of the well during its formation and spilled over the sides coating the circular dirt structure with a thick layer of shimmering ice before dropping back down to its normal depth. This was likely done on purpose to fortify the sides of the well. The resulting feature resembled a beautiful ice sculpture of a well, but there was nothing beautiful or pleasant about the purpose for this well.

Stephanie looked down at the boy she was carrying under her arm. She was confused about the boy's identity. Once moment she thought it might be someone named Samuel, who she believed she should know but did not, and other times she thought he was one of Marie's Livingston's dead sons and that she was Marie. For a while, she thought the boy might be one of her cheating husband's bastard children. And for one moment she even believed the boy might simply be an inanimate doll of some sort and not a living human at all. But that made no sense to her either. In fact, nothing seemed to make sense to her. And now, she had absolutely no idea who or what the child might be.

It was as if she were living in a dream world, where people and things were not cohesive and changed fluidly from one moment to another, depending upon the direction the dream seemed to take. Perhaps that was why she didn't fear the hideous creatures or could not concretely identify the thing in her arms. Perhaps in the dream she believed she was having, nothing was real and everything was simply symbolic. It all seemed to make perfect sense, because it made no sense. And it made no sense because it made perfect sense.

But one thing she did know was that it was her job to bring this boy or doll or unidentifiable package to the well, to Dwight and Marie Livingston. Stephanie wondered if the package was to be sacrificed in order that she would have revenge on her unfaithful husband, Dwight. No, she thought. Her husband's name was Jason, and Marie's husband's name was Dwight. Or was it Marie's husband who was named Jason and her husband who was named Dwight? Stephanie wasn't even sure who she was let alone who her husband might be, if she even had one. Sometimes she thought one thing then a moment later she thought another. Perhaps she was no longer Stephanie or Marie but had evolved into some new type of being; a conjoining of two separate beings: one living, one dead. Perhaps she was some new type of hybrid species.

But whatever or whoever she was or was not, she knew what she had to do and understood that once the thing she carried was placed in the well everything would be all right. The circle of blood would be completed. That is what the voices inside her befuddled mind told her so no matter how confused she might seem, it had to be the right thing for her to do.

As Stephanie approached the well, the creature she thought of as Marie Livingston raised her arms high in the air and began speaking in a loud and unearthly voice.

"We have waited for this night for almost a century. It has taken that long for the circle of blood to be completed. Dwight Livingston and I have been unwillingly bound together in death because of a curse placed upon us long ago by his sister, Amelia Miller.

"In this unfortunate union, he is in the role of master and I, his servant. I present this information at the behest of my master, Dwight Livingston. But neither of us is content in these roles and we have tried unsuccessfully all of these years to find a way to free ourselves of each other. And not only do we wish to be free of each other, but also free of this torturous limbo in which our tormented souls have been forced to exist. To watch others live their lives while we wallow in anguish. It is the act of existing, without existence, living without life and dying without death.

"We believe we have finally found a means to break the bonds which hold our souls captive and to accomplish this we must sacrifice the life of the one who can complete the circle of blood. And those who gave life to the child must also die in a manner similar to our own deaths so many years ago."

"Samuel Jason Wright, born on this day, December 19, is he who has completed the circle. The child carries the blood of Dwight Livingston, present in him from both his mother and his father. As such, he must be sacrificed on this night exactly ninety years from the date when Matthew James Livingston, Charles Edward Livingston, Marie Louise O'Hara Livingston and Dwight Charles Livingston died on this very same property, the Livingston Family Homestead.

"When the child dies it must be by his own mother's hand; that woman being Stephanie Sage Washburn Wright. The child's father Jason John Wright will then go mad with rage and will murder his wife before succumbing to remorse and taking his own life. This was how it happened so many years ago and how it must happen tonight. The parties gathered with me are here to assure that the ceremony of the blood circle is carried out before midnight, as it must be.

"Stephanie Sage Washburn Wright. Present the child, Samuel Jason Wright for submergence in the sacrificial well."

Stephanie lifted Sammy in the air directly in front of her and for the first time since leaving the loft, looked into his dark brown pleading eyes. Those eyes said, "Please, Mommy, don't do this. I love you, Mommy". She saw the sentiment in his expression and practically could hear the words in her head. Then she heard the boy's pleading. "Pease Mommy" he said pitifully. Stephanie began to feel like some force was playing tug-of-war with her mind. At one moment she was unaware of the child she held in her arms, then a moment later, she began to recognize him as her son. She struggled with her emotions upon hearing his tiny voice calling to her as if from the back of a long tunnel. "Pease Mommy" she heard him say.

Slowly, the recognition became clearer and the other voices, the once trying to control her, began to fade. The creatures had made a critical mistake by not continuing to maintain control of Sammy. They had no idea how special he was.

His voice was able to surpass their sinister control. His love for his mother had broken through the fog which surrounded her. And for the first time in what seemed like months, she was starting to feel like herself once more.

She looked over and saw the dreadful mob of beings now understanding not only what they were, but what their horrible plan was. She looked into the eyes of her son then held him tightly to her breast whispering, "Oh, Sammy. Oh my sweet baby boy. My poor son. Mommy loves you so, so much. I promise I would never do anything to hurt you my sweet, sweet baby boy."

Stephanie looked defiantly at the ghost of her great grandmother and shouted, "I know who I am now, and I now know who and what you are. I also know my husband Jason is a good man and not like your unfaithful husband Dwight. He could never do such a thing to me, and I could never ever lift a finger to hurt either Sammy or Jason. So all of you might as well give up your plans and go away, because I will never help you."

Marie Livingston let out an ear-splitting wail of anger and frustration. Dwight turned and looked angrily at Marie as if to indicate she had failed him. Marie suddenly bent over screaming as if suddenly racked with incredible agony.

"You know what you must do, woman," Dwight bellowed in a voice that shook the air like thunder. "You must do what she cannot do. You must complete the circle of blood, no matter the cost."

Marie stood upright to the best of her ability and Stephanie could see the look of fear on her face. She was terrified of Dwight and could do nothing to hide her terror. She pointed an unsteady hand at Stephanie, summoning all of her strength. Stephanie felt herself lose control of her motor functions. She held Sammy out in front of her, his eyes now filled with a new terror. She wanted to set him down and tell him to run away, but she was powerless to do so. It was apparent to her that Marie was now completely in charge of Stephanie's body. Then one shuffling step at a time, Stephanie began to walk closer to the well. She tried to fight against the force, but was helpless to do so.

Marie screamed, "I told you the circle had to be completed, and it must be. If you will not willingly kill the boy yourself, then I will force you to kill him. Your beloved Jason will not know the difference. He will find you with the body, mumbling like a mad woman, and he will assume you murdered your son. Then he will kill you and finally take his own life. It has been preordained and so it must be."

Resist as she might, Stephanie continued to shuffle forward, tears streaming down her face, practically freezing on her cheeks in the frigid night air. She would rather die herself that let anything happen to Sammy but was powerless to stop herself.

Marie Livingston bellowed, "I command you to throw the boy into the well and kill him."

From somewhere in the darkness behind her Stephanie heard a voice shout, "The hell you do, you rotten old bitch!"

Chapter 39

Jason ran from the shadows out into the light. He pointed an accusing finger at the phantom Marie Livingston, and shouted "No! No more! Get away from my family, you unholy sow!" Startled by Jason's outburst, the ghost lost her control over Stephanie. Then the creature suddenly realized there was more to her losing focus than simple shock or surprise; there was something about this man, Jason Wright, that had instantly depleted her strength and had taken away her ability to possess the woman. Stephanie turned and with Sammy held tightly against her chest, stumbled back toward her husband. Jason wrapped his comforting arms tightly around his wife and son.

"Steph! Honey! Are you alright?" he asked struggling to sound calm and reassuring.

She replied tearfully, "Y...y...yes...now...I think...thanks to you." Then she pressed her head against his shoulders and cried in his arms, "Oh my God. Jason, what has happened? What's wrong with me? I can't seem to remember anything...just bits and pieces...like a bad dream. What in the name of God have I done? And what are those horrible creatures?"

Jason kissed her forehead and said, "Shhh. Steph. Don't worry. I'm here, and now everything will be all right. I don't really understand all of this or know exactly what happened, but I swear I won't let anyone or anything hurt you or Sammy."

"Mommy cwy," Sammy said, obviously concerned about his mother.

"Yes, Sammy," Jason said reassuringly. "Mommy is crying, but she won't cry anymore because her big man Sammy is here to protect her from those bad people." He pointed over at the specters that appeared to be waiting for something.

Then for the first time, Jason looked directly at the unearthly gathering of demonic spirits taking in the details of each of them. It was only the briefest of glances, but the ungodly sites he saw would be burned into his memory for as long as he lived; whether that was for sixty more years or sixty more seconds. And at this point in time, Jason had an understanding that his life could literally be over in minutes.

The first creature he noticed was the one he had accosted, the wretched Marie Livingston. The madness was still present in her long-dead eyes.

He then saw the visage of his dead lawyer, H. Mason Armstrong standing next to Marie's right and looking much as he had the day Jason saw him in the field by the back of the property.

Standing behind Armstrong was an image Jason knew had to be that of Emerson Washburn. Although this being no longer resembled the photos Stephanie had found of the big man.

A charred, skeletal figure stood next to Washburn. Jason had no idea who or what this being might be as his hideous form was scarcely recognizable as ever being human. There was a thick length of rusted chain which passed right through the creature's neck bones, down its chest and into Washburn's hand. It suggested to Jason that whoever the pathetic creature had been in life, it was now the slave of Emerson Washburn.

Finally, Jason's eyes settled on the being, which he determined must be the master of the macabre assemblage. It was some warped and unimaginable incarnation of Dwight Livingston. Although Jason realized he and his family could be in grave danger from any single one of the creatures before him, he believed Dwight Livingston might pose the greatest threat. He was obviously the leader and as such would likely be the most powerful.

Jason's first instinct was to take his family and flee as far from these horrible beings as possible; to turn and run, never looking back. But he realized such an action would be futile. These creatures, these demons, had somehow controlled and manipulated events not only locally but had done so over a distance of more than fifty miles. He had no idea how far he and his family might have to run to escape their control; if they could escape the horrid creatures at all. No. Jason realized he would have to face the horrible undead, unholy beings right there and then or else he and his family could never hope to be safe again. He was going to have to find a way to drive them back into the hell from which they came and he was going to have to do so permanently, or die trying.

Anxiety took Jason in its grip as he comprehended their plight. He was an engineer, a man of logic. He had never believed in ghosts, spirits or any of the other supernatural mumbo-jumbo, which seemed to pollute pop culture. Jason knew he was about as ill prepared to go up against such creatures as anyone could imagine. But he also knew he had no choice but to do whatever was necessary to protect his family. If that meant he would have to die this night, then by God, he would do so fighting. He had too much to live for but would gladly sacrifice his own life and even his immortal soul, if that's what it took to save Stephanie and Sammy. He had no idea, however, what it was he could possibly do to fight against beings that were already dead.

"Jason John Wright," Dwight Livingston abruptly bellowed from his side of the menacing well. "You must bring the woman, Stephanie Sage Wright and the boy Samuel Jason Wright to us. I command it, and you must obey my will."

Jason felt a tugging sensation inside of his skull as if he were being compelled against his will to obey the specter's command. But then he suddenly realized he didn't have to do as Livingston ordered. He could resist the creature's psychic pull; he did have a choice. He could feel the force of the strange specter trying to influence his own body into doing its bidding, but Jason apparently had some previously unrecognized power of his own, as he was still in control of his actions. He could also tell by the strange look, which suddenly appeared on Dwight Livingston's face, that the ghoul was equally surprised to discover he could not control Jason. Dwight's face contorted with displeasure, and the attitude of confidence he originally displayed began to wane. Although Jason was not exactly sure what all of this might mean, he did unexpectedly get an idea, which he thought might be their only way out of the deadly situation.

"Steph," Jason said, "I have an idea. And I think I may be right; at least I hope I'm right. Listen. No matter what you hear or see. Try not to be afraid of them. I think that might be part of the secret of how we can beat them. I think they live on the fear and the hatred of others. That's why they tried to pit us against each other. They need us to be at odds with each other and not united. Because I suspect with the three of us here together and combined as one force they can't control us."

Stephanie looked perplexed for a moment as if thinking about something then said, "I think you're right, Jason. I can feel them trying to take back control...of me...of my body...like they did before...but they can't seem to do it. When it was just me they could, but now I don't think they can."

"Keep fighting them, Steph," Jason urged. "We can beat them together. I know we can. We love each other, and nothing is stronger than that. I'm sure of it. "

"You will bring the bitch and the child to me now!" Dwight shouted across the distance, his form was twitching and moving erratically like an old silent movie film as were the rest of the creatures. Jason could see something was now very different about the ghosts; something was happening to them, but Dwight still tried to assert his control: "You will do as I command or I swear I will order you all to rip out your own eyes and swallow them while we watch with pleasure!"

Fueled by a newfound confidence, Jason pointed his finger at Dwight once again and shouted, "Screw you, Livingston. Any powers you believe you have are now useless against us. We are a strong and unified force of unconditional love, and you can do nothing to harm us. You've existed without love for so long you have forgotten its power and its strength. We don't fear you, Dwight Livingston, nor do we fear any of your pitiful minions. We don't even acknowledge your right to exist."

Then Jason decided to push even harder, "We laugh at you as the pathetic lost souls you've become. You're all destined to spend your eternities in pain and torment because of the sins you've committed in your lives. My wife's soul is pure; my son's soul is pure and so is mine. And together we are immune to your ridiculous commands.

"We may have the blood of Dwight Livingston flowing through our veins, but we have souls which are uncorrupted. And you pitiable creatures don't have the power to separate us ever again. Jason shouted one taunt after another not even certain what he was doing, but he could tell that the more he showed his strength and lack of fear, the more disturbed the spirits appeared to get.

Then all of the ghosts began to howl like banshees and wale as if in the throes of agony. They continued to twitch and gyrate as if being hit with painful bolts of lightning. Jason realized he was definitely on the right track and decided he would continue to taunt the demons until they either fled or hopefully were somehow destroyed.

He shouted at the jerking group of hell-spawned demons, "I, Jason John Wright, illegitimate great grandson of Dwight Livingston, with the strength of my family's love now possess the power. And as such, I command all of you miserable creatures to go now and return to whatever corner of Hell you have arisen from. I order you to leave me and my family alone forever."

The specters were all contorting and screaming as if Jason's words were hitting them like a barrage of bullets one after another. Fresh blood began to ooze from each of the creatures' wounds. The gashes began to rip open further allowing more of the sickening blackish crimson fluid to flow.

Then a sound like that of thousands of buzzing insects was emanating from the opening of the well as suddenly an enormous black cloud made up of swarms of some type of tiny blackish flies flew from the fiery pit encircling the creatures then boring deep into their freshly weeping sores.

One of the insects flew close to Jason's face, and before it flew away a second later, he saw it clearly in all of its horror. The thing's body was similar to that of the type of fly Jason had seen many times before around garbage or dead animals; a mix of blue, green, black and other colors giving its skin the impression of an oil slick on a puddle of water. Its legs were double the length of a normal fly and appeared to have long, talons on the ends of tiny humanoid fingers.

Its hideous face was by far its most disturbing feature, resembling that of a balding old man with wispy grey hair, segmented insectile eyes and two long ram-like horns curving back from a hairless forehead. Its mouth was much too large for hits head, disproportionately oversized and was filled with hundreds of long pointy needle-like teeth. That single second of observation seemed like an eternity to Jason, and he was relieved when the creature flew away to return to the swarm, obviously not interested in either he or his family.

H. Mason Armstrong stood twisting from side to side all the while bellowing in agony. The hole where his heart had once been was black with the carnivorous insects and was obviously increasing in size as thousands of chomping mouths proceeded to devour him from the inside out. Likewise, the gaunt form of Emerson Washburn twitched and convulsed as the tiny creatures filled the gashes in his chest, while lapping up his oozing fluids. Some had zeroed in on the area between his legs and were chewing on the dangling threads of musculature which was all that remained of his severed genitalia. He slapped the palm of one hand against his chest while batting at his crotch in a useless attempt to stop the hungry things from enjoying their feast.

All around them, the ground suddenly began to tremble and the family found themselves in the middle of an earthquake. Then before his eyes, Jason saw the well begin to change shape. The ice holding the circular wall of soil together, which formed the shape of the well began to melt and the wall crumbled back to soil. The creatures screamed and howled uncontrollably as the insect-like scavengers devoured their mottled flesh.

Next, the place where the opening for the well had been was visible to Jason and Stephanie, but it too was changing its appearance. Instead of its original round shape, it took on the shape of giant slit in the soil, looking as if God had taken a giant ax and cleaved a gash in the earth. The frozen ground around the opening was thawing as a cloud of steam rose up all around the crevasse. The earth around the opening was becoming hot and molten. Jason could smell something foul and sulfurous coming from inside the crevasse. The small bubbling pools of lava spurted from inside the hole followed by occasional bursts of flames. Soon the flames were larger, almost twenty feet high, as the ground continued to shake with tremors.

Jason was not and could not possibly be prepared for what happened next. Long rope-like flaming tentacles sprang up out of the opening whipping and spitting flames like a nest of uncontrollable vipers. One of the whipping lava lariats wrapped itself around Dwight Livingston's throat and began pulling him toward the hole. Dwight screamed and howled "Noooo!" repeatedly while trying desperately to fight off the grip of the wild flaming loop. An instant later, another rope of molten lava wrapped around his arms and legs, and soon he was being pulled downward into the bubbling earthen caldron of pain. Just before Dwight disappeared from his sight, Jason witnessed the specter's head separate from his body as did his arms and legs as his spectral form was torn to pieces.

Jason heard a woman scream and saw Marie Livingston entwined in the fiery filaments, which melted the flesh from her ghostly body while simultaneously dragging her contorting form toward the volcanic pit. Her hair was ablaze and burning like a torch. She looked directly at Jason as if pleading for help, when her eyeballs exploded outward as a swarm of black insects streamed from her now vacant sockets. Likewise her scream mouth vomited a swarm of buzzing pestilence.

The charred skeletal remains of Jack Moran, the creature Jason had not been able to identify, was face down clawing and digging at the earth trying desperately to escape as ropes of flames wrapped around its ankles and pulled the creature toward the fiery threshold.

Within the next few seconds, the each one of the horrible beings were likewise pulled down into the flaming portal to what Jason assumed was Hell. He could not think of anything but what he imagined Hell to be that was capable of the unholy carnage he was witnessing. The earth continued to shake so violently; Jason found it almost impossible to remain upright. After a moment or two, Jason smelled something he feared almost as much as the horrifying sight unfolding before him. Despite the sulfurous stench coming from the flaming split in the earth, Jason was certain he smelled something he recognized, which was extremely dangerous and which was not from Hell but was of his own world. He smelled natural gas and suddenly realized the line which connected the main house to the hexagonal spa building had become ruptured by the earthquake.

With the conflagration of fire billowing from the crack in the earth, Jason knew he only had seconds to get his family to safety. He turned and tried desperately to lead Stephanie and Sammy away from the eminent explosion. But before they gotten more than twenty feet away, the spa building blew up sending deadly debris of flaming rock and timber flying high into the sky.

Chapter 40

The pressure from the blast knocked Jason, Stephanie and Sammy to the ground as a storm of flaming debris began plummeting down toward them. Despite his shocked condition, Jason managed to become a human shield, covering Stephanie and Sammy with his own body in an attempt to protect them from the rain of flaming hellfire. He prepared himself for what was to come, fearing he might die in the process but prepared to use his last breath if necessary to save his family.

He heard the fiery rubble of stone and rock fall around him and gritted his teeth in anticipation of the agonizing pain he knew was coming. But to his surprise he felt nothing. He heard sizzling sounds from above and cautiously lifted his head to try to see what was happening. All around them the formerly frozen meadow was ablaze as fiery debris continued to rain down like a vision from some hellish nightmare. Yet for some unknown reason, a small area immediately near them remained untouched.

"Jason?" Stephanie asked, "What's happening? Why aren't we dead?"

For a moment Jason began to wonder if they actually might in fact be dead. He replied, "I... I don't know, Steph. None of the stuff seems to be landing anywhere near us. It's like we are protected or something."

"Look!" Stephanie exclaimed pointing upward. She still was lying on the ground but had rolled over on her side. About ten feet above them the raining pieces of burning debris seemed to miraculously stop in the air, sizzle then turn to dust and slide down the outside of what appeared to be a giant translucent dome of some sort, which glimmered with millions of tiny sparkling lights. The large structure completely covered them, acting as a protective barrier. "Look at it, Jason! What in the world is it? Where did it come from?"

Sammy sat up and pointed to a place in the meadow about thirty feet away and said, "Boys."

Jason and Stephanie followed his gaze and saw two bright glowing forms of light, which seemed to be roughly shaped like two small boys. The brightness of their iridescent forms was almost impossible to look at directly. But through squinted eyes, shielded by his hand, Jason could make out a stream of luminescent particles extending from the shimmering beings linking them to their mysterious protective dome.

"Boys help," Sammy said. "Boys phone Daddy. Boys help Sammy."

Then before Jason and Stephanie had a chance to grasp the significance of what was happening, they heard another incredible explosion, even greater than the first. They turned to see their beautiful renovated farmhouse/mansion blasted into flaming rubble before their eyes. The shock wave from the blast shook the earth below them and nearly knocked them down. They saw the translucent dome wobbled from the blast but still maintained its shape. As before, the fiery remnants flew far and wide setting the remaining out buildings on the property ablaze. Soon every single building and outbuilding was being reduced to cinders.

"Oh my God no!" Stephanie cried. "Everything we own. Everything we have is burning up, Jason. Our house, our clothing, our furniture, it's all gone."

Jason's stomach sank with the frustration of the loss. But then he realized what they had just managed to barely escape and suddenly the burning buildings and all of their earthly possessions became nothing more than that: just a bunch of burning material and fallen stones. "Don't cry, Steph. All of that was just stuff. We can worry about it tomorrow. Right now all that matters is we are safe and alive." He knew Stephanie agreed with him, but she still needed to grieve for the loss of their belongings.

In a few minutes, the rain of debris stopped, and Jason saw the translucent sparkling dome which surrounded them begin to dissipate and fade away. In the distance, the two glowing boys stood quietly, arms at their sides.

"Go see boys," Sammy said as he squirmed in Jason's arms, wanting to be put down. He held Jason and Stephanie's hands, and the three carefully walked between the flaming remnants to the place where the boys quietly stood. Now they all could clearly see the Livingston boys in greater detail. They were dressed in bright white dress shirts and white pants but were barefoot. They wore a look of contentment which Stephanie believed came from their seeing the Wright family together and safe.

"All things happen for a reason," Stephanie thought. She found herself contemplating how because the spirit boys were here and had not moved on to whatever afterlife awaited them; she and her family were safe and alive. Had the two crossed over ninety years earlier, then the three of them surely would have died in the explosions. "All things happen for a reason," she thought again, smiling satisfactorily.

Stephanie stepped forward and said, "Matthew. Charles. Thank you so much for protecting me and my family. You saved our lives." The two spectral shapes stood looking at her but said nothing. "Had you lived, I'm sure you would have grown to be fine men, and I would have been proud to have had you as great uncles. God bless you both and thank you again for all you have done for us."

After a few seconds slight smiles appeared on their cherubic faces as they looked upward as if hearing someone calling to them. Then they began to slowly dissolve as Stephanie had seen the dome dissolve. Next, two long streams of effervescent particles streaked up onto the heavens. Stephanie thought she heard the boys calling to their Aunt Amelia Miller. Perhaps the time had finally come for the boys to join her and Amelia had come to lead them home.

"Bye bye, boys," Sammy said. He heard their voices inside his head distant and fading. "Goodbye, Sammy. You have been brave and have helped to free us so we can move on. Live a long and good life and maybe we will see you again someday."

Sammy didn't understand everything the boys were talking about, but he could tell they were both happy and were going to a place far away, where they would never be sad again.

Jason and Stephanie looked about them at the burning buildings, the billowing smoke and the debris strewn patches of burning meadow.

"What now?" Stephanie asked, staring around in stunned confusion.

"Well," Jason replied, pulling out his cell phone, "now I guess we call 911."

Epilogue

"Wright Industrial Consulting; Jason Wright speaking," Jason said into his desk phone. "No. Sorry. I have don't have need for that at the moment, but I'll keep you in mind. Thank you and goodbye." He hung up the phone and thought, "Salesmen! Well, I suppose they have to earn a living too." He had found since setting up his own business and working from his home office he seemed to be getting a lot of 'cold calls' from a variety of salesmen. This was probably because he had been doing a lot to promote his business through a number of professional and Internet resources. "I suppose since I put myself out there to try to gain some name recognition, I have to assume the push is starting to work by the number of sales calls I've been getting. Too bad most of them aren't from potential clients."

As he was about to return to the project on his desk he stopped for a moment and found himself once more reflecting back on how much had happened. And how much had changed over the past six months, since that unbelievable night.

After the firemen had managed to get the blaze under control and the gas company had capped the leak, he, Stephanie and Sammy had been taken to a hospital in the city of Yuengsville to be treated for shock as well as minor cuts and abrasions. The rescue workers were amazed the three had even survived the carnage. When they had arrived on the scene the workers had found them aimlessly walking toward the main road, down the driveway as a conflagration equivalent to a war zone could be seen burning behind them. One rescue worker described the sight as appearing like three survivors escaping from Hell. Jason had been carrying his son in one arm while his other was secured tightly around his wife. The fire trucks had proceeded up to the home site while the ambulance crew looked after the family near a large rock in the driveway which bore the inscription "Fallen Stones".

None of the Wrights seemed to have had much of a recollection of what actually happened, but somehow they had managed to survive a gas explosion which had destroyed every single structure on the property. Even the in-ground swimming pool and patio area as well as Jason's pickup truck in the driveway had been blown to bits.

Later Jason called his brother-in-law, Chuck, from the hospital to check on Jeremy and Cindy. He wanted to be sure the specters had not done anything to harm them. When he heard they were ok, he quickly filled Chuck in on what happened – being careful to exclude the mention of demonic ghosts - and asked him to keep the kids for another day until he and Stephanie could get some details worked out. He knew it would take months until their lives even came close to returning to normal, but he figured he could at least get out of the hospital and settled into hotel as a temporary measure by the next day.

The property was a total loss with everything being burned to dust in the inferno. All that remained of any of the building was rubble. Luckily for the Wright family, included in the tax escrow for the property was a clause for automatic payment of their homeowners insurance as well. Jason and Stephanie forgot about how Armstrong had explained everything to them on the day of the settlement. Since Armstrong's death, another lawyer had taken over his practice and assisted Jason and Stephanie in resolving matters. Eventually they received a settlement check for close to three million dollars for their loss.

After what they had been through, Jason and Stephanie both decided it would be best to move back to Berks County and begin again with a fresh start. Jason quit his job at the Ashton facility and pursued his dream of starting his own consulting business. He already had several lucrative client contracts, and since he had managed to leave his old job on good terms, the Ashton factory also agreed to become one of his clients.

He and Stephanie built a brand new home in Western Berks County in a new upscale subdivision with large homes on two acre lots. The home didn't compare in opulence to the one which was destroyed, but that was just fine with them. Jason had a home office from which he could run his business, and Stephanie had a small studio she could use to write her books. The kids each had their own bedrooms, a large family room and an in-ground pool in the back yard.

Stephanie's latest book was doing amazingly well in a very tough market. Fortunately for her, about a week before the fire, Jason had sneaked into her loft in the middle of the night and found her book and illustrations buried under a stack of papers. Unbeknownst to Stephanie, Jason packaged everything and then sent it to her publisher. About a month later a galley proof of the book arrived at the apartment where they were temporarily staying until their new home construction was finished. Jason had it mailed to him so he could surprise Stephanie with it, which he did one night while having dinner at their favorite restaurant.

He was delighted by her tearful reaction. He hadn't seen her so happy since their wedding day or the day Sammy was born. He supposed holding a new book that was personally created was distantly like holding a newborn. Stephanie was so inspired; she immediately began working on her next book. She had also been doing numerous book signings, readings and interviews with magazines, newspapers and blogs as well as television and radio.

Stephanie no longer had any desire to recreate her family history and told Jason perhaps it would be better if the kids didn't know about their ancestors. Maybe in a hundred years or so one of their dependents might take an interest and begin researching anew, but she didn't want to record what she knew or what they had been through. She thought once again, "Everything happens for a reason." All of her data was destroyed in the fire and so perhaps it was meant to be destroyed.

She and Jason almost never discussed the events of that horrible evening again hoping perhaps that time might erase the memories. But they both knew deep inside that on those nights when pleasant dreams turn unexpectedly to horrifying nightmares, the images would return. There would be little they could do to stop that but they could opt to not discuss it while awake. Sammy seemed to have forgotten completely about it or else with his brain's child-like resilience he simply found a way to block it out, which was just fine with his parents.

Since Emerson Washburn's will required they not be permitted to sell the property and must keep it in the family, Stephanie thought of a way to put the land to work, making at least some money for them. She asked Jason to hire a contractor to remove all of the debris from the property. Then, since the gas line was capped out at the highway, she had them dig up and eliminate the old gas line. They filled in the foundation and the in-ground pool remnants with top soil and re-tilled the entire forty acres, making it perfect for farming. Then they contacted a number of local farmers and found several interested in leasing a section of the farm for their own use. The income from the lease was not much, but it made Stephanie happy to know the land, which had once caused so much sorrow, was now being put to a good use.

Things were finally getting back to normal for the Wright family, now that they were settled in their new home. Jason could hear Stephanie and the kids in the back yard swimming in the pool, enjoying the start of their summer vacation. The scars of that horrible night were finally starting to fade and life was beginning anew.

Jason decided to check over the latest proposal he had prepared for one of his new potential clients. He reached over and removed the paperweight which held the pile of documents in place. He picked up the weight and smiled knowingly as he turned it about in his hand. It was a small flat, irregular-shaped piece of stone, about an inch or so thick.

To the casual observer it would look like a piece of marble or granite which might have once belonged to something larger, but had broken off. The back of the paperweight was smooth but the front bore a partial carving of some sort which resembled half of the face of an angel or cherub. It was the type of engraving one might find on the tombstone of a very young child. Jason picked up the report and placed the stone back on the stack of documents smiling once again.

THE END

Thomas M. Malafarina - September 2012

Lawrence Knorr's Original Ideas for "Fallen Stones"

(Remember unless you want some of the story spoiled - wait to read this until you finish the book.)

This Stephen King-style thriller starts with a young family with children moving onto a farm in upstate Pennsylvania.

An old family plot is discovered on the property in a copse of trees in the middle of the property

Meanwhile, the children begin to experience ghostly encounters from ghost children and a ghost mother.

The mother, who had been working on the family genealogy, decides to research the (long ago) former owners. (relatives)

She discovers a tragedy -- first determining this family all died around the same time -- tracing from census records to burial records, wills, and newspaper accounts.

She also discovers there is a genetic connection between the woman and herself.

Ultimately, an old letter is found in the county archives describing how the mother killed all of her children, drowning them in a well.

The husband came home, discovered this, killed his wife, and then himself.

The mother begins to lose her mind, and sets out to repeat history...

But, will the husband get home in time?

Will the spirits prevent her?

14913677R00185

Made in the USA
Charleston, SC
07 October 2012